EDWIN M. GRIFFITHS
NEWT & DEMON

I

aethonbooks.com

NEWT AND DEMON
©2024 EDWIN M. GRIFFITHS

This book is protected under the copyright laws of the United States of America. No part of this publication may be reproduced, stored in a retrieval system, or transmitted, in any form or by any means, without the prior permission in writing of the publisher, nor be otherwise circulated in any form of binding or cover other than that in which it is published and without a similar condition including this condition being imposed on the subsequent purchaser. Any reproduction or unauthorized use of the material or artwork contained herein is prohibited without the express written permission of the authors.

Aethon Books supports the right to free expression and the value of copyright. The purpose of copyright is to encourage writers and artists to produce the creative works that enrich our culture.

The scanning, uploading, and distribution of this book without permission is a theft of the author's intellectual property. If you would like to use material from the book (other than for review purposes), please contact editor@aethonbooks.com. Thank you for your support of the author's rights.

Aethon Books
www.aethonbooks.com

Print and eBook design and formatting by Kevin G. Summers.

Published by Aethon Books LLC.

Aethon Books is not responsible for websites (or their content) that are not owned by the publisher.

This book is a work of fiction. Names, characters, places, and incidents are the product of the author's imagination or are used fictitiously. Any resemblance to actual events, locales, or persons, living or dead is coincidental.

All rights reserved.

Also in Series

Newt and Demon

Newt and Demon 2

Want to discuss our books with other readers and even the authors?

JOIN THE AETHON DISCORD!

Chapter 1
The End of the World

The gentle slope of endless, desolate hills gave way to the Pacific Ocean down the drop of treacherous cliffs. The once-green landscape of Ecuador sat as a sprawl of dead trees, flattened buildings, and endless radiation. Devastation visited these lands months ago, rendering most of the country uninhabitable. While the outward signs of the strike left the landscape bleak, the oncoming fallout would be worse. It would stretch out across South America in the coming weeks, leaving all of it as deadly as the epicenter. None of this mattered, though, with the impending destruction of planet Earth.

Theo Spencer slung his rifle over his shoulder, gasping for breath that came labored in his environmental suit. While the systems were functioning perfectly, it was only a matter of time before their squad of five soldiers needed a rest. They plopped down on rocks and regarded each other with faces shielded by visors. The entire mission seemed pointless to him, but life back home was much worse. The sun overhead, swiftly growing by the day, saw to that. What little family he had left were distant cousins, all starving in the global famine. Working for the CIA had its benefits, even if it meant running operations that would never hit the books.

"How much further?" Yuri's voice came over the comms. He was the only man in the squad that Theo knew well enough to call a friend. Everyone else was just another face in the grim parade.

"Not far," Commander Morales responded.

Theo tried to remember what his squad looked like under the black environmental suit, but he came up short. He was happy that their faces were obscured by those dark visors, lest he might see the pain etched onto them. It would be more of a problem if they saw the grin that painted his face. While oxygen was hard to suck down in the suit, it was extremely comfortable. The environment outside the suit was not only radioactive but absurdly hot. He glanced at the sky to catch sight of the source of the heat, the growing sun, and smiled wider.

Things grew simpler when impending doom reared its ugly head. Survival boiled down to who was the strongest and who had the bigger gun. The appearance of an entity designated as "The Harbinger" brought an enemy that the world could fight, something that the nations of the world could throw nukes at to make themselves feel better.

"Maybe if we had worked on space travel, this wouldn't have happened," Theo thought.

"What are the chances this guy is the problem?" Theo asked, thumbing the communication button on his wrist.

"Exactly zero percent," Sergeant Bawa said.

Theo scoffed at the thought of rank. The government assembled them hastily, pulling in anyone with combat training to take out the threat. Most of his squad consisted of paper-pushers, long since retired from any active duty. Only Theo and Yuri had conducted black ops before the fall of civilized society. The incompetence of the government resulted in them being assigned the rank of private. Another cruel twist of fate.

"So, bullets are going to work better than nukes?" Theo asked, his grin widening.

"Shove it, Spencer," Morales said, his voice crackling and

hitching through the comm. "If you have a better idea, let me know."

Theo kicked back, reclining on his rock, and stared up at the growing star. His plan was to sit around, drink some shitty beer, and wait for the world to end. When his unit was assembled, those dreams were shattered. A week-long journey through towns controlled by as many gangs as rogue governments allowed him to witness the atrocities of the end times. He savored that one thing that made this all worth it. The completely over-engineered environmental suits that only a privileged few had access to. He didn't understand the technology, but the inside of his suit was cool, like a spring breeze. The air he breathed was crisp and free of radiation. It even had a little radio, but it had stopped working a few days earlier.

"We could just sit here," Theo said, staring up at the sky. "Let that big old sun eat us up."

"Damn," Bawa said, scoffing. "I mean, just look at the view! You really can't beat this."

He wasn't kidding. The view out west, toward the ocean, was beautiful. The waves lapped in the distance, sparkling like azure jewels among the flat sea. Theo sighed, content with this place.

"What are you gonna do when you die, Yuri?" Theo asked.

"I don't know about you, but I'm going directly to hell," Yuri said, shrugging his massive shoulders.

"I'm going to the big strip club in the sky," Belchev said. At least Theo thought the other person's last name was Belchev. He couldn't even remember, and he didn't care enough to find out either.

"Yeah, I think I'm going to hell, too," Theo said, adjusting his position to remove a rock from his impromptu resting spot. "Too many dead men who didn't deserve it. Too many secret missions to countries I can't even remember."

"This is getting a bit too nihilistic for me," Morales said, shaking his helmeted head. "Break's over. We're meeting the Harbinger today."

Theo rose to his feet slowly, stretching lazily and surveying the area. Before the bombs dropped, this area would have been a forest. The small village outside of which they rested had a small population, but enough to warrant notice. He thought about the tourists that would visit—perhaps eco-tourists coming to see the dense trees. His thoughts fell away as Morales struck his arm, forcing him into that familiar march.

The squad continued their walk down the sloping hills, through as many burnt-out villages as they had seen coming in. The closer they got to the coast, the more Theo wanted to feel the salty breeze of the sea on his face. He planned on popping his helmet off before the end finally came but kept this thought a secret, even from Yuri. They progressed through that barren landscape for hours, the sun having barely moved in the sky by the time they found a coastal road. Morales stopped, allowing them to rest again and determine their exact position.

"Damn GPS isn't working," Morales said, swinging his pack around to dig for a map.

They spent another hour waiting for the man to figure out where they were and where they needed to go. Then the marching continued. Theo fell further away from his squad as the sun grew larger. He could see ribbons of fire leaping off of the star, none large enough to grace Earth, and savored the star's beauty. A silver pendant, awkwardly pinned to the environmental suit, shimmered brilliantly under those lights. He ran his gloved fingers over the faded surface. The image had washed away long ago from exposure to radiation, the enlarged sun, or just time. A lost love's image, erased like the woman herself, now only lingered in his mind.

He was walking on the beach by the time he found his senses again, waves lapping the shore to his right while his squad marched forward. They had their weapons at the ready, and Morales was shouting something. His voice came with barking commands, and the soldiers fanned out. He joined them reluctantly.

Theo was surprised that their intelligence bore fruit. He spotted the Harbinger over a dune, standing and appreciating the waves. The entity didn't look very human. It was taller than a person and wore a black mask bearing the image of a white eye in the center. Its limbs were too long, with hands and feet bearing jagged claws. The robes the thing wore reminded him of fantasy media he had consumed over the years, flowing and resting against the wet sand. It held its arms wide, a motion that didn't seem very threatening. But Morales had already given the order, and his squad opened fire without hesitation.

Theo stood there, next to the firing soldiers, without discharging his weapon. He watched as the bullets seemed to bounce off of the creature, ricocheting into the sand and back at his squad. Something bit deep into his stomach, and he collapsed on his side, contentment flooding through his body as the same fate visited his companions. He rolled to his back painfully, trying to get a better look at the sun. Silence filled the surrounding air, broken only by the occasional lapping of waves.

"Anyone alive?" Theo said, gasping for air.

Footsteps joined the silence—bare, taloned feet on sand. Firm hands grasped the side of his helmet, lifting it off and revealing the blinding environment. The air stung his skin, spreading like electricity down his body. His lungs burned, and he gasped against the poison, failing to expel the deadly radiation. The Harbinger stood above him, tilting his masked face and tutting.

"Ah, I'm still learning," the Harbinger said.

The creature moved off, and Theo watched as it drew a circle in the sand. Motes of light rose from the circle, rising to the sky with a rush of wind. The burning faded from Theo's lungs, his skin no longer crawling with deadly radiation. He gasped at the fresh air, smiling as he saw the sun above grow larger. The pain in his abdomen was still there, but he was happy.

"Looks like you're going to die," the Harbinger said, coming to sit next to Theo. His voice was a monotone thing, devoid of accent or emotion.

"That's not unique," Theo said, coughing.

"Indeed."

"Is anyone else alive?" Theo asked.

"Barely," the Harbinger said, pointing to the downed men. "That one will see the transition through, I think."

Theo craned his neck painfully, watching as his friend Yuri clutched his chest, writhing on the ground.

"Who are you?" Theo asked, attempting to assuage his curiosity before it ended.

"You're calm for someone about to see their death. You're unaware of the transition, yes?"

"Transition? No idea what you're talking about—and you didn't answer my question," Theo said, another fit of coughing stealing whatever else he might say.

The Harbinger shrugged. "I'm a traveler. I visit places like this before they die. You're a soldier, correct?"

"Yeah, something like that," Theo said.

"A soldier looking for a peaceful life," the Harbinger said wistfully. "What a familiar story."

The pair sat in silence for quite some time. When the sun started growing, it was imperceptible. Whatever agencies were in charge of keeping track of how big the sun was didn't notice until it was too late, although there was nothing they could do. In the past week, it had started growing at an unpredictable pace. For all its destructive power, it was beautiful, taking up a fair portion of the sky even though it should have set by now. The creature sitting next to Theo seemed to enjoy the sight, casting its gaze toward the star with interest. It tilted its head back toward the prone private and shrugged, placing a finger on his forehead.

"A quiet life. You want a peaceful life, yes?" it asked.

"That'd be nice," Theo said, another fit of coughing taking over. "I think it might be too late for that."

"Not at all," the Harbinger said.

The creature pressed its finger harder into Theo's forehead, a strange sense spreading through his body. More motes of light joined that of the circle, swirling through the air in a vortex as the rush in his chest continued. The Harbinger removed his finger after a while, placing a comforting hand on Theo's shoulder.

"The transition will give you a chance at a new life," the Harbinger said. "Everyone who is still alive when the sun consumes your planet will get that chance. Millions of lives…"

"Sounds like a dream to me," Theo said, laughing, "or a bunch of bull."

The Harbinger shrugged, gesturing toward the sky. "It's happening. Perhaps we'll meet when you transition to the other side. Well, enjoy the view." He placed the helmet back on Theo's head, clasping it at the collar, and stood up. In a flash of light, the strange creature disappeared.

Theo watched as the sun grew, happy that the entity had put his helmet back on. He could see the details of the sun as it ballooned in size. Even the environmental suit could no longer hold back the burning tide. It swept over the planet in an instant, consuming Earth and destroying all life still present on it. However, as darkness assaulted Theo's vision, something strange appeared in front of him. Text crowded the center of his sight.

[Transitioning to World B71…]
[Running stored protocol: 'Harbinger's Gift']
[Resetting life…]
[Welcome to Iaredin!]

Chapter 2
Awakening

The first thing Theo remembered after the expanding sun was a sharp pain in his chest. Unconsciousness gave way to that sensation, followed by oppressive humidity and the scent of soot and sweat. He realized, before anything else came back to him, that it was his sweat. He stirred, forcing his eyes open. The scene that swirled around him was dizzying, a feeling that was made worse by the text in the middle of his vision. No matter where he tilted his head, the annoying text followed.

[Welcome to Paradise!]
Quest
You're dead!

Congratulations! Your world has been destroyed. The System has determined that you qualify for transfer to World B71, commonly known as Iaredin. A powerful entity has vouched for your transfer, upgrading your vessel with additional benefits.

Acclimate yourself to your new world and enjoy Broken Tusk!

Newt and Demon

Objectives:
Meet the villagers of Broken Tusk.
Sleep in your new home.

"Ugh, it doesn't feel like paradise," Theo said, swatting at the text. "What the hell—"

His words were interrupted by the same painful poke. As the shapes in the room resolved, he saw a massive woman standing over him and only now realized that he was lying down. She was a tall, well-muscled lady with short hair, ocher—almost red—skin, short tusks protruding from her bottom lip, and a scowl hanging on her face. Theo blinked away the sleep, frantically trying to drive away the woman through sheer willpower. She didn't go, simply glowering down at him.

"About time," she said. At least he could understand her. "You have a lot of questions, and I don't care. Well, here's the short version. You owe me money."

"Nice to meet you, too," Theo said, staring up at the ceiling. He desperately tried to avoid eye contact with the intimidating woman.

With his vision cleared, he took stock of where he was. Shoddy wood paneling on the walls, cracked boards on the floor, a roof with more mold than he'd ever seen, and a bed stuffed with straw. The uncertainty that painted his face upon awakening vanished in an instant. He wasn't dead. No matter how strange things were around him, the sun hadn't killed him.

"We found you in a field a week ago," she said. "My name is Miana Kell, Mayor of Broken Tusk. We figured you were integrated from another system, so I've had Luras prepare to get you situated. Wait here."

Miana rose from the side of the bed, stomping out of the room and off into the hallway. Theo rose to a sitting position on the bed, a shock running through his heart when he saw his hands. He frantically pushed back the rough cloth covering his forearms, inspecting his skin. It was rougher than he remembered, and purple. His fingers ended in thick claws, and as he pressed his palms against his face, he found horns. They traced along the shape of his head, swooping up at the back of his skull. The horns were rough and variegated, with ridges along their length. Then he felt the tail attached near his buttocks.

"All right," Theo said, his brow knitting tightly. "What's going on?"

His question hovered in the emptiness of the room. He rose to his feet and inspected his legs, ultimately letting out a sigh of relief. "At least I don't have hooves," he thought, inspecting his bare feet. With a wiggle of his toes, he shrugged.

"Greetings." A voice like coarse gravel came from the threshold of the room. "I'm Luras Trinner, a hunter and a trapper. I hope you transitioned well."

Luras was a mountain of a man, easily two heads taller than Miana. He wore what Theo could only conclude was leather armor. It looked well-oiled, hugging the man's massive frame, and layered for protection. A pair of daggers sat at his hip, with a bow held in his hand. His skin was darker than the woman's, edging toward a dark ocher color to contrast her pale orange. Something about the softness of his expression put Theo at ease. His shaven head even caught the light spectacularly.

"Not so sure about that, Luras," Theo said, letting out a nervous chuckle. "I appear to be a demon." He held his arms out as if to gesture, "You seeing this?"

"Ah, yes," Luras said, digging in the satchel at his side. He held a parchment out, squinting to read the text. "I tried to memorize this, but... you know. It says that most transitioned worlds don't have the number of races we have here. Right."

"Well, I was *human*," Theo said, shrugging.

"We have humans here. I'm a half-ogre... Well, we're not really half of an ogre, but that's just a name, just like how you're not a demon. You belong to the Dronon race—part-demons." Seeing Theo's concerned expression, he continued. "Come on, I'll give you a tour of the town while I explain things. Can you walk?"

The simplicity of the gentle way the man spoke smoothed away the rough edges of Theo's mind. His mind's eye produced images of ogres from fantasy. Towering brutes that would eat someone's liver as soon as they introduced themselves. Luras was very unlike that image, presenting a calm exterior that brought about more questions than answers. He wobbled on the spot, swaying around to understand his new body. His balance seemed worse than before the transition, the strength born of years of service gone in an instant. His mind, on the other hand, seemed more honed, able to process things quicker and come to an understanding. It was all strange.

"Let's go," Theo said, nodding to himself.

Luras led him through a short wind of halls, holding a rickety wooden door open for Theo to step outside. The exterior was more of an assault on his senses than the interior, with the humidity doubling in the open air. The scent of wet earth and manure filled his nostrils, along with the light bustle of other half-ogres walking along a central dirt road. Each building in Broken Tusk was of the same shoddy construction. Boards seemed nailed together in whatever manner pleased the builder, the cracks jammed with green mosses. A yellow sun blistered overhead, casting its light over the terrain.

Theo breathed in the air, a grin spreading across his face. It wasn't paradise, but he wasn't dead.

Luras led the way silently, stopping by a half-ogre-sized monolith in the center of a circular section of the road. It sat atop a stone dais hewn from some dark stone Theo didn't recognize, although he wasn't an expert on stone.

"I assume the System doesn't exist in your world," Luras said.

"Nope," Theo said, shrugging. "Hey, do you have a mirror?"

"No. The system gives everyone a chance to pursue skills and collect information. That's the only way I can put it generically enough for you to understand," Luras said with a meek shrug. "Consider this your introduction... You can access information about yourself with a thought. It should appear in front of you in a format you can understand."

Theo obeyed, sending a mental command that resulted in a box containing information crowding his vision. He took a moment to inspect it.

Belgar (Theo Spencer)
Drogramath Dronon

Level 1 Alchemist
Core Slots: 2

Attributes:
Health: 40
Mana: 10
Stamina: 50
Strength: 5
Dexterity: 5
Vigor: 9 (+2)
Intelligence: 8
Wisdom: 15 (+2)
Points: 0

"All right. This says I'm an alchemist. And it thinks my name is Belgar—a 'Drogramath Dronon' named Belgar," Theo said, chuckling.

Theo dismissed the screen, watching as Luras traced his finger over the scroll. "We don't see that breed of Dronon around here, but whatever. The System placing you in our town makes sense. We have an alchemist's workshop that's been abandoned for a while."

Theo folded his arms, racking his newly powerful brain. "I was a soldier in my world. Why did it make me an alchemist?"

His first thought was of the governmental bureaucracy assigning him the rank of private, but then his mind flung back to what the Harbinger said about living a peaceful life. Theo wanted to keep that information to himself for the time being. There was no need to rock the boat before he knew what this town was all about.

Theo instinctively grasped at the place where his silver pendant normally was, clutching the rags given to him. The quick search revealed that, like his old body, it was gone. Like his old life, it became nothing but a memory.

"You're the first person I've given this speech to," Luras said, shrugging helplessly. "I don't know how the System determines what to make you."

"Fair enough. On with the tour," Theo said.

There was no use fighting it. With trained familiarity, Theo fell in step with the large half-ogre. It was too much like one of his old *assignments*. Falling in line with strange people to do even stranger things. The outcome of those actions often resulted in casualties. A tour felt much less harmful.

The pair walked a path that looked much like the other paths. The smell of manure grew as they trudged, the path becoming muddier by the second. Theo regretted going barefoot, with the muck underfoot quickly becoming more animal droppings than soil. A sprawl of farms came into view after they ascended a sloping rise. Endless fields of a slender, unknown crop reaching toward the sun stretched as far as he could see. The view of Broken Tusk below revealed how small the village really was.

"You're looking south, toward the town. To the east is the river. West holds the marshes. This entire area used to be a marsh before a wizard came to visit. It was well before my time, but he diverted the river out into the ocean. He even raised these fields so our people could farm," Luras said.

"Your people being the half-ogres?" Theo asked.

Luras shrugged. "When the ogres left Broken Tusk almost five hundred years ago, they left behind their half-blood children. Those children formed an alliance with the marshlings. We consider those two to be the founding races of Broken Tusk, but everyone is welcome."

"Very utopian," Theo said. He was already impressed that no one on the street shrieked in terror at the mere sight of him. He would need a mirror to see how bad it really was.

"We get by," Luras said with a grunt. "I'll show you the blacksmith and your shop. We'll avoid the tannery. I guess you don't know how skills work."

"Nope."

"Everyone has access to skills based on their level. You want skills that work with the cores you have. You should have started with at least one core," Luras said.

"Let's see," Theo said, mentally sending the command "Core" to the System.

A screen blocked his entire vision, filling it with two ornate orbs that pulsed with purple light. He could see two empty slots on each of the cores, inspecting them one after the other.

[Drogramath Alchemy Core]

Legendary Alchemy Core
Bound
2 Slots
Level 1 (0%)

Alchemy core given to the descendants of Drogramath.
Effect:
Increases the synergy of Alchemy abilities.
+2 Wisdom

[Drogramath Herbalist Core]
Rare Herbalist Core
Bound
2 Slots
Level 1 (0%)

Herbalist core given to the descendants of Drogramath.

Effect:
+2 Vigor

The information made little sense to him. He understood that these were cores related to his ancestry, a bloodline that he knew nothing about, but the rest was nonsense. What a core was, or how it functioned, was still beyond him.

"I've got two cores. Drogramath Alchemy Core and Drogramath Herbalist Core," Theo said. Something twinged in his mind when he said the names of the cores, as though he were imparting the knowledge of those things directly to Luras.

"You started with a legendary *and* a rare core?" Luras said, scoffing. "That's absurd. I've never heard of that happening."

"Well, I don't even know what the hell a core is," Theo said, laughing.

"Damn. Right, well... A core is like a family of skills. You level your core separate from yourself. You can attach skills to a core, but they need to be of the same attribute. You can't put a fighting skill in your alchemy core."

"Makes sense. Where do I get skills?"

"You should have some by default. With your luck, I bet there's more legendary stuff," Luras said, narrowing his eyes on Theo.

Theo didn't want to disappoint the only person in this new world he could call an acquaintance. Inspecting his skills and sharing them with him might be a bad idea. How valuable were these skills, and could Luras be trusted completely? Without an answer to his questions, he mentally summoned his skill menu. There were two skills at the top and an endless list of skills underneath. The indicator showed that he didn't have any skill points and couldn't purchase a new skill. He reluctantly shared his two skills with his companion.

"Drogramath Distillery Specialty and Drogramath Herbalism," Theo said, grimacing.

[Drogramath Distillery Specialty]
Legendary Alchemy Skill
You claim heritage to the Demon King—Drogramath the Potioneer. The Demon King's specialty was distillation, which allows you to extract the essence of alchemical ingredients. Distillation produces a pure form of extract, although some claim it to be more unstable.
Effect:
Allows the user to operate distillery equipment with significantly increased efficiency.
Allows the user to visually gauge the exact quantity of mixtures in units.
+2 Wisdom

[Drogramath Herbalism]
Rare Herbalism Skill
Drogramath had an eye for reagents. His descendants have an easier time identifying plants that can be used as alchemical ingredients.
Effect:
You have a keen sense for identifying whether something can produce alchemical ingredients.
+2 Intelligence

"I knew it," Luras said, clapping in triumph and laughing. He saw the pained look on Theo's face and clasped a hand on his shoulder. "I'm not faulting you for this. You're just insanely lucky."

"Is this something that I shouldn't share freely?" Theo asked.

"I'd keep it quiet for now," Luras said. "If someone asks, just refuse to show them the skill. It's considered rude to force someone to show their skills. You should equip those two in your cores, by the way."

Theo obeyed, equipping the Drogramath Alchemy skill in the alchemy core and the Drogramath Herbalism skill in his herbalism core. He felt a noticeable surge running through his mind as he equipped them, receiving the bonuses the two of them had. He smiled at his friend, gesturing for the tour to continue. The pair trudged down the slope, waving at farmers as they went. They finally caught sight of the other races inhabiting the town. The half-ogres were about Theo's height, although it varied by person, while the marshlings measured somewhere above his navel.

"They're so cute," Theo whispered, garnering a smile from Luras.

The marshlings toddled around on stumpy legs, their smooth skin appearing like that of a salamander. Their fat tails swept the ground as they walked. They had webbed feet, and most of them appeared to prefer going shoeless. On the side of their lizard-like heads were protrusions that reminded Theo of axolotls, with little frills coming forth. The tone of their skin varied from person to person, with some having bright pink pigment and others having that of mud. The one thing they had in common was that they were all extremely polite.

Theo spotted a marshling crowding the shadows under a tree. It stared at him with an intensity he couldn't ignore, feeling a strange pull toward it. The sensation swelling in his chest was that of a magnetic attraction, pulling him inexorably toward the strange, pink creature. He managed to shake off the sensation and follow Luras's lead.

The blacksmith's shop sat on a raised platform of stone, the work area completely outdoors. Steel sang under the marshling's hammer, and the creature doused itself with water every few seconds of hammering. The work area itself was incredibly tidy, with hammers hung on shelves to the side and a coal-burning forge sitting in the center. An anvil sat on a small stump, low enough for the diminutive man to work the metal.

"Every town needs a blacksmith," Luras said. "Throk spends most of the day working on stuff for the farm, but you might be able to ask him about crafting skills."

"Right," Theo said, "because I'm a crafter."

"Yeah. You won't have much in common with a person like me in terms of skills," Luras said with a shrug.

The tour continued southward, the road becoming less crowded the further away from the square they went. Homes dotted along either side of the path, a squat building looming in the distance. It was a stone construction, standing out against the wooden buildings that seemed iconic for Broken Tusk. A sign hung on the outside, depicting a vial with red liquid inside. The paint had faded long ago, causing it to look dilapidated like the rest of the building.

Luras produced a key from his pouch, handing it to Theo. "This passing of the key represents your ownership of the alchemy lab. Do you know how to inspect items or buildings?"

"I'm guessing I just think about it," Theo said.

"With that intent in your mind, touch the building," Luras said.

Theo once again obeyed, holding the thought of inspection in his head as he pressed his finger against the mossy stone. A box appeared in his vision, displaying information about the building.

[Alchemy Lab]
Owner: Belgar (Theo Spencer)
Faction: Broken Tusk
Level: 1 (0%)
Upgrade Status: 0/20
Rent Due In: 7 days

"Oh. I have to pay rent," Theo said, frowning.

"Every week. Miana will probably give you a grace period while you get set up," Luras said.

"How am I going to afford food—or get water?" Theo said.

"I'll bring something for you later. You can get a meal at the inn for a copper coin," Luras said. "You can draw water from the river, but if you don't have high Vigor, boil it."

Theo knitted his brow. Suddenly finding himself in another

world was hard enough to deal with, but now he had to see to his own survival. Meals back on Earth were easy enough to come by, especially in the end times. Everything was provided by the agency, and before that, he could just go to a grocery store and buy whatever he needed. Without Luras's help in this new world, he'd starve.

The half-ogre handed him a waterskin and smiled. "This should tide you over for a while."

"I owe you, Luras," Theo said, nodding to himself. "Once I figure this alchemy crap out, I'll pay you back with interest."

"I wouldn't say no to a health potion," Luras said, grinning. "Let's head inside and take stock of what you have."

Theo followed the man through the threshold. As he passed into the dark interior, it felt as though a mantle had fallen from his shoulders. Crossing into that small building washed his old life away. He felt the cores in his chest sing at the thought, banishing that old title away. Like the faded image on his now-lost locket, his old life vanished. Now, Theo Spencer was an alchemist.

Chapter 3
Theo the Alchemist

The interior of the lab wasn't much better than the outside. There was a suspicious lack of dust that made Theo think Luras had been by to clean. He doubted that the brusque woman, Miana, would have done so. It was fairly small, twenty paces by ten, and crowded with tables and equipment. A door to the right led off somewhere—a place he assumed was the bedroom. The scent inside was musky, and he doubted that opening a window would help.

"Did you clean up in here?" Theo asked.

"I did," Luras said. "I organized whatever books I could find scattered around," Luras said, pointing to a neatly packed bookshelf near the back of the room. "Your bedroom is through there."

Theo spent some time walking around, inspecting all the equipment. Near the back corner of the lab was a copper still, something that he thought fortunate because of his distillery specialty. The thing that caught his eye was a strange-looking piece of machinery in the opposite corner. When he inspected it, he let out a laugh.

[Glassware Artifice]
[Alchemy Equipment]

Epic
Created by: ???
Feed the Glassware Artifice any mote, think about the glassware you need, and it will be produced!

The machine was a large box with a slot to accept a circular object in the front and a spout near the bottom. It didn't seem large enough to spit out anything larger than a small phial. It was made of bronze, as far as Theo could tell.

"This looks rare," Theo said, scoffing.

"It is," Luras said. "Most of the text is obscured for me. I don't have any alchemy specialization, but artifices are rare."

"I just feed it motes, and it spits out glassware," Theo said.

"That's fortunate. We have a lot of concentrated magic near the river and in the swamp. If it accepts any motes, you'll have an easy time generating whatever glassware you need."

"Right... What should I do now?" Theo asked.

"Every book on that shelf is about alchemy," Luras said. "I suggest you read them. There are candles in your bedroom. I'll be around later to drop off some supplies."

"I can't thank you enough," Theo said, chuckling.

"You'll thank me plenty when you start making potions," Luras said, grinning.

The pair exchanged more pleasantries before the half-ogre departed, leaving Theo with a sense of unease. He didn't know what he had done to deserve such a great start in this new life. He could have been thrown into many different, crappy, scenarios, and yet his circumstances were amazing. Even with the threat of a hefty debt, rent to pay, and food to buy, he was in a much better situation than he was on Earth.

The books on the shelf varied drastically in topic. There were advanced topics he couldn't hope to understand, but also basic tomes regarding swamp plants and a general guide to alchemy. He picked up a book titled "Essential Alchemy" and started reading. The text was written in a language he shouldn't have understood. The blocky characters made up groups that were read as syllables, similar to Korean back on Earth. And yet, he could understand every word and even felt some insight on the topics.

While *Essential Alchemy* focused on the classical preparation of alchemical ingredients, Theo knew that most of it didn't apply to him. The milling of herbs and creation of poultices were things relegated to standard alchemists. Even the creation of potions was done in a fashion that seemed antithetical to the innate knowledge that lingered in his mind. He settled in for hours, reading at speeds he could never hope to achieve in his old world, although he wasn't much of a reader back then.

Mid-afternoon struck when he finished thumbing through the first book, and he settled in with the next. *Wild Plants of the Swamplands* was a much more productive tome, revealing the traits of many common reagents in the marsh. According to the book, the swamps wouldn't produce the common healing leaves present in the highlands to the north. He would have to rely on a plant called Spiny Swamp Thistle to produce healing ingredients. The method of processing these ingredients was elusive, as *Essential Alchemy* had a very brief section on distillation.

Only after reading for several hours did Theo notice that something appeared in the upper-left corner of his vision. A set of three bars, red, blue, and yellow, floated and followed his sight. The yellow bar lost a bit of its length, and he concluded that the rigorous study had depleted some of his stamina. He went searching in the bedroom for something to write on when he realized that the important information from the books had not left his mind. It wasn't a photographic recall of what he had read, but the high-level concepts stuck with ease.

Theo found a short knife among a pile of things in the bedroom, inspecting it before tucking it into his belt.

[Copper Alchemy Knife]
[Alchemy Equipment]

Common Basic copper knife. The copper in this blade won't react with any reagents.

He was confident that he could identify the ingredients in the wild without a problem and set off. The thick marsh to the west seemed like a more dangerous place than the river to the east. Sticky mud and looming cypress trees made the path uninviting. He wasn't walking for long before he spotted a cluster of trees and the spiked leaves of the Spiny Swamp Thistle. Theo knelt near the plant for a moment, remembering the warnings included in the book. The Spiny Swamp Thistle's leaves weren't poisonous, but they could easily draw blood. The spines on the leaves made that idea obvious, but the stalk of the plant was safe to touch. He bent it over, drawing his knife and cutting it below the leaves, and discarded the dangerous part.

The gnarled roots of the Spiny Swamp Thistle were fat and oozing a red liquid. Theo smiled to himself before regretting not bringing along a bag to store the ingredients. He reflected on the fact that he had found the thistle so easily, quickly concluding that it was because there were simply no other alchemists in the town. The muddy hills were his to harvest, and he found a goldmine. He pulled his shirt off, already threadbare and full of holes, to hold the roots.

Drogramath Herbalist Core gained experience (1%).
Theo Spencer gained experience (0.5%).

During his digging, he located several fat orbs of pulsating green energy the size of ping pong balls. Upon inspection, he learned that they were the motes he needed for glassware.

[Earth Mote]
[Mote]
Common The most common mote. A mote of pure earth

magic, condensed by magical forces. Earth Motes can be found anywhere in the world.

These were the items he needed to shove into the Glassware Artifice. Standing there among the trees and the dirt, he spotted a beady pair of eyes once more. The marshling's skin was pink, but those deep-set eyes stared with knowledge. He felt drawn into them, even if he couldn't explain why. But then, a crack of a branch caught his attention, some half-ogre stumbling through the woods nearby. When he turned to look at the marshling again, they were gone.

When the sun was getting low, threatening dusk, he returned to his lab to inspect his roots.

[Spiny Swamp Thistle Root]
[Alchemy Ingredient]
Common
The root of a Spiny Swamp Thistle.
Properties:
[Healing] [???] [???]

Theo stood there, staring at what he had collected for some time. His mind raced, looking for the best way to process the roots, but there were gaps in the knowledge that sat innately in his mind. *Essential Alchemy* contained a lot of information regarding the processing of leaves and the creation of crude poultices, but nothing about how to extract essences. He popped the lid off the Copper Still and nodded, appreciating that the last owner had cleaned it before abandoning the lab. His mind went back to Earth and a friend who died years ago from the famine. Before everything went to hell, he tried his hand at creating liquor at home.

This memory was a distant thing, and the entire process wouldn't return to Theo. He understood that whiskey was made with some kind of mash, a combination of the fermented ingredients and water, before running it through the still. The job of the still was to concentrate the ingredients, bringing out as much alcohol as possible. Theo collected a wooden bucket from his supplies and found a barrel of Purified Water near the Copper Still.

[Purified Water]
[Item]
Common
Water that has been purified. Perfect for stable alchemical reactions.

The discovery of the water was fortunate, as his current plan was simply to use the water from the skin that Luras had given him. He dumped his haul of Spiny Swamp Thistle Root into the bucket, found the nearest heavy wooden object, and started smashing it. The thought of cutting the roots up flashed past his mind but was quickly dismissed by his innate knowledge. It made sense when he thought about it. If his plan was to extract as much of the [Healing] property from the root as possible, he would need to smash it up to get at that red liquid inside.

His stamina drained as he smashed away, finally turning the mass of roots into a chunky paste.

A knock sounded at the door, startling him. "Hello?"

Luras's massive frame came through the door, a surprised look on his face. "Wow, you're already getting into it?"

The half-ogre held a bag in his hand, hoisting it up onto a table and coming to inspect the mash.

"Yeah, the books were helpful, but there are a lot of gaps in my knowledge," Theo said. "Hey, I can remember most of what I read. Isn't that cool?"

"You have high Wisdom, so it's not surprising," Luras said. "You'll eventually be able to remember everything you read, if you get it high enough, that is. It also affects your thinking speed."

"That's awesome," Theo said, suddenly feeling his stomach growl. "I hope you brought food."

Luras smiled, retrieving long strips of dried meat from the bag and handing one to Theo. The alchemist didn't hesitate, biting into the tough meat and swallowing it with some chewing. It was lightly salted and tasted of wild game. He didn't dare ask what creature produced the meat; he was just happy to have something to eat. He gulped at his waterskin, devouring the food without sharing a word with his new friend. After a while, the half-ogre flashed him another grin.

"Thanks, man," Theo said. "Oh, do you have a mirror?"

Luras produced another item from the bag—a small piece of polished metal. Theo took it, happy to inspect himself. In his eyes, he was a demon. The horns swooped over his head, following the path of his slicked-back black hair. His eyes had no pupils, and their shade was an almost-glowing violet. Even as he smiled, he winced at his fangs.

"I look like a monster," Theo said.

Luras shrugged. "You look like a Dronon."

With tremendous effort, Theo waved his tail from side to side. "I wonder if this thing does anything for my balance."

Luras laughed at that. "It's like watching a child learn."

"I *feel* like a child. I'm going to need some new clothes, too."

Luras produced clothes from the bag, and Theo frowned. There was a black linen robe, a loose-fitting shirt, and a pair of slacks. The thing that the alchemist was most interested in was the pair of leather gloves, remembering the sharp spines of the thistle.

"Again, I expect repayment in the form of potions," Luras said.

"Right. About that," Theo said, putting off swapping his clothes for the time being. He was still standing without a shirt and in hole-filled slacks. "I think I have a good idea of how this works."

The Copper Still sat under a flue in the ceiling meant to vent the smoke of a fire outside. Theo wished that there was a magical solution to heating his still, but he had to take what he could get. He smashed the roots a few more times before dumping them into the still, using a ladle to wash the rest of it out of the bucket. He added the Purified Water to match the level of the roots before returning the lid and positioning the condenser over a fat glass flask. Luras watched as he worked. The alchemist darted around the lab to collect the flask, wood for the fire, and a few books from the shelf.

"Do you know how to make a fire?" Theo asked sheepishly.

Luras silently collected the wood, taking a quartered log and scraping off the tinder with a knife. The section underneath the Copper Still protected the floor from the heat. It was made of perfectly hewn flagstones, arranged underneath in a decorative pattern. The hunter broke the logs down further, arranging them underneath and applying sparks with a flint and his knife. After only a few moments, a small fire crackled underneath.

"You mean like that?" Luras said, grinning.

"I have a lot to learn," Theo said, laughing. "Right... That's going to take an hour or two. I'm going to get changed."

"All right."

Theo retreated to his room, far too modest to change in front of his new friend. Behind his closed door, he inspected himself further, finding that all the sensitive anatomy was where it should be, and donned his new clothes. The shirt and pants were extremely comfortable compared to his burlap rags, and there was even a pair of moccasins made of the most supple leather he had ever felt. He felt like a wizard after pulling the robe over his shoulders. There was even an opening for a tail in his slacks.

"How do I look?" Theo asked, holding his arms wide in the alchemy lab.

Luras had lit a few candles, setting them in lanterns around the room as dusk fell over Broken Tusk. He regarded the alchemist with a discerning eye, smiling after a moment. "Like someone wearing second-hand clothes. The still is making noise."

Theo ran across the lab, leaning in to listen to the sound. The contents were boiling a little too vigorously. He instructed the half-ogre to reduce the intensity of the flames, bringing the pot to a low simmer. He didn't want the roots to burn against the bottom, fouling the extract. The pair found seats around the bubbling still, watching as a few drops of liquid fell into the flask.

"Do you miss your family?" Luras asked.

"I had little family left," Theo said with a shrug. "Most of my world's population had already died."

"That sucks."

"I was pretty all right with the whole arrangement," Theo said. "I was just enjoying every new day. This transition is a welcome change."

"I lost my mother recently," Luras said.

"Sorry to hear that."

"It's nothing compared to an entire world, I guess."

"You're right. It's a lot worse."

They sat in silence for some time before Luras brought up a new topic. He talked about his interests outside of hunting, and the people in Broken Tusk. The farmers were the real backbone of the town, being the only people besides the hunters who produced resources for them to sell.

"Alchemy is going to be big," Luras said, nodding to himself. "You seem like a really calm person—I like calm people—but you'll make a massive impact on this place. We have dungeons to the east, west, and north. Adventurers pass through often. Once they hear about a potion shop, they'll come in droves. It would be nice to have the first pick of the stuff you produce."

"A relationship of convenience? I can appreciate that," Theo said, smiling. "At least you're honest."

The condenser on the Copper Still sputtered a few times, the last drop falling into the flask below. Luras and Theo cleared away the fire to inspect the product. It was a clear pink substance, and the alchemist understood it was approximately five *units* of liquid, whatever those units were. Pressing his fingers against the flask, he got a pop-up describing what he had produced.

[Healing Essence]
[Essence]

Common
Created by: Belgar
Quality: Poor
5 units (liquid)
Concentrated essence of healing, used to create healing potions.

Drogramath Herbalist Core gained experience (5%).
Theo Spencer gained experience (2%).

"It worked!" Theo shouted, holding his hand out for a high-five.

Luras narrowed his eyes, raising an eyebrow.

"Slap your hand against mine," Theo said hastily, a stupid grin hanging on his face.

Luras obliged, hitting Theo's hand with force and sending him tumbling to the ground. This didn't diminish the alchemist's good mood—he had just made an essence.

"Not a potion, though," Luras said.

Theo ran to the shelf of books, retrieving one and bringing it back. *Essential Alchemy* had a small section on distillation, but it only had the basics. Essences were the basis of distillation alchemy, but they did nothing on their own. An alchemist needed to combine essences, water, and a catalyst to create a potion. Catalysts came in many forms, but the one listed in the book was Copper Shavings, which he remembered seeing in the drawer in the lab. He ran off to retrieve a pinch of the flecks, setting them down on the page of the book before approaching the Glassware Artifice.

Theo judged the contents of the potion he would make to be about two units after the reaction, something he didn't know how he knew. He retrieved the Earth Mote, shoving it into the artifice and closing his eyes to imagine a narrow vial with a glass stopper on top. The things would fit perfectly together, preventing any of the valuable liquid from leaking out. The machine vibrated, the aperture in the front expanding to eject a glass vial.

"Perfect!" Theo shouted. Luras watched as the alchemist returned to the flask of essence, grinning the entire time.

He found a narrow glass tube among the endless glassware strewn on the tables, something that he could easily use to measure out quantities. With one unit of the Healing Essence, one unit of Purified Water, and exactly two flecks of the Copper Shavings, he filled his new vial. The reaction was immediate and violent. A plume of smoke exploded out from the top of the vial, filling the room with a flowery scent. Theo proudly stoppered the vial, appreciating the dark red bubbling liquid and handing it over to his new friend.

Drogramath Alchemy Core gained experience (5%).
Theo Spencer gained experience (2%).

[Lesser Healing Potion]
[Potion]
Common Created by: Belgar
Quality: Poor
A lesser healing potion. Drink to restore health.
Effect:
Instantly restores 20 health points.

A surprised look washed over Luras's face. He took the potion from Theo and held it up to the candlelight, letting out a whistle. "You actually did it. I was certain you were going to blow us up."

"It's poor-quality, but that's my first potion!" Theo said, wagging his tail and pumping his fist. "I'm an alchemist!"

Chapter 4
Pay Your Debts

The sun broke through Theo's window, pulling him from a peaceful slumber. Despite the bed's rough construction, he had slept well. His stamina bar was at full once again, and he was ready to meet the day. He couldn't remember the last time he had gone to sleep shortly after dusk, and awoke with the dawn, but it made sense. Without electricity, he was bound by the whims of his candles. Something about the way the light flickered made him drowsy, and Luras had departed shortly after the sun had set below the horizon.

[Quest Completed: Welcome to Paradise!]
Reward: 10 Copper

A weight fell into Theo's pocket. He scooped out the ten coins, inspecting them. They were stamped with an image of a laurel and the number 846. He shrugged, returning them to his pocket.

Theo's stomach growled when he rose, stretching and sating his thirst with the last of his waterskin. The problem of drawing water directly from a river would have to wait until later. He couldn't stand by while his lab was such a mess. After creating his first potion, he gained a sense of where things should go. While eating the mystery jerky, he went around and tidied up. Glassware piled high in the room's corner, his makeshift pipette being the only one spared. Four units of the light pink Healing Essence remained, but he reserved those for later.

The three long wooden tables stood in the open, cleared of all the clutter. Only his two books stayed in a place of prominence, the remaining space reserved for stages of his production. With his lab sorted, he wanted to take care of a few more problems. His supply of water would have to wait, but he had an idea for that. Before departing the night before, Luras informed him he would have to meet with Miana and discuss his debt. After doing that, he would get a lay of the land and determine what the fair prices for his potions were.

It was easy to assume that farmers wouldn't have an interest in his healing potions, but it was impossible to imagine a swamp without some widespread disease. *Essential Alchemy* mentioned combining ingredients with [Healing] and [Cure Ailment] properties, and *Wild Plants of the Swamplands* had detailed drawings of a tree that could produce an ingredient with the [Cure Ailment] property. Focusing his mind on completing these tasks helped him adjust to the strangeness of the situation. He kept a single thought in his mind.

This is way better than being dead.

Theo pulled his light robe around himself. Despite the heat outside, he felt more comfortable wearing the robe. It made him look more like an alchemist, and that counted for a lot. The simple white shirt and gray trousers did little for him, but the moccasins were incredibly comfortable. He wondered if the leather used in the creation of his shoes had been gathered by his new friend, but he dismissed the idea and left the lab, locking it behind him.

The town was already buzzing with activity, with marshlings that smelled more like death than the marsh moving up the road in a small group. They greeted him all the same, smiling and baring rows of their fanged teeth. He winced at the sight but forced a smile before they could notice. Miana's house was also the mayor's office and was situated in the circle near the small monolith. He knocked and waited for her, listening to the angry stomping of her feet before stepping back to avoid the door.

"What?" Miana asked.

"Luras said I should see you about my debt," Theo said, smiling.

Miana's scowl vanished, a smile spreading across her face. "Come on in, then. Are you done setting up?"

"I'm working on it," Theo said.

She led him through the building and into a small sitting room near the back. With no fanfare, she handed him a scroll, which he immediately unraveled.

[Debtor's Notice]
It is noted by Miana Kell and the witnesses noted below that the Dronon named Belgar of transitional origin is hereby indebted to Miana Kell until such time as his debts are cleared. The debts shall accrue interest at a rate determined at Miana Kell's discretion and dependent on the betterment of Broken Tusk.
Below is an itemized list of services rendered in the acclimation of the Dronon Belgar to Iaredin.
Medical Services Rendered: 1 Silver
Room and Board (1 week): 10 Copper
Alchemy Lab (to be paid in installments): 1 Gold
Equipment (to be paid in installments): 1 Gold
Service Charge: 5 Copper
So it is noted, 873rd Year of Balkor's Betrayal in the Third Week of the Season of Blooms.

Theo gawked at the ridiculous price of everything, a twinge filling his mind as a box popped up in his vision.

[Pay Your Debts]
Quest

Miana Kell has overseen your transition into the new world, and you owe her a lot of money!

Objectives:
Pay the following debts:
Medical Services Rendered: 1 Silver
Room and Board (1 week): 10 Copper
Alchemy Lab (to be paid in installments): 1 Gold
Equipment (to be paid in installments): 1 Gold
Service Charge: 5 Copper

"That's a lot of money," Theo said.

"I don't expect you to pay it all at once," Miana said, rubbing her hands together.

"Isn't it enough to have an alchemist in the town?"

"What, you think I don't have taxes to pay? Half of what I collect from you will go to the crown. You know, you should appreciate what I've done for you."

Theo held up a silencing hand, a broad smile spreading across his face. He was too excited for this new world to let something like crippling debt get the best of him. "I will pay off my debt as quickly as I can. I've already made my first potion."

"Good for you," Miana said, sneering. "Now get the hell out of my house."

The brusque woman shoved him out of her home, his moccasins skidding along the wooden floor as he went. He stumbled out onto the muddy street as she slammed the door behind him, parchment still dangling in his hand. It must have been a common occurrence because none of the people passing by paid any attention to the scene. Theo shrugged and trudged northward toward the farms. Just like on Earth, farmers were up before dawn on Earth, working the fields until the light faded from the day. He could probe them for information.

After ascending the hill, he watched the half-ogres work the strange crop. Theo didn't know what season it was, but the southernmost fields weren't ready for harvest. As he wandered further north, he saw that a similar crop was being reaped by the massive farmers with sickles taller than him. The green fruit that grew on top of thin shoots looked like a clustering of giant corn kernels, three per plant.

Theo watched a large man ply his sickle on the crops, bringing a score of them down with a single stroke. Their eyes met, and the alchemist smiled. "What?" the farmer said crudely.

"I'd like to buy some... uh, whatever this is," Theo said, grinning.

It would leave a poor impression if he didn't at least offer to buy some of the farmer's hard work. The last thing he wanted to do was make enemies with the people who provided food for the town. They might even become good customers, if he could figure out how to make their crops grow larger or faster with alchemy.

"You're that lad who transitioned, aren't you?" the half-Ogre asked. "The name's Banurub, you can call me Banu."

Banu strode across the field, holding out his massive hand for Theo to shake. Like Luras, the farmer shook too hard, almost sending the alchemist tumbling into the mud.

"Nice to meet you, Banu. I was very excited to see your farm, but I'll be honest... I know nothing about this place," Theo said.

"Well, this field holds Zee. Sturdy crop. Grows in all seasons down south. You can mill it like a grain to use in many different things or eat it as it is," Banu said.

Theo couldn't imagine milling the fruit. Each kernel on the stalks was as big as his head. He remembered going to farmers' markets before the end times, buying absurd amounts of produce for cheap directly from the people who grew them.

"How much do you sell them for?"

"By the kernel? I couldn't say... We sell them by the bushel—typically exported north. Twenty kernels to the bushel, 10 copper for the bushel. Well, that's the price we get to export them for," Banu said.

"Would you take 6 copper for a bushel? And another copper upon its delivery to my alchemy lab?" Theo asked, smiling.

"Aye, I can do that," Banu said, reaching out his hand to shake once more. "That'll avoid the export tax."

Theo winced as he shook the man's hand before fishing 6 copper from his pocket. Banu counted it out and nodded at the alchemist, saying, "I'll have one of my boys deliver it."

"Thank you," Theo said, turning on the spot and walking along the fields once more.

He didn't have a use for that much Zee, and he didn't know if it was useful for anything. What he gained from the exchange was information, and a positive impression in the farmers' eyes. If people in town thought of him as a productive member of society, they would be more likely to work with them. He now knew that twenty kernels of Zee sold for ten copper. It was easy to reason that there was 100 copper to a silver, and 100 silver to a gold. Perhaps there was 100 gold to something else, but he couldn't speculate further. Because of the specialized nature of creating potions, and the scarcity within Broken Tusk, he could demand five copper per flask easily, ten if he was greedy.

The town of Broken Tusk was cleared of trees, a fact that Theo thought a shame. A wizard might have diverted the river away from the town itself, but water still soaked the ground. A few well-placed willows, or the equivalent of this new world, would do wonders to rid the roads of the mud. He filed the thought away before it got away from him, focusing on his next project. The area to the west seemed inherently dangerous, but it was easy to spot his next target. His book detailed a tree that was common enough in the swamplands, the Ogre Cypress. The familiar name helped center him, and they were easy from spot at a distance.

Wild Plants of the Swamplands had detailed drawings of the tree, and the harvestable parts of it. It had a thick outer bark that was useless, with seams of silver sap-laden bark underneath. This made up the bulk of the useful material of the tree—the Ogre Cypress Bark that the book described to have the [Cure Ailment] property. His intended use for the reagent was twofold. He planned to experiment by combining water purification with an essence derived from the bark and create a potion combined with the Healing Essence for portable affliction curing.

"These resources are untapped," Theo said. He shrugged it off, spotting a towering cypress to the west.

It was a short walk from the center of town, towering over the edge of the wetlands. Theo's moccasins were treated with animal fat to prevent water from seeping in, but he trudged through knee-deep water and muck to approach the trunk of the tree. Peeling back a layer of the outer bark with his Copper Alchemy Knife, he saw the problems with his plan. Only a small amount of the inner bark bore signs of usefulness, thin seams running underneath the outer layer. The alchemist stuffed his satchel and pockets full of the reagent, inspecting a piece as he removed himself from the mire.

[Ogre Cypress Bark]
[Alchemy Ingredient]
Common
The bark of the Ogre Cypress. Known for its restorative properties.
Properties:
[Cure Ailment] [???] [???]

"You're a busy man," Luras said.

Theo whipped around, finding Luras standing in the mire. A grin spread across the hunter's face, a gesture that the alchemist returned.

"I have a plan to improve the town's drinking water situation," Theo said, struggling against the suction of the knee-deep mud. "Mind giving me a hand?"

"If it means I don't have to boil water every day, sure," Luras said with a shrug.

The help that Theo hoped to get came in the form of the hunter's ability in combat. If he was comfortable enough to roam the swamps daily, then he could handle himself. The notion came true within two hundred paces of the Ogre Cypress. A massive turtle burst from the water and covered them in a spray of muck. It was huge for a turtle, larger than a horse, its shell covered in a layer of moss. The head of the creature snapped back and forth, pushing itself through the swamp and toward Luras. Theo focused on the monster, and an information box popped up as the half-ogre hunter positioned himself between it and the alchemist.

[Ogre Snapper]
Monster-type Turtle
Level 5
Ogre Snappers lurk in the swamp, waiting for unsuspecting travelers to step over them. Their beaks are powerful enough to snap bones. Many inexperienced adventurers have fallen prey to this monster.

Theo watched as Luras released a series of arrows, all finding their mark under the hard shell. The monster shrieked in pain, its blood flooding and staining the water. All the alchemist could do was watch in amazement as the hunter disassembled the creature methodically. His mind went back to his days working for that clandestine organization and taking part in covert operations with a fireteam. He didn't miss it. The creature fell to the mud after a few minutes of fighting, letting out one last sonorous cry before dying.

"What does it mean when it says 'Monster-type Turtle'?" Theo asked.

"Animals can become monsters, although I don't understand why," Luras said. He moved to inspect the turtle, digging under his shell and retrieving a small circular object covered in slime. "Sometimes they have a monster core, which is like a proto skill core."

"What good is a core from a monster?" Theo asked.

"Artificers can use them to create magical objects. You can feed it to a house to upgrade it—or a town," Luras said. "A Level 5 monster core isn't all that useful, but they sell for a decent price."

"How much would you get for one?" Theo asked. He trusted his newly honed memory to lock the information in.

"Anywhere from 20 to 50 copper, depending on the trader," Luras said. "How much are you planning on selling your potions for?"

"10 copper," Theo said, trudging over to inspect the downed turtle.

"You could get more," Luras said.

"I need to establish my name first."

"Speaking of which, you should name your lab," Luras said, holding the core out for Theo to take. He narrowed his eyes when he saw Theo's reluctance to take the object. "I expect free potions."

Theo smiled, taking the core and inspecting it before shoving it into his already-full bag.

[Monster Core]
[Proto Core]
Common
Level 5
A lesser monster core.

"I don't have any idea what to name my lab. I eventually want to have a shop," Theo said.

"You'll want to upgrade it, then," Luras said. "If you feed it enough cores, you can change the way it looks. Regular buildings exist in Broken Tusk, but your lab was created with cores. You'll get bonuses the higher rank your building is."

Luras withdrew a knife and dug around in the turtle's insides. He withdrew an organ and handed it to Theo with a smile. The alchemist almost lost his breakfast as the squashy thing fell into his hands.

[Ogre Snapper Spleen]
[Alchemy Ingredient]
Common

Spleen of an ogre snapper.
Properties:
[Poison] [???] [???]

"This is gross," Theo said.

Luras simply laughed, returning to butchering the creature. Despite its size, there wasn't much meat to speak of. Theo doubted that whatever meat was extracted was without parasites, his mind going back to the jerky he had been eating. He pushed the thought away, joining with the half-ogre as they continued trudging through the swamp. Midday came by the time they left with enough Ogre Cypress Bark to execute the water purification plan.

Theo dropped his ingredients off at the alchemy lab, and Luras helped him carry four buckets down to the river. The edge of the river was a long stretch of rocky beaches, the water coming to lap against a little cove where the town drew its drinking water. It flowed cool and clear, but he knew too much from watching survival shows on television to trust it. Inspecting the buckets of water, his fears were realized.

[River Water]
[Item]
Common
Water drawn from a flowing river.
Properties:
[Disease] [Parasites]

"Do you see that this stuff gives you diseases and parasites?" Theo asked, throwing his hands up in exasperation.

"I can't," Luras said. "Your alchemy skill must give you the ability to identify the properties that stuff has."

"Well, this stuff is riddled with crap," Theo said.

On their way back to the lab, Theo instructed Luras on the proper way to harvest Spiny Swamp Thistle. They returned to the unnamed alchemy lab with enough of the root to make a double batch of healing potions, a fact that the hunter was excited about.

"I already used the first potion you gave me," Luras said, dumping the roots in an empty bucket. "Found a fairly rare swamp wolf and tested my luck."

"I still have four units of the Healing Essence. We'll whip up four more potions after we figure this water thing out," Theo said, moving to consult *Essential Alchemy*.

The book detailed standard uses for essences but also mentioned more unconventional uses. In theory, he could use the pure essences to impart an effect on something. The example given in the text was that he could drip Healing Essence directly onto a wound to close it in a pinch. It wasn't as effective as making a Lesser Healing Potion, but his intent was different with this approach. The plan was to instill the property of the essence directly into the water, but how much of the essence he would need was a mystery.

Theo brought out a ream of parchment, laying it down on the table and holding it there with empty flasks. He drew out columns and rows, writing "Bucket (100 units)" in the first column, and "Essence (0.01 units)" in the second. He would work his way up from the tiny amount to find the most efficient ratio for water purification, if it worked at all. He urged the Glassware Artifice to create a tiny pipette capable of drawing partial unit–sized doses of the essence.

Luras helped load a spare bucket with the Ogre Cypress Bark, mashing it down and adding it to the Copper Still with enough water for the process. While the hunter made the fire, Theo created four vials of Lesser Healing Potion, all of which were of the same—poor—quality. He would need to refine the process if he wanted to produce better potions.

"I wish I had something to control the fire better," Theo said, watching as Luras stoked the flames to life.

"That's something for an artificer to make," Luras said. "Keep an eye out for people passing through town. You might get a magical flame from a passing trader."

"Right. I have to make money first," Theo said. "How do I add this monster core to the lab?"

"Just hold it up and think about it," Luras said.

Theo did just that, holding the slimy core above his head and focusing his thoughts on adding it to the lab. After a moment, the core vanished, and a screen appeared.

[Alchemy Lab Upgraded]
Belgar's Alchemy Lab gained 25% experience toward Level 2.

"Four cores to get Level 2." Theo groaned. "That's a lot of cores."

They waited there for some time as the Copper Still did its work. Theo controlled the flame better this time around, letting it smolder the coals before moving it under the still. Then he added wood as needed. The result was a longer distillation process, but it didn't sputter or burn like his first attempt. He inspected the ten units of liquid in the flask.

Drogramath Alchemy Core gained experience (8%).
Theo Spencer gained experience (3%).

[Purifying Essence]
[Essence]
Common
Created by: Belgar
Quality: Decent
10 units (liquid)
Concentrated essence of purification.

Not only had he made more of the essence, but it was of a better quality. Luras watched as Theo took notes, applying his trade to the buckets of river water. The first dose of 0.01 units was almost impossible to measure and had no effect on the tainted river water. He wrote his findings and moved onto the second bucket, applying 0.1 units, which was easy enough to measure by eye, but there was no reaction besides a faint sizzling sound. By the time he moved to the last bucket, after failing with 0.3 units on the third bucket, he applied half a unit of the Purifying Essence, and the reaction took place. The water bubbled, releasing a foul odor that had both men coughing and gagging. They opened the windows and the door before inspecting the bucket.

"Purified Water!" Theo shouted, holding his hand out for Luras to high-five.

"You have a knack for this," Luras said, gently slapping his hand against Theo's.

Chapter 5
Paying Customers

Theo and Luras filled their waterskins with the freshly purified water in the bucket. It tasted pure enough, and the alchemist was satisfied with the process. From the short run on the still, he had created enough essence to purify twenty buckets of water. It was hardly enough to keep the entire town from catching diseases, but it would do for the time being. At least he could ensure that he had water to use for both alchemy and keeping himself away from dehydration.

A knock came from the door. When Theo answered it, he found a burly farmer waiting with a crate of Zee that he had bought earlier in his arms. He accepted the delivery, allowing the worker to stow the heavy crop in the corner of his lab before paying him the copper coin and bidding him farewell.

"Already working with the farmers?" Luras asked.

"I like to get a head start on establishing relationships," Theo said, grinning. "At least now I'm fed and watered for a time. The next problem is earning money to pay my debts."

"How much do you owe?" Luras asked.

Theo inspected his quest and summed the totals. "2 gold and change."

"Wow, she really got you," Luras chuckled. "I guess you worked out that there's 100 copper in 1 silver."

"Yeah," Theo said, waving his hand dismissively. "And likely 100 silver to a gold."

"There's something bigger, but I've never seen it. Maybe diamonds?" Luras said.

"Well, I've got 4 copper to my name." Theo tapped his clawed finger against his chin.

"I've got some errands to run, but I'll stop by later to see how you're doing," Luras said.

"Don't forget your potions. I can't express how much I value your help."

"What are friends for?" Luras said, stepping out of the lab and heading up the road.

Theo centered himself before moving forward. He had consumed half of his stamina bar but already accomplished a lot. He was going to level up soon, as were both of his cores, a thought that brought him a fresh sense of excitement. The results of his work were tangible things that he could observe, improvements made in percentage points and knowledge. As he considered his next move, he stoked the fire under the still, cleaning out the copper vessel in preparation for another batch of Healing Essence.

The fire burned low this time around. During his last run to make Lesser Healing Potions, the fire had been way too hot. It had sputtered and spat the entire way through, burning the bottom of the still before he could extract most of the effect. This time, he monitored the fire closely, only feeding it enough to heat the mixture until the condenser slowly dripped into the conical flask. By mid-afternoon, he had a flask with ten units of Healing Essence, sitting at "decent" quality. He used all the motes that he had collected with Luras during their adventure in the swamp to create ten small vials and ten potions within each. He was on the edge of leveling his alchemy core, and himself, when he inspected the improved potion.

[Lesser Healing Potion]
[Potion]
Common
Created by: Belgar
Quality: Decent
A lesser healing potion. Drink to restore health.
Effect:
Instantly restores 25 health points.

The improved quality came with a 5-health boost in health recovery. Since Luras had already tested the effectiveness of the lesser-grade potion, he was confident that he could sell these. The only thing he needed now was adventurers to buy them.

Theo locked up the alchemy lab and headed north, toward the tavern. If there were adventurers in town, that was where they would be. He passed familiar faces along the way, mostly the half-ogre farmers who were standing around the central monolith. They waved happily as he made his way to the tavern. Looming over the square with its wooden plank construction, the building was one of the few two-story buildings in town. A sign hung out front in that strange language, claiming it was the "Marsh Wolf Tavern," which sounded ominous. The interior was a haze of smoke and a roar of sound, the tables crammed in the tight space. All heads in the tavern, including that of Miana's, turned to look at him before returning to their business.

Theo made his way to the counter, putting on a brave face as he got the attention of a woman behind the counter. She was a half-ogre, far shorter than Luras and Miana, with darker skin and softer features than either. She smiled and said, "What can I get for you?"

"What are you serving?" Theo asked, returning the smile.

"We have turtle stew today—1 copper."

Theo forked over the single copper and received a bowl of greasy soup that looked less appetizing than the jerky he had been eating. It was hot inside, or everywhere in Broken Tusk for that matter, but it was the first warm meal he had since arriving in this strange world. He accepted the bowl eagerly, digging in before prying about any adventurers in the tavern. The soup was decent. Although the flavor was bland, the turtle meat was tender. He cast his eyes around the patrons, noticing that shadowy pair of eyes staring at him from the corner. He had seen them before.

He dismissed the thought, turning his head after sipping the stock, and got the barmaid's attention once again. "Do you know if there are any adventurers here?" Theo said, managing a sheepish smile. "I'm Theo, by the way. I just transitioned to this world."

"Nice to meet you, Theo. I'm Xam," she said, smiling back. "There's actually a group headed to the swamp dungeon over there."

Theo followed her gesture to a table in the back. A group of humans sat huddled together, poring over a map. His satchel rattled as he spun around, the potions shifting with the speed of his turn. "I'm not much of a salesman, but..."

"A man's gotta eat," Xam said, chuckling. "Suck it up and put your best foot forward. The road to Broken Tusk is long, and most adventurers don't account for fighting on their way here. Chances are, whatever potions they prepared are long gone."

"I guess word gets around, huh?" Theo said. "I never said I was an alchemist."

"Yeah. Small town."

Theo finished his turtle soup, thanking Xam for the information before striding across the room. The group of humans fell into hushed silence as he approached. He wondered if his appearance had anything to do with their hesitation.

"Hello," Theo said. "I heard you're adventurers planning on entering the swamp dungeon."

"That we are," a man, presumably their leader, said. Theo could see his piercing eyes from under a leather cowl and a shaven head.

"My name is Theo. I'm the alchemist here in Broken Tusk and—"

"Broken Tusk doesn't have an alchemist," another adventurer spat.

The leader held a silencing hand up, casting a glare at his companion. "My name is Jarson. I led this rabble south in search of riches, but..."

"But you're fresh out of potions," Theo said, grinning.

"Well, I certainly didn't expect a Dronon this far south, let alone an alchemist," Jarson said, letting out a heavy sigh. "What are you selling?"

"I'll be honest. I'm a very *new* alchemist. I've crafted my first batch of Lesser Healing Potions, and I've got rent to pay. I have ten that I'd let you have for 5 copper each," Theo said.

Theo's initial plan of selling the potions for 10 copper apiece fell apart in the face of a paying customer. He didn't want the adventurers to know how desperate he was, or that he lacked any negotiation experience. But debt was debt.

"Sounds like poison to me," an adventurer said, receiving a swift fist to the arm from Jarson.

"Let me see one," Jarson said, trying and failing to hide the excitement on his face.

Theo produced one potion, allowing the adventurer to inspect it. Jarson nodded to his companions, casting a pleading look back at the alchemist. "These are worth far more back in the capital."

"But you're in the swamp now. And I'm broke," Theo said, shrugging.

"We'll take them all, but it feels like a robbery," Jarson said, grimacing. "We didn't come south to take advantage of small-town folk."

Theo didn't see it that way at all. He could live for months on 50 copper at his current pace. This wasn't so much about the sale, as much as it was the principal. The alchemist was untested and unsure about his wares. For anyone, let alone those going out to risk their lives in adventure, to buy his potions was a boost to his confidence. It was a drop in the bucket compared to his debts, but that quest would take time. He removed the remaining nine potions from his satchel and handed them over, receiving several stacks of copper for the exchange.

"Nice doing business with you," Theo said, pocketing his earnings.

As he was turning to leave, Jarson whistled, forcing him to turn back around. "We'll be here for three days before departing. Could I convince you to make us a few more potions?"

"What do you have in mind?"

"As many health, mana, and stamina potions as you can craft," Jarson said. "At your current rate of 5 copper a potion, if it's all right with you."

"Sounds like a deal to me," Theo said. He didn't know how people sealed deals in this world, but Jarson held out a hand for him to shake, which he did.

It took every bit of Theo's willpower not to hoot with excitement as he turned on the spot, departing from the adventurer's company. Xam caught his attention before he left, beckoning him over to the bar.

"I guess you made yourself a sale," Xam said, smiling.

"Big city people have big city money, I guess. They acted as though 5 copper a potion were low. They must be loaded," Theo said.

"That's the way it is out here," the female half-ogre said, laughing. "I hope you gave them a good deal."

"I did," Theo said, shrugging.

"I've never bought or sold a potion, so I wouldn't know," Xam said.

"Fifty copper seems like a fortune," Theo said. "I'm rich!"

"Theo." Luras's voice came from behind. "A word?"

Theo spun on the spot, the grin on his face washed away by Luras's piercing gaze. He followed the half-ogre outside, into the humidity and wash of pale light cast by dusk. They were standing in the square by the time they stopped to talk.

"Jarson is a good guy. I've talked to him already. Helped him scout out the dungeon even," Luras said. "But you're going to learn that not all adventurers are created equally. Careful who you strike deals with."

Theo thought about it for a moment. In all his excitement at making money to pay off his debts, he failed to consider the implications of such a deal. He laid claim to exactly zero combat skills and doubted that he could defend himself from anyone with his Strength. It was a bad idea to rely on the good graces of the town to see him through, and he would need to be more discerning when making agreements with strangers.

"Thanks," Theo said. "You're right. I got caught up in it. Fifty copper seems like so much money, though."

"And you'll make a lot more," Luras said, nodding. "The nearest person specializing in alchemy is a week-long journey north. You have a knack for it. You'll make a name for yourself quickly. Then you can charge more."

"And I still need to name my lab," Theo said. "I guess I want to expand it into a store and a lab, eventually."

"Good idea. The name should be something meaningful," Luras said.

"Or something silly," Theo said, rubbing his hands together. "Local Alchemy Demon. Devil and Herb. Swamp Thing."

"Those are stupid," Luras said. "I like the play on 'demon', though. People like a shop with a cheeky name."

"We're going to need to brainstorm this," Theo said, stretching and yawning. "Listen, do you think I could get your help with this project?"

"Does it pay?" Luras asked.

"Naturally. Half of our profits. A better rate than I'll give you in the future. This is to repay you for all the help," Theo said.

Luras managed a weak smile. The honesty in his eyes told Theo that the half-ogre didn't enjoy taking advantage of his friends, but the alchemist's insistent smile was irresistible. "Fine. I know you're just going to bother me until I help anyway."

"That's the spirit," Theo said, slapping his hand on Luras's back. "Meet me at the lab bright and early. We're going to run batches nonstop for three days."

"Sure thing, boss," Luras said, shaking his head and departing.

Theo left the meeting with a feeling of excitement, despite his draining stamina bar. He hadn't experimented with potions that restored someone's stamina, but he could really go for one right about now. It was easy to imagine someone with an absurd Vigor attribute could stay up all night with no rest. The thought lingered in his mind as he returned to the lab. With the candles lit, he settled in on his bed to thumb through *Essential Alchemy* before bed.

According to the book, only high-level potions using complex ingredients caused long-term issues. Even the highest-level restoration potions could be taken back-to-back with no problems. It was the elixirs that altered a person's status that were the issue. The book gave an example of a potion that allowed the imbiber to grow five times their normal size. Repeated use of the Giant's Elixir caused permanent damage to the drinker's heart, inflicting an incurable disease. It also noted the abuse of stamina-restoration potions. The mind still needed to sleep, and repeatedly staying up all night would inflict the same problems that came with the lack of sleep.

Theo spent the hour before and after dusk planning the next day. The first step would be to gather the ingredients needed for the potions. Luras needed to be instructed on which herbs to gather and how to gather them. His book had enough information on the Moss Nettle used to make the stamina potions that he could easily relay the information. The half-ogre would know where the herbs would grow because of his extensive hunting knowledge. The issue came in the form of finding motes and creating a workflow that would maximize the time they had.

Theo thought about the mountain of debt hanging over his head. It was easy to dismiss Miana's posturing when faced with a simple fact. He would easily turn to the swamp to provide all he needed to bring him out from under her thumb. The arrival of the adventurers was fortunate. The citizens of Broken Tusk were unlikely to pay 5 copper for a potion, even if it would save their lives. Adventurers had the advantage of fighting through dungeons, which he could only assume were incredibly lucrative. A band of fighters could travel a week south, raid a dungeon, and make a profit. That meant they had money to throw around, although the cost of doing business must have also been high.

The deal that Theo struck and the ridiculously low price of the potions was a calculated move. Once this group moved out, heading back north, they would spread the word that Broken Tusk had an alchemist. There must have been people with cores specialized in healing magic. It only made sense, but those people would need mana potions all the same. At every turn, he had an advantage, starting with his incredibly powerful cores and skills. He had a feeling that his ridiculously high Wisdom attribute—at least for his level—had a lot to do with his success.

As his mind was spinning with the possibilities of tomorrow, he collapsed into his straw bed. Every time he was about to fall asleep, however, another aspect of potion-making logistics popped into his mind, robbing him of rest. This went on for an hour before not even the most pressing matter could rouse him from slumber, and he finally fell asleep.

Chapter 6
The Vast Swamp, The Shy Marshling

Theo rose before the sun did, but not of his own accord. A loud banging roused him from his slumber, as repeated fists on his door cut through the lab and echoed in his bedroom. He stumbled out of bed, flinging the door to the alchemy lab open and glowering at Luras, who stood fresh for the day. Through a hooded gaze, Theo invited him inside.

"This world doesn't happen to have coffee, does it?" Theo asked.

"You're the alchemist," Luras said. "I don't even know what coffee is."

"It's a drink that helps you wake up," Theo said.

"We have something like that. You can make a tea from Moss Nettle," Luras said.

"Funny, that's one of the ingredients we'll be looking for today," Theo said. "Let me figure out how to prepare this giant corn before we go."

"Zee kernels? Here, I'll show you," Luras said.

The half-ogre strode to where the crate of Zee rested, hefting one of them up and withdrawing his knife. He cut it into slivers, moving the Copper Still out of the way and starting a small fire. Theo watched, sating his thirst from his waterskin before refilling it from the barrel of Purified Water. The strips of Zee went directly on the fire, sizzling as the flames licked them. Luras seemed proud of his work, producing two charred lengths of the vegetable and handing one to Theo.

"Dig in," Luras said. "This is the life's blood of Broken Tusk. The farmers replace the soil on the farm when it gets baked by the sun. Only that muck out in the swamp allows this stuff to grow."

Theo took a bite of his food, surprised at the complexity of the flavors. It was somewhere between an avocado and corn, striking a strange savory-sweet balance through the flesh of the vegetable. He had to put it down before he could finish it, however. He nearly jumped when a window popped up, informing him that he had discovered an additional effect of the Zee Kernel.

[Properties Discovery!]
You've discovered an additional effect of the Zee Kernel by eating it.
[Cure Poison] discovered.

Theo dismissed the screen, tapping on the kernel to inspect its properties.

[Zee Kernel]
[Alchemy Ingredient] [Food]
Common
Zee is a crop grown in the rich marshlands' soil.
Properties:
[Regenerate Health] [Cure Poison] [???]

"Wow, Zee is an alchemical ingredient," Theo said, scoffing.

"That's news to me," Luras said. "I can't see the properties of ingredients like you can."

"Well, good thing I have a ton of the stuff," Theo said. "All right. Time for my plan. It's pretty simple. We make as many potions as we can before those adventurers leave."

Newt and Demon

"So, we need to gather a bunch of stuff," Luras said, shrugging. "Easy enough."

Theo retrieved his books and went over the plants they would be targeting. It was fortunate that Luras knew what a Manashroom was and where they could be found along with the Moss Nettle. The mushroom would make a potion that restored mana, if the books could be trusted, while the nettle sorted out stamina. The bulk of the effort would come from collecting the plants, but processing had its own challenges. They set a target of fifty units of each essence in order to produce fifty of each potion.

"They'll have the money, too," Luras said. "Groups clear that dungeon and return to the north. The tales the traders tell say they can make up to a gold per attempt."

"And you can't really put a value on your life, can you?" Theo said, grinning.

The pair settled on lighter topics, waiting for the sun to rise before they set out. Luras warned Theo that there might be people coming to seek apprenticeships in his lab once word really got out. The fear was that someone from afar would come to usurp a spot that the citizens of Broken Tusk saw as their own. It would be seen as an act taking the wealth away from the town, something that Theo wanted to avoid at all costs. He hadn't met everyone in the town, but it was already growing on him. He wanted to embrace this new place as his home and see it prosper. He vowed to keep the wealth of his abilities within the small town.

The sun crawled lazily over the eastern horizon, casting the town in shadows of pink and orange. The heat was already on the rise for the day, a layer of sweat accumulating on Theo's body the moment he stepped out into the open air. Thinking about it, he didn't even know what time of year it was. Seasonal changes in swamps could be tricky to determine, but it certainly felt like summer to him.

"What season are we in?" Theo asked.

"The Season of Blooms," Luras said.

Theo knitted his brow, not sure what he had been expecting.

They certainly weren't going to call it "spring", but he could assume it was spring with the blooms and all. "Are we in the season that comes after the cold one?"

"That's right. All the seasons are 'Season of'. The Season of Blooms, Fire, Death, and Ice," Luras said. "Although we don't get any ice here. Or death—none of the plants die here like they do up north."

"Right. We call them spring, summer, autumn, and winter," Theo said.

"I like ours better."

"I don't like the one about death," Theo said, grimacing.

Luras shrugged.

The pair trudged north to the town square before departing. Luras assured him that anything interesting that happened in the town started in the square, but nothing interesting was going on. Throk was setting up his shop for the day, and the tavern had a barker outside that was advertising their specials. It was turtle soup, again. Miana burst from her home, narrowing her eyes on Theo and stomping through the mud. She still wore her nightgown, the hem already soaked in mud.

"Now that you're settled, I expect you to start paying," Miana said.

Luras cast her a dangerous glare, and she shrank under his withering gaze. "New arrivals get a grace period. It's in the contract."

Miana sputtered for a moment, straightening her nightgown and glowering. "Two weeks. Then I expect you to start paying."

She stomped off without another word, slamming the door behind her.

"She's behind on taxes," Luras said, shrugging. "We just don't get enough trade here."

"Broken Tusk pays taxes to whom, exactly?" Theo asked.

"The capital in the north. Qavell—the Kingdom of Qavell, to be exact," Luras said. "We have taxes on the Zee exports, as well as the cores I sell to traders, but it's not a lot. Miana collects property taxes as 'rent' weekly, then pays the full sum to the crown once a month. Not sure why they call it rent, though... Anyway, you're the first hope we've had in a long time."

"That's not a lot of pressure or anything," Theo said.

He had been in charge of people before—people fighting for their lives against impossible odds—but this was different. This wasn't some dictator who needed to be overthrown discreetly. This was the life of honest people. Theo couldn't picture the kingdom in his mind. He had learned so little of it. If the southlands were so distant that it would take seven days to arrive from the capital, and people acted as though that was far, they were in the backwaters. It stood to reason that overland trade was the best way that people could move goods, as he hadn't heard about any ships or other vehicles. Making a name for the town might not be enough to see it prosper. It needed roads, better infrastructure, and word of mouth.

Theo pushed those thoughts out of his mind. He pressed that sense of responsibility deep down, forcing it away. He wondered if his high Wisdom attribute helped with that, as the feelings vanished immediately. Reorienting himself to the present, he cast his eyes over the road leading into the southern swamp.

"Which would you like to collect first?" Theo asked.

"The Moss Nettle. It's going to be the worst to collect," Luras said.

"Lead the way."

Luras did exactly that, turning on the spot and marching down the road. Theo looked at his moccasins and grimaced, not looking forward to the sensation of mud squishing underfoot. They passed by the tall Ogre Cypress and deeper into the swamp, avoiding monsters where they could. Whatever monsters attacked were quickly put down by the hunter, his skill with the bow and dagger shining. All Theo could do was stand back and give a thumbs-up when the monsters fell.

Most of the trees had been cleared out of the town, but the swamp to the west was littered with trees Theo had never seen. There were more cypresses, but also low-hanging trees that looked like willows with far broader leaves. They looked brutish compared to the ones he remembered from Earth. While they hung low, it wasn't low enough that the pair could snatch the spiny moss from the boughs, and neither was certain of their climbing ability. Luras decided that boosting Theo into the branches was a good enough plan, hoisting the alchemist up by the feet and watching him wobble and shout his objections.

"Hold me steady!" Theo shouted.

"Grab a branch!" Luras shouted back.

Theo frantically snatched at the boughs, his inferior Dexterity making the task difficult. If not for Luras's incredible strength, he would have plunged into the mud below. Theo finally got his hands around a branch and hoisted himself into the canopy, pushing away smaller twigs and sputtering as a leaf inserted itself into his mouth. It tasted like mud and salt. He spotted the Moss Nettle, his superior Wisdom allowing him to recall the general shape of the plant from his book. The branch wobbled ominously as he moved out along the limb, pressing his body against it and holding on with both hands. He reached out a hand and touched the moss, intent on identifying it.

Drogramath Herbalism Core gained experience (2%).

[Moss Nettle]
[Alchemy Ingredient]
Common
A spiny moss that grows among the boughs of many swamp trees.
Properties:
[Stamina Recovery] [???] [???]

Theo almost lost his grip as he hooted with excitement, his heart skipping a beat. He wrapped both hands around the branch again. Waiting a moment for the drum of his heartbeat to settle down, he reached out and worked his clawed fingers under the moss, where it connected with the bark. He brought the moss to his face and inhaled the earthly aroma, somewhere between mud and a lemon.

"Look out below!" Theo shouted, tossing the clump of moss down to Luras, who caught it deftly.

"Keep your balance!" Luras shouted back. "I don't want to scrape you up from the mud."

Shimmying across the branches was tedious. Theo wasn't about to risk it with his horrible agility to get the task done sooner and took as much time as he needed. He moved on his belly, not daring to rise to his feet on those shaky limbs, and repeated the process over the course of an hour. Once all the Moss Nettle was cleared out of the first tree, the pair sized up another stout tree and did it again. It was easy to see why Luras wanted to get the moss out of the way, and without him, the entire ordeal would have been impossible. Every so often, a monster would come to investigate what the commotion was, instigating combat with the hunter immediately. Without someone to guard his back, Theo would have been dead before he got his first ingredient.

They spent the entire day filling their bags with Moss Nettle and fighting monsters. Theo's stomach was growling by midday, but he pushed through. Only when he started feeling woozy did they decide that they had done enough and plan to return to Broken Tusk. Before leaving, Theo received his first core level-up.

Drogramath Alchemy Core has reached Level 2!

Luras informed him that nothing happened at such a low level, but as his cores grew stronger, they would gain additional effects and more potency. Gaining a level in his Herbalism core was just a bonus for the entire journey.

The alchemist's stamina bar was drained, with only a sliver remaining. Luras propped him up as they deposited their ingredients at the lab before retreating to the Marsh Wolf Tavern for dinner. True to the barker's word, the tavern was once again serving turtle soup.

"Good to see you again, Xam," Theo said, grinning.

The half-ogre's soft features were a sight compared to the grueling day out in the swamp. She smiled the way she smiled at everyone, flashing her white tusks. "Nice to see you're not dead."

"Two of your finest turtle soups, please," Theo said, producing two copper coins from his pocket.

While he was covered in muck, the entire floor of the tavern was more mud than wood. Xam smiled and poured two bowls of the soup before returning from the hearth. Sliding them across the counter, she chuckled.

"You know, we're thrilled to have you here," Xam said, taking the coins. "People are already talking about how you're going to put us on the map."

"I'm afraid that I won't be enough to see Broken Tusk prosper," Theo said with a sigh.

"Don't pretend like you're alone," Xam said. "Miana is a spiky woman, but the rest of us are ready to elevate this swamp town. You're the kick in the pants we need to make that happen."

"Thanks," Theo said, smiling. "I'm going to go eat before I pass out."

Theo brought the two bowls to a table that Luras found near the back. It was further away from the hearth and near a window, a fact that he appreciated. The sun hadn't set yet, and the heat was still in full effect, but the breeze was nice. He didn't want to eat the hot soup, making himself hotter and sweatier, but it was delicious. The pair finished their bowls before speaking, reclining back in their chairs and taking in the surrounding conversation. The townsfolk's words came as a sea of aspirations, small hopes that would blossom into bigger things. Broken Tusk was filled with those little dreams, all coming together to create a bonfire.

The contentment that Theo felt at that moment was overwhelming. Combined with his low stamina, he found himself just watching. The life that he had wanted for so long was right in front of him. He hadn't lived in the town for long, but the scene of destruction and radioactivity seemed like a lifetime ago. The Harbinger was a distant dream that he could cast out of his mind and breathe in the fresh air of peace.

"Alchemist. I'm an adventurer." A small voice came from somewhere near the ground.

Theo turned to see a small marshling, their wet pink skin catching the light. He couldn't get over how cute the pink protrusions at the side of its head were. They wore a small black cloak that flowed over their fat tail, complete with leather adventurer armor. The alchemist noticed something in her eyes that felt familiar.

"You're not an adventurer, Tresk," Luras growled. "If your father hears you say that, he'll kick you out."

"Is it rude to say that the marshlings are absolutely adorable?" Theo said, letting out a heavy sigh.

The marshling called Tresk went a deep shade of violet, pressing their webbed fingers against their face and turning away. The marshling scampered off through the tavern, keeping their face covered the entire way.

As the little salamander-like creature ran off, Theo felt a deep sense of familiarity. He resisted the urge to grab his silver locket.

"You embarrassed her," Luras said, laughing and slapping his knee.

"Her? How can you tell?" Theo asked.

"Now *that* is rude," Luras said, grinning.

"I'm still learning," Theo said. "Does she have a crush on me or something?"

"Ah, well... Marshlings don't really work like that," Luras said. "I think she's looking for work."

"I think she's been spying on me," Theo said, that magnetic sensation pulsating in his chest. "I've seen a strange set of eyes staring at me from the shadows since I got here. Hard to shake the sensation of attraction."

"Surely not romantic attraction," Luras said, raising an eyebrow.

Theo waved him off. "No, not romantic attraction," he said. "Something *weird*. A pull from my chest. A sense of... familiarity."

Luras eyed him curiously. Theo could tell there was something the half-ogre was holding back, but couldn't put his finger on it. "I'm sure it's nothing."

Theo didn't feel as though it was nothing. He wanted to know more about the strange marshling girl. He wanted to find out what the urgent feeling building in his chest was, as though there was a dam ready to burst. It was as though a thread connected them, invisible to everyone but quickly retracting. The alchemist shook the thoughts away, deciding they were better met on a different day.

"I'd hire her if I needed an adventurer," Theo said with a shrug.

"Well, keep that in mind. She got her hands on some combat cores and insists on being an adventurer, despite Throk's protests."

"Oh. She's Throk's kid?" Theo scoffed.

"She's an adult, but yes," Luras said. "We really could have used her for the trees, actually. She's a rogue and has high Dexterity."

"Yeah, we're definitely hiring her," Theo said. "How much fallout can I expect from Throk?"

"Some. He knows that she's going to be an adventurer. He's just fighting it as long as he can," Luras said. "It's really just a matter of protecting his child. He has other kids to take over the business, but parents can be really protective. Especially marshlings."

The pair sat there for some time as the sun hung low outside. It wasn't even dusk, and Theo was ready to turn in for the night. The moss was the most difficult part of the harvest, though. Luras didn't think that the mushrooms would be much of a problem, and they already knew easy spots to find the thistle. If everything went according to plan, they would have enough materials to craft by the end of tomorrow.

Luras helped Theo to his feet, and they made their way to the door, only to be waved over by the group of adventurers they had missed. Jarson was reclining in his chair, a grin hanging on his face, as they came over to talk.

"I tested your potion, Alchemist," Jarson said, his grin widening. "You're a hidden gem."

"Thank you," Theo said.

"I'm not sure how much you know about alchemy, but distillation is an advanced skill. Most alchemists start with very simple concoctions that don't really get the job done," Jarson said. "Everyone eventually specializes in distillation, but that comes way later."

Theo hadn't even thought about his path in alchemy yet. *Essential Alchemy* described many processes to create useful things from plants, but he didn't really consider the idea that he was ahead of the curve. It made sense when he thought about it, as the book lingered on those other processes and glossed over distillation.

"I wasn't aware of that, actually," Theo said, grinning. "Thank you."

"No problem," Jarson said, waving a dismissive hand. "We might even come back, if you're still here."

"I have no plans to leave," Theo said. "Now, if you'll excuse me, I'm about to collapse."

Jarson laughed and waved them away. Theo's mind wavered in and out, the journey back to his unnamed alchemy lab a blur. He climbed into bed with his friend's help, kicking off his muddy moccasins and pulling the sheets up. The sun dipped below the horizon, casting the room in shadows as Luras went to leave. The alchemist was asleep before the half-ogre had even left the building.

Chapter 7
The Newt and Demon

Theo woke up the next day feeling refreshed. He was up well before dawn, and his stamina bar was full once again. It was impossible to tell how many hours it would be before dawn, and he didn't even know if this new world worked on a 24-hour day. He considered the differences in the world he had already discovered. It was impossible to shake the feeling that things were so similar. Whatever system deposited him in this spot knew exactly what he needed to be happy, and he was grateful.

As he blinked the sleep away, he heard something out in the lab, his heart immediately hammering hard in his chest. Theo padded across the room, pressing himself against the wall and peeking around the corner. He didn't want to take any chances. A small pink form came into view, clad in the same black cloak he remembered from the day before. Tresk sniffed the air, turning to meet his gaze. She toddled across the lab, coming to peek around the corner as the alchemist stood, trying not to laugh.

"Hire me, alchemist!" Tresk said, a burning intensity behind her eyes.

"I don't need an adventurer," Theo said, smiling.

The pair were nose-to-nose at the threshold. Tresk smelled like flowers, similar to the effect of a Lesser Healing Potion. Theo simply took the situation in.

"I can help," Tresk insisted.

Theo considered his options before responding. Broken Tusk's fear that he would take an outsider under his wing came to mind, and he didn't want to offend the people of his new home. There was the problem that Throk, Tresk's father, would get involved in the situation. But he didn't need to hire her as an adventurer—he didn't even need the services of an adventurer yet. What he needed was someone who could climb trees and collect reagents.

He had to consider actually paying her as well. He couldn't offer her any kind of salary yet. The 50 copper that he had gotten from the adventurers would dwindle quickly if he didn't make inroads into selling more potions. But there lay the biggest issue. He needed materials to make potions. Every moment he spent out in the field was a moment he wasn't crafting potions. It came down to this need that he decided to hire the cute marshling. How long Luras would continue to work alongside him was unknown, and he didn't want to force the half-ogre to work for him forever. People often had their own aspirations.

"Can you collect reagents?" Theo asked. "I expect hard work from my employees."

"You don't have any employees," Tresk said, grinning.

"Not yet, but when I have them, I'll expect them to work as hard as I do," Theo said.

Tresk giggled at that. She shook her head, the feathery pink things on the side of her head flopping with the motion. "I don't want any pay, but I'll work hard."

"I *have* to pay you," Theo said, frowning. "Luras has a stake in our current contract, but I can pay for the materials you gather. I can give you a copper coin for every ten potions we make in this contract, and later on we can renegotiate."

"I don't care," Tresk said, finally leaving the doorway and entering the bedroom. Theo watched as she eyed up the room, nodding to the corner opposite his bed. "I need a place to stay."

"You want to live in an alchemy lab?" Theo asked.

"Yeah. Father is going to kick me out when he hears you hired me," Tresk said with a shrug.

"I don't want to strain my relationship with anyone," Theo said.

"He'll be mad at me, not you. And he'll get over it. I'm 20 years old—old enough to leave the nest by marshling standards," Tresk said, her gaze confident. "Now, hire me, alchemist."

"Done. Luras will be here soon, and we can discuss our plans," Theo said. "We'll get you a more agreeable sleeping arrangement when we can."

"The floor is fine," Tresk said.

Theo sighed and shrugged, leaving the bedroom with the marshling close on his heels. The alchemist went around the room, lighting the candles until the sun rose. He realized that he didn't know what they ate or if she would find Zee offensive, but he started preparation anyway. Piles of useful stuff littered the edges of the lab, still without a permanent location. There was a tea set among the junk. He set about making a small fire and tossing the cast-iron kettle filled with Purified Water on, and waited for it to come to a boil. With his knife, he cut small pieces of the Zee Kernel and set them on the flames, just like Luras had done.

Tresk watched intently the entire time, hovering behind him and making surprised sounds at his every motion. Theo laughed it off, cutting a small portion of the Moss Nettle to steep in the boiling pot. The pair sat down next to the fire, digging the sliced kernels out of the coals and eating in silence. After a while, the tea was ready, filling the room with the scent of citrus. Theo poured two cups and tested his own, noting the subtle orange flavors and sudden rush of energy. It wasn't coffee, but it would do for now.

Being in Tresk's presence brought a sensation of strange familiarity. She was a stranger, but he knew her. Theo wanted to let himself get washed down that river of nostalgia, of old feelings, which should have been dead but were still burning even a decade after *her* death. The closer she got, the stronger he felt the tug in his chest. The more she lingered, the more he worried their souls would join without their consent.

"What is your world like?" Tresk asked, sipping her tea.

"It was dying before it was destroyed," Theo said. To his surprise, he finished his entire slice of Zee Kernel. It was incredibly filling, but the busy day yesterday left him feeling drained.

"Bummer," Tresk said. "Do you have marshlings there?"

"Nope, just humans," Theo said.

"Double bummer. Sounds boring." Tresk snorted.

"It had its moments," Theo said.

"What did you do?"

Now that was a hard question to answer. Theo wanted to shed his past life completely. The faster he stopped thinking about it, the better. He wouldn't tell her about the horrors he had witnessed, or the ones he had caused. The parentless families he had left, or those wiped out completely. "Assassin" wasn't a good term. That implied confidence and poise that he never had. "Brainwashed child soldier" was more accurate but didn't convey the growth he had made at the end of his life. He died when he was in his forties.

Tresk's question was born out of genuine curiosity, not a prodding intent meant to make him relive those times. It was small talk, never meant to crack open those dark things still lingering in his mind. No, she just wanted to know what he did. She was too innocent.

"I was a killer," he said, finding the word too easy to say.

Tresk tilted her head, looking him up and down. She grabbed at his arms, almost able to wrap her tiny hands around his stick-thin biceps. "You? Killer? You look like a clerk more than anything."

Theo burst out laughing, clutching at his sides as Tresk nervously joined with a chuckle. "That wasn't the reaction I was expecting. Murderers aren't seen very favorably where I'm from."

Tresk shrugged. "People have to survive. I'm a rogue, I've killed a couple people."

Theo laughed again, slapping the marshling on the back. "No, you haven't."

"Okay, maybe, but I could!"

"Then we're going to get along well," Theo said, grinning.

Tresk grinned, suddenly busying herself with the tea. Theo watched her reactions and wondered if she had any romantic intent. He had only just met her but had absolutely no interest in dating anyone in this new world. His life on Earth was a series of disastrous relationships that he repeatedly sabotaged. The door swung open, Luras leading with a lantern and sighing.

"I knew you'd be here," he said.

"I need work," Tresk said, hissing.

"I know. This was bound to happen, but your father won't be happy," Luras said.

"He'll get over it," Tresk said, glowering.

Luras crossed the room, setting down his lantern and sitting near the pair. He cut himself a piece of Zee and started roasting it. "I know what you're doing, Tresk."

"Shut it."

"You made some tea?" Luras said, shifting uncomfortably and changing the subject.

"Help yourself," Theo said, gesturing to the pot.

Luras busied himself with the tea, removing something from his satchel and adding it to the liquid. He sipped it and let out a heavy sigh, casting his gaze to the ceiling. "Of course your tea would be the best I've ever had. You're an alchemist."

Theo hadn't thought about it before, but his alchemy core might influence the brewing of teas. It wasn't exactly alchemy, but perhaps it was close enough. The trio sat for some time, mostly in silence, only exchanging the occasional word. When pale orange light flooded through the windows, the silence was broken entirely. The day started.

"As your minder, I need to ask your new hireling a question," Luras said, staring Tresk down.

"Mind your own business, Ogre," Tresk growled. "I'm trying to get to know him before I decide."

"You plan on performing the Tara'hek, don't you?" Luras asked. "Are you saying you knew at first sight?"

Something flared in Theo's chest. That string that had been tugging suddenly pulled taut. Whatever the Tara'hek was, it called to him. It was like a siren song, something he couldn't avoid no matter how hard he tried. The way the pair were staring at each other told him that it was something serious, but he was afraid to inquire. After a tense moment of staring, he broke the silence. "What's that?"

"It's a bonding ritual," Luras said. Tresk flushed a deep shade of violet.

"What? You want to get married?" Theo asked with a chuckle.

"It's not marriage!" Tresk shouted, returning her attention to her tea.

"It's more of a legend," Luras said, letting out a sigh. "The bond only happens when two people are a perfect fit. I don't mean they get along well, or something like that. They exist to serve each other. The legend guarantees both parties will rise to greatness. But this is just a young woman's fantasy. You would have sensed her from afar, Theo."

Theo's face went blank for a moment. He *had* sensed the woman the moment he got into town. That pull was only drawing him closer by the moment, and he didn't know if he could resist its gravity any longer. Luras read the alchemist's face, his mouth falling open.

"I might have felt a little something," Theo said.

"You're kidding," Luras said. "Sure. Just drop into town with a legendary core, throw in a legendary skill to complement it, and then take up a legendary bond with a Broken Tusker right away. Makes sense."

"The bond is strong, Luras," Tresk said. She looked sheepish about her words. "I can already taste the power it will provide."

"This isn't something to take lightly," Luras said.

"I do not take it lightly!" Tresk shouted. "I have watched Theo from the moment he arrived. I know the bond is perfect."

"Get to know each other before you take the plunge," Luras said.

"That's a good idea," Theo said, smiling. He had no intention of following his own words. Romance didn't interest him at all. Whether it was his new body or his old mind, the bond seemed more attractive than anything else. Luras didn't need to know that, though. "I think I just figured out what I'm going to name the lab, though."

"What's that?" Luras said, crossing his arms.

"The Newt and Demon," Theo said.

Luras burst out laughing, slapping his hand against the ground. "All right. This might be perfect."

Tresk sat there, burying her face in her hands and shaking her head. Theo didn't understand how serious being a marshling's life partner was, but weighing the options, it seemed like a decent idea. She could help with herb gathering and one day delve into dungeons. He could only imagine what ingredients they could find in the swamp dungeon.

"She's going to live here, so I guess that's the first step," Theo said.

"Yeah, Throk will kick her out for sure," Luras said, confirming Tresk's earlier words. "All right. How about we get down to business for the day?"

"Please!" Tresk pleaded.

Theo went to the table, bringing his tea along. The moss had a powerful effect, and he was completely awake by the time he consulted his books. Tresk was a very studious person, taking notes as he explained her role in the collection of ingredients. She was tasked with the collection of the Spiny Swamp Thistle Root, the easiest of the reagents to collect. The Manashroom was more difficult to collect, but nowhere near the level of difficulty of foraging the moss. Tresk copied the drawings from the book onto a ream of parchment, noting the characteristics and nodding through the alchemist's explanations.

"I've seen them before but didn't know they were alchemy ingredients," Tresk said.

"That makes it easy," Theo said, craning his neck to look outside the window.

The sun was up, the last vestiges of dawn giving way to a clear blue sky. Tresk departed to collect reagents on her own, hoisting a satchel over her shoulder and leaving the lab. Theo and Luras spent some time strategizing their collection effort. The Manashroom would be in a cave to the north, past the farmer's fields. The half-ogre only remembered seeing them there because they glowed in the dark, illuminating the darkness with a pale blue glow.

"It's an hour's walk, but we'll get more than we need from the cave," Luras said.

"Let's get to it," Theo said.

The pair departed northward, stopping in the square to see if anything was going on that day. Miana burst from her home, spotting them through the window, but quickly retreated under Luras's glare. They shared a laugh and continued on. Theo's clothes were dirty, strewn with muck and smelling foul. It was another problem that he wanted to solve with alchemy, but his first plan to purify the water of the town had seen little use. The contract with the adventurers saw him chasing down useful reagents, unable to unfurl the purification plan completely. He would have to try dropping a unit of the Purifying Essence on his clothes when he got back to the lab. If everything else fell apart, he could start a laundromat.

Farmland passed on either side, and Theo regretted not making stamina potions. It wouldn't drive away the need for sleep, but at least it could help the fatigue he felt in his muscles. Luras seemed at home while traveling, even when the dirt path disappeared and gave way to an open forest. Fortunately, it wasn't a marsh like the land to the west. The area was a dense pack of lowland trees, steep hills, and rocky terrain. It was easier to move through than the swamp, but it still had its challenges. They were attacked by several monsters, some kind of wolves, but Luras had no trouble putting them down.

They spotted the cave after an hour of mostly silent travel. The entrance was cut into the side of a stout hill, naturally formed in stone that appeared to be shale. It flaked off the edges of the yawning entrance, leaving messy piles on the ground.

"We'll rest here for a moment," Luras said, dropping his satchel and sitting on the rocky ground. "I've never seen someone try the Tara'hek. There's this story... Ah, well it's dangerous. Do you swear that you felt the pull?"

Theo thought about that for a moment. He wouldn't embarrass himself by admitting that it felt like a connection as deep as the one he had with his dead wife. Nonetheless, he couldn't deny the pull. That was a great way to put it, as though the cores in their chests wanted to join together.

"I swear."

Luras rolled his shoulders, staring off into the distance for a moment. "You should seriously consider performing the Tara'hek. If you feel the pull, it's real. You could become *powerful*."

Theo already planned on accepting, but his friend's words solidified the idea. The name he came up with was enough to give Tresk a stake in the lab, but having an adventurer as a partner was a very powerful reason. Some innate knowledge in his mind told him that alchemical finds in dungeons were valuable. It would give him an edge in the future, when his skill was renowned.

"If she likes me enough to do it, I'll accept," Theo said, once again pushing those familiar feelings aside.

"Good. She's a good person. Although, I don't know if '*like*' has anything to do with it. According to the legends, you know," Luras said. "Anyway, the rest is over. Let's get some mushrooms."

Theo would have been perfectly happy in a cave filled to the brim with snakes, wolves, or whatever other horror this world had to offer. He wasn't happy with the fact that it was packed with monster versions of insects. Their strangely jointed limbs made him want to vomit. As the pair delved into the cave, they skittered along the ceiling and attacked. The monsters were no match for Luras's prowess, easily falling to either his bow or his dagger, but the alchemist couldn't stand to look at their corpses. He averted his gaze as they passed by the dead monsters, grimacing the entire way.

"Most people don't like insectoid monsters," Luras said with a shrug, "but the prize will be worth it."

It didn't take them long to see that promise come true. The cave was littered with Manashrooms. They were scattered along the ground, emitting a faint light even after being harvested. Theo inspected the first mushroom before continuing with his companion.

[Manashroom]
[Alchemy Ingredient]
Common
A mushroom emitting a pale blue glow.
Properties:
[Mana Recovery] [???] [???]

"This is it," Theo said, confirming what they already knew. "At least my book is accurate."

"It's going to have all the base-level materials. Once you need more exotic ingredients, it's going to be trial and error."

Luras worked them deeper into the cave, easily slaying the insects as they went. Theo hadn't even thought about what level his friend was at. He had taken advantage of the half-ogre's prowess for days without even thinking about it. With a thought to inspect the man, he reached out with his mind and received a pop-up that confirmed his suspicions.

[Luras Trinner]
Half-Ogre

Level 12 Ranger

"It's considered rude to inspect people without their permission," Luras said, turning to meet Theo's gaze. The alchemist's face went pale. "I don't mind. Just a word of advice."

"Sorry. I realized I didn't even know what level you were," Theo said with a sheepish smile. "I should have realized you were far more powerful than me."

Luras grunted a response, pushing further into the cave. With the next mushroom harvested, Theo saw his first personal level-up. A screen similar to the one that had appeared when he leveled his core popped up.

Drogramath Herbalist Core gained experience (2%).
Theo Spencer gained experience (2%).
Theo Spencer reached Level 2!
Theo Spencer received one free point!

"I got a free point!" Theo shouted excitedly. "What's that?"

"You can put a point in any attribute you want. I think your primary attribute is Wisdom," Luras said.

Theo didn't hesitate, mentally commanding his personal sheet to appear and dumping the point into Wisdom. He looked over his sheet, noting that his Wisdom was extremely high compared to his other attributes.

Belgar (Theo Spencer)
Drogramath Dronon
Level 2 Alchemist
Core Slots: 2
Attributes:
Health: 40
Mana: 12
Stamina: 50
Strength: 5
Dexterity: 5

Newt and Demon

Vigor: 9 (+2)
Intelligence: 10 (+2)
Wisdom: 18 (+4)
Points: 0

Theo waved his noodle arms around for a moment, knitting his brow. "Should I put any points into Strength?"

"Not likely," Luras said. "I don't know many people around here who have their points into anything but Strength or Dexterity. Going outside of your focus isn't a good idea."

"I guess I need all this Wisdom to know what the hell to do with these ingredients," Theo said.

Luras chuckled, fording deeper into the cavern. The journey into the cavern wasn't as exhausting as climbing the trees. Theo just had to follow behind his friend and collect the mushrooms, but neither of them was interested in being outside of the town when dusk approached. By the alchemist's judgment, they had collected enough Manashrooms to make more than fifty potions. They left the cave with bags glowing with a blue light and bulging at the seams. The weight of their haul made the journey back much more difficult.

The farmers were done in their fields, and the familiar sounds and smells of the swamp returned. While the area north of Broken Tusk had the advantage of northerly winds sweeping off the high mountains, the swamp was set low to sea level. The crickets sang, getting a head start on their nighttime routine, and townspeople chattered in the town square. The duo made their way back to the alchemy lab to deposit their goods, finding Tresk with an absurd amount of Spiny Swamp Thistle Root, piled high on a table. Theo judged, with his alchemy ability, that there was enough root to make several hundred health potions.

"You've been busy," Luras said. "You don't even have the Herbalism skill."

"It's easy once someone tells you what to look for," Tresk said.

"Also, I might have convinced my big brother to help me. Also, I'm homeless. Yay."

"No, you're not," Theo said, unloading his Manashrooms. "You live at the Newt and Demon now."

"I like that name," Tresk said, fiddling with her cloak.

The sun was getting low outside, the dusk threatening to settle in over the town. Theo commanded his friends to join him at the Marsh Wolf for dinner, insisting on paying for everyone's meal. To his surprise, they were serving a different stew tonight. The wolf meat stew tasted exactly like the turtle meat stew, but he didn't mind. They found a table near a window and ate their meal, partaking in light conversation until dusk hung over the town.

"I'm going to head out now that you have someone to haul you home," Luras said.

"All right. Stop by tomorrow, although I'll just be distilling all day," Theo said with a wave.

Luras left with a smile, leaving Theo and Tresk alone in the tavern. They ate in silence for some time, still feeling each other out. The arrangement that she was proposing was strange to him, but the idea grew on him by the second. Those long moments of silence stretched out, and he questioned why he hadn't thought of such an arrangement before. He needed a companion to take partial ownership of the business. He couldn't be everywhere at once and would need someone to run errands for him or help with the lab. It just made sense.

"Shall we?" Theo said, breaking the silence.

"Yes. I'm very tired—my stamina is nearly gone," Tresk said, beaming.

The pair walked in time down the muddy street, the marshling dragging her wide tail through the mud. She hummed a song as they went, skipping every so often. Whatever hopes she had for the future, Theo would help see them through. Just like every person in Broken Tusk who would benefit from the alchemy lab in their town, she would get some piece of the fame. With the lab locked up, they brought a lantern into the bedroom to sort out new sleeping arrangements.

"The bare floor is fine," Tresk insisted.

"Nonsense," Theo said. "There's so much junk in here, there's bound to be... Ah! There we go."

Theo found a spare bedroll tucked away among the pile of junk. It sat under various linens and discarded flasks, stained from years of use but still comfortable. He cleared away the things cluttering the far end of the room and laid it out for her. It wouldn't be a permanent place for sleeping, but it was good enough for now. The bed he slept on wasn't much better than the floor. A straw-stuffed mattress wasn't comfortable to sleep on, the wood slats underneath him pressing up at odd angles.

"We'll do great things, Theo," Tresk said. "Once I get to the point where I can go into a dungeon, you'll see."

"For now, I'm happy to have another pair of hands in the lab," Theo said.

Tresk extinguished the flame as dusk set in, quickly giving way to night. She settled into her bedroll, curling up like a cat and casting him an excited look. He realized that this was likely her first time away from home. Pain mixed with excitement in his chest, the innocence of youth painted plainly on her face. There were still a lot of things he needed to understand about this world, but he understood something very clearly. He needed to protect his little pink marshling.

Chapter 8
Alchemy

Theo woke in the morning to a dry mouth and an empty bedroom. After a moment, blinking the sleep away, he heard clanging out in the lab. Dawn hadn't broken yet, but he could tell by the faint glimmer outside that it was close. It took him a while to get to sleep last night, his mind darting between ways he could improve the town, but it came eventually. His stamina was fully restored, and he felt rested, if not a little groggy. Stepping out into the lab, he stretched and saw that Tresk was preparing breakfast. She turned her head and smiled at him.

"I made tea," Tresk said.

"Have you been up long?" Theo asked.

"Not really," Tresk said with a shrug. "If you get higher Vigor, you'll need less rest."

"Good to know," Theo said.

He ran his hand through his hair, still finding it awkward to smooth it back with the swoop of horns in the way. He crossed the lab, sitting next to the fire and breathing in the scent of the cooking Zee mingling with the citrus tea. His mind raced with the coming of the day, jumping from problem to problem. He would need to organize the distillation process to run as smoothly as possible if they were going to make the order. The large barrel of Purified

Water would be enough for this run, but he would need to refill it afterward. They collected enough motes during their harvest, filling several buckets in the room's corner, but things were getting messy.

"We're going to need to organize this place after this run," Theo said.

"Yes. We need shelves. We need to upgrade this place—maybe add a shop area?" Tresk suggested.

Theo hadn't even considered the idea that he could do that. He understood monster cores allowed him to upgrade the place, but he wasn't aware that it could do such a thing. "How does that work?"

"The building will reshape itself a little when we upgrade it," Tresk said. "We should expand it out, toward the river, until we can create separate rooms. One for the shop, one for the lab."

"That's a great idea," Theo said.

He poured himself a cup of the moss tea and sipped on it, feeling the flood of satisfaction rush through him. Tresk was already carrying her weight. She looked at the world in a different light than him and wasn't reserved in sharing her opinion. Luras was always hesitant to provide information unless asked. He wouldn't fault the half-ogre for it—it simply wasn't his job to hold Theo's hand the whole way through. The advantages of taking the marshling up on the offer of Tara'hek were evident, the ritual becoming an inevitability.

"Right," Theo said, rising to his feet. "There's quite a lot of work to do, and I'd like to get started."

"Teach me, Alchemy Man," Tresk said, grinning.

Theo beckoned her over to the Glassware Artifice. She tilted her head at the machine and shrugged.

"This is what we use to make the glassware. We're kind of screwed if we don't have this. You don't need any alchemy skill to run it—I think—so you're in charge of making our vials," Theo said. He produced a mote and created a flat-bottomed vial with an ornate stopper using the machine before handing it to Tresk.

"We're going to need a lot of these, but let me get the first run going before you start."

"Sounds good, boss," she said.

Theo started his process with the Spiny Swamp Thistle Root. The amount that Tresk gathered was far too much for their purposes and would take most of the day to process. He started by washing away the dirt that clung to the roots and cutting them into a more manageable size. He recalled from his last attempt at making healing potions that it was difficult to bring them into a good-sized mash. The sharpness of his memory only increased as his Wisdom grew, a fact that he loved. With the roots cut and deposited into a bucket, he began smashing them with the large piece of wood he had used the last time.

"What are you doing?" Tresk asked.

Theo chuckled between breaths, already winded by the process. "We're making a mash. We'll mix the root paste with Purified Water and distill it. This will give us our essence."

Tresk watched intently as Theo transferred the mash to the Copper Still, rinsing the bucket out into the mix and standing back for a moment. It was the largest batch he had tried so far, easily five times what he had attempted previously. He carefully leveled off the water, coming up to cover the mash, before returning the lid and positioning the condenser over a large conical flask. The fire that Tresk used to make breakfast had burned down to coals, but he stoked it back to steady life.

"We're going to keep the fire really low," Theo said. "You don't want to burn the bottom."

"I've seen magical fire before," Tresk said.

"Yeah, if you can find a fire artifice, get it," Theo said. "I'd love to have granular control of this part."

Tresk nodded, eyes glued to the still.

With a hiss of steam, the first batch of Healing Essence was being cooked. If he could keep the flame low enough, it was reasonable to assume he would extract fifty units of the essence, making 50 Lesser Healing Potions. Theo tended the fire through the cooking process, with Luras arriving half-way through. He came through the front door with a smile on his face, watching the pair crowd around the flame.

"Already working?" Luras asked, laughing. "You two are funny."

Theo looked out the window, seeing that dawn broke sometime after they started. He really wished there were clocks in this world. "First run for the day—it's going a lot faster than I expected."

"Well, since I'm not needed, I have some errands to run," Luras said. "If you don't mind."

"By all means," Theo said. "We might be done by noon."

"What's noon?" Luras asked.

"Midday," Theo said.

Luras departed with a wave, leaving the pair to their work.

The first run went well, but the fire was temperamental. Theo had a better sense for what the Copper Still needed to run at maximum efficiency, constantly removing or adding wood to keep it at a steady pace. Tresk was the perfect assistant, running off to grab fuel when needed. By the end of the run, the alchemist beamed at his fifty units of Healing Essence.

[Healing Essence]
[Essence]
Common
Created by: Belgar
Quality: Great
50 units (liquid)
Concentrated essence of healing, used to create healing potions.

"Great quality." Theo sucked in a breath of air. "That's amazing."

"Good job! What do we do now?" Tresk asked.

"Start making the glassware. Make sure the bottoms are flat so we can stand them on the tables, then lay them out. I'm going to start the batch of moss," Theo said.

Tresk nodded, hoisting a bucket of motes and retreating to the Glassware Artifice. The machine started cranking away immediately, spitting out perfectly acceptable vials.

Theo filled the still with enough water to wash it out, dumping the contents out the window before returning to start the next mash. The Moss Nettle was easy to turn into a paste, and he judged the amount he would need to make the fifty units. He filled the still with the mash, added enough water, and covered it with the lid, another flask positioned under the condenser. While the still was heating, he turned his attention to the row of vials Tresk was lining up. She set them down on the table, removing the stopper and setting it in its matching vessel.

"Right, now we start the alchemical reactions," Theo said. "This recipe needs one unit of the essence, one unit of water, and two flecks of Copper Shavings."

Tresk nodded, continuing to line up the vials in perfect rows.

The first reaction took place, filling the lab with the familiar scent of flowers. Theo felt as though he measured the quantities out better than before, the potion taking on a darker shade of red with more bubbles. He inspected the first one before continuing.

[Lesser Healing Potion]
[Potion]
Common
Created by: Belgar
Quality: Great
A lesser healing potion. Drink to restore health.
Effect:
Instantly restores 30 health points.

"Great quality again! This is perfect," Theo said.

"Yay!" Tresk shouted and immediately focused on her task again.

Theo ran back and forth between the still and the row of vials, tending the fire and setting off the reactions. Tresk watched him after she had created the fifty vials, nodding as though she understood what he was doing. She switched to tending the fire alone after a while, and he could finish the rest of the reactions, reaching Level 3 of his Drogramath Alchemy Core. It didn't come with any additional benefits, but the experience gained from running such a large batch was excellent. With all the reactions done for the healing potions, Tresk organized them before joining him to wait for the Stamina Essence to finish.

"This is extremely efficient," Theo said. "It's a lot easier with another person helping."

"That's the power of friendship," Tresk said, grinning up at him from the fire.

The pair worked in a whirlwind, setting aside the clutter of Lesser Healing Potions in a crate and moving on to extracting the next essence. As Theo had predicted, he made fifty units of the liquid, and after closer inspection, he began the process again.

[Stamina Essence]
[Essence]
Common
Created by: Belgar
Quality: Great
50 units (liquid)
Concentrated essence of stamina, used to create stamina potions.

His excitement for the quality was tempered because they had 100 more potions to craft, his stamina bar draining accordingly. Theo cleaned out the still once more and prepared the mushrooms. His Drogramath Herbalism skill told him that the entire mushrooms could be used to produce the Mana Essence, so he went about turning them into a paste within his bucket. The process was significantly easier than either of the other ingredients. He had the entire batch of the mushrooms, with some to spare, smashed to pieces within a few minutes. He filled the still with the mushrooms and water before stoking the fire.

Tresk moved to tend the fire while Theo started the reactions for the Lesser Stamina Potions. The vials erupted into yellow smoke, filling the room with a pleasant citrus smell. He smiled upon inspecting the potion, unable to spare more time for celebration.

[Lesser Stamina Potion]
[Potion]
Common
Created by: Belgar
Quality: Great
A lesser stamina potion. Drink to restore stamina.
Effect:
Instantly restores 30 stamina points.

"This will earn me a good chunk of change," Theo said, moving down the line and setting off the reactions, "but this is a lot of work."

"How much are they paying you?" Tresk asked, tossing another stick onto the fire and poking it.

"7 silver, 50 copper," Theo said.

"That's a lot of money," Tresk said. "The smithy would take forever to earn that amount."

"Adventurers need their potions," Theo said.

"Swamp prices," Tresk said, sneering.

The condenser sputtered to life, the first of the Mana Essence splashing into a flask. Theo finished with the reactions, gaining a significant amount of experience, before swapping with Tresk to tend the fire. The alchemist was sweating profusely, even after opening all the windows and the front door. A breeze swept through the lab but did little to combat the stifling heat. Midday passed, and the pair was still working, finally extracting the fifty units of Mana Essence and moving on to the reaction process. His supply of Copper Shavings was running low, but there would be enough to see the order through.

Theo barely had time to inspect the essence before moving on to bottling.

[Mana Essence]
[Essence]
Common
Created by: Belgar
Quality: Great
50 units (liquid)
Concentrated essence of mana, used to create mana potions.

The alchemist moved in a frenzy, ignoring the window that informed him of skill experience gains and focusing solely on the task. His plan to produce so many potions was a gamble. He relied on his ability to create 150 potions for the adventurers but underestimated the amount of work. By the time he bottled his fiftieth Lesser Mana Potion, he was exhausted. Both of his cores sat at Level 3, along with his personal level. He dumped the free point into Wisdom without a thought. Luras arrived with Jarson near the end of the day, both of them standing at the door and watching Theo work. Wiping sweat from his brow, he stacked the last of the potions into a crate and managed a weak smile for the adventurer.

"Done," Theo said, heaving a breath. "Only just."

"How many did you end up making for me?" Jarson asked, moving to inspect the potion.

Theo held one up for him to look at, inspecting it himself.

[Lesser Mana Potion]
[Potion]
Common
Created by: Belgar

Quality: Great
A lesser mana potion. Drink to restore mana.
Effect:
Instantly restores 30 mana.

"Fifty of each," Theo said, finding a cloth to dab his forehead free of sweat.

"You distilled 150 potions in three days?" Jarson asked, raising an eyebrow. "Are they all of 'great' quality?"

"Every single one," Tresk said, striking a heroic pose. "We're a team."

"A damn good team," Jarson said, setting the potion down on the table. "I expected five, maybe ten of each."

"I told you Theo had talent," Luras said, smiling.

"And I helped!" Tresk shouted.

"I don't have to talk to a paladin to see you're from the Drogramath lineage," Jarson said. "I've heard tales of the Drogramath Alchemists. They're the stuff of legends. I told you before, but distilling is an advanced alchemical art. Do you mind if I start taking my potions?"

"By all means," Theo said, gesturing to the crates heavy with vials.

Jarson produced a small satchel, far too small to contain all 150 potions, and shoved them inside. Theo watched in amazement as the bag didn't fill up. The man just continued to put the vials inside without rest.

"Dimensional bag," Luras said, noticing Theo's confused expression.

"A perk of being an adventurer," Jarson said. "Listen, Theo... My team and I will be back now that we know you're here. We'll spread the word to Qavell—people are going to fall over themselves to visit Broken Tusk."

Jarson finished stuffing his bag, digging into it to retrieve a handful of coins. He counted them out and set 11 shining silver coins, embossed with a coat of arms, on the table.

"We agreed on a rate of 5 copper per potion," Theo said, knitting his brow.

"And even 11 silver for this batch is a daylight robbery," Jarson said. "I suggest you find a mercantile core whenever you gain a spare slot. It will allow you to assess a fair price for your items."

Theo stood there, staring at the pile of silver coins for a moment. Eleven silver seemed like an embarrassment of riches to him. Whatever the adventurers pulled out of the dungeon must have been worth a fortune.

"Nice doing business with you," Tresk said with a grin.

"We'll be at the tavern tonight," Jarson said. "Until then..."

The adventurer departed, leaving the trio in stunned silence. Luras broke out of the stupor first, casting his gaze to Theo and smiling. He moved over to the pile of silver and took two of the coins, even though he was entitled to five. "This will do. A half-year's pay in less than a week is greedy enough."

Theo wouldn't push the matter. He knew that he would establish a very close relationship with the half-ogre, specifically buying any monster cores he found in the wild. Tresk was looking at him expectantly, even though she didn't ask for any of the earnings.

"I suppose you want to be paid, too?" Theo asked.

"I mean... I was a superb helper, right?" Tresk asked.

Theo took a single coin from the pile and handed it to her, bringing his earnings down to 8 silver. She took the silver coin excitedly, stuffing it in a pocket and dancing on the spot.

"I'd like to talk about buying your monster cores," Theo said, patting Luras on the shoulder.

"Of course. You're going to upgrade the lab, right?" Luras asked.

"Exactly," Theo said.

"At a discounted rate," Luras said, grinning.

"First, let's go get some food," Theo said. "Then I'm going to pass out."

They left the shop, walking together to the tavern. Tresk seemed as though she were in a good mood, but then again, she was *always* in a good mood. Luras had a devious grin on his face the entire way, bordering on giddy. Theo dismissed it as excitement after the job they had completed, but suspected that something was going on. Miana accosted them at the square, and they ignored her. Tresk made a few rude gestures, gestures that Theo could only assume were rude based on the mayor's response. The Marsh Wolf Tavern was buzzing the way it always had.

"Three of whatever you're serving, Xam," Theo said, ordering their food while Tresk and Luras found a table. They settled in near the back, finding a space with a window. A suspicious object wrapped in burlap sat behind the table, the half-ogre failing to hide it behind his bulk.

"It's wolf meat again today," Xam said, serving up three bowls of steaming stew.

Theo paid the 3 copper and retreated to his friends, eying Luras suspiciously. He set the bowls down on the table and placed his hands on his hips. "What's going on?"

"I had something made for you," Luras said, hoisting the burlap-wrapped thing on the table. "What shop is complete without a sign?"

Luras pulled back the cloth dramatically, revealing a sign shaped like a downward-faced spade. At the top of the sign was a painting of a newt with horns. Below the image, it read "The Newt and Demon." Theo took in the thing's artistry, at a loss for words. Sat on the top were iron chains for hanging the sign. The half-ogre watched, still holding his dramatic pose. Tresk was hopping on her chair, shrieking with excitement.

"Well?" Luras asked.

Theo couldn't find the words to match his appreciation. He crossed the distance between him and his friend and pulled him into a hug. Tears formed in the corners of his violet eyes, but he refused to let them break. He pulled back after a moment and shook his head. "This is amazing," he said. "I cannot think of a better gift."

Some patrons in the tavern voiced their approval of the gesture, cheering for Luras. Others paid no attention, too consumed with their wolf meat stew to care.

"Woah! This is so cool! This makes it look official!" Tresk shouted.

"This is a big step for you," Luras said, raising his voice for the entire tavern to hear, "but this is also a massive step forward for Broken Tusk. Coins will flow from the adventurers who flock here."

More of the crowd cheered, and the trio finally sat down to eat their meal. Theo was in love with the design of the sign. The tongue-in-cheek reference to both him and Tresk was perfect, and the image at the top sealed it. He made a promise to himself to make the most of the name. He would make sure that the Newt and Demon was on the tongues of alchemists in the capital.

Jarson made his way over to their table. His adventuring party planned to set out with the dawn, wasting no time in clearing the swamp dungeon. Theo knew nothing about how dungeons worked, but it must have been dangerous. Still, the conversation didn't linger on things related to dungeons or alchemy. They spoke lightly of the things they hoped to do in the future. Tresk was even more firm with her proposal of the Tara'hek. The alchemist didn't want to shut her down completely, but he wanted to wait. It felt like he was running off to be married in Vegas, although he felt the magnetic pull the woman had.

The group stayed there later than normal, even lingering past the setting of the sun. Theo's stamina still had ten percent to go, and he was happy to celebrate after the difficult job. Luras departed, leaving Tresk and Theo to spend more time bonding. They left shortly after, carrying the sign and finding their way to bed after locking the lab up. Sleep came easily enough after the day. He nodded off quickly, exhaustion overtaking him.

Chapter 9
Perpetual Ledger

Theo rose before Tresk in the morning. She might have put on a brave face the preceding night, but the difficulty of the order had worn her down. He took a moment to watch her sleep, still not over how cute she was curled into a little ball. After a while, he left the bedroom, pulling the door closed quietly and coaxing the fire to life. While cutting the Zee into strips, his mind swirled with possibilities. The biggest problem he had with supplying potable water to the town was storing it and retrieving it from the river.

With the cast-iron kettle settled on the fire, he added the stimulating moss to get him started. His barrel of Purified Water was getting low, but it would be easy enough to purify it himself. A gigantic metal water container entered his mind for a moment— Something like a water tower that could supply the city with fresh water. The old problems he considered came back again, namely transporting it from the river. Theo let out a heavy sigh, dropping the Zee strips next to the kettle and pushing his mind further. He could imagine a series of people running back and forth to the river, but it seemed labor-intensive.

The bedroom door creaked open, and Tresk stepped out. She stood on the spot and stretched, yawning before padding across the room. "Good morning," she said, flopping down beside him and resting her head on his arm.

"Morning. I'm trying to figure out how to solve the town's water problem," Theo said.

"What problem?" She scratched at her lower back absently

"Well, the river water is tainted," Theo said. "I wanted to purify it."

Tresk snorted. "Marshlings don't need purified water. We could drink it from the swamp and we'd be fine."

Theo let out a sigh. "But I assume that humans and half-ogres can't."

"No, they boil their water," Tresk said. "You're going to burn the food."

Theo rushed to take the strips of Zee off the fire, setting the charred vegetable down on two plates and pouring the tea. The pair ate in silence as the question hung unanswered. The alchemist finished his food before saying, "My problem is transporting the water."

"Maybe we could get one of those fancy dimensional bags," Tresk said, shrugging. "They're actually common enough. Most adventurers have at least one."

"Do you have one yet?"

"No," Tresk said, slurping her tea. "There are abilities that do something similar. Demons are extra-planar things; maybe you have something like that."

Theo raised an eyebrow, kicking himself for not checking out new abilities sooner. He had gotten free attribute points but no option to select a new ability. With a mental command, he summoned the skills screen and started looking through them. It was an endless scroll of abilities, organized in a list format that made him dizzy. They scrolled by, and he read the descriptions, finding nothing that seemed to be useful. Out of frustration, he thought, "Why can't it just show me the Drogramath skills," and the system obeyed. The endless list was replaced with a short one, his two current Drogramath skills already there in green.

"Oh, I can get one," Theo said, spotting an ability and mentally sharing it with Tresk.

[Drogramath Inventory]
Legendary Universal Skill
Your heritage gives you access to the extra-dimensional spaces claimed by Drogramath. This ability changes to suit the user, giving them access to a pocket dimension presented in a way that matches their true origin. Items can be stored in the dimension at will; the only limitation is based on your origin's manifestation. Items stored do not encumber the user.
Effect:
Inventory (32 slots, item stack count varied by item)

"Oh, that's interesting," Tresk said. "Universal skills can slot into any core. Most of them are a waste of a slot, but that'd be very useful."

"Now I just need a skill point..."

"You should get one when your personal levelreaches Level 5," Tresk said. "While I'm sure there's a lot of neat stuff you can get for alchemy, the utility of that one is so good."

Theo imagined what he could do with Drogramath Inventory. He would save himself a lot of stamina, assuming that no encumbrance meant he could plop thirty-two barrels of river water into his pocket dimension. It seemed like an obvious choice, and he dismissed the screen. He was well into his personal Level 3 and had no plans on slowing down. The ability just gave him more drive to push harder.

"I have a goal, now," Theo said. "Tresk, what level are you?"

"I'm Level 8," Tresk said, beaming. "And a rogue, as you know."

Theo fell back into his thoughts, setting the idea of the purified water aside for the moment. Upgrading the lab would be his next move, along with making enough potions to sell if another set of adventurers came around. He would need those adventurers if he wanted to establish a real business in Broken Tusk. Despite their well-wishes, the citizens of the town were broke. If he sold potions to them, they wouldn't pay what he needed to make decent money.

"Do you have any plans for the day?" Theo asked.

Tresk sipped on her tea, tilting her head. "Not really. I was thinking of going into the swamp and farming monster cores."

"Can you handle yourself out there?" Theo asked.

Tresk laughed, grinning at him. "I'm out in the wilds most days. I'll be fine."

"Still... You should let me brew you some potions before you go," Theo said.

"Great idea!"

They had a pile of Spiny Swamp Thistle Root left over from yesterday, sitting in a crate in the corner of the room. Theo started the familiar process, intent on making a full fifty-unit batch of the stuff before she set off. He needed the experience points, but most of all, he needed peace of mind. If his partner ran off into the swamp and died, he didn't know what he would do. Luras arrived half-way through the process. Tresk was laying out the vials, and the mash was almost completely cooked through. He laughed, shaking his head. "You guys never take a break, huh? Couldn't have asked for a better partnership," Luras said. "I brought some cores for you to buy."

"How many?" Theo asked, looking up from the fire.

"I've got five," Luras said. "You can have them for 10 copper each."

"Chump change," Theo said. "Take a silver for the bunch."

"I'm not about to argue with you. The merchant who normally buys them hasn't shown up, so I've been sitting on them. I'd be lucky to get 20 copper for them at this point..."

Theo left the fire for a moment, fishing a silver coin out of his pocket and handing it to his friend. "We're going to burn all our money upgrading the lab."

"We need more damn space," Tresk said, having finished with the vials.

"Since it's an alchemy lab, you'll get some bonuses to alchemy as you upgrade it," Luras said.

"That's perfect," Theo said, setting the five monster cores on the table.

He inspected the cores, finding that all but one were Level 5. The last one, a Level 8 core, glowed with a distinct energy. Theo wasted no time, hoisting the first three cores above his head and watching them disappear. Swirls of white energy raced around the lab, a satisfying *ding* playing as though over an intercom.

[Alchemy Lab] has advanced to Level 2!
Select a direction you wish to expand the lab into (north/south/east/west).

"We wanted to expand toward the river, right?" Theo asked. "Eastward?"

"Yep," Tresk said, nodding.

Theo mentally chose the direction, and the building rumbled under their feet. In an instant, the space inside the lab expanded, adding two or three paces of room near the back wall. He almost fell over when it moved, the boards shifting underfoot.

[Alchemy Lab]
Owner: Belgar (Theo Spencer)
Faction: Broken Tusk
Level: 2 (0%)
Rent Due: 4 days

"No bonuses yet," Theo said.

"But we have more space! We can fit a row of tables in the front to hawk our wares," Tresk said.

"Speaking of, I have something for you," Luras said,

rummaging through his bag. He hoisted a large tome, setting it down on the table and gesturing for Theo to inspect it.

[Perpetual Ledger]
[Shopkeeping Equipment]
Rare
Transactions that take place inside a core building will be recorded in this ledger. It will never run out of space and can infinitely expand itself to accommodate new transactions.

"That's awesome," Tresk said. "Where did you snag one of those?"

"It came from the capital when Theo arrived," Luras said. "Just like the instructions I got to acclimate him to the world. I forgot about it—too caught up in all the excitement."

"This is for tax purposes, isn't it?" Theo asked, laughing.

"Yeah, they want to make sure that you're paying what you owe," Luras said.

"Well, that's fine. I don't want to get in trouble for not paying my fantasy-world taxes," Theo said. "How much do they take?"

"Not a lot." Luras shrugged. "The merchants I know don't pay over ten percent of what they earn annually."

"Wow. That's way better than it was in my world," Theo said.

Luras lingered, agreeing to accompany Tresk into the swamp to collect monster cores. They agreed to split them down the middle, including the other items harvested from the creatures. Theo was extremely happy that his partner wouldn't be going into the dangerous wilds alone, especially since the half-ogre was Level 12. He finished firing off the reactions for the day and sent both of his friends off with five potions each. Luras tried to refuse, but he insisted.

Theo departed shortly after them, intent on settling a few things before they returned. He wanted to smooth things over with Throk and put money toward his debt with Miana. The blacksmith was setting up shop, several of his children darting around to start the fire in the forge and arranging various hammers around the anvil. He looked up and regarded the alchemist with a glare.

"You stole my daughter," Throk said.

"She was bound to leave eventually," Theo said. "She's too intent on being an adventurer. Fortunately, she picked a Tara'hek that can make healing potions."

Throk stood there for a moment, the gears in his head turning. It was clear that the marshling hadn't considered that fact. Tresk could have ended up with anyone as her partner, but she was drawn to Theo by some mystical force. Something in the young adventurer shouted that he would make the best Tara'hek. It likely had to do with the fact he just stated. He could easily craft her life-saving potions that would see her through most scrapes, and his skill would only improve. There was no safer place for an adventurer than by the side of an alchemist.

Throk narrowed his gaze at Theo. There was a glimmer of disbelief there, but the gruff man didn't verbalize anything. Maybe other marshlings could sense the viability of a Tara'hek?

"I hadn't considered it," Throk said, shocking Theo with his honesty. "An outworlder *and* a Dronon... Well, I guess the only thing that matters is the Alchemist title. Fine, is that all you came to say?"

"No, I'd like to commission a water tower," Theo said. "I'd like you to sort out its construction, if it's at all possible."

"How many units does it need to hold?"

"As much as possible," Theo said. "I'd like it to be in the 2,000-unit range."

"That's positively massive," Throk said. "You really are ambitious, aren't you?"

"Just trying to make Broken Tusk a better place," Theo said. "How much for materials and labor?"

"Let's see... Copper is *cheap* right now—absurdly cheap. Everyone wants stuff made of northern steel. 1 silver coin worth of materials, 1 silver in labor, and Gods know how long."

Newt and Demon

Theo didn't hesitate in bringing two silver coins from his pocket, handing them to Throk. He had a look of shock on his face, his gaze darting between the coins and the alchemist. "Really?"

"You're hired," Theo said, turning on the spot and walking to the mayor's house. He felt Throk's gaze on him as he left and smiled.

The mayor was in as she always was. She flung her door open as he approached, searching for Luras before berating him. Theo held up a silencing hand, withdrawing a silver coin and handing it to her before she had a chance to shout. She was just as shocked as the blacksmith, bringing the coin between her teeth and biting hard. Theo felt a twinge in his mind and knew that his quest had been updated.

"You're full of surprises, Dronon," Miana said.

"Please work with Throk on the water tower project," Theo said.

"What water tower?"

"I hired him to build a water tower to provide fresh water for Broken Tusk," Theo said. "Find a nice spot for it, please."

As Theo was walking away, he heard her mutter, "Full of surprises."

[Pay Your Debts]
Quest

Miana Kell has overseen your transition into the new world, and you owe her a lot of money!

Objectives:

Pay the following debts:
Medical Services Rendered: 1 Silver **(DONE)**
Room and Board (1 week): 10 Copper
Alchemy Lab (to be paid in installments): 1 Gold
Equipment (to be paid in installments): 1 Gold
Service Charge: 5 Copper

The only thing left to do for the day was to harvest ingredients.

While they targeted three specific reagents for their adventurer project, the swamp was riddled with useful ingredients. He also wanted to experiment with effects, drawing out the secondary properties like the one he had found in the Zee Kernel. He was down to 5 silver, but at least his water purification project was underway. Theo retreated to his newly expanded lab to consult his compendium of reagents.

His books detailed the range of plants that grew in the swamp, and he had only collected a fraction of what was available. He wanted to investigate potions that enhanced a person's attributes, and some that boasted powerful poisons. He had an Ogre Snapper Spleen, but it didn't seem practical to run a monster's organ through the distiller. The smell alone already drove him to throw the slab of meat away, but the book offered another answer. The Widow Lily was a flowering plant that grew near the edge of swamps.

Essential Alchemy told him that poison potions could be applied to an adventurer's weapon, allowing them to inflict the Poison debuff on hit. It seemed like the perfect pairing with Tresk's Rogue class, and he couldn't resist whipping her up a batch. With much of the day left, he planned to scout out the rare attribute-enhancing flowers along with the Widow Lily. The flowers matched an element associated with the attribute. Strength to fire, Dexterity to wind, Vigor to earth, Intelligence to lightning, and Wisdom to water. The book didn't have any information about where they could be found.

Theo left the lab, locking up and thinking about how he could get a spare key made for Tresk, before heading off to the southern section of the town. He hadn't been down that way, advised against it by Luras, and he immediately found out why. A stench like death crept up with the wind, washing over him in a putrid wave. The further south he went, the worse it became. Then he saw the source of the smell. A group of half-ogres were standing outside of a building, the sign hanging out front claiming it was the tannery.

"Good lord, what's that smell?" Theo asked.

"The tannery," the half-ogre responded with a snort.
"Do all tanneries smell this foul?"
"Yep."

Theo shook his head, departing west toward the swamp. *There has to be some alchemical solution for that.*

He filed away the thought before finding his first Widow Lily, a small flowering plant with white flowers. A bold black streak rode down the petals of the flower, striking a stark contrast. Theo carefully removed the plant before placing it in his bag. He made a mental note to clean the bag out before using it for anything else, not wanting to risk it. While crouching low to harvest the reagents, he got a smell of himself. He looked down at his stained clothes and frowned. While he had planned to figure out a solution to laundering his clothes, he hadn't found an answer yet.

Another problem for alchemy.

After an hour of picking the deadly flowers, he wandered back toward the road and returned to the lab. He placed the Widow Lily in a bucket, covering it with a lid and setting it aside. It would be unfortunate if someone accidentally ate it. Tresk came to mind.

Theo rummaged through the disorganized buckets and crates of reagents, finding the Ogre Cypress Bark and considering what to do. It was the reagent with the highest chance of producing a useful property for his plan. When sampling the Zee Kernel for the first time, he had discovered an additional property. He didn't think that the bark would have any negative effects and took a bite of the smallest piece in the bucket. It tasted like dish soap in his mouth.

[Properties Discovery!]
You've discovered an additional effect of the Ogre Cypress Bark by eating it.
[Cleanse] discovered.

Theo felt something in his stomach. It rumbled angrily for a moment before settling down, and he went to consult *Essential*

Alchemy. It had a short list of common properties, [Cleanse] among them. The property was the first one that didn't have an effect when a user imbibed it. This was something that affected the world, instead of a person. [Cleanse] was used to restore something to pristine condition, removing all dirt and odor. He considered the fact that he was drawn to the bark for testing, leaving the rest of the reagents and going straight for that one. His Wisdom was at 19, and it likely had an effect. There were also his Drogramath skills to consider. Whatever the reason, he studied the book's information on the strange reaction. The deeper he read, the more he understood.

"Distillation uses my alchemical ability... Extracting the essences has to be about intent, right?" Theo asked, scratching his head around his horns.

Every distillation he had done so far was intended to extract the first property of a reagent. His mind begged to start the experiment, and he obliged. The coals from the fire were long dead, and he stoked another one to life. Theo processed enough Ogre Cypress Bark to make five units of the new essence and started the distillation process. He studied his books as he waited, committing more of the information to his permanent memory with his improved Wisdom attribute. The small batch meant that it was finished within half an hour, a significant improvement from when he first started.

Theo inspected the essence, grinning as the theory about intent proved true.

[Cleansing Essence]
[Essence]
Common
Created by: Belgar
Quality: Great
5 units (liquid)
Concentrated essence of cleansing.

He retrieved his tiny pipette and found another flask to start his testing. The conical flask was filled with five units of Purified Water, the barrel starting to run low, and he drew the smallest possible amount of the Cleansing Essence, starting with 0.01 to be thorough. To his surprise, a reaction occurred. It was the smallest essence-to-water ratio he had found so far, and he made a note of it. Theo inspected his new reaction.

[Cleansing Scrub]
[Cleaning Agent]
Common
Created by: Belgar
Quality: Great
Cleansing Scrub instantly restores clothes, surfaces, skin, and so on to a clean state. Leaves behind the smell of Qavellian berries.
Effect:
Cleans anything it touches.

After washing his pipette, Theo took off a muddy moccasin and drew 0.1 units of the Cleansing Scrub. He set the shoe on the table and let the drops fall into the mud, caked on the surface. Steam rose from the leather, and the alchemist watched as the liquid glowed white, slowly spreading across the muck and breaking it down. The light faded, and what remained was a completely pristine moccasin.

Theo hooted with excitement, eagerly drawing another 0.1 units of the solution and cleaning the rest of his clothes. The lab was filled with a scent somewhere between a strawberry and a raspberry. He removed his robes, applying another drop to his forearm and watching bright light race across his body. The days of grime that accumulated were washed away in a moment, even spreading through his hair and cleansing his scalp. Next, he tried the miracle potion on the floor. The same 0.1-unit dose seemed to have enough steam to clear through half of the muddy floor, and he simply applied more to finish the job.

The alchemist went into a cleaning frenzy. He darted into the bedroom and cleansed his bed, Tresk's bed, and then the walls. He collapsed into his sheets, letting the pristine material rub against his skin. Potions that halted mortal wounds or refreshed someone out of exhaustion were nice, but this was amazing. He could sell this.

"Why does it smell like berries?" Tresk asked from the door.

Theo rushed out to meet her, a wide grin painting his face. He could smell her from the door—like week-old sweat and muck. He drew more of the solution and placed one drop on her head, and one on her clothes. She giggled as the light raced across her body.

"I made the most amazing thing," Theo said, holding up the flask. "It's a bath in a bottle—that's what we'll call it."

Tresk had her eyes closed, savoring the cleansing sensation before responding, "People will buy this."

Theo stared at her for a moment, the excitement tingling through the air. "How was the trip, by the way?"

"We got some cores, but screw that," Tresk said, pointing at the flask. "I want more of *that*."

Chapter 10
The Tara'hek

Theo was nose-blind to the stench of the swamp by now. Only the discovery of the Cleansing Scrub was enough to pull him out of it. He was glad that Tresk could appreciate how amazing the new creation was, although he was not entirely certain how her nose worked. The feeling of freshly laundered clothes pressing against his body was amazing, and he couldn't go back. They would need to keep a supply of the Ogre Cypress Bark on hand to manufacture as much of the scrub as possible. Not every half-ogre in town would care about feeling clean all the time, but there would be an interest.

"Luras wanted to hang out at the tavern," Tresk said. Her excitement remained, but she had a concerned look on her face. "We've been gabbing about this new Cleansing Scrub for too long—he's waiting."

"All right, hold on," Theo said, grabbing a few motes and approaching his Glassware Artifice.

The alchemist imagined a dispenser for the liquid. He held an image in his mind before inserting the mote. It would have the vial-shape he used for his potions, but the stopper on top would have a rod that went down into the inside. The artifice spat out three vials according to his specifications, and he filled each with one unit of Cleansing Scrub.

"Just pull the stopper off, and use the little rod to apply the scrub," Theo said, handing Tresk one vial.

"Genius," Tresk said, nodding. "Let's go."

The pair left the lab well before dusk started settling in over Broken Tusk. Theo felt the warmth of friendship spreading through his chest, his tail waggling in sync with Tresk's the entire way to the Marsh Wolf Tavern. They even received a vile sneer from Miana and shrugged it off. Luras was waiting for them at their normal spot near the window. Where he expected to see bowls of stew, there were three plates with a fat steak on each.

"Wow, something other than stew," Theo said, sitting down.

The scent of the meat was overwhelming, causing his mouth to water immediately. He hadn't seen a solid cut of meat since he had arrived in the town, and he didn't care what kind of creature it came from. Without waiting for an invitation, he cut into the meat and took a bite. It tasted exactly like a medium-rare steak back on Earth. Tresk was also eating, shoving large chunks of meat into her mouth and chomping noisily.

"Why do you two smell so clean?" Luras said, raising an eyebrow.

Theo's nose was already adjusted to taking in pleasant smells again. The tavern had the stench of mud and sweat, but it hardly diminished his appetite. He withdrew a bottle of the Cleansing Scrub and handed it over to the half-ogre.

"Put a drop on your skin, and a drop on your clothes and boots," Theo said through a mouthful of steak.

"Yeah, you stink," Tresk said, almost halfway done with her meal.

Luras had a skeptical look on his face but did as the alchemist said. He shouted when the light spread across his body, joined by the surprised yells of the tavern's patrons. After a moment, the Bath in a Bottle did its work, and the half-ogre smelled fresh, the muck on his clothes and boots scrubbed away.

Newt and Demon

"We're calling it 'Bath in a Bottle,'" Tresk said, grinning.

A small crowd formed around their table, some patrons running their fingers over Luras's clean armor. They were amazed that he had been covered in a thick layer of swamp muck just moments earlier, but now appeared as though he had just washed himself and his armor. All eyes fell on the alchemist, who grinned through a mouthful.

"Stop by the Newt and Demon tomorrow, and you too can purchase some Bath in a Bottle!" Tresk shouted, leaping up onto the table.

She pulled her bottle out and started dripping it on random patrons. Theo just watched as shouts of excitement filled the tavern, the flash of lights almost blinding. The stench that filled the tavern slowly abated, giving way to that berry smell that the scrub left behind. Patrons returned to their seats, eventually, just after the alchemist finished his meal.

"Well, that's one way to drum up interest," Luras said. "I'm guessing this bottle is mine to keep."

"Naturally," Theo said, waving a dismissive hand. "What's this steak, anyway? I was just settling into the stew."

"The tavern put in an order from the northlands months ago for some aged Karatan steaks," Luras explained. "Xam wanted 5 copper per plate, and I gotta say, it was worth it."

"It was *so* worth it," Tresk said, letting out a heavy sigh.

"So, when are you two going to do the Tara'hek? Seems like a perfect match to me," Luras said.

"When *he* is ready," Tresk said, narrowing her eyes at Theo.

"I don't even know what it is," Theo said, scoffing. "I understand it's a bond, but that's about it."

"It's a lifetime bond between friends," Luras said. "You're basically making a promise to forego romance with anyone and focus on making each other better people."

"There are benefits, too," Tresk said, nodding. "We can talk to each other from anywhere. I think there's other stuff, but a bond is rare enough that I haven't seen it."

"That sounds useful," Theo said.

The reality of his companion running off to adventure was that he would never know if she was all right until she returned. If he could speak to her from anywhere, that would ease his fear. As far as romance went, he had no interest in pursuing it. He had ruminated on the topic for a while, but it was just something that he couldn't bring himself to do. If he had a companion that he could share his successes and failures with, bound by the Tara'hek, he would be much happier.

"All right. I'll do it," Theo said. "Is there some grand ceremony?"

"Nope," Tresk said. "It's a very personal thing. We can do it before bed tonight, if you want."

Theo shrugged. "Sounds good to me."

The conversation switched to lighter topics from there on. Dusk settled in over Broken Tusk, and Theo's stamina bar was still a quarter full. He would have enough energy to undertake the Tara'hek and spend time with his friends without worrying about getting exhausted. Conversation died down as dusk gave way to nightfall, Luras looking exhausted. He bid the pair farewell and departed before them. Theo and Tresk stayed for some time before leaving. They walked in tandem, step for step, down the muddy roads.

"I was thinking about how we could make stone roads in town," Theo said, stopping at the monolith.

"Well, we can upgrade the town if we feed it enough monster cores," Tresk said. "Here, inspect the monolith."

Theo obeyed, reaching out his hand to touch the monolith with the intent of inspection.

[Small Town]
Name: Broken Tusk
Owner: Kingdom of Qavell
Mayor: Miana Kell

Faction: Qavell
Level: 2 (31%)
Features:
Alchemy Lab
Blacksmith
Large Farm
Tannery
Tradesmen
Upgrades:
None

"Wow, I didn't know towns had a level," Theo said. "Why isn't it higher than Level 2? Hasn't it been here for a long time?"

"We're dirt poor; that's why," Tresk said. "People want to sell their monster cores, not dump them into the town."

"I wonder what level paved roads would be," Theo said.

"I don't know, but that'd be nice. We wouldn't be tracking mud everywhere," Tresk said. "We're already hoarding monster cores, we might want to think about putting some in."

"The mayor decides what to do with the upgrades, right? She's basically the owner," Theo said.

"I think that's how it works," Tresk said.

They left the monolith behind, and Theo fell into thought. He didn't know if he could trust the mayor to do the right thing with his investment, but upgrading the town seemed like a great idea. The bigger the town was, the more customers he would get in his alchemy lab. It made sense to split his efforts between the town and his lab.

Theo locked the door behind them, lighting the candles in the corners of the room to prepare for the Tara'hek. Tresk seemed giddy with excitement—or perhaps a little anxious, he wasn't sure —and he reserved himself to trust her judgment on the matter. He had weighed his options and selected this one as the most likely to benefit him in the long run. She cleared away a section near the bedroom and laid her bedroll there before setting out candles in a circle.

"Sit," she said, taking a spot on the far end of the bedroll and gesturing to the other.

He sat cross-legged on the bedroll, and Tresk reached her hands out for him to take. She didn't say a word, simply grasping his hands and staring into his eyes. They sat like that for some time before anything happened. He felt himself drawn into her gaze, his head swimming. The deeper he fell, the more he felt a connection with the marshling, as though he were understanding the contents of her soul. It seemed like a vague thing until he felt the ground fall out from under him, plunging him into a black void.

Theo tried to let out a shout, but nothing came. The darkness was all around him, although vague shapes roiled in the distance. After what felt like an eternity, something appeared before him. Specks of light pink light formed out of the darkness, the mist swirling to create a ball-shaped form. He recognized it as Tresk's soul and noticed that a red mist had formed around him to create his.

"Gaze into her soul and judge its contents," a voice spoke into his mind.

The alchemist found himself unable to do anything else. He saw Tresk's ambitions laid bare for him to prod. She wanted nothing more than to prove herself to her family, showing that one of their line could rise to be an adventurer. There was fear of failure and a hope that lingered like a fire. The hope she held was in Theo, and his ability to elevate her to that status. At that moment, he could sense the potential in her, more than he had ever seen before. She had all the traits of a powerful rogue, maybe even an assassin. Her decisiveness shone through the brightest, then her tenacity, and finally her loyalty.

She will make you great. There is no better pairing for your Tara'hek.

Theo didn't know where the voice was coming from, but he

knew it was right. It spoke into his mind in a monotone voice, echoing through his skull with reverberating truths.

[Tara'hek, Life Partner Proposal]
Tresk would like to be your Tara'hek. If you accept, you'll be bound to them forever. You gain experience by accomplishing tasks together and have access to more powerful abilities as you grow as partners.
[Do you wish to accept the Tara'hek? YES/NO]

Theo didn't hesitate to accept the offer, mentally affirming his bond with Tresk. A painful rush flooded through his mind as the darkness fell around him. He was left gasping for breath on the floor of the alchemy lab, the marshling also having difficulty breathing. After a moment, it faded, and he noticed a new notification from the system.

[New Tara'hek Bond]
You've performed a Tara'hek with a marshling, gaining a new core slot. This core slot can never be changed for any reason. Only the Tara'hek Core may be placed in this slot, and it can never be removed.

"Oh! We got a core!" Tresk shouted.

Theo examined his core screen, finding a new slot already filled.

[Tara'hek Core]
Legendary
Tara'hek Core
Bound
1 Slot
Level 1 (0%)
Tara'hek cores are given to those who accept a marshling

life partner. You cannot change the skills inside the core or remove it.
Effect:
+2 Strength

A skill was already slotted in the core, and he inspected that as well.

[Tara'hek Communication]
Marshling Bond Skill
Rare
The first step to a Tara'hek is communication.
Effect:
Allows you to communicate with Tresk, no matter how far away they are. Others cannot hear your conversation.

"We can talk into each other's brains!" Tresk said without moving her lips.

"This is weird..." Theo said, shocked at how easy it was to use the ability.

"Yeah, let's use our faces to talk for now," Tresk said, grinning.

The bond that Theo already felt with the woman was absurd. It transcended anything he had felt before; it was like having another half of him sitting there on the bedroll. The sensation of ascendence he felt in her presence was unlike anything else, trumping that of any girlfriends he had had in the past, as well as that of his parents, brothers, or friends. The downside was that the process left him feeling exhausted. He didn't know how much time had passed, but the darkness outside told him it was late.

"I think it gave me a Strength bonus because you're always calling me weak," Theo said, smiling.

"Yeah, now you're less weak. It gave me a Wisdom bonus," Tresk said.

"I think it's time to go to bed," Theo said, yawning.

Tresk nodded, moving around the room to extinguish the

flames before dragging her bedroll back into the room. Theo laid on his clean bed, savoring the scent of berries. He wouldn't miss the times when everything smelled like stale laundry and rotting vegetation.

Sleep threatened to overtake him quickly. His eyes got heavy even before the marshling settled down in her bed. He closed his eyes and felt the familiar tingle of Tresk speaking into his mind. *"Good night."*

Chapter 11
The Tannery Job

Theo was the first to wake up the next morning and went about his daily ritual of preparing tea and food. Before the fire was even lit, he was considering how to sell his new product. He would price it at a single copper coin per unit, banking on the fact that the townspeople were poor and were unlikely to pay any more than that. It was a business move designed to improve the lives of the citizens of Broken Tusk rather than turn a profit. His immediate concern was the tannery. The stench he had experienced while in its close proximity was horrid. It was a problem perfect for an alchemical solution.

Tresk woke up in time for breakfast, stretching at the threshold and flashing a broad grin. Theo could somewhat feel her emotions now, but only faintly. Nonetheless, it didn't require a Tara'hek to see the excitement on her face.

"What's the plan today, boss?" Tresk asked, sitting cross-legged on the ground and helping herself to the food.

"I'm not the boss—we're a team, right?" Theo asked.

"Yeah, but someone has to call the shots."

Theo let out a sigh. "All right. I'm going to talk to the tanners and understand their process. That's an industry that needs alchemy. I'd like you to get some motes—we're getting low—and push these tables toward the back of the lab."

Since they expanded the lab, there was a small gap near the back wall that sat empty. Theo wanted to shove the three rows of tables back there, creating a clear walking space near the entrance.

"Right, what about our new product?" Tresk asked.

"The motes are for glassware. I'd like to make 50 vials of Cleansing Scrub and set it out front with an honor box," Theo said.

"Honor box?"

"A little box that people can drop their coin in and take a vial," Theo said. "I don't care if they steal it. We're only going to ask for a single copper coin."

"I like the idea of helping the town out that way," Tresk said, nodding and sipping her tea. "Seems like a waste of our talents to just seek profit."

"Agreed. After I talk to the tanners, I'll come back to the lab and work on something for you, as well as some research," Theo said.

"Oh! A present?" Tresk asked.

Theo smiled, patting her on the head. "Some poison for your daggers."

"I like this idea," Tresk said.

They ate their breakfast, sharing the excitement they both felt for the new partnership. It was as though they were two hands reaching for the same goal. This fact brought a new warmth to Theo's heart, as though he were more complete than before. He couldn't deny that Tresk would be useful for his goals, but she was more than just someone to run errands. He could bounce ideas off her and listen to hers in return.

Theo finished his tea and bid farewell to his companion, fording down the road southward to the tanners. He didn't have to wait long for the wind to pick up, carrying with it the stench of the tanner's building.

"This smell is worse than I remember," Theo said to Tresk in his mind.

"They say you get used to it."
Somehow, I doubt that.

A half-ogre tannery worker was standing outside, looking out over the rising dawn and leaning against the building. She waved at Theo as he approached. The smell didn't seem to bother her.

"Good morning, I'm Theo," the part-demon newcomer said.

"The new alchemist? Nice to meet you—I've seen you in the tavern. My name's Perg. I run this tannery," she said.

"A pleasure," Theo said, plugging his nose.

"You get used to the smell," Perg said with a shrug.

"Right. Can you tell me about your process?" Theo asked.

Perg shrugged, gesturing to the backside of the building. Theo followed reluctantly, the stench growing stronger the further back they went. There was a pile of rotting hides resting over a cobbled yard, baking in the rising sun. It took everything in his willpower not to vomit at the sight.

"We usually process wolf hides for export," Perg said. "They come in from the hunters, and we trim the fat off and lay them here after soaking them in water."

Theo felt the bile sting his nose, but he maintained his composure. "What's the purpose of letting them rot like this?"

"We need to remove the hair, and this is the best way," Perg said.

"Right. Step one, remove the hair without destroying the hide," Theo said, counting on his superior Wisdom to lock the information in.

"Then we need to cure the hides," Perg said, gesturing for Theo to follow her. She rounded the corner of the building, where two bay doors sat. They were already open, revealing a massive warehouse inside. Pits were dug in the ground and lined with stones, leathers in different stages of processing within. "They sit in a secret mixture that preserves them and gives the leather a pleasant color."

"The purpose of the curing process is to... what?" Theo asked.

"We're basically preventing the hide from rotting, making it softer, and adding some color." Perg shrugged. "That's the last step for our process, by the way... Why are you so interested? People usually find this disgusting."

"I want to find an alchemical solution to your problem," Theo said. "I assume from the size of your warehouse that this process takes a long time."

"It can take up to a year," Perg said.

Theo nodded, walking up toward the road. The wind blowing from the south cleansed some of the stench from his nose. Perg followed. "If I understand your process, I think I can find a cleaning agent sort of potion that'll do the job. Well, two, if my intuition is right."

"Let me guess, you want a piece of the action?" Perg said, grinning.

"Not until I have something that makes your life easier. And gets rid of this smell," Theo said.

"If you can make this process easier, then we can come to some kind of arrangement," Perg said.

"Whatever we decide, I'll be fair. My only interest is getting rid of this smell... And improving Broken Tusk, of course," Theo said, laughing. He almost lost his breakfast, holding his hand to his mouth and heaving.

"I can't wait," Perg said.

Theo left, sprinkling some Cleansing Scrub on himself when he got out of range of the smell. He mentally reported back to Tresk, who seemed hopeful that he would find a solution. He would focus on finding a reagent that would have a property similar to "stripping" or "removing"—something like that. Then he would have to find a property that was close to "preserving." When he returned to the shop, his companion already had a small wooden box with "Honor Box" written on it in a strange, blocky text. She bid him farewell, leaving him to his research while she collected motes.

Essential Alchemy had a section on combining essences that came with a warning. The combination of essences wasn't well documented in the book, but the warning stated that it was a volatile reaction. Essences that didn't combine would sometimes explode. Theo decided that this was an experiment for another time and focused on scanning his catalogs for useful plants. While he browsed the books, he started cooking a small batch of Widow Lily. The entire process of creating essences became second nature to him, and he could easily move between the Copper Still and his books.

Theo finished cooking down the last of the foul-smelling Widow Lily, propping the door and opening the windows half-way through before returning to his books. Two reagents stood out to him. The first was a tuber that grew among cypress trees, which had the [Preservation] property. Next was Swamplight Spider Silk, which the book claimed to have the Supple property. If he could combine these two ingredients, he would have something that would preserve and soften the leathers. That would cover the second step in the tanner's process. He wiped the sweat from his brow, committing the information to memory before inspecting the Poison Essence.

[Poison Essence]
[Essence]
Common
Created by: Belgar
Quality: Great
5 units (liquid)
Concentrated essence of poison.

The essence would be too dangerous to leave out in the open, despite its dangerous neon-green color. He stowed it away in a chest and cleaned out the Copper Still. The barrel of Purified Water was getting dangerously low, but he had no intentions of running another large batch today. Theo surveyed what few ingredients he had left, determined to discover more effects before he went hunting for reagents. The gnarled Spiny Swamp Thistle Root didn't look appetizing, but the Manashrooms were inviting enough. He took a bite, feeling a cold sensation rush through his body, followed by stomach cramps. A screen popped up, informing him that he had discovered a new property. Theo read it from a prone position.

[Properties Discovery!]
You've discovered an additional effect of the Manashroom by eating it.
[Freezing] discovered.

The ability to freeze something wasn't useful to him at the moment. After the painful sensation in his stomach passed, he plucked up the courage to take a bite of the root. While the Manashroom tasted like nothing, the Spiny Swamp Thistle Root tasted like a copper penny in his mouth. He scrunched his nose up and swallowed, but no pain followed. The familiar window popped up, and he read.

[Properties Discovery!]
You've discovered an additional effect of the Spiny Swamp Thistle Root by eating it.
[Regeneration] discovered.

While the new property was useful, it wasn't something he could use for the tannery process. He made a note in the margins of his book and prepared to move on, but was interrupted by Luras entering the lab unexpectedly. The half-ogre didn't say a word, striding across the room to grab the sign and leave. Theo shrugged and turned his attention back to his books.

"*Any idea where I could find Swamplight Spiders?*" Theo asked Tresk telepathically.

"*Basically, anywhere in the swamp that's low to the water. The Swamplight Spiders like to build their webs near the Ogre Cypress,*" Tresk replied.

The mental communication ability was incredibly useful. There was a lot Theo still didn't know about the swamp, and having access to a native's knowledge at any time was beyond useful. He stepped outside to find Luras hanging the new sign, banging on the lab with a hammer.

"Thanks for that," Theo said with a chuckle.

"Not a problem," Luras said.

A farmer came trotting down the dirt road from the north, waving his arms in the air. "Hey! Do you have that cleansing potion you showed us last night?"

"We're working on getting it ready. I'll leave the vials outside my shop," Theo said. "Hey, want to make a copper?"

The farmer shrugged. "Sure."

Theo knew that the farmers likely dumped all their points into Strength and Vigor, the two attributes that made the most sense for farmwork. The big half-ogre would have no trouble carrying his water barrel to and from the river. He fished a copper coin from his pocket and flicked it to the man, who caught it deftly.

"If you could fill my barrel with water from the river, I'd appreciate it," Theo said.

"Yes, sir," the farmer said, scrambling inside the lab and hoisting the barrel before darting off to the river.

"It's a good idea to delegate tasks if you have the coin," Luras said, hammering the last nail to hang the sign.

Theo stepped back and looked at the sight, smiling at the design. Both the name and the icon of the demon-newt were perfect.

"We need more streams of revenue if we're going to upgrade the town," Theo said.

Luras raised an eyebrow. "That's an interesting plan. Very selfless."

Theo waved his hand dismissively. "The bigger the town gets, the more business we get."

Luras nodded, casting his gaze over the swamp to the west.

"I need to harvest some Swamplight Spider Silk and Marsh Tubers," Theo said. "We're working on a project for the tannery."

"You'll find both near the cypress," Luras said. "Need an escort?"

"I mean, are you doing anything today?" Theo asked.

"Nope. I don't want to see you dead at the claws of a wolf," Luras said.

"Got your water, sir!" the farmer called from around the lab.

It had only been a few minutes since the farmer left. Theo was stunned by the way the half-ogre hoisted the barrel effortlessly, despite it being full.

"Thank you," Theo said, watching as he disappeared into the lab and returned. He wasn't even winded.

"Let me know if you have any more odd jobs like that. My name's Oruk, by the way. Of course, I know your name," he said, chuckling.

"I will, Oruk," Theo said. His mind spun with the possibilities that a brawny hand could get done. He filed it away for the moment, focusing on the tannery job. The half-ogre turned on the spot and left.

"Let's go," Theo said, mentally informing Tresk where he was going.

"Sounds good to me... I've got quite a few motes. We're going to need a storage system in the lab," Tresk replied.

Perhaps we can get our hands on a dimensional bag... Or maybe a dimensional cupboard, Theo said.

The pair departed for the marsh to the west, quickly finding themselves among the massive cypress trees. Luras killed a pack of marsh wolves and began processing their bodies while Theo busied himself with the trees. He dunked his face in the muck, digging for the tubers below. According to the literature, he would find them among the roots of the cypress trees. It was foul work, but he knew that banishing the filth was easy now. A window appeared, detailing his core leveling up.

Drogramath Herbalist Core gained experience (2%).
Drogramath Herbalist Core reached Level 4!

The level-up came without additional benefits. Theo had a theory that he would see something at Level 5, but disregarded the notion for the time being and inspected the Marsh Tuber.

[Marsh Tuber]
[Alchemy Ingredient] [Food]
Common
Marsh Tubers grow near the roots of Ogre Cypress Trees. Their taste is disgusting, but palatable to those desperate enough.
Properties:
[Preservation] [???] [???]

Luras finished skinning and butchering the wolves, hoisting his haul over his shoulder and approaching Theo.

"Could I buy the hides you get today?" Theo asked. "I'm going to improve the tanner's process."

"Sure," Luras said, shrugging. "I usually sell them for 5 copper each."

"And you'll get your 5 copper," Theo said, nodding. "I don't want to get into the habit of taking advantage of our friendship. If this process works out, I'll stand to make a lot of money."

Luras shrugged. He wasn't a man who cared about money and seemed to live his life by the day. The half-ogre was stoic most of the time, only showing emotion when it really counted.

"There it is," Theo said, pointing at a faintly glowing spider web nestled between the jutting roots of the cypress.

"The spiders are venomous, but they're hiding under the bark during the day," Luras said. "Never harvest the webs during the night."

The web was extremely thick for spider webs. Theo wrapped it around his glove and removed it in a big wad before placing it in his bag. He looked forward to the inventory ability more than anything else. Without a high Strength attribute, he couldn't carry much.

The pair moved through the swamp, collecting as many tubers and webs as they could carry before heading back at midday. Tresk was already back at the lab, praising the Cleansing Scrub as a miracle of modern alchemy. Theo laughed out loud, gaining the attention of Luras.

"You're talking to Tresk? With your brain?" Luras asked. "I've heard about that ability, but I've never seen a marshling take a life partner."

"It's really nice," Theo said. "It feels more like having a copy of yourself than being in a relationship."

"It sounds nice," Luras said, adjusting the bag of dead wolf parts on his back.

Theo explained how the Tara'hek created a new core, granting him a free slot. He explained the quirks of the new core, including how he couldn't change the skill that was slotted inside.

"That's unexpected," Luras said. "You can basically level up your relationship."

They returned to the lab to find Tresk organizing an absurd number of motes into a few crates. There were several hundred, most of them a shade of blue Theo hadn't seen before. Inspecting them, he found that they were Water Motes. They looked like spheres of water, held together by an invisible barrier. He held one in his hand for a moment before the marshling approached him. She beckoned him down, and he obeyed, doubling over. Tresk pressed her forehead against his for a moment before backing off and smiling.

"That's how you say hello to your Tara'hek," Tresk said, beaming.

Theo couldn't deny the powerful warmth that flowed through his body from the gesture. It was like seeing an old friend for the first time since childhood.

"I like it," Theo said. "You got a lot of motes…"

"The river is lousy with them. People down here have little need for them. The fishermen left an enormous pile near the shore. I just scooped them up," Tresk said, giggling.

Theo fished 15 copper from his pocket and handed it to Luras. "Please leave the hides outside," he said. "I don't want them stinking up the place."

"Wait! Let's try the Cleansing Scrub on one," Tresk said, withdrawing her vial of the liquid.

Luras produced one hide and held it out. The fat was still attached to the bottom, the gray-brown hide catching the light of the sun in a beautiful display. Tresk placed a drop of the cleansing agent on the hide, which glimmered with the familiar white light. It was left as it was before, but at least it smelled good.

"It was worth a shot," Theo said. "Out the back they go."

The half-ogre took the three hides outside, returning only to announce that he would depart for the day. They bid him farewell and focused on creating the glassware needed to make the Cleansing Scrub. Tresk manned the Glassware Artifice, and Theo turned his attention to the barrel of River Water. He easily judged the contents of the barrel and applied the correct amount of Purifying Essence, resulting in a level-up of his Drogramath Alchemy Core to Level 4 and a barrel full of Purified Water. He then worked on creating fifty vials of the Cleansing Scrub, chatting idly with Tresk as they worked.

The pair finished the reactions and carried a side table outside. They placed it in front of the shop with a crate containing all the Cleansing Scrub and set the honor box next to it. It was the easiest-to-make recipe they had discovered so far. They could easily produce tons of the potion.

"Next step," Theo said. "We're going to try some volatile reactions."

"That sounds dangerous."

Theo gathered his remaining Cleansing Essence, Purifying Essence, and several empty flasks. Tresk followed him behind the lab to a wide gravel yard he hadn't understood the purpose of until now. It was littered with shards of glass and burn marks, while the hides Luras had delivered rested in the corner. He understood now that it was an area meant for testing reactions. He placed an empty flask on the far side of the yard and drew the smallest unit from his Cleansing Essence. The reaction would be sudden, if it happened at all, and he prepared to retreat after drawing some Purifying Essence.

"All right, stand back," Theo said, positioning his pipette over the flask.

The reaction happened before he could retreat to a safe distance. The flask shattered from the force of the explosion. Theo patted himself down to check for shards of glass before inspecting Tresk. They were both unharmed, and the marshling was hooting with excitement.

"That was awesome!" Tresk shouted, dancing and hopping around.

"Not the intended reaction, though," Theo said, cupping his chin in his hand.

Instinct said that there was an issue with the combination being unstable. He used his superior memory to search his books, finding a mention of agent stabilization. The pair retreated to the lab, waving off concerned citizens and consulting the books. He remembered one page that had something on the matter and quickly flipped to it, hoping to find the answer to his problem. Purified Water could be changed to Stabilized Water by introducing Flaky Agate—an agent he had seen among the various reagents left in the lab by the previous owner. He followed the instructions and created a flask with five units of Stabilized Water, moving back outside. Tresk followed the whole time, nodding to his mutterings with interest.

"So, the reaction was unstable," Theo said, "but my intuition says that this should work."

"And you have really high Wisdom, so you must be right," Tresk said.

"Yeah... So let's try a five-unit solution of Stabilized Water and work our way up with the other ingredients," Theo said.

"Yeah, let's do that," Tresk said.

The first few attempts didn't result in a reaction, but it also didn't result in an explosion. Theo reset five times before he found the right combination of the essences. The flask sputtered for a moment, and he ran back to safety, only to find that it was a success. His intuition was correct, resulting in the perfect thing for the first step of processing wolf hides. Theo and Tresk inspected the solution.

[Stripping Solution]
[Cleaning Agent]
Common
Created by: Belgar
Quality: Great
Remove surface imperfections based on the application. Commonly used in material-processing trades such as silk manufacturing and hide tanning.
Effect:
Smooths out the surface it is applied to.

"Smells gross," Tresk said, making a sour face.

Theo agreed. It smelled like industrial-strength cleaner, leaving his nose stinging long after he had pulled away from the flask. Eager to test his new potion, he placed a hide on the gravel and splashed the contents of the flask onto it. The reaction was immediate. The liquid worked its way across the hide, letting off a steam that smelled far better than the solution itself. It sizzled for a while; the solution moved across the hide on its own before stopping. He smiled upon inspecting the result. The hair didn't just fall off the skin, it completely evaporated. The fat underneath also saw a similar fate.

"Perfect!" Theo shouted, holding it up for Tresk to see.

"That's step one," Tresk said, nodding.

"Let's find a way to preserve this bad boy," Theo said, looking at the sheet of leather in his hand with a bright smile.

Chapter 12
Rivers and Daub

Theo and Tresk spent the rest of the day distilling the Marsh Tuber and Swamplight Spider Silk into their respective essences. The spider silk was incredibly easy to prepare into a mash, while the tubers required quite a lot of work. They looked and smelled like slightly rotten potatoes, but they didn't break apart easily. Each one needed to be diced into small chunks before being ground with the heavy "mashing stick," as Tresk called it. The alchemist gained another personal level, hitting Level 4 and dumping his point into Wisdom without a second thought. He felt a tangible surge in his mind, tipping over the 20 mark.

"I can think faster," Theo said, laughing. "Twenty points must be a threshold..."

"That's what I've heard," Tresk said with a shrug. "I've been pumping points into Dexterity, mostly."

Theo wiped the sweat from his brow, inspecting his dwindling stamina bar. He suspected that his companion was also feeling exhausted, but he also knew that she would never show it. Dusk was a few hours off, but the alchemist's stomach was already rumbling. He inspected both of his flasks of essence before they departed for the tavern.

[Preserving Essence]
[Essence]
Common
Created by: Belgar
Quality: Great
5 units (liquid)
Concentrated essence of preservation.

[Supple Essence]
[Essence]
Common
Created by: Belgar
Quality: Great
5 units (liquid)
Concentrated essence of supple.

The Supple Essence had the silliest name of anything he had seen so far, but if he could get the two ingredients to play nice, it would make the perfect tanning solution. As Theo made for the door, he noticed fifteen new lines in his Perpetual Ledger. Various townsfolk had put money in the honor box, and the pair went out to investigate. The people of Broken Tusk were apparently as honorable as they seemed. Fifteen potions were missing, and 15 copper sat in the unlocked box. Theo split the money between him and Tresk before they left for the tavern.

"How much do the tanners sell their finished work for?" Theo asked.

"I'm not much into leatherworking myself," Tresk said, shrugging. "Luras might know."

"I'll ask him," Theo said. "If the next step of the tanning process works as fast as the first, we're going to reduce their work time by about a year."

Tresk laughed, slapping her knobbly knees. "That's insane."

Miana wasn't at her house to glower at them as they passed, which was a welcome sight. They entered the tavern and greeted the familiar faces. It was still fairly empty because of the early hour of the evening. Xam had no more Karatan steaks tonight, and the pair settled for more mystery stew. Theo suspected that whatever meat the tavern claimed was in the soup was merely Xam's best guess. It all tasted the same and had the same texture. He ordered two bowls of "wolf meat stew" and retreated with his companion to their regular table.

"Did you have wolves in your world?" Tresk asked, noisily slurping her stew.

Theo found the way she ate funny. Back on Earth, the loud lip smacking would have annoyed him. He couldn't tell if it was his new circumstances, or because Tresk was his Tara'hek, but the noise didn't bother him. He only found it a bit silly.

"Oddly, we do. I've only really seen three different creatures here, and we have all of them in some form," Theo said. "Our turtles are a lot smaller, and we don't have giant insects... But the wolves seem exactly the same."

"That's weird," Tresk said, gnawing on a gristly piece of meat.

"Mind if I join you?" Perg asked, approaching with a bowl of stew.

Theo went to hold his breath but caught the familiar scent of berries as she approached. She must have been one of the townsfolk who had bought the scrub. It was incredibly potent stuff if it could wash away the smell of the tannery. He gestured for her to sit down. "Of course."

"We've made a lot of progress on the tannery project," Tresk said, grinning.

Perg let out a long breath. "A Tara'hek. In the flesh. I guess a legendary bond makes you more focused."

"We have a potion that will strip the hair from a hide in a few minutes," Theo said, finally taking a moment to taste his stew. It tasted exactly like all the stews he had tried before, reinforcing his mystery meat theory.

"What?" Perg said, sputtering. "You work fast, don't you?"

"No sense wasting time," Theo said, waving a dismissive hand. "We have a lot of things to improve in this town."

"How much do you sell your leather for?" Tresk asked. She could be quite rude, but Perg seemed accustomed to curt people.

"Marsh wolves are actually pretty rare," Perg said with a shrug. "They produce a very soft leather for what they are. Most people in the north are used to the Karatan leathers, but even after treatment, those can be rough. Broken Tusk leather is soft. Very soft. We can get up to a silver per leather, depending on the buyer. Typically, between 50 copper and 1 silver."

"Wow, that's awesome," Tresk said, gawking.

"Except it takes a year to make a single leather," Theo said.

He understood the delicate nature of their work. They had to sit on a batch of leathers for over a year, considering that traders didn't visit Broken Tusk often. They ate the cost year-round and prayed that someone showed up with enough coin to buy what they had. His alchemical process for the trade would give them flexibility, and he considered the price he should claim for this luxury.

"That's the biggest problem of our industry," Perg said, letting out a heavy sigh. "I suppose those Karatan leather makers in the capital have access to fine alchemists such as yourself."

"Wait until they see what Broken Tusk can do with their new alchemist," Tresk said. "How much hide do you decline to process every year?"

"Tons," Perg said. "We have a deal with a few hunters in the area, but my warehouse is only so big."

Money created money in this situation. He would streamline the tannery's process, and the hunters of Broken Tusk could sell more hides to the tanner. The tanner could sell more leather, and the hunters could sell more hides. Theo sought to create cycles like these within the town, things that only improved the lives of the townsfolk.

"We'll turn it into a volume game," Theo said. "You'll be

putting out more leather than you ever thought possible when we're done."

"I look forward to it," Perg said.

The group settled on idle chatter for a while as the tavern filled up. Luras found his way in eventually, surprised to see his friends already seated with Perg. He bought a bowl of the stew and sauntered over, pulling up a chair. They chatted for a time before the tanner needed to leave.

"You're always making connections," Luras said. "I'm headed up north tomorrow, so you won't see me for a while."

"Off to Qavell?" Tresk asked.

"Not quite. I'm going to visit Rivers and Daub," Luras said. "I have a friend up there that I'd like to check on."

Theo thought about the idea of traveling outside of Broken Tusk. He had no interest in leaving the muddy confines of the town, finding everything about it comforting. He would live his entire life here if he could, never venturing further than he needed to. It was another thing that drove him to turn the alchemy lab into a shop. A constant flow of coin meant that he could afford hirelings to do the running around, leaving him to focus on experimentation.

Even the debt that hung over his head was nothing. Once he worked out a deal with the tannery, the coin would flow. Since Miana agreed he could make regular payments, it would be simple to gradually pay it back. His primary concern was upgrading his lab and the town. Something in his heart told him that the fast progress he was making with the tannery job was beyond his own aptitude. The legacy of Drogramath ran through his veins, and the Drogramath Alchemy Core was likely a driving force in his progress. There was an innate knowledge in his mind that let him see a clear path forward in all things alchemy.

"I hate Rivers and Daub," Tresk said. "Pompous folk there."

Luras smiled, shrugging. "I think most of the southlands hate them. They're not nearly northern enough to be city folk, but they act like it."

"If you're going to wallow in the mud, you may as well go all in," Theo said.

"Actually, that gives me an idea," Tresk said, knitting her scaly brow. "Theo, what do you think about making a double batch of Cleansing Scrub tomorrow?"

"Oh, people up in Rivers will pay an arm and a leg for that," Luras said. "I'll gladly hawk your wares."

"Works for me," Theo said, grinning. "You can have half the haul, of course."

"You're too generous," Luras said, shaking his head. "How do you expect to make a profit working like this?"

"I'm only generous to my friends," Theo said. "Everyone else gets fair rates, but that's it. Nothing wild like half my total profit. If you can sell them for over 2 copper, I'll still get more than I get here."

"Good point," Luras said. "Plus, I have to carry 100 vials of a potion up a dangerous road."

Luras excused himself for the evening after more light conversation. Theo and Tresk only lingered for a while before departing, heading out as dusk gave way to night. The alchemist couldn't stop thinking about how nice the city would be to walk through if not for the muddy roads. Once he had more money, he would focus a lot of effort on upgrading the town.

"Don't look now, but my father is giving you the eye," Tresk said telepathically.

Theo's head instantly snapped to the smithy, Throk's gaze meeting his with fiery conviction. The marshling stomped across the muddy square, beckoning for the alchemist to bend to his level. Without thinking about it, Theo obliged. Throk had the same piercing gaze as his daughter, those ruby eyes of his boring a hole into Theo's soul.

After a moment, the blacksmith nodded. "The Tara'hek took. Despite my best advice, I knew the girl was too much to handle."

"I'm panicking. What should I do?" Theo said in Tresk's mind.

"I dunno! I never expected him to accept you as my partner,"

Tresk replied. Even through the mental link, he could hear the panic in her voice.

"You're talking to her with the Tara'hek core, aren't you?" Throk said, smiling. "Those tools are only going to get more powerful as you grow closer. The system wouldn't have allowed this to happen if you weren't meant to grow together."

"We could feel it right away," Theo said. "I just knew that she'd make me better at everything."

"Well, if you're willing to give up your life of romance to take the bond, you're worth keeping around," Throk said. "You're welcome to come home, Tresk, but I doubt you'll take me up on the offer."

"Thanks, dad," Tresk said, grinning. "I knew you'd understand once you saw us together."

"You're two sides of a blade," Throk said, nodding. He always seemed so sage-like. "The things you two will accomplish... They're going to be grand."

Tresk waddled through the mud to give her father a hug before departing. Theo was stunned by the exchange. The connection that the Tara'hek created was absurdly deep, and as he reflected on the process, he knew another marshling would understand. While it was rare, it seemed deeply rooted in their culture.

"I knew he'd come around," Tresk said. "He's such a blowhard."

"Seems kind of poetic," Theo said, unlocking the lab. After stepping inside, he lit the candles. He still had a portion of his stamina bar and assumed that Tresk did too.

"How do you figure?" Tresk said, locking the door and settling in on the ground near the burnt-out fire.

Theo grinned. "A blacksmith as hard as iron? Come on."

Tresk laughed, slapping her knees and doubling over. Theo came to sit next to her and leaned in to press his forehead against hers. They stayed there for some time before coming apart.

Tara'hek Core gained experience (5%).

"We got experience," Tresk said, chuckling.

"I guess we get experience points for bonding," Theo said. "Seems kinda silly."

"Yeah, we gotta level the Tara'hek Core just like our other cores," Tresk said.

Theo settled down on the ground, leaning his back against the wall and looking around the lab. It could use some additional seating, but it was crowded as it was. The space required for making potions was greater than the need to be comfortable. There was also the issue that they wanted to turn it into a store, which would consume a fair amount of floor space. Assuming that the expansions on the lab were uniform, they would need at least three more levels before it could be used as a shop.

The three rows of tables dominated the space, but the junk that littered every corner wasn't helping. They lacked shelf space and storage areas. The crowded space got more crowded with every new project they took on, adding to the mess. Theo let out a heavy sigh, casting his gaze over the lab. The ownership was still solely in his name, which didn't sit right with him. He thought for a moment, mentally adding Tresk to the list of owners. To his surprise, it worked.

Tresk is now an owner of the [Alchemy Lab]

A key appeared in Tresk's hands, and she shrieked in delight. She wiggled on the spot for a moment before concentrating.

Tresk has named the [Alchemy Lab] "The Newt and Demon"

"I didn't want to push the issue," Tresk said. "I knew you'd make me a co-owner in time. Hey, it says you have two names here."

"The system gave me a name when I came here—Belgar. That's why all my potions say they were made by 'Belgar.'"

"Theo Spencer... Yeah, Belgar sounds a lot cooler," Tresk said. "And a lot more like a Dronon name for that matter."

Theo smiled, his mind drifting back to his demonic heritage. "I imagine there's people in this world that might not like me because I'm a Dronon."

"Maybe somewhere in the world, but there are so many races that most people really don't care," Tresk said. "Some people seek demon-born folk, but they're very knowledgeable on the subject. The Order of the Burning Eye handles all the demon lords—keeps them in check."

"Are they going to come for me?" Theo asked, grimacing.

"Maybe one day," Tresk said, "but come on... What demon would undertake the Tara'hek? They'll take one look at us and be like, 'Oh, nevermind. This lovely little marshling can vouch for him.' I heard they can test to see whether you're a terrible person."

"That's comforting. Hopefully, we'll have made a name for ourselves by the time they come knocking," Theo said.

His mind wandered again, tiredness slowing his thoughts. Every turn in Broken Tusk seemed to open a gateway to more opportunities and more work. They would have to rise early the next morning to make more of the Cleansing Scrub before experimenting with their new essences. Fortunately, Tresk had harvested enough motes to last them a while. They could easily craft enough for Luras to make a killing in Rivers and Daub and complete the tanner's job.

"We'll need to get up early tomorrow," Theo said. "Seems like a rude thing to keep Luras waiting."

"I agree. It's a day or so of travel north for Luras. But he's a fast guy, so he'll want to go early," Tresk said. "Hey, why don't we make the vials now?"

Theo shrugged. This was exactly why he needed a partner. He had enough stamina to keep going for an hour and didn't even consider the concept of getting a head start on the next day. "Brilliant idea."

The pair spent the next hour creating Cleansing Scrub vials

and arranging them neatly on the table. They had more than enough Cleansing Essence for the job, as it was a 0.1:5 ratio of essence to water. They would distribute the 5-unit result into 1-unit bottles, stretching it even further. If Luras really could get a decent price in Rivers and Daub, this would be their lowest-effort money-maker.

"That'll do it," Tresk said, wiping her brow and taking out her Cleansing Scrub from a satchel. "Time for a bath."

Theo retrieved his vial and did the same, placing one drop on his forearm, one on his clothes, and two on his two moccasins. The white light filled the lab, followed by the pleasant smell of berries. He instantly felt clean, as though he had just gotten out of the shower. Tresk beamed, nodding toward the bedroom. The alchemist extinguished the candles and followed her in, pressing his forehead against hers before crawling into bed.

"Goodnight," Theo said telepathically.

Sleep came quickly that night. The allure of adventure the following day did nothing to stave off his slumber.

Chapter 13
Tanning

Tresk woke before Theo the next day. The smell of grilled Zee wafted into the bedroom, darkness still looming outside. The alchemist emerged from the bedroom, stretching and taking in the mingling of scents. With their lab cleaned by the Cleansing Scrub, the smell of the tea wafted in strongly. The citrus was more distinct than before, permeating the air and stinging his nose. He took a seat next to his companion and rubbed the sleep from his eyes.

"Plenty of time to make the Cleansing Scrub," Tresk said, serving him a slice of Zee. "We're going to need to get more food. That Zee you bought is going to rot before we eat it."

"If we weren't so busy, I might have a solution for that," Theo said. "The Manashrooms have a [Freezing] property on them. We could create a storage area."

"Another time," Tresk said. "Let's take care of Luras's job first, then we can sort the tanner's job out."

"I have a good feeling about the two new essences," Theo said, finishing his food and approaching the Glassware Artifice with a mote in hand. He produced two flat-bottomed vials and set them on the table. He idly created a reaction in both vials, mixing 1 unit of Purified Water, 1 unit of Poison Essence, and Copper Shavings in each. The reaction was immediate, stinging his nostrils in a puff of smoke. Theo handed Tresk the vial, and her face lit up.

[Basic Poison]
[Poison]
Common
Created by: Belgar
Quality: Great
Coat your weapon to deal additional damage to an enemy.
Effect:
Applies the poison damage over time effect, whose strength is contingent on the poison's quality.

"You're getting good at this," Tresk said.

"I have an intuition about things now," Theo said, "but something tells me these reactions are basic."

"That's likely your Drogramath heritage and Wisdom attribute," Tresk said.

"To have a Legendary core at Level 1... Yeah, it has to be my Drogramath cores. I can tell, just by thinking about it, that the Supple Essence and Preserving Essence will generate something that the tanners can use."

"But you don't know the quantities, so we need to test," Tresk said, nodding. "I'm getting used to the way you work. The next time a trader comes to town, we need to ask them to bring back advanced distillation books."

"Good plan."

Theo went around to the 100 vials that Tresk arrayed last night and started the simple reactions. He used a flask to start the five-unit reaction before distributing it among the vials. The process was extremely simple compared to his new recipes that required Stabilized Water, and he only gained partial percentages for each flask full of Cleansing Scrub. The entire process only took half an hour, and shortly after he was done, Luras arrived.

"Just in time," the half-ogre said, setting a heavy bag down on the table. "Load me up, boss."

Tresk and Theo went about setting the vials in the bag, separated by small wooden crates. They found what they could to pad the individual vials in the bag, finding cloth and pieces of wood to keep them from clanking together. Luras looked extremely excited for the trip, flashing a grin and heading for the door without a word.

"Hold up," Theo said, reaching for his Basic Poison potion. "Another gift."

Luras took the vial and smiled. "You're getting into poison-making now... You're going to be a generalist by the end of the year."

"Anything that helps you survive out on the road," Theo said.

"Thank you," Luras said, waving and departing.

The pair stepped outside to watch the half-ogre march northward toward the farms. Dawn had just broken over the eastern horizon. Theo took a deep breath of the damp, warm swamp air and let out a heavy sigh. The smell of mud and vegetation felt somewhat invigorating. He called Broken Tusk his home, and every day was a new adventure. Tresk joined him, mocking him by taking a deeper breath and letting out a heavier sigh. She flashed a devious grin at her companion.

"You're a clown," Theo said, laughing.

"What's a clown?" she asked.

"You."

They brought the ingredients for the next reaction to the back of the lab, in the gravel yard. Theo held a flask of his Stabilized Water with the Supple Essence and Preserving Essence. Tresk carried the spare flasks, still worried about the volatile reaction from last time. Her fears proved correct. The first flask exploded, despite the stabilizing agent, sending shards scattering in all directions and sending the pair running for cover.

"Why did it explode? You used the safe water," Tresk said.

"Yeah, this one is going to be tricky," Theo said.

His intuition told him that the Preserving Essence was the volatile essence in this reaction. It didn't like something about the Supple Essence and fought against it when they came into contact. He switched up the way he added the essences to the solution, starting by adding the less reactive one first and letting it sit for a moment. The liquid reacted after a moment, getting released into the vial without fully consuming the Stabilized Water. Theo pressed his fingers against the side of the flask and nodded to himself—it was extremely hot.

"We'll let that cool for a minute, then add the next essence," Theo said.

"How is someone supposed to figure this stuff out?"

"Experimentation, I guess," Theo said. "This is why alchemists have such a high Wisdom attribute... We have to know when to keep pushing and when to stop."

"Should I write this down?"

Theo waved a dismissive hand, watching the flask with interest. "My memory is pretty good now. I can remember most of what I've read. I'm quickly approaching a photographic memory."

"Fancy boy," Tresk giggled.

They waited for the flask to cool down to the ambient temperature, which was still pretty warm, before adding the last essence. This time it reacted immediately, sending a plume of clouds in the air that smelled like shoe polish. Tresk and Theo waited at a safe distance before they approached the flask, moving to inspect it.

[Alchemic Tannin]
[Leatherworking Agent]
Common
Created by: Belgar
Quality: Great
Replaces the traditional tannins from the leather working process.
Effect:

Apply it to a dehaired hide to cure it and make it more supple.

"I wish I had your level of intuition," Tresk said, shaking her head.

"It's easy. Just start with a legendary core given to you by a demon god," Theo said.

Tresk slapped her knees, doubled over with laughter.

The sun hung low in the sky by the time they rolled out the dehaired hide from yesterday. Theo did the honors, pouring a portion of the Alchemic Tannin over the hide. They watched as it worked its way into the material, sending puffs of smoke up as it went. After a few minutes, the potion did its job, leaving the hide in perfect condition. The smell it exuded was much like the shoe polish smell of the potion itself. The leather that remained was soft, and Theo would be happy to put the alchemical version of the process up against the natural one any day.

Tresk wanted to spend the day in the marsh, testing her new poison and collecting monster cores. Theo bid her farewell and made a new batch of the Stripping Solution to show Perg. A part of him felt reluctant to offer to replace her entire industry with a simple alchemical solution, but he had learned that the half-ogres didn't have pride to harm. They were practical people who took the best route to all solutions, and he knew she would appreciate his contribution.

Theo made his way south, plugging his nose when he got close to the tannery. Perg was waiting outside, leaning against her building with a smile on her face. "I had a feeling you'd fix this problem fast."

Theo couldn't hide his smile. "Care to join me for a demonstration?"

"Of course," Perg said, pushing off against the wall and trudging across the mud. They walked northward, and he could feel her excitement. "People said there'd be big changes when you got to town. Didn't realize they would come this quick."

"Tresk is helping a lot," Theo said.

"The bond you two have is a powerful thing," Perg said. "I've never seen it before, but I've heard stories."

They arrived in the gravel yard, and Theo handed Perg the hide he had completed. "This is obscenely soft," she said. "How long did it take you?"

"Two days for the research, but the reaction only takes a few minutes," Theo said.

"You've boiled my year-long process down to 'a few minutes,'" Perg said, shaking her head with amazement. "You understand how ridiculous that sounds, right?"

"These are the wonders of alchemy," Theo said, embarrassing himself by making jazz hands. "Anyway, want a demonstration?"

"Please do."

Theo retrieved a rotting wolf's hide, dragging it into the middle of the yard. It was already stinking, even if it had been freshly skinned just the day before. "The first step uses Stripping Solution, which removes the hair and fat," he said, pouring the first-step liquid over the hide.

Perg stood back, giving an approving nod after a minute of the potion doing its work. She moved to inspect the hide, flipping it over and saying, "Wow. It takes care of the fat too."

"The second step is the Alchemic Tannin, which works just as quickly," Theo said, pouring the next solution over the hide.

They stepped back and watched it work its magic, finding its way into the cracks and fizzling. Perg was amazed at how fast the potion worked, voicing her surprise and pointing out how it found its way into the grain of the leather. When it was done, she moved to inspect it. She pressed it against her face and inhaled its scent, turning to Theo with her mouth agape.

"I thought it would be fast, but... Wow, this is amazing," Perg said. "What do you need me to do to start mass production?"

"Come with me," Theo said, beckoning for her to follow him into the lab. He found his books and laid them out, rolling a piece of parchment to scribble on. "The first step requires Ogre Cypress Bark; we'll need a lot of that."

"The white bark in the inner layer of the ogre cypress trees?" Perg asked. "That's an ingredient in our process. I have a stockpile in the warehouse."

"Lucky you," Theo said. "I don't suppose you have Marsh Tubers and Swamplight Spider Silk as well? That's what we need for the second step."

"That I don't."

"We'll need equal parts of both," Theo said, using his intuition to calculate how much he would need per hide. By his estimation, one unit of either solution could cure one hide. One unit of tubers by weight would produce one unit of essence, and a quarter unit per essence for the spider silk. He scribbled on the parchment, describing what the Swamplight Spider Silk and Marsh Tubers were and where to find them. "You can collect these yourself, but I'll need to distill them and perform the reactions."

"I've seen the goods. You've proven yourself, but we haven't come to an arrangement," Perg said, knitting her brow.

"What's fair to you?" Theo asked.

"Would you do ten percent off the top?"

"Works for me," Theo said, reaching out a hand for her to shake.

Perg shook his hand vigorously, a grin spreading across her face. "You're so easy to work with. My guys will have all the ingredients you need by tomorrow."

"Pleasure doing business with you. Now we need to get some traders in town."

Perg departed with a bounce in her step, and Theo breathed a sigh of relief. He wasn't interested in doing the collection part of the job for them and was happy that she agreed to handle it. He wanted to expand his potion-making, branching out to more than just restoration potions. The alchemist planned on making attribute-enhancement potions, which his books claimed were harder than the base-level potions.

Before leaving to find Stone Flowers, he separated out his supply of Zee, targeting the kernels that were getting close to rotting. The second property on the kernels was [Cure Poison], something that seemed out of place for a farm-grown ingredient. Theo prepared the still for a run, creating a mash from twenty units of the usable crop and filling his Copper Still. He cooked it down easily, finding that the kernels were perfect for distillation. Something about the way they mingled with the water without becoming too soaked prevented them from burning on the bottom.

It took less than an hour to cook down, even though he kept the fire burning low, and it barely fit in the conical flask placed under the condenser. He inspected the new essence before running off to search for his flowers.

[Cure Poison Essence]
[Essence]
Common
Created by: Belgar
Quality: Great
20 units (liquid)
Concentrated essence of poison cure.

Theo tested the new essence by creating a Potion of Cure Poison.

[Potion of Cure Poison]
[Potion]
Common
Created by: Belgar
Quality: Great
Drink to remove poison.
Effect:
Remove one instance of poison from the drinker.

Theo's goal, now that he was waiting for Perg to collect his materials, was to create a few different potions for any adventurers passing by. It was nice to have the baseline restoration potions, but he wanted a selection for them to pick from. The plan also gave him a variety to sell to any passing merchants, although he had not met any of those yet.

"Perg will work with us. How goes the core hunting?" Theo asked, enjoying his mental link with Tresk.

"These poison potions are awesome! I'm getting a lot of experience," Tresk replied into his mind.

"Just stay safe. I'm going to look for some Stone Flowers," Theo said.

"I've seen them growing north of the farmer's fields. Just be wary of the wolves."

"Understood."

Theo nodded to himself. The area north of the farm had those horrible insectoid creatures. They were much further north than the fields themselves, but he shuddered at the thought of the strangely multi-jointed limbs. Monsters like that existed to defy what should be possible. He made a plan to stick to the area directly north of the fields.

Miana bothered him at the square, and he waved her off. The woman was all bark and no bite, and he had no obligation to pay her the massive sum of money all at once. The rent on his lab was due in a few days anyway, although how he could owe a mortgage *and* rent was beyond him. The familiar scent of manure and dirt wafted through the air as he approached the farmlands. Theo could only help the farmers if he came up with a way to accelerate the growth of plants, and he wasn't willing to put more work on his plate.

The lowland fields that stretched beyond the gentle slope of the farmer's fields were a strange place. Theo chalked it up to whatever magic the wizard had used to raise the farmer's land, sending the area into a dry habitat relative to the rest of the marsh. The Stone Flowers were easier to find than he expected. They grew like lilies among shale outcrops, their roots dug deep into the stone. The alchemist core allowed him to determine the best part of the plant to harvest, which was the flowers. The delicate petals crumbled if he grasped them too hard, forcing him to place them in his bag.

[Stone Flower]
[Alchemy Ingredient]
Common
Stone-like flower that grows near shale outcrops.
Properties:
[Increase Vigor] [???] [???]

The unknown properties of the flower would need to stay undiscovered. The flower was much like the shale it grew in and didn't look very appetizing. Theo continued to harvest the flowers, picking up the Earth Motes that he found and shoving them into his bag. He roamed the fields for a while, and his Drogramath Herbalist Core even reached Level 5.

Drogramath Herbalist Core gained experience (2%).
Drogramath Herbalist Core reached Level 5!
Drogramath Herbalist Core gained an additional bonus to Vigor (+1).

His herbalism core now provided +3 Vigor. His other core was on the verge of leveling up as well, which would cascade into a personal level-up. Theo looked forward to picking the inventory skill, hoisting the bag over his shoulder and straining under its weight. He had collected more motes than expected, spurred on to return to the lab by the sound of wolves baying in the distance. The alchemist entered the farm quickly, huffing for breath as his stamina dropped from the strenuous activity. Tresk was right about the wolves. Had there been this many wolves when he arrived?

"Is it me, or are there more wolves around?" Theo asked, waving

to a farmer as he held his silent conversation with Tresk using telepathy.

"Tell me about it. I ran into a pack of five just now. Glad that I have the poison and healing potions."

Theo felt his heart skip a beat at the mention of so many wolves. Tresk was putting herself in danger—but that was what adventurers did, right? There was a war raging in his heart; one side demanding her safety and the other happy to see her accomplishing her goals. He resolved to create more powerful potions, something that could shield her from danger even more. What he needed more than anything was a strong revenue stream and as many cores as he could buy. If his cores were anything to go by, the lab should get an upgrade at Level 5.

Throk waved Theo over as he was passing the blacksmith. The marshling smiled, gesturing to a massive pile of copper sitting in his workshop. "Progress is being made, alchemist," Throk said. "Your order for a water tower is coming along."

"When was a trader here?" Theo asked, knitting his brow.

"Earlier today," Throk said, casting his gaze over the copper. Theo pegged him as a man who liked a challenge. He had no doubt the water tower would be difficult to construct. "I have a metal trader come from Rivers and Daub every few days, and he came through on the copper. Like I said, it's not in demand at the moment. I got it for a steal."

Theo looked at the massive pile of copper and nodded. He suddenly understood that distance might not mean the same thing for traders as it did for others. After he discovered he could get an inventory ability, it was reasonable to assume that if there was a trader-style core, an inventory would be necessary.

"Did Miana sign off on it?" Theo asked.

"She doesn't have a choice," Throk said, croaking a laugh. "I own a fair amount of the land on the square. I can do whatever I want with it."

"And you want to put the water tower on your land?"

"Some of us are interested in seeing Broken Tusk prosper, just like you," Throk said. "You roll into town, transported from another world, and start making improvements as your first move. That says a lot about you."

Theo smiled, nodding and turning away wordlessly. He felt the beaming smile of the marshling on his back even as he left, and contentment spread through his body. He dove into the problems of the small town without giving thought to his own desires. His heart became tied to those people instantly, and he never looked back.

Chapter 14
Alchemy Lab Advancement

The Newt and Demon was empty when Theo returned. He mentally checked in with Tresk before peering out the window, trying to find the sun in the sky. It was some time after noon, and he had plenty of time to cook down his Stone Flowers before his companion returned. She apparently had a haul of monster cores, remarking that she had never seen that many wolves in the marshes before. The alchemist pushed the thought to the back of his mind, focusing on the task at hand. He was eager to get his new inventory skill, and his Drogramath Alchemy Core was on the cusp.

The Stone Flowers were incredibly easy to grind down. Theo could crush them in his hand over the Copper Still, cutting out the mashing process entirely. He set a small fire, added enough Purified Water for a five-unit batch, and sat down near the still. Something about the way it bubbled was soothing to him. He closed his eyes and listened to the crackle of the fire. By the time he opened his eyes again, the condenser was spitting and hissing, signifying the end of the process.

Theo moved the fire from underneath the still with his smashing stick and inspected the flask. The Vigor Essence was a light brown color and smelled like the earth. His intuition said that it followed the simple recipe, and that as he advanced in his alchemy, things would become less simple. The Glassware Artifice spat out five flat-bottomed vials, and he arranged them on the table before adding Purified Water and two units of Copper Shavings to each. While he noted his imminent need for more shavings, the five reactions were going off without a problem, and he finally achieved what he was hoping for.

Drogramath Alchemy Core gained experience (5%).
Drogramath Alchemy Core reached Level 5!
Theo Spencer gained experience (2%).
Theo Spencer reached Level 5!

He dumped his free point into Wisdom without a thought and immediately brought up the skills menu. It claimed that he had one free skill point, and he bought [Drogramath Inventory] without hesitation. His excitement reached a crescendo when he slotted it in the free slot of his Drogramath Alchemy Core. It didn't really matter which core he put it in, he just wanted to use his new inventory.

Theo fiddled around with his new ability for a while, finding it difficult to summon the screen at first. Four rows of eight slots sat in an ornate pop-up box, styled to look like a leather bag. The alchemist reached out for the Lesser Vigor Potion he had just crafted and stowed it away. The potion gained a simple icon, falling into the first slot with a satisfying sound. He repeated the process for the other four potions, and they stacked with the first.

Theo spent the next thirty minutes running around the shop and cramming everything he could find into his inventory before returning it to where he found it. The water barrel fit in easily, as did his bed. Only when he went outside to shove an entire boulder inside did it complain, filling his ears with an objecting beep. Tresk arrived in time to find him standing at the side of a massive chunk of shale, as though he were trying to lift it.

"Did you go insane while I was gone?" Tresk asked.

"No! Check it out," Theo said, producing a Lesser Vigor Potion from thin air.

Tresk shrieked with excitement, bouncing up and down and screaming in Theo's face. "That's so awesome!"

"I know!" Theo shrieked back.

The pair gained the attention of a half-ogre who was passing by. He gave them a weary look, making more room on the road than he needed to. They calmed down after a while, and Theo finally looked at the new potion he had crafted.

[Lesser Vigor Potion]
[Potion]
Common
Created by: Belgar
Quality: Great
Drink to temporarily enhance your vigor.
Effect:
+5 Vigor for 1 hour.

"That's fantastic... Does that mean you can make one for every attribute?" Tresk asked.

"Yes, the swamp biome has all the flowers," Theo said, "which is rare, apparently."

"There are a lot of rare things about the swamp," Tresk said, pulling her satchel around and revealing fifteen monster cores. "Including a strangely high number of Marsh Wolves."

"What do you think? Should we put all of them into the lab?" Theo asked. "I think we'll get some kind of upgrade at Level 5."

"Yeah, I think that's a safe bet. We can focus on the town later," Tresk said.

Tresk pressed her forehead against Theo's before they went into the lab, adding a few percentage points to their Tara'hek Cores. The marshling held the monster cores up one at a time, feeding them into the lab. The Level 5 monster cores gave the shop 25% of the experience bar at Level 1, but only 10% at Level 2.

Tresk concentrated when it reached Level 3, expanding the lab a few paces toward the river yet again. Compared to the original layout, the Level 3 lab expanded the space near the back by about Tresk's height.

[Alchemy Lab]
Owners: Belgar (Theo Spencer), Tresk
Faction: Broken Tusk
Level: 3 (40%)
Rent Due: 2 days

"The cores gave 8% experience at Level 3," Theo said. "We're going to need a lot of cores."

"I'd really like to get my hands on a dimensional bag," Tresk said, shrugging. "I could carry a lot more stuff."

"We'll put some feelers out for those," Theo said. "Those adventurers—how long should it take to clear a dungeon?"

"They're not from the swamp. It's going to take them a day to get there, at least two days to clear it, and a day to get back. I could get there in a few hours," Tresk said, grinning.

"The water tower project will come together soon. Your father has the copper he needs. The tanners are going to bring us reagents, likely tomorrow. What's our next plan of attack?" Theo asked.

"We should stock up on some potions," Tresk said. "I think we should take a break for the rest of the day, but tomorrow I can go core hunting again and get ingredients for more potions."

Theo inspected their stock of Spiny Swamp Thistle Root, then rifled through Tresk's bags without her objections. She had one health potion and no poison potions left. He handed her a Potion of Cure Poison and started preparing a mash for more Lesser Health Potions.

"You're afraid I'm going to die out there, aren't you?" Tresk said, smiling as she watched him work.

"Of course I am; you're my Tara'hek. I don't even know what cores you have," Theo said.

The alchemist cut the Spiny Swamp Thistle Root and started mashing it down in the bucket with his stick. Tresk came beside him and grinned.

"I have a common rogue core, and a common tracking core," Tresk said. "They're really not great."

Theo scrunched up his nose, feeling a pang of guilt in his heart. He felt as though he flaunted his rare cores around her, making him feel disgusted at himself. "Can we upgrade your cores somehow? I really don't know how that works."

"If we find another common-grade core that matches mine, we can," Tresk said. "Cores can be pretty expensive, though."

Theo waved his hand dismissively at the mention of price, transferring the crushed roots into the still. He scooped the perfect amount of water into the drum and replaced the lid, moving to stoke the fire back to life. It crackled at the perfect heat, just low enough to warm the mix without burning it.

"Keep an eye out for ability cores," Theo said. "I'd be happier if you had something higher than common... It goes common, uncommon, rare, epic, legendary, right?"

"There's something above legendary—well, that might just be a myth," Tresk said, scoffing. "I think it's an excellent investment, but I didn't want to push."

"Please push," Theo said. "I'm still really stupid about a lot of stuff in this world, and I didn't even ask you about your cores."

"It's okay. We'll get there," Tresk said.

"I have 5 silver and 20 copper," Theo said. "Just let me know if a trader stops by with cores, and we'll buy them."

Tresk nodded without responding, her eyes focusing on the flames. She stood near him during the cooking process, just watching the fire. The twenty-unit run took about an hour, but they spent most of their time idle. Only when the essence was distilled did the marshling get to work creating the vials. She arrayed them on the tables, and Theo followed up with the reactions. He quickly stored them in his inventory after setting five aside for his companion to keep on her at all times. He mixed the rest—4 units—of Poison Essence into Basic Poison and gave the resulting batch to her as well.

"Now you're armed to the teeth," Theo said. "I don't have to check up on you every five minutes when you're out hunting."

Tresk giggled, only stopping when a knock at the door came. Theo answered it, finding Perg standing there with a heavy satchel over her shoulder.

"My people are calling it quits for the day, but they collected a few things," Perg said, tossing the bag on the floor. It hit the ground with a resounding thump.

Theo's eyes went wide as he opened the satchel, finding an absurd amount of ingredients inside. It was all mixed, but he judged it was enough to make 200 units of both essences. "I'm going to need a bigger still," Theo said, shoving the items into his inventory. To his surprise, the Marsh Tubers stacked over 200, the slot they were taking up showing a small "215" in the corner. The Swamplight Spider Silk, which produced more essence by volume, showed the number "50".

"You have an inventory power now," Perg said, nodding. "That's incredibly rare if you're not a shopkeeper or a trader."

"Magic demon powers," Tresk said.

"If I can take the Ogre Cypress Bark from your warehouse, I can have 200 units of all the potions made tomorrow," Theo said.

"Sounds good to me," Perg said. "You're going to turn my group of tanners into glorified herbalists. Most of them have Laborer Core, anyway, but some have the Farmer Core. This one guy has the Stonecutter's Core. I guess it's not much of a waste."

"Just think of the profits, Miss Grott," Tresk said, wringing her hands together.

Theo realized he didn't even know Perg had a last name. He understood that marshlings didn't take a surname, but most of the half-ogres he had met did.

"We're going to blow the trader's mind when they come," Perg said.

"I need to skin the wolves that I kill," Tresk said. "I just never learned how to do that. I left fifteen wolves out in the marsh today."

"I can show you how to do it, if you want," Perg said, shrugging. "But tomorrow. The day is getting too late for me to care."

The heat had that effect on people. The longer the day got, the less Theo felt like working. They exchanged pleasantries for a while before locking up the lab and heading up the road to the tavern. Dusk was a few hours away, but no one seemed to have the will to work anymore for the day. Perg was in especially high spirits. She held her cards close to her chest at first, but her desire to see alchemical tanning through was obvious the further along they got.

Xam was serving meat stew yet again, and Theo bought three bowls for his friends. They settled in at the same table, propped the window open, and began eating. The tavern slowly filled. Partway through the meal, the door swung open, revealing someone that caught Theo's eye. The familiar shaven head and tightly drawn cowl of the human adventurer Jarson appeared, flashing a grin at them before sauntering over. He took a seat without saying a word, shaking his head and smiling.

"I guess this means you're done with the dungeon," Theo said, sipping his soup.

"It was a wild ride. Compared to the dungeons in the north... I can't even explain it," Jarson said. "It was so dense with monsters—we got so much loot that we were throwing stuff out by the end."

"Hopefully the potions served you well," Theo said.

"We almost burned through them all," Jarson said. "I went to your lab to give you my thanks but figured you'd be here when it was locked. Those potions saved our hides, Alchemist."

"Just doing my job," Theo said, smiling. "I don't know if you've met her, but this is my Tara'hek, Tresk."

"We met when I came for the potions, but I didn't know you

two were life partners," Jarson said, smiling. "A Dronon and a marshling... That has to be the first pairing of its kind."

"It just might be," Tresk said through a mouthful of meat.

"Anyway, I wanted to give you my thanks," Jarson said. "I'll be spreading the word to Qavell that Broken Tusk is open for business."

"If we could just get a road between here and there, that'd be perfect," the half-ogre tanner said. "I'm Perg, by the way."

"A pleasure," Jarson said. "You could find someone specializing in earth magic, but they're expensive."

Jarson reached into his dimensional bag and pulled out a smaller leather bag. He set it on the table and smiled at Theo, pushing it forward. "This bag is only worth a few silver in the big city." He reached in again and produced five Level 20 monster cores. "*These* are worth more, but I want you to accept them as my thanks."

Theo looked over the spoils, his mouth agape. He inspected the bag, finding it to be a Small Dimensional Bag.

[Small Dimensional Bag]
[Dimensional Bag]
Epic
A dimensional bag with 18 slots.

"This gift is too generous," Theo said, shaking his head. "How can I accept it?"

"You can accept it because we collected several hundred monster cores, and a few of these bags," Jarson said. "The reason we could get this stuff is your potions. We would have stopped at the tenth floor if not for you. The party ended up pushing all the way to the fifteenth."

Tresk whistled, shaking her head. "I haven't been past the fifth floor. We should accept this man's generous gift, Theo."

"All right, but since we're exchanging gifts," Theo said, withdrawing a Lesser Vigor Potion and handing it to Jarson. "Another taste of what Broken Tusk alchemy can do."

Jarson shook his head, accepting the potion and stuffing it in his bag. "You don't know how rare attribute-enhancement potions are, do you?"

"Nope."

"I've heard stories about the swamplands and the alchemical bounty they hold, but now I've witnessed it with my own eyes," Jarson said. "Well, my companions and I are traveling through the night to the north. The sooner we get back, the sooner we can sell this loot."

"Don't be a stranger," Perg said, fluttering her eyes at the human. He swallowed hard before taking a deep bow, leaving the tavern in a hurry.

"Most humans are afraid to get with half-ogres," Tresk said, laughing.

Theo laughed, putting the monster cores in his inventory and placing the Small Dimensional Bag in front of Tresk. Her eyes went wide as she pulled the item close to her, looking back and forth between the bag and the alchemist. "My very own dimensional bag... I thought I'd be Level 20 before I saw one of these."

"Now we both have dimensional storage," Theo said.

Tresk hooked the bag to her belt, standing up to admire it with a massive grin on her face. Perg was still looking longingly at the door, finally letting out a heavy sigh. "What I wouldn't give to jump that human and—"

"Ew," Tresk said, scowling. "Keep your dirty talk to yourself, lady."

Perg laughed, casting a hooded gaze over the marshling. "You took the Tara'hek, so I guess you'll never understand. You've never been in love."

"How can you be in love? You just met the guy," Tresk scoffed.

"Love at first sight," Theo said mockingly. "*Love* drove me to the Tara'hek. I've had too many good relationships ruined by adding that layer of romance."

"Maybe I need to find a strong marshling to take the vow with," Perg said, frowning.

Tresk shoved her soup into her Small Dimensional Bag and tugged on Theo's arm. "Let's go use those cores."

Theo followed suit, curious if the soup would keep its heat inside his inventory. Fortunately, it did. They beckoned for Perg to follow, but she waved them off, lost in her imagination. The pair moved at speed southward, toward their lab. Excitement bubbled over inside Theo's mind. He couldn't imagine how much experience Level 20 cores would give his little shop.

Tresk locked the door once they were in, withdrawing her soup from her inventory and setting it down on a table. She took idle sips as she passed by to light the candles, eagerly bobbing her head the whole way. Theo removed the five cores from his inventory, holding them in his hand for a moment. He could feel the raw power coming off of them—some malevolent energy that radiated in turgid waves. They were all troll or goblin cores and images of what the vile beasts looked like flashed through his mind.

"All right, let's see how much experience we get," Theo said, holding the first core up.

The alchemy lab vibrated under their feet. A window popped into Theo's vision.

[Alchemy Lab] has advanced to Level 4!
Select a direction you wish to expand the lab into (north/south/east/west).

"Woah!" Tresk shouted. "Almost there."

Theo nodded, selecting the window to expand northward. The lab vibrated under their feet, shifting to expand to the north. They went inside the bedroom to find that both that room and the main lab had gotten another two to three paces of space. The alchemist eagerly hoisted another monster core for the lab to consume.

[Alchemy Lab] has advanced to Level 5!

Select a Level 5 specialization:
[Alchemy Shop]
[Root Cellar]
[Experimentation Room]

"This is awesome!" Tresk shouted. "You can inspect each option, but I want the shop."

Theo did as his marshling Tara'hek suggested.

[Alchemy Shop]
Split-level design housing a space for a shop on the first floor with a lab and bedroom on the second.

[Root Cellar]
A cellar for preserving reagents housed under the lab. Reagents placed inside of the cellar decay at a slower rate.

[Experimentation Room]
A reinforced room placed behind the lab, creating a safe place to conduct explosive experiments.

Theo observed that the Level 5 upgrade had more to do with additional rooms rather than enhancements to the lab itself. The shop was the clear winner. If the description could be trusted, it would double their current floor space. "It's settled then. [Alchemy Shop]."

The lab vibrated violently under their feet, sending the pair tumbling to the ground. None of the tables or objects on those tables moved at all. The ground below their feet rocketed upward, passing through their bodies as another floor appeared under their feet. Theo watched the bedroom vanish, replaced with a set of stairs that led to the second floor. Tresk was shouting with excitement the entire time. They were shoved out of the way as a counter appeared in the middle of the room, shelves and tables springing throughout the shop.

Theo and Tresk raced up to the second story lab, finding all of their tables, equipment, and ingredients where they left them. The bedroom was now at the back of the building, accessible by a hallway at the top of the stairs. The door leading to the east was the bedroom; north was the lab. They made their way back downstairs to admire the new shop.

Tresk ran her hands over the long counter, shouting, running up the stairs, and returning with the Perpetual Ledger. She placed it on the counter and smiled.

"We need to get a bell," Theo said. "If we're working the lab upstairs, we'll need to know someone requires our service."

"Yeah, maybe!" Tresk shouted. "Let's use the rest of the cores."

Theo hoisted the remaining three cores one by one, gaining two more levels for the shop and expanding it out the back two more times. The building was massive by the time they were done, allowing enough room for a new row of tables upstairs. They would need to organize the lab, but it was an enormous improvement. Even though both of their stamina bars were nearly depleted, they spent hours running their hands over the surfaces in amazement.

Theo inspected the shop before they turned in for the night.

[Alchemy Lab] [Alchemy Shop]
Name: The Newt and Demon
Owners: Belgar (Theo Spencer), Tresk
Faction: Broken Tusk
Level: 7 (31%)
Rent Due: 2 days
Expansions:
[Alchemy Shop]

The pair retreated to the bedroom, sharing in their excitement. Their bedroom was big enough to fit two beds side-by-side now, and Theo felt guilty that Tresk was still sleeping on the bedroll. She said it didn't bother her, but he would like to find her a proper bed. He closed the bedroom door and settled in for the night. They lay there in silence for some time, both consumed with their excitement for the new shop. Jarson's gift was beyond anything they could have expected, and neither would forget his generosity.

"That guy is getting so many discounts the next time he's in town," Tresk said before they both fell asleep.

Chapter 15
Blacksmith's Wares

A small crowd formed outside of the Newt and Demon the following morning. Theo and Tresk grinned from the second story, peering out the window and eating their breakfast. They had used the last of the Moss Nettle to make their morning tea, but the spectacle outside demanded their full attention. If the townsfolk weren't aware of the alchemist's presence before, they were now. It was a rare morning where the pair rose after dawn, the excitement from the previous night clearly stealing away their sleep.

"Do you think they're going to disperse?" Tresk asked, finishing her tea.

"I'm happy to glower down from our gigantic shop the whole day," Theo said, waving at the crowd.

"Too bad we have some potions to synthesize," Tresk said.

Theo thought about the plan for the day. An issue came to the front of his mind quickly. Their alchemy lab had a problem with production capacity. The Copper Still could handle fifty units at a time, but no more. He planned to distill an absurd amount of essence to fulfill the tannery job, but he would need to run several batches over the day to get it done. With the time to cook fifty units of anything being at least an hour, he had a better idea.

"I think I'll pay your father a visit before I start," Theo said. "I think I should have commissioned another still a while ago, but here we are."

Tresk cast her eyes to the ceiling, nodding in agreement. The flue that caught the smoke from the fire had grown large enough to accommodate another still, if not two more. "Does that mean I get to go adventuring?"

"It absolutely does," Theo said, moving to press his forehead against hers. They remained there for a moment, gaining some experience in their Tara'hek Cores before departing. They didn't need the time for long farewells, as they could keep in communication with their abilities. Tresk departed, moving through the crowd and heading west into the marsh. He watched her go before leaving himself.

"You just grew your building," Perg said, following him through the crowd.

Theo locked up before leaving, not that any of the townsfolk would trespass. Perg followed him up the road north. "Those monster cores were absurd. The lab is... Well, it's a shop now, and it's Level 7."

"I forgot that old building was a seed core building," Perg said. "So, are you working on my job today?"

"Yeah, I need to commission some new stills from the blacksmith," Theo said. "I underestimated the volume of the job."

"Not like my people are doing anything, anyway... Should I get them to harvest more of the materials?"

"That's a good idea," Theo said.

Perg nodded before heading down the road back to the tannery. Theo approached the blacksmith, spotting the beginnings of the water tower project off to the side. He found Throk hammering away at some glowing metal and got his attention.

"Tower isn't done, yet," Throk said, grimacing.

"I have another job for you," Theo said.

"More work, huzzah," Throk said, rolling his eyes. "Well, you're officially my best-paying customer, so what is it?"

"Two copper stills. Somewhere near 200-liquid-unit capacity," Theo said.

"Well, guess who ordered more copper than he needed? This marshling," Throk said, pointing at himself with both thumbs. "I've seen the still in your lab. I can make the entire thing easily, including the condenser unit. Hell, I can make a more efficient condenser if you want to pay more. Materials will be 20 copper and I'll take 5 for labor. I can have it done by tomorrow."

Theo dug in his pocket, kicking himself for keeping the coins in his physical pocket for so long. He stuffed four of the silver coins and all the copper into his inventory space, watching as a coin counter appeared at the bottom of the bag. He flicked a silver coin through the air, which Throk caught. His eyes went wide, and the alchemist grinned.

"I want you to go wild with it. Give me the fanciest stills you can think of. As fast as you can," Theo said.

"Alchemist... You really do speak my language," Throk said, dropping the hot iron and hammer. "Give me about two hours. I'll show you what a master blacksmith can do."

Theo couldn't hide his smile as he turned to walk away. The greatest motivator for anyone living in Broken Tusk was coin, especially lots of it. He mentally told Tresk about his purchase, which she approved of. She was loving her new dimensional bag, already climbing the trees to harvest more Moss Nettle for their tea. Without the need to shove it in a satchel at her side, she could harvest the moss faster. While her goal was to collect more monster cores, she picked up whatever herbs she could find along the way.

Tresk reported that the number of monsters in the swamp had evened out for the day. While she still found packs of five wolves, they weren't expanding. Theo didn't know how the generation of monsters worked in this world and hadn't thought to ask. Every time the topic entered his mind, he pushed it away. The only thing that allowed it to linger was his concern for his partner's safety. One day, he would have to face that problem, but today wasn't it.

Theo returned to the shop, locking the door behind him and

standing near the front counter. Waiting for the blacksmith to complete his order might have been a welcome reprieve, but it felt like agony to him. Two hours of waiting around didn't sit well with him, but there was no sense in running his Copper Still while new ones were on the way. Instead of languishing in the lab, he left to find herbs. The idea of testing out his inventory in a real scenario was enticing enough, and he was off toward the river to the east. Before leaving, he checked the table outside the shop, finding that the rest of the stock had sold.

The Spiny Swamp Thistle Root was a staple of his crafting endeavors. Everyone needed health potions, and he would gladly provide for them. Perg's offer to supply exorbitant amounts of Ogre Cypress Bark meant that he could skim a little off the top for his Cleansing Scrub. While he made a lot of money up front from the adventurers, they weren't coming in a steady stream. The citizens of Broken Tusk and their sudden desire to stay clean would go a long way in bridging that gap. He had rent to pay, after all.

Theo plucked a spiny thistle out of the ground, cutting the roots away before stowing it away in his inventory. He grinned the entire way toward the river, harvesting the roots and making them vanish never lost its appeal. The best part was that when he approached the rocky shore of the flowing river, he wasn't overly encumbered, despite the massive quantity of the roots he had gathered. He sat by the edge of the river and watched its flow, several marshling fishermen passing by and giving their idle greetings.

The great river had been, according to legend, redirected by a powerful wizard ages ago. He gave the people of Broken Tusk a place to create their own fortune. The lost sons and daughters of the uncaring ogres struck out on their own, reforging their fates with their own hands. Theo appreciated the mirror that the tale held up to his situation. He owed the mysterious Harbinger everything, and it was hard not to think about what happened to that entity. He couldn't even remember how many days he had spent in the town. Things were simply moving too fast.

The sun crawled across the sky as the alchemist sat at the

river's edge, taking in its sound and smell. A comically large trout jumped in the distance, flopping in the air several times before diving back into the turgid swell. Theo couldn't estimate how much time had gone by, but it could have been two hours. He collected more roots along the way, planning to keep them in his inventory. His theory was that they wouldn't rot in there because his soup kept all of its heat while inside.

As he came around the alchemy shop, he heard banging on the door. Turning the corner, he saw Throk staring up at the second-story windows and scowling. He spun on the spot and grinned. "How's this for service? I'm all done."

"That was fast," Theo said, laughing.

"I'm a blacksmith," Throk said, waving him away. "Come to the smithy and collect your new stills."

Theo followed him up the muddy hill and into the blacksmith's workshop. Two shiny stills sat on the workshop floor, and the alchemist's jaw dropped. They were massive compared to his current still. Each one was made of two parts. The main boiler of the stills looked like a giant copper pot with a tube coming out. It sat on an iron frame with enough space to light a fire underneath. The tube fed into another device that looked like a smaller still, and Theo didn't recognize what kind of condenser it was. His original Copper Still simply had the tube curl to condense the essence, but this looked like a bucket where the tube fed and coiled around before coming out the side.

"You did go wild with the condenser," Theo said, laughing.

"The point is to cool down the vapors, right?" Throk asked. "So the condenser line feeds into the bucket there, and you pour cold water into it."

"That's genius," Theo said.

"Thank you. They're all yours—do you need a hireling to carry them home?"

"No need," Theo said, approaching the Custom Copper Stills and placing them in his inventory.

"Of course you have an inventory power," Throk said, rolling his eyes. "Well, I have your *other* order to work on, so if you'll excuse me."

Theo marched back down to his shop, inspecting the new items in his inventory as he went.

[Custom Copper Still]
[Alchemy Equipment]
Rare
Created By: Throk
A 200-unit-capacity copper still with advanced condenser attached. The advanced condenser allows for more efficient cooling of essences, decreasing the time needed to distill.
Effect:
Distillation time reduced.

Theo kicked himself for not commissioning new stills earlier. The capacity was one thing, but the reduction in crafting time was also really useful. He made his way to the second floor and into the lab, quickly stowing his old still in his inventory. He positioned the two new stills so that the condenser buckets could rest perfectly on the table, setting flasks under the output nozzle. The new equipment struck an impressive image in the lab. It was looking more like an alchemy lab and less like a hodgepodge of equipment. He left the alchemy lab, looking over his shoulder one last time at the gleam of copper before heading to the tanner.

Perg was standing outside, leaning against the wall the way she always did. She smiled and waved when she caught sight of him. "Coming for your bark?"

"Yes, I am," Theo said. "I've got my new stills, and I'm ready to cook."

Perg led him inside the tannery, the alchemist plugging his nose the whole way, and into a small storage area in the back. There was a mountain of the chalky white Ogre Cypress Bark piled in the back. He stretched his mental intuition as far as it would go, trying to figure out the correct amounts of materials to collect for the reaction. His Drogramath Distillery Specialty ability fell short, however. He knew that 0.1 units of Cleansing Essence and 0.1 units of Purifying Essence mixed with Stabilized Water would produce 5 units of Stripping Solution. His mind just couldn't do the mental math to figure out how much he needed. He scratched his chin for a while before settling on taking 100 units of the best bark he could find.

"With two stills, this shouldn't take long to cook," Theo said. "I'll have everything ready by tomorrow."

"Good. I've started buying up all the hides everyone brings me—and there's a lot," Perg said. "The dehairing yard is getting cluttered."

Theo didn't doubt that fact, given that the smell had intensified since the last time he was there. He bid farewell and placed a drop of Cleansing Scrub on his head when he was out of the building's foul range. He took a deep breath and savored that berry scent before returning to the lab.

"I'm going to make the potions for the tanner," Theo said, mentally checking in with Tresk.

"Let me know how the new stills do. My dad might be a backwater guy, but he's an amazing blacksmith. He's like... Level 20," Tresk said.

Theo's eyes went wide for a moment, but he shook his stupor away. He wasn't good at judging the age of a marshling, but Throk didn't look that old. The climb to Level 20 must have been brutal, but servicing the farmers for years on end did the trick to elevate him. He shook his head, refocusing on the task at hand.

The alchemist wouldn't be pushing his new stills to their capacity today, but the extra space made them easier to work with. He started by splitting his stack of 100 units of Ogre Cypress Bark in half. When he removed them from his inventory, a pile of bark appeared in the air and fell to the floor. Theo mashed whatever would fit in the bucket, transferring it to the still and repeating the process until everything had been processed. He repeated the act again, placing the mash in the second still. The bark was versatile and would produce both his Cleansing Essence and his Purifying Essence, which would later be used for Stripping Solution.

Theo filled the condenser buckets with water from the barrel before continuing. The iron frames that the Custom Copper Stills rested on made it easy to start a fire underneath. The expanded alchemy lab even had a metal plate for the fires to burn on, preventing him from burning down his home. Theo started the fires and let them burn as low as possible, the flames gently licking the bottom of the stills in unison. It was more work to keep the twin fires going, but he managed. The seventy-five-unit flasks he produced were comically large, almost as big as small barrels. Instead of the characteristic sputtering that his old still had, the new versions simply produced a steady drip.

While the result came out quicker, Theo could do nothing other than tend the fires during the run. When he scooted the fires out from under the still with the smashing stick, Tresk returned from her run through the forest. She applied a few drops of Cleansing Scrub to her body and joined him at the side of the table. Theo watched her admire the new stills for a while. She was initially speechless.

"My father is superb at his job," she said, nodding in appreciation.

"That's no joke," Theo said. "The condensers he came up with work really well. They cut the time down quite a lot."

"Right, well... I'm here to help now," Tresk said. "I'll show you the loot later... Just more of the same."

Theo washed and rinsed the stills, finding it much harder to dump the fouled contents out of the window, and set up for the next run. He realized it would have been impossible without Tresk's help and made a mental note for the next iteration of the equipment. Tresk got to work cutting Marsh Tubers up while he found a spare bucket to process the fifty units of Marshlight Spider Silk. They planned to run the stills' maximum of 200 units of Marsh Tubers to see how the increased capacity worked.

"This goes faster with another hand," Theo said. "I'll need an assistant when there are ten stills running up here."

Tresk laughed, finishing the last of her cutting and starting the mashing process. She had to work in stages, just like with Ogre Cypress Bark. The final mash of the tubers came dangerously near the top, and Theo filled it with water to match. The spider silk was much easier to prepare, and before long, both fires were going at a slow pace. During the run, they had to swap out the oversized flask for the still containing the tubers. The entire process happened faster than either of them could have expected, and the tables were soon cluttered with flasks.

The pair washed the stills before heading off for the evening dinner at the tavern, both of their stamina bars threatening to deplete completely. Theo wanted to put off the reactions until the morning, as it required them to mix the ingredients in the gravel yard out back. They left everything where it was before heading off for dinner.

"You'll be surprised to know it's wolf meat stew," Xam said with a smile.

Theo bought two bowls and joined Tresk in their traditional spot. They were both too tired for conversation, only sending the occasional mental message to each other. The Tara'hek communication seemed to consume less of their energy, and by the time dusk threatened over the western horizon, they had left the tavern. Their pace back to the shop was sluggish, and they fell into bed and into a deep sleep immediately.

Chapter 16
Ten Percent

Theo woke well before dawn the next morning, finding Tresk curled up on her bedroll. She was snoring loudly when he stepped out into the lab, so he carefully pulled the door closed behind him. He stood at the second-story window for a time, lording over the sprawl of the town below. He started a small fire near the stills, sighing as he realized they were out of Moss Nettles and most of the Zee was rotting. The alchemist shoved the last three usable kernels into his inventory after slicing off strips and tossing them onto the fire. He set the cast-iron kettle on fire as well.

Tresk came through the doorway, holding a clump of moss in her hand and grinning. "Thought we were out of this delicious stuff?" she said, bounding over to toss it in the boiling kettle. She took a seat with him near the fire, pressing her forehead against his and sighing.

"Big job today," Theo said, "but this should hold the tanners over for a while."

"We should get the shop in order, too," Tresk said. "We have some potions lying around, and we have to get the townspeople used to the idea of coming in to get their Cleansing Scrub."

"Well, we're going to need a hireling," Theo said with a sigh. He pulled the Zee strips off the fire and onto a plate. Tresk blew on her portion, nibbling at the edge. "How much should we pay them to work the shop?"

"It would be nice to have someone with a Shopkeeper Core or a Mercantile Core. But that's not gonna happen in Broken Tusk. A laborer in our small town would charge 2 copper a day."

"Seems like a robbery," Theo said, "since a meal at the tavern is a copper."

"That's how I know you're still green," Tresk said, tutting. "The tavern charges way too much. You can get by for a week on a single copper if you try hard enough."

Theo leaned back, lamenting the delicate economy in Broken Tusk. Everyone was dirt poor besides him. Traders were irregular, making exporting anything hard, and work didn't come easy. The advantage they had over the northern towns seemed to be the dungeons and the abundance of reagents in the nearby swamplands. They needed his plan to work for a more stable future.

"All right. We'll find someone to man the shop," Theo said. "Do you have anyone in mind? You have more insider knowledge than I do."

Tresk busied herself before answering, pulling the pot off the fire, and pouring two cups of tea. "We can post a for-hire bulletin in the tavern," she said.

"Fine with me," Theo said. "We'll give them a week's advance so we don't have to worry."

"Absolutely not. Pay them by the day until they show that they're good," Tresk said, shaking her head. "Broken Tusk laborers are fine at laboring, but none have shopkeeping experience. We might need to fire them."

Theo frowned, sipping his tea. "All right. Until we have a chance, we'll finish out the tanner's job."

The companions took their time eating breakfast, the threat of dawn still a far-off thing. They stoked the fires, preparing to make a batch of Healing Essence to stock the shelves of the shop with Lesser Healing Potions. They had an excess of Cleansing Essence that could make a good amount of Cleansing Scrub to bolster their stock. Theo prepared the mash of Spiny Swamp Thistle Root, while Tresk worked the Glassware Artifice. They devised vials that would work perfectly for the tanner, allowing them to just dump the contents onto the hides to process them.

"Watch the fires, and I'll start the reactions outside," Theo said. "I'm not confident enough to do it here."

"Understood, boss," Tresk said, smiling.

Theo knew she wanted to show him the spoils of yesterday, but he wanted to get a head start on the two different potions for the tanners. He started the first set of reactions in small, five-unit measurements until he was confident enough to scale them up. The technique that he used when first working with the essences was to make the reaction in pre-measured amounts. He would add one unit of the essence and one unit of water to a vial for his restoration potions. The problem with that technique was that it was time-consuming. It was too hard to do the math in his head for how much of each ingredient he needed for a large reaction, a problem he needed a pen and paper to solve.

The alchemist plied his trade in the gravel yard, starting his first 100-unit reaction in a sizzling eruption of smoke that rose into the sky. Theo was excited when his math was right, uncertain of how large the explosion of a reaction of this size would have been. He performed the same reaction again, leaving him with 200 units of Stripping Solution in two massive beakers. They were too heavy to carry, and he simply stored them in his inventory along with the entire barrel of Purified Water and Flaky Agate.

Drogramath Alchemy Core gained experience (10%).
Drogramath Alchemy Core gained experience (10%).

The larger reaction gave more experience, which made sense. The Stripping Solution gave him less experience last time, a fact that he chalked up to the levels he had gained in his alchemy core.

While it didn't scale one to one, he would take the hit in overall experience to get the job done faster. Theo was resetting for the next reaction when Tresk spoke into his mind.

"*I have a better idea for the distribution of the solution,*" she said.

"What's that?" Theo asked, looking up at the second-story window to see his companion pressing her face against the glass.

"*We just give them a measuring beaker to pour out the solution. That way, we don't need to make 200 vials... That's 400 motes total we'd need.*"

Theo kicked himself for not noticing the flaw in his plan before. Motes were easy enough to come by, but they didn't have 400 motes. Perg was a smart-enough person to use a measured pipette. Tresk had a way of boiling everything down to the simplest, most cost-effective solution. He grinned up at her and waved. "*You're a genius.*"

"Yeah, I am."

The alchemist realized that he would run out of water before attempting the next reaction. With his water barrel stored in his inventory, he alerted Tresk that he was running down to the river and padded through the muddy forest. He awkwardly withdrew the barrel and rolled it into the river, almost losing it to the current as it filled. The water barrel was completely submerged and drifting away when he slapped it, returning it to his inventory. He ran back to the gravel yard, constantly grinning at how powerful his new ability was.

Theo withdrew the barrel from his inventory, satisfied that it came out upright and filled with River Water. After purifying the entire thing, he repeated the process for the Alchemic Tannin, hoisting those flasks into his inventory when he was done. Four hundred units of liquid, double the size of his water barrel, now sat in his inventory. He retreated to the lab, where Tresk tended the fires.

"That was a lot faster," Theo said, nodding to himself.

"I need you to make the measuring equipment. I don't have an innate grasp on units like you do," Tresk said.

Theo nodded, moving to his Glassware Artifice to generate a small flat-bottomed vial that measured exactly one unit. He made five, counting on the fact that some would be lost or broken. The pair tended the fire for another half an hour, filling two fifty-unit flasks with Healing Essence as the dawn rose outside. By the time they were ready to leave for the tannery, the day had broken over Broken Tusk.

Perg was waiting outside of the tannery, and Theo had to wonder if she did anything other than wait for him against that wall. She had a grin on her face and cast them a knowing look. "Delivery day?"

"Indeed," Theo said. "Two hundred units of tanning potions, which should last you a while."

"It requires special instructions," Tresk said.

Perg gestured for them to follow her around the back to the dehairing area. Theo took it as a bad sign that he was getting used to the stench, but looked forward to a time when the process wouldn't smell at all. The half-ogre tossed a rotting hide on the ground and folded her arms, waiting for instructions.

"Do you have a lot of Strength?" Theo asked.

"I'm almost at 20," Perg said, flashing a grin.

"Good, hold out your hands," Theo said, watching as she obeyed.

The alchemist withdrew the first flask from his inventory, and Perg caught it deftly with one hand. They repeated the process for the next three flasks, setting them gingerly to the side.

"You should be able to tell the difference between the solutions by inspecting them," Theo said.

Perg confirmed that she could, nodding and smiling.

Theo withdrew the glass stopper from the flask of Stripping Solution and produced his measuring vial from his inventory. He carefully withdrew some solution until it reached the rim of the vial. "One unit per hide," he said, dumping the contents onto the rotting hide. The potion did its magic instantly, deftly working through the fat and hair. Within a minute, it was done sputtering, sending plumes of vapor into the air. Perg shook her head in amazement.

"That hide was only there for a day—this stuff really does work," Perg said.

"You doubted us?" Tresk asked.

"Same thing for the next solution," Theo said, heading off any confrontation. He was certain it was just friendly banter, but he didn't want to risk it.

The alchemist produced another vial from his inventory. "Don't mix the vials up. Wash them out with Purified Water if you need to use the same vial. I don't know what kind of reaction will happen if you mix the two, but it can't be good." He measured out a unit of the Alchemic Tannin and dumped it on the stripped hide. Something about the shoe polish smell seemed nostalgic to Theo, but he snapped out of it in time to watch the raw wolf's hide turn into a supple sheet of leather.

A small crowd of the tannery's workers gathered to watch the alchemy work its magic. They marveled at how quickly the potions worked, chattering excitedly among themselves.

"You've really outdone yourself, Alchemist," Perg said. "Both of you. We'll go through our entire stock of hides by the end of the day with this."

"Thanks, Perg," Tresk said, beaming.

"Our agreement still stands—ten percent of the profits," Perg said. "I can't wait to see the trader's face when I present him with hundreds of hides instead of the usual ten or fifteen."

"Hopefully, it puts you on the map," Theo said.

The group exchanged pleasantries, watching as the workers came over to inspect the leather. They wouldn't stop talking about how soft the leather was, running their rough hands over the surface constantly. Theo and Tresk excused themselves after a while, finding their way back up the road and to the alchemy shop. To their surprise, Luras was waiting outside.

"Hey," he said, managing a weak wave, "got any stamina potions?"

Luras looked haggard, as though he hadn't stopped to rest on his way back from Rivers and Daub. Tresk darted inside to grab a potion while the half-ogre swayed on the spot.

"Rough journey?" Theo asked.

"It always is," Luras said with a heavy sigh. He pulled a stack of silver coins from a satchel, handing them over. "Your pay for the Cleansing Scrub. Anyway, I'm here to fetch you, Tresk, and Perg. Miana wants to meet with the biggest business owners in town."

"What? Why?" Theo asked, storing the coins in his inventory.

"Well, since we're technically somewhere between a mercantile town and a farming town, the businesses that make the most money have a say in important matters," Luras said. Every word seemed to strain him further, but he went on. "Your Perpetual Ledger reports back to the mayor, so she knows you've been making some serious money."

"Good to know," Theo said.

Tresk returned with a small vial of the yellow potion, and Luras consumed it immediately. He perked up, his hooded gaze vanishing as his back straightened out. The half-ogre rolled his shoulders a few times before pointing up the road. "I'll meet you at Miana's house. Gotta go grab Perg."

Theo and Tresk departed up the road, casting each other confused looks.

"I didn't know we had a say in the town," Theo said, not willing to voice his words out loud.

"I knew we had some sway, but I didn't expect us to get a seat at the table so soon. My father has a seat as well, seeing as his smithy makes good money," Tresk said.

They arrived at Miana's house quickly, finding their way inside. The brusque woman was waiting at the threshold, and simply gestured for them to find their way to the back room. They sat down in the mayor's office, finding themselves in familiar company. Throk, Banurub, and Xam were already seated in a row of ornate wooden chairs. On the far side of the room sat a lacquered wooden desk with a chair behind it, as well as bookcases lining the wall.

"Well, you sure found a seat quickly," Throk said. "The rest of us have been building these businesses for decades."

"Alchemy is a powerful art, you old toad," Banurub said, snorting a laugh.

"What do you think Miana wants to talk about?" Xam asked, fidgeting nervously.

"The wolves," Tresk said, shrugging. "Monsters in the swamp have gotten out of control."

The group talked for a few minutes before Luras arrived to deposit Perg. She took her seat while Luras lingered around the door, his arms folded but standing at attention. Miana entered some time after that, a permanent scowl on her face.

"The life's blood of Broken Tusk," she said, gesturing to those gathered, "or something like that. I got some big news from those adventurers that just departed. What was his name?"

"Jarson," Tresk said, nodding.

"Right, Jarson... Well, our Swamp Dungeon has hit a threshold. During their delve, it leveled up to 25," Miana said.

The murmur that spread across the group told Theo that Level 25 meant something. But it was logical to assume that like his personal level, a dungeon's level increasing meant it would be stronger. "So—outworlder here—someone is going to have to explain how dungeons work to me."

Luras spoke from the back of the room. "Dungeons spawn monsters. They have floors to them, going underground. A dungeon's heart is its core, but most are indestructible. They level up like people or buildings, gaining power over time. Higher-level dungeons have higher-level monsters and loot. We have three dungeons around us. Swamp, River, and Hills."

Theo appreciated the rapid-fire way Luras delivered the information.

"Right," Miana said, idly adjusting the paperwork on her desk.

"This new level signals a new opportunity for Broken Tusk. We're going to see more monsters in the surrounding area, and more powerful ones, but also more adventurers."

"Should we have a mind for defense?" Throk asked.

"We should, but the flow of monster cores has been slow," Miana said.

"Well, we had a plan to pump the town with cores," Tresk said, grinning. "We finished the tannery job, so we're going to focus our efforts on that."

Miana sneered for a second, finding her composure in a heartbeat and shifting her expression to placidity. "The Level 5 upgrade should give us some walls. The core they used to establish the town wasn't very strong, which is why it's such a pile of mud."

"What we need is more adventurers living in the town," Theo said, tapping his chin. "We need to attract a population that can survive here and patrol the swamps. I mean, the swamps aren't even safe to begin with, let alone with a Level 25 dungeon."

All eyes turned to him, and he felt his heart skip a beat.

"He's right," Luras said, breaking the awkward silence. "We have a few hunters in town but only two that you could call adventurers. Walls would help, but they'd only delay an attack."

"Hey, I'm behind any plan that gets me more hides," Perg said, chuckling.

Miana steepled her fingers, casting her stony gaze over the group. "Banu, Throk, do you have an opinion?"

"Nope," Banurub said.

"I don't," Throk said, shrugging.

Miana stayed silent for some time, tapping her foot. "Qavell gave Broken Tusk a supplement to spend how I see fit. I can see that the problem can't be solved with a simple approach, so I have a solution. Every monster within the borders of the town will have a 2-copper bounty on their heads. All adventurers that claim residence here will get a 5-copper-a-week stipend."

Tresk was the most excited out of the bunch, hopping in her chair excitedly.

"That'll draw attention from the north, all right," Luras said, nodding in agreement. "Are you going to issue a quest?"

"Yes, anyone who wants to take the bounty quest can find it at the tavern later today," Miana said. "I'll be paying out the bounties weekly."

"Just so everyone knows, I'm buying all the hides," Perg said.

Miana scoffed, shaking her head. "This meeting is over. We've come to a solution. Kill the monsters, cram cores into the town. That is all."

The group slowly filtered out of the mayor's house, finding their way onto the muddy square and talking in excited tones. Theo wasn't sure how he missed it on his way in, but a massive water tower had been built since his last visit to the blacksmith. Throk dug his bony elbow into his side, laughing at how he gawked.

"Ten thousand units of water storage," Throk said. "How's that for a water tower?"

"You really don't mess around, do you?" Theo said, still staring up at the structure. "Do you have any barrels I could borrow?"

Throk gestured toward his workshop, where ten barrels sat lined up neatly. "I really am the best, aren't I?"

Chapter 17
The Bell

"You got your inventory power," Luras said, watching as Theo shoved ten barrels into his inventory.

Tresk approached, unhooking the dimensional bag from her belt and holding it out for the half-ogre to see. "I got a bag too!"

"Luras, shouldn't you get some sleep?" Theo said, knitting his brow.

While Theo's tasks were many, he had had a good night's sleep and a square meal. He felt Luras's intention to help him with the barrels but wanted to avoid the conversation that would inevitably follow. Whatever adventures the man had in Rivers and Daub could wait another day.

"I should," Luras said.

Despite the effects of the Lesser Stamina Potion, he looked tired beyond reason. He turned on the spot and shambled up the hill, dragging his feet through the mud as he went. Theo felt bad for a moment, but the big guy just needed some rest.

"Stamina potions don't remove the need to sleep," Tresk said, shaking her head knowingly. "It just gives you a jolt that doesn't last long. Your stamina bar could be full, but you'll still be dead tired."

Theo made his way around the water tower and behind the

blacksmith's shop, toward the river in the east. He turned on the spot, beckoning for his companion to follow. Filling the barrels at the river would be easier if someone with more than 7 Strength came along to help.

"Ten barrels at 200 units each—we'll need to make five trips to fill the tower," Theo said.

"You don't have to fill it all the way," Tresk said. "This is work for a hireling anyway."

Theo stopped and sighed, turning back again to look at the water tower. The tank of the tower was a perfect cylinder of wrapped copper perched atop a wooden frame. It was two half-ogres high and caught the rising sun perfectly. He could easily hire someone to collect the water and bring it to the lab to be purified, but he wanted to do it himself.

"I want to do the first filling myself," Theo said. "This was the first idea I had to make Broken Tusk better, and I want to see it through."

Tresk hopped over to him, grabbing his arm and pulling him toward the river. "Then let's get this done."

The pair arrived at the river, spotting the same marshling fishermen Theo had seen before. They waved and smiled at Tresk, heading southward toward the ocean. Filling the barrels was significantly easier when Tresk held them steady in the water. Despite her slight build, she kept them in place with ease. Compared to his attempt at filling his personal water barrel, this went well. They had all ten barrels filled in a matter of minutes, quickly returning to the lab to pick up their leftover Purifying Essence.

Theo had the Purified Water reaction memorized and withdrew the barrels outside of the smithy. In a matter of moments, he turned 2,000 units of River Water, with its deadly pathogens, into Purified Water. Tresk volunteered to dump them into the top of the water tower, stowing the barrels into her bag and ascending a rickety ladder. Her superior Dexterity and Strength meant that she had no trouble handling the heavy barrels and was back down with the alchemist in minutes.

Theo turned the spigot at the bottom, causing a torrent of water to rush out. He put his face under the tap and let it wash over him, guzzling the water and turning to cast a beaming smile at his companion. She laughed and shoved her head under the tap to drink the fresh water. A crowd gathered as they frolicked in the pure water, absorbed in their celebration of accomplishment. Oruk, the half-ogre laborer, was the first to voice his confusion.

"What's this?" he said, cocking his head.

"Fresh water," Theo said, turning the spigot off and addressing the crowd. Only after the flow had ceased did he realize that most of the town was gawking at him.

"Free Purified Water," Tresk said, bouncing up and down. "For everyone to drink. No more boiling your drinking water."

A ripple of excitement spread across the crowd. Townsfolk rushed off to their homes, shouting about retrieving buckets to collect the precious water. Theo had easy access to as much drinkable water as he needed, aided by his powerful alchemy. The marshlings didn't have a need for the pure water, but every half-ogre in town needed to boil their water before consuming it. Tresk and Theo grinned at each other, heading back toward the river for another run.

While they had originally had no intention of filling the water tower to capacity, they did exactly that. Each time they returned from the river, different people gathered to fill their buckets. Only on the fifth run did the crowd disperse, the excited murmurs still flowing through the town like the surge of the river. Tresk returned the barrels to her father, giving him her thanks while Theo ascended the ladder. His Drogramath Distillery Specialty skill allowed him to judge that only a barrel's worth of water had been taken in the initial surge. The massive capacity of the water tower would last a long time.

"How many cores did you find on your adventure?" Theo asked, climbing down from the ladder.

"Fifteen cores and a bunch of other junk," Tresk said. "I was thinking of picking up the quest once Miana posts it... Could've made 30 copper yesterday."

"Not to mention the money you'd make selling the hides to Perg," Theo said.

"I'm still not good at skinning the beasts," Tresk said.

Tresk cast her gaze over the water tower, admiring her father's work. Theo fell into his thoughts, going through the things he still needed to do. Food was an issue again, and he didn't have a suitable solution. The Zee was already overstaying its welcome as a part of his diet, and he didn't have an alternative. As he weighed his options, his inventory came to mind. The assumption was that food didn't rot when it stayed there, and until he found a proper storage solution for his shop, it would do.

"Well, we're almost out of Zee... I think I'll sort our food situation out before moving on to other projects."

"If you don't mind, I'd like to spend the day adventuring," Tresk said, grinning.

"That's perfect. Even if you can't skin the wolves, bring some meat back. We can try our hand at wolf meat stew," Theo said.

"That works for me," Tresk said, beckoning for him to bend to her level. She pressed her forehead against his before departing toward the swamp.

Theo went around the water tower, finding his way to the blacksmith. Throk hammered away at a bar of red-hot iron. The alchemist had to wave his hands to get the man's attention. "Do you sell pots?"

"Copper pots, sure," Throk said. "You know you can go inside the store—this is just the workshop."

"I didn't know that," he said, his violet face flushing a deeper shade of purple.

Throk simply smiled and gestured to the front of the building. A bell jingled as he entered, and he made a mental note to get his hands on one. A small marshling stood at the counter, tapping his foot impatiently. He was the spitting image of his father, and Theo pinned him for Throk's son.

"Hello, I need a pot," Theo said awkwardly.

"Copper pot? How big?"

"Somewhere between 20 and 50 units," Theo said.

The marshling disappeared for a moment, returning with a cauldron slightly larger than his head. "Five copper."

"Do you sell those bells?" Theo asked, pointing back toward the door.

The marshling disappeared behind the counter again, returning quickly and slapping the jangling bell on the counter. It had the mounting bracket with it. "Eight copper total."

"And what about a stand for the pot?"

"Needy, aren't you?" the marshling said, disappearing and reappearing with a stand. It was an iron tripod with a ring of metal in the center to hold the pot in place. "Ten copper. Anything else?"

"That's all," Theo said, retrieving 10 copper from his inventory and presenting the coins to the shopkeeper.

"Pleasure doing business with you," he said, affecting a shallow bow.

Theo stored the items in his inventory, gaining a judging look from the marshling. He departed before the man could ask him about the power and made his way south down the muddy road. The Newt and Demon was empty, as expected, and he placed the copper pot along with the stand upstairs, leaving the bell on the ground level until he could figure out how to mount it. Even on Earth, he was bad with tools, could never drive a nail straight. The food would have to wait until later, as the lab had nothing edible. Instead, he focused on organizing the shop downstairs.

The alchemist started by working the Glassware Artifice to create fifty of the vials meant for Cleansing Scrub. Using his new technique, he kicked off a fifty-unit reaction in a large flask before distributing it into the individual vials. He laughed at himself for ever doing individual reactions the way he had before and had the entire batch sorted in less than a half-hour. Theo brought the entire stock of his potions into his inventory and made his way downstairs to place his wares. He propped the door open as he grouped them on the shelves. The stock was pitiful, with only four Lesser Vigor Potions, thirteen Lesser Healing Potions, and fifty units of Cleansing Scrub.

"We're going to need an 'open' sign for the store," Theo said.

Tresk took a moment to respond. Her voice came with ragged gasps, and his heart stopped for a moment. *"Ten wolves at once! If they were higher than Level 5, I'd be in trouble... Good idea with the sign, though."*

"Are you all right?"

"I still have health potions, so yeah!" Tresk said.

Theo let the matter go. He had loaded her up with enough potions to survive out there and had to trust that she was a good adventurer. He couldn't see himself taking on a single wolf, let alone a pack of ten. It seemed like an impossible feat, but his cores were focused on crafting and gathering. The alchemist jumped when a voice came from the doorway.

"Got any work, boss?" Oruk said, grinning from the threshold.

"Actually, I do," Theo said, laughing. "Can you mount this bell?"

Oruk entered the shop, striding over to the counter and inspecting the bell. He swiveled his head to look at the door frame and nodded. "Yeah, no problem. Can't swing a hammer?"

Theo held up his thin arms before shrugging. "I'm more likely to hit my fingers than drive a nail, friend."

"Sure thing, boss. Let me go grab a hammer and nails," Oruk said.

Theo withdrew a copper coin from his inventory and flicked it toward the half-ogre. He caught it from the air and grinned, darting out the door. Mounting the bell might have been too much of a job for him, but he was fairly certain he could write a sign that said "Open" and "Closed" on either side. Lacking paint, he trudged down the road toward the tannery. The stench hadn't subsided yet, but it would take them days to process all the hides.

"Perg?" Theo called. She wasn't at her normal perch.

"She's in the warehouse," a tannery worker said, peeking his head out from around the building.

Theo plugged his nose and walked around the building to find the woman using his potions on a pile of hides. She turned and grinned at him. "Hey, what's going on?"

"Do you have any paint? I need to make a sign for my shop," Theo said.

"Begrut!" Perg shouted.

A rotund half-ogre came around the corner.

"Help the alchemist out. He needs some paint," Perg said, going back to her work.

"Follow me, sir," Begrut said, trundling out of the warehouse.

Theo followed him to a small storage shed, where the man produced a bucket containing a tar-like substance and a brush.

"Thank you," Theo said.

The alchemist retreated to his shop with the paint and found a small bit of wood on the outside of his shop. When he wrote "Open" on one side, he found the action strange. He had never written in his newly adopted language and didn't even know what the people of the land called it. The blocks of letters came out looking strange, but the sign would have to do. He wrote "Closed" on the other side, leaving it to dry as he returned the paint. He didn't find Begrut there, so he just left the paint where the half-ogre had retrieved it from.

Theo returned to the lab, finding Oruk banging on the inside frame of the door. He slid past the laborer and went upstairs to retrieve some string. Among the many piles of junk that littered the lab, he found a length that would do. By the time he made it back downstairs, Oruk was done with the job. He opened and closed the door a few times, producing a pleasant jingling noise.

"Could you hang a sign for me?" Theo asked.

"Sure, just don't pay me," Oruk said. "You always overpay people."

Theo's face flushed again, and the half-ogre followed him to the drying sign. He grunted something and retrieved a hand drill from a wooden toolbox, drilling two holes in either side of the plank of wood. Oruk then placed a nail in the center of the door, hanging the sign and turning to grin at the alchemist.

"See? Easy," Oruk said. "Looks like a kid wrote it, though."

"There's a disconnect between speaking this language and writing it," Theo said.

"I always forget you're an outworlder," Oruk said, scratching his chin. "You fit in far too well here at Broken Tusk—I even forget you're a Dronon."

"Do people in the wider world fear the Dronon?"

"I wouldn't know," Oruk said, "I've lived my whole life here. Seen everything from elves to goblins pass through, and the only thing I learned from them was that a jerk is a jerk. No matter the race."

"Good to know," Theo said. "I may have more work for you later. That's all for today."

"Thanks, boss." Oruk grunted, waddling up the muddy road.

Theo retreated into his shop, smiling as the bell jingled. He mentally updated Tresk on the shop's new features, which she seemed excited for. The alchemist went upstairs, working on a list of the potions he wanted to stock up on, when the faint tinkle of the bell issued from downstairs. He perked up, descending with the expectation of seeing Perg or Luras. A half-ogre woman he vaguely recognized stood behind the counter, her eyes snapping to him as he descended the stairs. She had a chipped sword fastened to her belt and a tattered leather armor covering her body.

"Oh! I've seen you at the farm," Theo said, suddenly realizing where he had seen her.

"Yes. I need some potions, Alchemist," the woman said.

He shrugged, coming to stand before the counter. "Are you planning to go out adventuring?"

"Yes. The bounty quest on the wolves is too good," she said.

"I'm guessing, on a farmer's wage, you have little coin," Theo said, smiling.

The woman rummaged through her bag, producing ten copper

coins and placing them on the table as though they were a fortune. Theo's heart ached at the destitute nature of the farmers. A two-copper bounty on wolves was an amazing opportunity for them. They would earn that with a day of hard labor out in the fields if they were lucky. Oruk's words of the alchemist being too generous rang through his mind, but he couldn't help himself.

Theo found the shelf with the Lesser Healing Potions and plucked five of them before grabbing a single Lesser Stamina Potion. He laid them out on the counter and smiled. "I won't lie to you, adventurer. I'd expect to charge 5 copper per potion, minimum."

"I'm not looking for charity," she growled.

"And I'm not looking to give it. Consider this an 'adventurer starter pack', until you can bring in some bounties," Theo said. "There's no shortage of wolves. You'll stand to make a farmer's yearly wage in a week if you can kill the wolves."

She hesitated for a moment before taking the potions, stuffing them in her bag. Her gaze locked onto Theo's eyes, her cold, piercing look sending a shiver up his spine. "The next time I come in here, I'm paying full price."

The bell jingled merrily behind her, and the alchemist let out a heavy sigh. The half-ogres hated getting things for free. They seemed to have honor that was sorely lacking back on Earth. He knew that she would return to the shop and buy the potions at full price, and that she would be able to afford it them she spent her days in the swamp, slaying wolves. Theo just couldn't stand the thought of hearing about a citizen of Broken Tusk dead in the swamps because they went unprepared. He added the 10 copper to his inventory before the thoughts got out of control, returning to the second floor.

"Something unexpected happened," Theo said to Tresk. He underlined the entry on his parchment for Lesser Healing Potions and turned to assess their stock of Spiny Swamp Thistle Root.

"What's that?"

"A farmer came in, fancying herself an adventurer. I gave her

potions for a steal—I don't think she can handle herself out there," Theo said.

"They have one thing on their side. Farmers put their points into Vigor and Strength," Tresk said. *"The wolves are usually Level 5, and the farmers aren't dumb."*

Theo thought for a moment before he responded. Assuming that every backwater farmer was an idiot was his fault. The allure of more coin was strong, but the half-ogres were strong and smart. They lived in Broken Tusk their entire lives and would be familiar with the local monsters. Armed with five Lesser Healing Potions, she could get out of most scrapes.

"You're right. I'm going to craft more healing potions. I have a feeling we're going to have a surge of would-be adventurers soon," Theo said.

Chapter 18
Wolf Bones

The lab's stock of Spiny Swamp Thistle Root was low. Theo could make a twenty-unit batch but had a mind to run a much larger amount. He left the shop, flipping the sign to "Closed" and locking the door before delving into the sparse forest in the direction of the river. Something interesting happened in that loose knot of trees before the stream. The roots that he had harvested days ago had regenerated, already grown to their adult form. The alchemist wouldn't have paid any attention to this, simply gathering the herbs and calling it a day, but he had concerns about how much supply he could get.

While Theo dug in the mud and harvested the precious roots and Earth Motes, Tresk adventured away in the swamp. The alchemist liked the swamp least of all the four areas to gather herbs in. It was full of snapping jaws and lurking turtles, something he wanted nothing to do with. The area to the east was the safest and thick with healing roots. It was past midday, and he had enough roots and motes to make a large batch of Lesser Healing Potions. His herbalism core also reached Level 6 as he harvested the last few reagents.

Drogramath Herbalist Core gained experience (2%).
Drogramath Herbalist Core reached Level 6!
Theo Spencer gained experience (2%).

Theo had already expected that his core wouldn't get anything new at Level 6, banking on Level 10 giving him something interesting. When he returned to the shop, a short marshling man was standing outside. The alchemist didn't recognize him from the town, but the mud encrusting his bare feet gave him away as a local.

"Here for some potions?" Theo asked.

"Aye, I am," the marshling said.

Theo unlocked the door, getting close enough to the man to see a pair of old daggers stuffed in his belt. He wore light clothes that wouldn't do as armor. He gestured for the man to wait at the counter and pulled five Lesser Healing Potions off the shelf. Their stock of Lesser Stamina Potions had run dry, and there was no time to make more. The marshling's eyes glittered as Theo set the potions on the counter.

"Looking to become an adventurer?" Theo asked.

"Naturally," the man said, nodding his head. "I've seen you by the river—I'm a fisher by trade."

Theo smiled. He wasn't sure how useful fishing skills would be against the wolves. "I suppose we're running a special for new adventurers. Five Lesser Healing Potions for 10 copper—Broken Tusk residents only."

"Only 10 copper?" the man asked. "I've seen traders running through town asking for sixty. Are they poisoned?"

Theo let out a heavy sigh, shaking his head. "No, they're not poisoned. I don't want to see the citizens of Broken Tusk die in the swamp. You get a discount on your first visit, then you pay full price."

"Full price as in 60 copper?"

"Five each." Theo shrugged.

The man tilted his head, nodding in agreement, fishing 10 copper out of his pocket and placing it on the counter. "You're doing a fine service for the town."

Theo put the coins in his inventory, waving as the brusk marshling left the shop. He didn't know if he would ever get over how much he enjoyed the jingling of the bell. He flipped the sign to "Open" before retreating upstairs.

The alchemist withdrew the roots from his inventory in batches of twenty, appreciating that the system allowed him to split the stack. They fell to the ground with a dull thud, and he scooped them up. The most important thing about the Spiny Swamp Thistle Root was to remove the mud and trim it up for mashing. While his Dexterity attribute was low, he could quickly trim the roots and smash them up in a few minutes. The huge pestle slammed against the bottom of the barrel, turning the first batch into pulp. The massive quantity of roots he had collected took ten such cycles of cutting, smashing, and dumping into the Custom Copper Still.

Right as Theo lit the fire, after filling the still with Purified Water, the gentle tinkling of the bell issued from downstairs. He placed a flask under the condenser before rushing downstairs to find another person he vaguely recognized waiting. It was another half-ogre, a man this time, with his arms crossed. He was far better armed than his previous customers, with a well-maintained sword at his hip and freshly treated leather armor. The mud gathered up to the inseam of his leather pants gave him away as a resident of Broken Tusk.

"Greetings, Alchemist," he said.

"How are you? Looking to get into adventuring?" Theo said, smiling.

"I've dabbled in the past. Fancied myself a military man years ago. Got rejected from the Qavelli Irregulars and turned to farming. I have the Swordsmanship Core and most of my points have been put into Strength," the man said, delivering the information as a matter of fact. "My name is Aarok Thane, by the way."

Newt and Demon

Theo looked the man over for a moment before responding. While the other would-be adventurers had the smell of failure on them, Aarok was well put together. He was a broad man, even by half-ogre standards, and carried himself with a poise uncommon in Broken Tusk. He had pale red skin, an oiled, slicked back head of hair, and a sleepy gaze that betrayed his intelligence.

"Very nice to meet you, Aarok," Theo said. "I'll be honest, you're the first new adventurer to enter my shop that I can say looks like an adventurer."

Aarok looked at the sword on his hip, shrugging. "I've kept up with my swordplay, maintained my armor... Nothing more."

"It's impressive," Theo said. "Well, I'm running a special for new adventurers. Five healing potions for ten copper coins."

"That's a steal."

"So I've been told." Theo shrugged. "The deal is only good for the first time, then it's 5 copper each."

"You're trying to get the new adventurers started. That's incredibly honorable for a Dronon," Aarok said.

"I'm an outworlder," Theo said, chuckling. "I don't know how Dronon are meant to behave."

Aarok fished ten copper coins out of his pocket, placing them on the counter. Theo retrieved five Lesser Healing Potions from the shelf and returned to the half-ogre. He also plucked one of the four remaining Potions of Vigor from his inventory and set it on the counter, adding the coins to his inventory.

"That should get you started," Theo said, gesturing to the six potions.

Aarok gathered the potions and put them in his bag. He locked his gaze on the alchemist again and nodded. "I'll be back to pay the full price. Count on it."

Theo followed him out the door, switching the sign to "Closed" before locking up and darting upstairs. The fire was dying by the time he got back, a steady trickle of essence dripping into the flask. He stoked the fire, adding several twigs and coaxing it back to life. The alchemist propped up the two back windows before swapping out the massive flask for a fresh one. Once the fires died a few more times, the entire batch was done. He left the task of cleaning the massive stills until Tresk could help him move them around.

With the storage drawers empty of Copper Shavings, Theo left the shop. Fortunately, no one gathered outside, awaiting more potions. He trudged up the muddy hill to the blacksmith's shop. Throk brought his hammer down on something glowing red-hot before meeting the alchemist's gaze.

"You'd better not be here to give me another job," Throk growled. "Those adventurers are looking for weapons, and it's been years since I've made a sword."

"Just looking for Copper Shavings," Theo said.

"Well, I've got a heap of those out back from your job," Throk said, grunting. "Help yourself."

Theo simply nodded, finding his way around the building. There was a massive pile of the shavings lying on the bare ground, mounded up near rusting iron castoffs. He placed his hand on the pile and sucked it into his inventory. It occupied a box in the leather bag–themed screen that crowded his vision, a number well over 10,000 sitting under the single tile. He made his way back to the lab, shaking his head. If the shavings didn't stack to such an absurd number—he would have needed to take multiple trips to the blacksmith, not that he could imagine using so much of the material.

"I just saved a townsperson," Tresk said, her voice filling his ears as he marched back to the shop.

"What happened?" Theo asked, stopping in his tracks. *"You all right?"*

"Some marshling tried to take on a pack of wolves. He got too greedy and needed me to bail him out," Tresk said. *"This is going to be dangerous for them."*

"That's what I was worried about. The bounty seems nice in concept, but these people are going to throw themselves into the swamp and die," Theo said.

The alchemist decided to keep the shavings in his inventory for now. Even if the lab was already cluttered, he didn't want to add to the piles of junk lying around everywhere. He fell into a rhythm at the Glassware Artifice, settling on using half of his Healing Essence to create Lesser Healing Potions. They had a lot of the Water Motes, but burning through them all seemed like a waste. He set 100 flat-bottomed vials across several tables and made a flask to use for the reaction. It was easier to withdraw an exact amount of Copper Shavings from his inventory. He could mentally select the exact number—200 in this case—and drop it in a pile at the bottom of the flask. He then added 100 units of Purified Water and 100 units of Healing Essence, the massive flask looking more like a glass barrel than anything else.

Theo was happy that he had propped the windows open earlier. The smoke that rose from the flask might have smelled nice, but it wafted in a thick red cloud that hung in the air. Several minutes of coughing and fanning the smoke out of the windows later, he started distributing the Lesser Healing Potion mixture. It still sat at "great" quality, but it was good enough for the adventurers in Broken Tusk. He would need to improve his process even more if he wanted the potion to be of even better quality. By the end of the bottling process, sweat gathered on his brow and he gained another level in both his alchemy core and his personal level.

Drogramath Alchemy Core gained experience (5%).
Drogramath Alchemy Core reached Level 6!
Theo Spencer gained experience (2%).
Theo Spencer reached Level 6!
Theo Spencer received one free point!

The alchemist inspected his personal sheet before applying his free point.

Belgar (Theo Spencer)
Drogramath Dronon

Level 6 Alchemist
Core Slots: 2
Attributes:
Health: 42
Mana: 10
Stamina: 53
Strength: 7 (+2)
Dexterity: 5
Vigor: 10 (+3)
Intelligence: 10 (+2)
Wisdom: 21 (+5)
Points: 1

Theo considered putting a point somewhere other than Wisdom, but it was a hard sell. The more Wisdom he had, the more ingrained his innate sense for how things worked would be. His memory sharpened with every point in the attribute, already pushing him beyond anything possible back on Earth. The only other attribute he could consider putting points into was Intelligence, mostly because his mental math was pitiful. Being an excellent judge of himself, or perhaps because of his Wisdom attribute, he estimated that he was currently at the intelligence level of a straight-C student in college. He could remember almost everything that he read, but his ability to extrapolate information was lacking. He sucked it up and dumped the point into Intelligence, feeling a gentle tingle run through his brain.

The alchemist retreated downstairs, filling the shelves with his potions in time for Tresk to return. She stomped in the door, a broad grin painting her face.

"You stink," Theo said.

With a flourish, Tresk withdrew her Cleansing Scrub, placing several drops of the liquid on herself before moving further into the shop. She wordlessly inspected the ledger and shot Theo a surprised expression. "You made 30 copper today."

"From three hapless adventures," Theo said. "How deep into the marsh was that marshling you saved?"

"You sold him potions, didn't you?" Tresk said, laughing.

"I did. Chipped daggers. No armor. Said he was a fisherman."

"He was about ten paces into the swamp," Tresk said. "Spotted a pack of wolves and went in without thinking."

Theo shook his head, groaning. "Well, how much did you get paid in bounties?"

"30 copper. But I brought back more wolf game this time, including three usable hides," Tresk said.

"Hopefully you have meat and bones," Theo said. "I bought some cookware from your father."

"Oh, yeah, I do. Bones and meat," Tresk said proudly.

The pair locked the door and went upstairs. Theo stoked the dying embers from the fire back to life, positioning the pot stand, which Throk had sold him, over the flames. Tresk produced several bones from her inventory, dropping them in the pot before filling it with water. They chatted idly as the pot came to a boil, both lamenting the lack of vegetables in their stew. Before long, the bone broth was done, and they added strips of fatty wolf meat.

"Monster wolf stew," Theo said, grimacing. "Can't be worse than the stuff that Xam makes."

Tresk snorted a laugh, stirring the soup with a long wooden spoon. A knock came from the front door, and Theo rose to answer it. Luras was standing there, arms folded with a grimace on his face.

"You weren't at the tavern," he said.

Theo stuck his head out the door, finding the sun to be in its pre-dusk position. "It's still early."

Luras shuffled awkwardly on the spot, casting his gaze to the ground. "I smelled your soup from the street."

"Ah, an honest confession," Theo said, beaming. "You're welcome to try it, if you don't mind sitting on the floor of my lab."

Luras wordlessly pushed past him, ascending the stairs, with

Theo close behind. Tresk gave him her greetings, gesturing for him to take a place by the fire.

"How was Rivers and Daub?" Tresk asked.

Luras sat there for a moment, and Theo could see the gears turning in his head. It was the thing the half-ogre did when he wasn't willing to share all the details. "The dungeon gaining a few levels is going to be the least of our concerns soon."

"That sounds grim," Tresk said, scooping out bowlfuls of the stew to pass out. She handed a bowl to Theo and Luras. They both set it down to cool.

"Qavell is going to war, if the rumors are true. Veosta to the west are rattling their swords."

"How does war affect us all the way to the south?" Theo asked.

The alchemist picked up a wooden spoon and prodded the stew. The meat looked tender enough, having boiled for a fair amount of time, and the scent wasn't bad. It smelled like bone broth and little else, which made sense. He took a spoonful of the liquid and sipped it. Despite his negative experiences with bone broth in the past, this iteration was delicious. It had a deep, savory flavor that lingered on the tongue. The fat from the wolf meat danced on top of the yellowed soup, adding to the flavor.

"Nothing direct, of course," Luras said. "They'll fight their war, and we won't feel it. But war breeds deserters, and those result in bandits."

Tresk scowled. "We haven't had a bandit problem down here since my father was a child."

"And Broken Tusk was still young enough to go unnoticed," Luras said. "With the recent waves we've been making, we'll become a target. For people looking to lie low or for an easy mark."

Theo took a bite of wolf meat, looking to avoid the topic. It was unreasonably tender and split into stringy sections under just the force of his bite. The flavor was mundane, only soaking up the bone broth and adding nothing more to the dish. The flavor of the soup was leagues ahead of the swill that Xam served and cost them nothing to make.

"We'll be overtaken by a rabble," Tresk said. She told the story of the adventurer she saved and how disorganized he was.

"Aarok seemed put together," Theo said, looking up from his soup.

"I know Aarok," Luras said. "We shared the dream of soldiery before... Well, that's water under the bridge."

Theo should have known that Aarok didn't give him the full story but wouldn't pry. Whatever secrets Luras wanted to keep were his to hold onto. Reopening old wounds was something that he avoided at all times, preferring to keep things smooth among his friends.

"Militia!" Tresk shouted, unprompted. "We should make our own little army."

"That's not a horrible idea," Luras said, shrugging.

"How many worthwhile adventurers do we have in town? Three? Two of them are in this room," Theo said, sighing. "Not much of a militia."

"They're useless now, but give them time," Luras said. "You can't judge someone by the first step they take on a journey."

"I'll leave that judgment to you guys," Theo said. "If you can whip the other people into shape, that's a reasonable approach."

"I smell the invisible 'but' in your statement," Tresk said.

"But we should level the town up," Theo said. "Right? We should upgrade it until we have walls. I'd feel safer with walls."

"Walls are definitely a great idea," Luras said. "An unprotected town like this is easy to attack, and the core they used to create the town should get a stone wall upgrade at Level 5."

"I'd really like roads," Theo grumbled.

"I have thirty cores I was going to use on the shop," Tresk said. "We won't get another upgrade until Level 10, so we may as well use them on the town."

"I've got a large stock of cores at my house," Luras said.

"I didn't know you had a house," Theo said earnestly, returning his attention to the soup.

"Did you think he lived in the woods?" Tresk asked, snorting a laugh.

"Yes."

The rest of the group turned their attention to the soup, voicing their surprise at how good it was. They whittled away the late afternoon hours with strategies and plans for training the adventurers. Theo was only interested in obtaining more cores and conducting more alchemical experiments. He lit the candles when the day grew into dusk, the conversation shifting rapidly between topics. The group settled on using the training to collect cores, allowing the training adventurers to collect the bounty while they kept the game.

"The soup was unreasonably good," Luras said, rising from the ground, "but we need some chairs. I'm going to post a notice at the tavern. Training starts tomorrow."

With Luras gone, Tresk and Theo pressed their foreheads together and gained a level in the Tara'hek Core. Unlike their individual core progress, the specialized core advanced at exactly the same pace for both of them. The alchemist extinguished the candles as night fell over Broken Tusk. With the entire pot of still-hot stew in Theo's inventory, they settled into bed, and he kicked himself for not sorting out Tresk's sleeping situation yet.

Sleep should have come easily, but the threat of bandits and dungeon monsters weighed heavily on Theo's mind. Nonetheless, exhaustion ultimately won this battle.

Chapter 19
Creeping Rot

Theo was the first to wake up the next morning, and he was getting good at creeping out of the bedroom without disturbing Tresk. In his previous life, he would never have considered waking up before dawn, but in Broken Tusk, it was a regular thing. He lit the candles and started a small fire for the tea. The cast-iron teapot bore scorch marks on its side from the repetition of use, burning deeper as he set it down on the flames. As he settled down near the fire, a notification filled the middle of his vision.

> **[Rent Is Due!]**
> Rent for **The Newt and Demon** is due in the amount of 10 copper coins, payable to Miana or the next acceptable functionary.

The rent was less than he expected, but the mayor would want him to make good on his debts as well. Theo had 4 silver, 39 copper to his name. With each day, his expenses mounted without traders to properly buy his goods. He let out a heavy sigh and took stock of his materials. There were smatterings of reagents here and there, but not enough to make a full batch of anything. He ran through each ingredient in his mind, his superior Wisdom allowing him to recall each one with clarity.

Ogre Cypress Bark had the [Cure Ailment] property, which he took to mean diseases and would be useful if monsters used afflictions. Zee Kernels were also useful in that regard, providing the [Cure Poison] property—a similar application. Everything else seemed to be of dubious use or too dangerous to eat. He could discover more properties by eating something, but the only thing that seemed worth trying was the Moss Nettle. He pulled some of the soggy moss from its storage crate and took a tenuous bite. His head rushed, sending him tumbling to the ground before a message flashed.

[Properties Discovery!]
You've discovered an additional effect of the Moss Nettle by eating it.
[Stamina Surge] discovered.

As with most things in the system, it didn't give him a description of the property. He couldn't make assumptions about how the stamina would surge and shrugged it away. Theo made a mental note to run a small batch of the moss to discover its effect but pushed it aside in his mind. The only other ingredient he could taste was the Marsh Tuber. The description even said it was edible, highlighting the fact that it was foul-tasting. Moments after taking the smallest bite, his stomach twisted into a knot. The taste was exactly as foul as the description claimed, sending the alchemist rushing for the barrel of Purified Water to cleanse the acrid sting on his tongue. It was like battery acid, and he didn't know how it was palatable. The message flashed regardless of how vile it was.

[Properties Discovery!]
You've discovered an additional effect of the Marsh Tuber by eating it.
[Barkskin] discovered.

Theo didn't need an in-depth explanation of that effect. Knowing the tenuous nature of the world as he did, the alchemist assumed that hardening one's skin came with drawbacks. It was still the perfect potion to brew for new adventurers, giving them an edge over the hordes of wolves outside their town. He was preparing thirty units of left-over Marsh Tubers when Tresk finally stepped into the lab. She stretched at the threshold, smacking her lips, before shambling over to the tea.

"Good morning," she said, still groggy.

"Morning. I'm going to start a potion batch," Theo said.

"What about breakfast?"

Theo withdrew the still-hot cauldron of soup from his inventory, his hands burning on the sides. He quickly set it on the ground, wincing at the pain. "I hope you fancy more soup."

"Soup is perfect," she said, finding a bowl and filling it.

The tubers were slightly more difficult to process than most things and needed to be cut into small pieces for the mash. Tresk sat near the fire, barely moving as she ate her soup. Theo poured two cups of tea, handing his companion one before mashing the tubers. His low Strength made the task difficult, but he managed. He dumped them into the clean still and started a fire using one under the boiling kettle. He focused on extracting the second property of the tubers. With a flask placed under the condenser, he joined Tresk and grabbed a bowl of the soup.

"We're going to be eating soup for days," Theo said, peering into the cauldron. It was only half-empty at this point.

"Yeah," Tresk said, yawning.

"You seem extremely tired," Theo said, placing his hand on her forehead. It was clammy and hot. "Are you sick?"

"Maybe," Tresk said. "Marshlings are extremely resistant to disease and poison, though."

"I think you're just exhausted," Theo said, testing the soup. It was still as perfect as it was last night.

"Maybe we should brew some potions to cure diseases," Tresk said. "Just in case."

Theo helped her to her feet and escorted her to the room, tucking her into his bed. "I'll brew the potions, you stay here."

Tresk groaned in response, and Theo rushed back into the lab, pulling the door closed behind him. He didn't want her to see the panic on his face, but she was too out of it to realize how concerned he was. The second still was still caked with yesterday's mess. He scrubbed the edges of the still, scraping off the edges with his knife, before returning the still to his inventory. The tables were heavy, but he shoved all his weight against one and brought it to the window. Theo removed the still from his inventory, and it fell with a clatter on the table.

It was only a matter of opening the window, and tipping the contents of the still out into the gravel garden below. He used his inventory to return the still to its original position, drinking some tea before starting a new fire under the second still. Theo zipped around the lab, frantically preparing a mash of the Ogre Cypress Bark left over from the tannery job and dumping it into the cleaned still. He leveled it off with ten units of Purified Water and inserted a flask under the condenser.

Theo left the lab, cracking the bedroom door open to find Tresk heaving breath. He let out a whispered curse before closing the door and returning to the lab.

"Why don't I have these supplies on hand?" he asked. The empty lab responded with the sputtering hisses of dual condensers.

The alchemist waited at the edge of the table, tapping his foot impatiently as the stills did their work. He tried to rationalize the situation, forcing his mind to realize that [Cure Ailment] was the best property for the job. She could have a marshling cold, and he wouldn't know what to look for. The only thing he could reach for was alchemy, and it left him feeling vulnerable. The ten units of mash cooked down quickly, Throk's amazing still doing its work.

Theo shoved the fire out from underneath the still and snatched the Purifying Essence. He approached the Glassware Artifice and created his standard flat-bottomed vial. The reaction was immediate when he added the ingredients together. It smelled like wood polish, but the description gave him hope.

[Lesser Potion of Purification]
[Potion]
Common
Created by: Belgar
Quality: Great
Low-tier purification potion that removes common ailments.
Effect:
Remove one instance of affliction from the drinker.

Theo returned to the bedroom with the potion in hand. Tresk's forehead felt hotter than it did before. "Tresk, can you hear me?"

She stirred slightly, but only groaned in response. Theo tipped her head back and forced the potion into her mouth. Tresk tried to object, but even with her high Strength, she couldn't resist after the affliction had sapped it all away. He saw her swallow the potion and stood, his heart hammering hard in his ears. The marshling was enveloped by ribbons of light swirling over her body with a buzzing sound. After a moment, they vanished, and her eyes snapped open.

"What the hell is [Creeping Rot]?" she asked, coughing.

Theo let out a sigh of relief, falling to the ground and chuckling.

"What happened?" Tresk asked.

Theo explained what just happened, the marshling growing paler the further he got into the story. She then flushed a deep shade of pink and busied herself with the bedsheets.

"A monster wolf got hold of my arm yesterday," Tresk said. "It was such a scramble, I must have missed the notification."

Theo let out another steadying breath, kneeling by the bedside and smiling at his companion. "We need to make sure the adventurers have these potions. I'm pretty sure you were dying."

"My health bar says as much," Tresk said, groaning into a seated position. "Only about 25% left."

"Drink a potion," Theo said, scowling.

Tresk obeyed, taking out a Lesser Healing Potion from her bag and downing it. She smiled at him before laughing. "I picked the right Tara'hek partner, that's for sure."

Theo scoffed, returning to the lab to tend to the other still. Tresk followed close behind him, taking a seat by the fire. The pair sat there for some time, only tending the fire and finishing their breakfast. The tea did a lot to calm the alchemist's nerves, but he was shaken. He blamed himself for the mistake—being unable to keep his mind off of making money when he should have been preparing his partner for adventuring. Even if she claimed she was seasoned, she had spent her early years in her father's smithy. Now, as Tara'hek, they were growing together, and that came with pain.

"Adventurers face a lot of stuff like that," Tresk said, breaking the silence.

The condenser on the still sputtered into silence, and Theo went over to remove the fire beneath it. He let out a sigh and regarded his companion. "I know. I'm beating myself up because I feel like you should have every potion under the sun. It's not reasonable, but I want you to have everything you need at the ready."

"It's not reasonable, but I understand," Tresk said.

"This might help with that, though," Theo said, inspecting the flask.

[Barkskin Essence]
[Essence]
Common
Created by: Belgar
Quality: Great
30 units (liquid)
Concentrated essence of barkskin.

"Would you mind making me thirty vials?" Theo asked. "We'll make half now, and half later."

"Of course," Tresk said, moving off to use the Glassware Artifice.

Theo found a flask large enough to contain the sixty-unit reaction, rinsing it out with Purified Water. He added the water, shavings, and essence, gaining a volatile reaction for his efforts. It bubbled and sputtered before emitting a cloud of smoke that smelled like the forest. The alchemist fanned it out the window, his heart thumping in his ears again. It was a pale brown color, fizzing with effervescence. He approached the reaction like the other low-level ones, assuming that it was one-to-one like Lesser Healing Potions. The fear that his lab would explode crossed his mind the moment that plume of smoke came out, but he breathed a sigh of relief and inspected the solution.

[Lesser Barkskin Potion]
[Potion]
Common
Created by: Belgar
Quality: Great
Imbiber's skin is turned to bark, significantly increasing their defense at the cost of mobility.
Effect:
Drink to gain the [Barkskin] effect for 3 minutes.

Theo began distributing the potion into the vials that his companion had made. She scooped one up and inspected it, her eyes going wide. "This is amazing," she said.

"I thought Barkskin might be useful," Theo said. "Another potion you can drink if you're in a bind."

The pair distributed all thirty units of the solution into the vials, jamming the glass stoppers in the top, before going downstairs to place them in the shop. In the early morning light, Theo could finally appreciate how much he liked the shop. The orange sunlight filtered through the front windows, casting a pale glow on the room. They placed the potions on a shelf and stood there, taking in the sight.

A knock came from the door, and Theo let Luras into the shop. The half-ogre looked over Tresk and knitted his brow. "You look pale."

"Almost died," Tresk said, smiling.

"A wolf inflicted her with [Creeping Rot]," Theo said.

Luras titled his head. "They must have evolved since the dungeon was upgraded. They're essentially scouts. None of the really nasty stuff, like goblins, are going to hit the surface."

"At least there's that," Theo said.

"I'm guessing you made a potion that cured the affliction," Luras said. "You'll want to stock a supply of that, unless we want to see dead villagers everywhere."

"Are you ready to go train the adventurers?" Tresk said, undaunted by her recent brush with death.

"Not so fast," Theo said. "You both need to take a Lesser Barkskin Potion and a few Lesser Potions of Purification before you leave."

Theo retreated upstairs without waiting for their responses, bottling the rest of the cure and returning downstairs. He distributed it among the two, finally satisfied that they could handle the deadly wolves.

"You're like our mother," Luras said.

"If that's how you feel, take a few Lesser Healing Potions, too," Theo said. "Seriously, I almost had a heart attack with Tresk."

Tresk smiled, scooping a few of the healing potions into her bag before coming to press her forehead against Theo's. They gained some experience, likely because of the harrowing experience upstairs, and the two adventurers departed. The alchemist intended to go to the tavern before opening the shop, hoping to find someone to run the shop so he could free up his time. Making money was nice, but the fuel that powered that engine were the potions he had been neglecting.

The Marsh Wolf Tavern was mostly empty, and Theo found the notice board tucked away near the counter. Xam greeted him as he read over the notices, most of them concerning the bounty on the wolves outside of the town.

"I need someone to run the shop. Anyone come to mind?" Theo asked.

Xam pressed her finger into her chin and hummed. She stood there for a moment before shrugging. "Most people in town are laborers. That work force thinned out when the wolf notice went up, but I know someone who would want the job."

"How good are they with people?" Theo asked.

"Fine, just fine," Xam said. "He's my brother, so I'll vouch for him if you're concerned."

"Send him to the shop," Theo said. He didn't want to post a sign in the tavern, having no desire to wait for help with the shop. "I offer laborer wages for the time being, but it's simple work."

"Azrug likes simple work," Xam said, sighing. "Doesn't even have his cores yet."

"What does that mean?"

"I forget you're an outworlder sometimes," Xam said. "People don't get their cores until they come of age. Depends on the person, but that usually happens around fifteen years old."

"Good thing there are no child labor laws here," Theo scoffed.

Xam smiled. "He'll be around soon, if you'd like to wait."

"I need to grab some materials," Theo said. "We're going to have a plague of Creeping Rot soon."

"Anything you want to share?" Xam said, raising an eyebrow.

"The wolves inflict the [Creeping Rot] effect, that's all I know," Theo said.

"Then by all means," Xam said, gesturing to the door.

Theo left, not really knowing how to take the woman's tone. He shrugged it off and made his way down to the tannery, intent on purchasing Ogre Cypress Bark from Perg. With the threat of wolves so close to town, he wasn't willing to delve into the swamp itself. He didn't want any part of that danger and knew he couldn't handle himself against a Level 1 monster, let alone something above Level 5.

"Perg," Theo said, waving at the tannery owner. She was standing in her customary spot, arms folded, with a bright smile on her face.

"Well, if it isn't the alchemist. Came to check up on our progress?" Perg asked.

"Not exactly," Theo said. "Although, now that you mention it, how's the processing going?"

"I cleared out my entire warehouse," Perg said. "We did a year's worth of work in a day."

"Perfect. And it doesn't smell like death anymore," Theo said. "Now all we need is some traveling merchants."

"Right, so what's the real reason you're here?"

"I need to buy some Ogre Cypress Bark from you," Theo said. "The wolves inflicted Creeping Rot on Tresk. Almost killed her."

Perg pushed off from the side of the warehouse and knitted her brow. "You know that you're welcome to just take the bark."

"Come on. That's not fair," Theo said.

"Let me say this again. We processed a year's worth of hides in a day," Perg said. "You're taking just ten percent of what I sell this stuff for. That's not nearly enough. Also, you're going to use the potions to cure the townsfolk. Just take the bark. I've got my crew running around stockpiling supplies anyway."

Theo shuffled his feet, eager to take the free Ogre Cypress Bark. He still felt guilty that he wasn't paying for it, but marched into the warehouse. Piles of perfectly cured leather could be seen in all corners of the place. The pits in the center of the building were empty and drained of the foul liquid. The pile of bark had grown larger since he was here the last time. He eagerly shoved the ingredients into his inventory, only stopping when they went over the stack limit of 400.

"The traders will show up soon," Perg said. "Word should be out by now. I hope your shop is ready for it."

"We are. I'm hiring Azrug to run the shop part of it," Theo said.

"Xam's kid brother? He's smart," Perg said.

"Good. As long as I don't have to babysit him, I'm happy," Theo said.

Chapter 20
The Kid

Theo returned to the shop to find a short half-ogre waiting patiently by the door. He looked a lot like Xam, with the same dark red skin and soft expression. The kid perked up when the alchemist approached, as though he were standing at attention. Eagerness was good, and whoever watched the shop didn't need to be a master negotiator.

"Azrug?" Theo asked, noting the boy's mud-stained clothes. He must have spent most of his life working in the fields.

"My sister sent me," he said, shuffling his feet awkwardly. "Said you had some work?"

Theo unlocked the shop and entered, gesturing for the boy to wait by the counter. He retrieved a bottle of Cleansing Scrub and handed it to Azrug, quickly explaining its use. The boy stood there for a moment before the alchemist encouraged him to use it, which he did. The effect startled him, but the cleansing effect of the potion washed away all the dirt from the fields, leaving him in pristine order.

"Now that you don't smell like manure," Theo said, taking a spot behind the counter. "It's a simple job. I'll give you a price list on the potions, and you sell them."

"So, I stand behind the counter? For how long?"

"From an hour after sunrise to noon, if that's all right with you," Theo said.

He didn't see a need for the boy to man the shop all day. The alchemist simply needed a few hours to get his other duties done, then he could take customers as they came. With Tresk off adventuring—where she truly belonged—he just needed someone to hawk his potions in the morning.

"What's the pay?" Azrug asked, narrowing his eyes.

"Two copper a day," Theo said. It was more than the laborers in the fields earned, most of the time.

"Seems suspicious," Azrug said. "I won't end up in some alchemist's cauldron, will I?"

"I honestly don't know if half-ogres are useful for potion making," Theo said. "If you have an issue with the arrangement, I can pluck another laborer from the fields."

Theo was feigning confidence. He wanted nothing more than to have the matter sorted. He couldn't tell if Azrug was reluctant to accept because the deal was too good or because he was a Dronon. It was easy to rule out the second option when he considered the good nature of half-ogres. They were the most welcoming bunch he had ever met.

"Sit behind the counter and sell potions," Azrug said, knitting his brow. "Pay me up front for today so I know this isn't a ruse."

Theo produced two copper coins from his inventory and placed them on the table. "Going forward, you'll be paid at the end of the day. If I'm not here to do it, simply take the money from the day's earnings and leave the rest under the counter."

"You trust me that much?"

Theo pressed his index finger into the Perpetual Ledger and grinned. "Anything you sell in the shop will be logged here. It has the date, what you sold, and how much you sold it for."

"Fine," Azrug said, nodding. "I'll give it a try."

"Good. Perch yourself behind the counter," Theo said. "I'm going to work in the lab upstairs. Flip the sign outside and wait around. You're free to... bring a book, or whatever it is people do in this world to pass the time."

"Really?" Azrug said. "Could I have a chair, too?"

The alchemist looked around the room. While the upgrade provided shelves and a counter, there was no chair for the boy to sit on during the long day. He furrowed his brow and sighed. "I don't have any chairs."

"You should get some chairs. There's a woodworker near the foot of the farmer's mound."

"Care to run an errand?"

"Sure."

Theo produced five copper coins from his inventory and handed it to the boy. There was no way five chairs would cost more than 5 copper. If they did, it was robbery. "Five chairs."

Azrug took two of the coins and smiled. "He sells them two for a copper, but I can talk him down."

The alchemist raised an eyebrow as the kid bound through the front door and up the street. If he wasn't lying about his ability to talk the carpenter down, that was a good sign for the boy running the store. Theo went upstairs to tend to the stills, cleaning them out before he heard the bell tinkle downstairs. When he went back to the first floor, he was surprised to see the small half-ogre with five hardwood chairs, tastefully carved and decorated. Azrug had a beaming smile on his face, setting more chairs than a boy should be able to carry down with a clatter.

"Two copper," Azrug said, producing the remaining three copper coins, "like I said."

"Well, you've earned your seat, then. Let me write a few things down for you," Theo said. He wrote a detailed list of the prices, highlighting the fact that new adventurers had a discount. The prices were set at what was fair for a local to pay, 5 copper for a Lesser Healing Potion, the Lesser Barkskin Potion at 8, and the Cleansing Scrub at 1. He also told the boy to find him if someone from out of town arrived.

"Looks good, boss," Azrug said, reclining in his chair.

Theo scoffed, putting the remaining four chairs in his inventory and ascending the staircase. Tresk updated him on the situation with the adventurers. Ten of them arrived for the training session in dire need of help. It was going well after a few missteps by the new fighters, leading to a few close calls. He told her to be careful before depositing his new chairs in the lab. The alchemist sat there for some time, appreciating being off his legs for once.

The stills were a mess from the morning run. Theo used his new technique of shoving a table against the window to clean everything, dumping the fouled water into the gravel yard below. He placed them back in their spots and considered performing more experiments. After some deliberation, however, he cast those thoughts aside and decided to focus on curing the inevitable plague of Creeping Rot that would come. Today was another false start, though, as his water barrel barely had enough Purified Water to make a ten-unit run. He placed it in his inventory and made to leave the shop, hearing the tinkle of the front door's bell.

"Welcome to the Newt and Demon," Azrug said, holding his arms out and beaming at the customer.

The man who stood at the threshold was a meek-looking half-ogre, casting his gaze over the shop in awe. It was immediately apparent to Theo that Azrug was a good fit for the shop clerk job.

"I take it from that pig-sticker on your hip that you're a new adventurer," Azrug said. "We're running a special today." He glanced down at the parchment Theo left him for only a moment, making the action look natural. "Five potions for 10 copper. You won't find a better deal anywhere."

"Of course," the man said, nodding. "Just can't resist that bounty."

"Who can? But you know—just for you—I'll add a Lesser Barkskin Potion and a Cleansing Scrub for 5 copper. What do you say?"

"All right. Not looking to die out there," the man said, fishing the money out of his pocket.

Azrug smiled, moving to collect the goods, and set them on the counter. He counted out the coins that the man set down, clamping one between his teeth, before smiling again. "Pleasure doing business with you, sir. Tell all your friends that the Newt and Demon is open for business!"

The man left with a wide smile on his face. Theo scoffed, descending the last of the stairs and placing a hand on the boy's shoulder. "Yeah, I have nothing to teach you. I might sit in on your sales and get a few pointers for myself."

"I've been hawking garbage to the fine folks of Broken Tusk since I could walk," Azrug said, waving Theo away. "Not that it's hard to sell stuff that actually does something."

In a flash, Azrug went from a nervous boy to a master salesman. Theo was amazed at the level of poise the boy showed. The way he upsold the additional potion was perfect, reminding him of those annoying people back on Earth. He remembered going into the electronics store looking for something and leaving with an armful of useless junk. The difference here was that all the potions they sold were life-saving things. They were the razor's edge that protected these people from certain death out in the swamp.

"Right. Be on your toes if there's someone from outside of Broken Tusk," Theo said. "That Lesser Healing Potion you sold for 2 copper goes for 50 in the capital."

Azrug nodded, knitting his brow as though committing the information to memory. "The traveling merchants might be out of my league, but I'll do my best."

"You're a natural, kid," Theo said. "I need to run errands. Keep being awesome."

Theo saw the wide smile on the kid's face as he left, feeling warmth bloom through his chest. He would leave the money with Azrug to test his loyalty. Fifteen copper was a tempting sum for a person used to working the fields and scraping by. It seemed like a cruel thing to do, but if they were going to have a long-term relationship, it was necessary.

The alchemist made his way to Throk's smithy, finding the marshling banging away on something in his workshop. He got a good deal on four water barrels, only paying 2 copper for them. He stuffed them in his inventory and made his way to Miana's house, finding her leering through the window. She threw the door open and gave him a scowl.

"Rent is due," she said, stone-faced as always.

Theo produced 25 copper, handing the sum to her. He wanted to clear out some of the lower-cost items on his [Pay Your Debts] quest while he was there. She seemed to understand the gesture, snatching the coins out of his hand and slamming the door in his face. He inspected the quest before departing for the river.

[Pay Your Debts]
Quest
Miana Kell has overseen your transition into your new world, and you owe her a lot of money!
Objectives:
Pay the following debts:
Medical Services Rendered: 1 Silver **(DONE)**
Room and Board (1 week): 10 Copper **(DONE)**
Alchemy Lab (to be paid in installments): 1 Gold
Equipment (to be paid in installments): 1 Gold
Service Charge: 5 Copper **(DONE)**

Two gold seemed like an absurd fortune to him. The long road that stretched ahead seemed daunting, but at least he could pay it in installments. Theo found the river and the fishermen that patrolled its shores. He filled all five of his barrels before returning to the shop. Azrug found a book somewhere and was reading it when he returned. The boy barely looked up at him when he entered, but the alchemist didn't mind. He didn't hire the half-ogre for idle chatter.

Theo placed all five barrels along the northern wall of the lab, purifying them one by one. With the window still propped open, he wafted the disparate fumes outside, although he didn't mind the smell of that reaction. The thing he appreciated most about the day was the comfort that the chair brought when processing the Ogre

Cypress Bark. His back didn't hurt as much in this world as it did on Earth, but spending hours hunched over a barrel still took its toll. Seating in the fine wooden chair made the task simple, and he spent the next hour processing 200 units of the bark, cutting it into smaller pieces and mashing it with his stick.

The fire crackled under the still, and Theo heard the bell downstairs. Azrug's boisterous voice, far too commanding for a boy so young, came from downstairs. The alchemist reclined in his chair, kicking his feet up onto the table as he tried to follow the conversation. Even with the door opened, it was too muffled to hear the exchange, but he listened anyway. The bell tinkled again after a few minutes, and the shop was silent again.

The Ogre Cypress Bark concoction took over an hour to distill. While Throk's invention was extremely efficient, it struggled to churn through the huge load he put on it. The bell tinkled several times during the run. Theo had to swap out the flasks several times, unwilling to deal with the barrel-sized glassware and favoring ones that could hold fifty units. The end of the run resulted in 200 units of Purifying Essence and Theo's new shopkeeper poking his head into the lab.

"It's closing time, boss," Azrug said. His eyes sparkled, sweeping the room. "Wow. That's some fancy equipment you got in here."

"I manage," Theo said. "Let's go see what you've sold."

The pair descended the stairs, and Theo immediately spotted the pile of copper underneath the counter. Azrug stood by the Perpetual Ledger, running his finger over the log and nodding to himself. "All new adventurer sales. Some of them went for the additional potions, and others refused."

"You made five sales today," Theo said, scoffing. "People are starting to learn about the shop, aren't they?"

At the end of his short workday, Azrug had sold twenty-five Lesser Healing Potions, three Lesser Barkskin Potions, and three units of the scrub. Theo counted out the pile of copper coins, cross-referencing them with the ledger to check if the amount was accurate. The shop had made 65 copper under the young half-ogre's watch.

"Well, I'll see you tomorrow," Azrug said, waving and leaving out the front door.

Theo added the copper coins to his inventory, shaking his head in disbelief. He mentally informed Tresk about his new shop-keeper, and how much of a burden it had lifted. She was wrapping up the day in the swamp, eager to return to the shop after a long day of fighting. He kept the shop open until his companion returned, heading back up to the lab to create vials. The single downside of the Glassware Artifice was its inability to generate more than one vial at a time, but he had to overlook that problem, unsure of where he could source glassware otherwise.

The bell rang downstairs, just after Theo completed 200 flat-bottomed vials for the Lesser Potion of Purification batch, but it was Tresk. She was filthy from the swamp and applied some Cleansing Scrub to herself before pressing her forehead against his.

"Luras donated all the cores he found to the cause. So did the other adventurers, but that was part of the agreement," Tresk said. "Fifty-five cores, all around Level 5. Should be enough for a level or two."

"Makes sense. The town is much bigger than our shop," Theo said.

"More good news. I have more wolf parts, and we stumbled onto some wild Swamp Onions," Tresk said, removing a small vegetable from her inventory. It looked like a tiny version of a regular onion, with gnarled roots coming out of the bottom. Theo inspected it.

[Swamp Onion]
[Alchemy Ingredient] [Food]
Uncommon
Swamp Onions grow near the mossy embankments
common in the marsh. They blend in with local flora and
can be extremely difficult to spot.

Properties:
[???] [???] [???]

It was the first item lacking at least one revealed property. Without asking for permission, he took a bite out of the side. Tresk grimaced. The flavor reflected her expression. It was as though someone condensed the essence of a large red onion into a tiny package, unleashing all the flavor in a small package.

[Properties Discovery!]
You've discovered an additional effect of the Swamp Onion by eating it.
[Stench] discovered.

"It has the [Stench] property," Theo said, tears forming in the corners of his eyes.

"Yeah, those are potent things. You don't see them that often," Tresk said. "We found an entire bed of them near a peat bog in the middle of the swamp. I picked a lot."

The flavor lingered in Theo's mouth, refusing to go away for a long time. He flipped the sign to "Closed" before locking up for the day. The pair retreated upstairs to make their dinner. Dusk was a way off, but they were both exhausted from the day. Theo knew Tresk was significantly more tired than he was and wanted to make sure she had something to eat before sleeping. He checked her forehead, causing her to giggle, and dumped the contents of their old stew out the window. It seemed like a waste of food, but he got over it.

"Chairs!" Tresk shouted, hopping into a chair. "You bought chairs!"

"That was Azrug's idea," Theo said.

They settled in, stoking one fire to life and placing the cauldron over it. Tresk prepared the onions, using them sparingly, while Theo got the cauldron ready.

"More barrels," Tresk said, nodding to the north-facing wall of the lab. "That's a great idea."

"Your father sold them to me," Theo said, laughing. "I felt like I went on a spending spree today, but then we made a ton of money."

"Maybe not a *ton* of money," Tresk said, "but it was a good amount. Luras and I made half a silver killing wolves."

"Are you sure you don't have Creeping Rot again?" Theo asked.

"I'm sure. Anyway, I see you're setting up to combat that problem," Tresk said. "What should we price those potions at?"

"Free if someone has the rot," Theo said. "Otherwise, a copper? I really don't care."

"You're too generous. If some haughty northlander comes down here, you'd better gouge them," Tresk said.

"Absolutely. I even gave our new shopkeeper instructions to do exactly that," Theo said.

The alchemist added the onions first, quickly understanding the [Stench] property of the vegetable. The smell filled the air, and he was immediately glad Tresk had only cut one of them up. Any more than that, and they would need to evacuate the room. It cooked quickly, caramelizing in the cauldron and crackling amid the dancing wolf fat. Tresk cleaned the cuts of meat she brought this time, minimizing the amount of fat sitting on the strips. They added the bones and water before letting it all boil away for a while.

"Future plans?" Tresk said, stirring the mixture.

"Our immediate goal is to upgrade the town," Theo said. "How long before the wolves get into town?"

"Not long," Tresk said. "They're edging closer to Broken Tusk by the day. Even with the new adventurers, it's going to be rough."

"Right. Make money and collect cores," Theo said. "We owe 2 gold on this place."

Tresk grimaced. They hadn't spoken at length about the debt that he owed. "Small steps."

Theo would have preferred to sear the wolf meat before placing it in the stew, but this worked last time. They cut the strips of meat into little chunks, adding more than they needed, and let it simmer for some time. It smelled far better than the last time they made it. Swamp Onions were the key to making a wonderful stew, as far as he was concerned. As if on cue, a knock came at the front door. The alchemist wasn't surprised to see Luras craning his head to see inside.

"I smelled the soup," Luras said honestly.

"What if it is a stew?" Theo asked.

"Beats me. Can I have some?" Luras asked, grinning.

Theo invited him in, leading him upstairs. The half-ogre was surprised to see the chairs arranged around a table. He gladly took a seat and smiled at his companions. He was in better spirits than he had been the other day. Either the news of war had faded, or his weariness from travel was gone. Luras took a bowl of the soup when it was ready and helped himself, making satisfied sounds with every bite.

"This is so much better than last time," Luras said. "The onion really does wonders here."

"Agreed," Theo said, nodding. He took his first sip of the soup and couldn't disagree with the half-ogre's words. Something about the potent Swamp Onion brought out the best flavors of the wolf meat. Even the broth seemed richer than last time, elevating it beyond anything he had thought possible. Xam's stew seemed like a distant memory, overshadowed by their new recipe.

"No offense to Xam, but her soup sucks," Tresk said.

"She makes a perpetual stew," Luras said. "It boils away for weeks at a time."

Theo grimaced, his brow knitting tight. That sounded disgusting. "That's vile."

"It's pretty common in poorer areas," Luras said. "The wolf population was low when you got here. Now that we have a steady supply, everyone is getting fat."

"I'd rather get fat on coins," Theo said.

Luras poked him in the stomach, grinning. "I don't think you'll ever get fat. You're like a twig."

Tresk grabbed Theo's thin arm and shook it around. "Look at these noodles."

Theo cast a glare over the pair, feigning anger. "You're lucky I don't collapse under a stiff breeze, Tresk."

The marshling erupted in laughter, almost spilling her soup in her lap. The conversation switched between topics, never lingering on anything long enough to produce depth. Tresk intended to use every monster core in her possession the following day, but Luras doubted it was enough to get the town to Level 5. They planned on going out again in the morning, Theo insisting they take as many Lesser Potions of Purification as they could carry.

Luras left when dusk threatened outside, bidding them farewell and patting his newly rounded belly. Theo stowed the cauldron in his inventory and shoved Tresk toward the bedroom. She might not have been acting tired, but he knew it was catching up with her. His own stamina bar was nearly drained, and he hadn't spent the entire day out in the fetid swamp like she did. She objected the entire way, but the moment he pulled the blanket up over her in the bedroll, she was out cold.

Theo was left alone with his thoughts for a while before sleep came. There had been a lot of progress made in Broken Tusk during his first week, but it paled in comparison to what was to come. Word was out about the new alchemist and the Swamp Dungeon. Rivers and Daub was a day's journey north. Traders would arrive soon, and he could finally start checking things off of his wishlist. On the top of the list was some manner of fire artifice. Managing the flames for the stills was his biggest weakness. His intuition told him that temperature control was going to become necessary the higher he got in alchemy.

All of those worries washed away, stolen by the inevitability of sleep.

Chapter 21
Well-stored Soup

The soup tasted even better on the second day. Theo knew that while it was stored in his dimensional inventory, it didn't age, but that didn't stop him from further marveling at its flavor the next morning. He sat with Tresk around the fire, finally able to enjoy the comfort of a nice chair, sipping his energizing tea. The effects were nothing like coffee, making it a ritual that he enjoyed. His marshling companion didn't show the signs of Creeping Rot the next morning. That fact didn't stifle his urge to make 200 Lesser Potions of Purification. Vigilance was required when dealing with the wolves baying at the non-existent gates.

The first order of business was to use Tresk's entire stock of monster cores on Broken Tusk. Before using them, Theo inspected the monolith.

[Small Town]
Name: Broken Tusk
Owner: Kingdom of Qavell
Mayor: Miana Kell
Faction: Qavell
Level: 2 (50%)
Features:

Alchemy Lab
Blacksmith
Large Farm
Tannery
Tradesmen

Upgrades:
None

Theo's superior memory allowed him to recall the town's total experience the last time they had been here. It was at 31% into Level 2 when he last visited, meaning someone had been feeding it cores. Tresk said that most of their cores had been donated by Luras. The marshling added each core individually, resulting in the town gaining varied experience points depending on the level of the core. She nodded her head when she was done, having dumped all fifty-five of the cores into the town.

"Not bad," Tresk said. "Level 3 with 35% experience."

"Agreed... Not bad, but also not good. We're very far off from our goal," Theo said, knitting his brow, "and I'd still like to see some stone walkways."

"We might need to hire some laborers for that. Mine the stone from the northern hills, process them into blocks, and set them with mortar along the roads," Tresk said, frowning. "That sounds expensive."

"Yeah, it does. Less expensive than a wizard, though," Theo said.

"Wizards are so expensive," Tresk scoffed. "That's what I heard, anyway."

Luras joined them at the monolith, departing with Tresk shortly after dawn broke. Theo got a glimpse of the would-be adventurers. All but Aarok seemed out of place, as though they were pretending to be adventurers. To his delight, none showed the torpor of someone infected with Creeping Rot, and he considered that a success.

Azrug was waiting for Theo at the shop, leaning against the

wall and reading a book. The alchemist couldn't see the title and was afraid to ask what the tome was about. The boy seemed eager to get back to work. He even cleaned himself with the Cleansing Scrub before arriving for his shift.

"Have you eaten this morning?" Theo asked.

"Sure have, boss," Azrug said.

"I'll make sure you have food available if you need it," Theo said. "Help yourself to the water from the barrels above."

"Since you built that water tower, I've had plenty to drink," Azrug said, beaming. "The copper you gave me yesterday will feed my family for a week."

"You're the sole provider?" Theo asked, furrowing his brow.

"Don't be dramatic," Azrug said. "Xam has more wolf stew than she knows what to do with, and my parents work the fields. I'm just trying to get a head start on things."

"Well, we should keep issues like that in mind," Theo said. He said it more to himself than anyone else. "We live and die by the strength of Broken Tusk and its people."

"You're in a mood today," Azrug said.

Theo wished he hadn't been called out by a child, but it was true. He was trying to shoulder the burdens of an entire town, and he didn't even hold the position of mayor. Miana was doing a horrible job of managing the place, but he didn't know if he could do any better. The alchemist wasn't even sure if he had such lofty aspirations. Until now he had been content to work in the lab and sell potions. Just as things were kicking off, he had dangerous thoughts about providing for the people of Broken Tusk.

"Why hasn't Miana done more for her people?" Theo asked.

"No one *wants* to be mayor," Azrug said, chuckling. "Not in a backwater place like this, anyway. She's been running this place as long as I can remember, and nothing has changed. Change only came when you showed up."

"Don't go putting dangerous thoughts in my head like that," Theo said, narrowing his eyes.

"What? Everyone's saying it," Azrug said. "From the day you arrived, all you've done is make everyone's life better."

"All of that was a stroke of luck," Theo said. "I got reincarnated with a lot more than most people in town. Then I was given a core building, an alchemy lab, and the tools to succeed. It would be more amazing if I failed."

"Whatever you say, boss," Azrug said. "All I know is you'd be a better pick to steer this ship."

Theo waved him off, not wanting to entertain the thought any longer. No matter how hard he pushed against the idea, it came back. The problem lay with his understanding of the political structure of the realm, or lack thereof. Taking the role would distract him from his alchemy, and he couldn't have that. No, the only thing he wanted to do was sit in his lab and experiment. The shop was hard enough as it was.

"Well, the shop is yours," Theo said. "I'll be upstairs making purifying potions if you need me."

"Sounds good," Azrug said, reclining in his chair and going back to his book.

Theo returned to his lab, the sour taste of the prospect of becoming mayor still on his tongue. He didn't want to be the person to do the paperwork or pay the taxes for the town, but he wanted to steer it. If the town grew, perhaps there'd be a position under the mayor, similar to the mercantile seat he held currently. *That* was a position he could get behind. None of the problems that came with politics, and all the ability to help those he wanted to help.

The 200 units of Purifying Essence Theo crafted yesterday would make 400 individual Lesser Potions of Purification, a number that seemed ridiculous in hindsight. He had already made and arranged the flat-bottomed glass vials, staged with their stoppers nearby, and planned to set off a 200-unit reaction. The other half, he would use later. He propped the windows before looking for four fifty-unit flasks, coming up short and generating the rest with the Glassware Artifice. The smaller reaction size would help with the immense cloud that erupted from the flasks.

Fifty units of Copper Shavings, twenty-five units of Purified Water, and twenty-five units of Purifying Essence went in each flask. The moment the flakes dropped into the glass containers, the liquid inside erupted with bubbles and steam, gathering in a cloud that hung in the lab. Theo waved the acrid smoke out the window and repeated the process four times. The Lesser Potion of Purification was still of "great" quality, no matter how much he tweaked his process. Heat was his biggest culprit, but he suspected that the catalyst he was using might be the limiting factor. *Essential Alchemy* listed a wide range of catalyzing agents, most of which he had never seen, but those would have to wait.

The reaction part of the alchemy process was the quickest, at least with the base-level recipes. Theo understood that his Stripping Solution and Alchemic Tannin sat in the middle ground between entry-level and more advanced reactions. That threshold sat somewhere near Level 10, a fact he could determine from observation and his keen intuition. What he really needed were hard facts provided by an alchemist who knew what they were doing. Broken Tusk was lacking any comprehensive libraries or other sources of information. He would settle for doing things the painful way for now.

Theo spent most of his morning on the Lesser Potions of Purification in his lab, also going over his books to see if he missed anything. The issue with *Essential Alchemy* was its simplicity, the contents aimed at traditional alchemy. They brewed potions the old-fashioned way by boiling things in cauldrons until they were sludge, creating salves from the result. Brewing potions was within the realm of a distiller, and the topic was sparse in the tome. The notes he took, both mental and physical, were enough to write a book on their own. The alchemist suspected that more comprehensive works existed in the world, just out of his reach.

Midday approached when the shop's bell finally jingled. Theo heard Azrug's voice from downstairs, lacking its normal poise as he stammered. Then there came the clattering of footfalls up the stairs, the boy emerging into the lab with panic on his face. "Fancy-pants trader from Rivers and Daub. I recognize those ruffles anywhere."

Theo's heart hammered in his chest, adrenaline suddenly dumping in his system. He stared wide-eyed at the boy and tried to calm himself.

"A trader from Rivers and Daub just came in the shop," Theo said, sending the words to Tresk's mind.

"Stay calm and milk him for every copper!" Tresk responded. *"I'm commanding the adventurer party to a halt—Luras is with me so ask any questions you need."*

Theo nodded, gesturing for the boy to return to the store section of the lab. When the shop came into view, he saw what the kid was talking about. The man stood at about his height, the pointy ears sitting under a fluffy hat betraying him as an elf. The cap he wore had a feather stuck in it—the long sweeping thing mottled with a rainbow of colors. His body was covered in more ruffles and fluff than Theo had ever seen, even on Earth. Purple crushed velvet on his chest, a jacket with pauldrons made of fluffy animal hair, and pantaloons that flared out near his pointed shoes. It was hard not to laugh.

Theo managed a smile and approached the counter. "Welcome to the Newt and Demon."

"Ah, the *demon* part of the name," the man said, bowing slightly. "I hardly expected to see a Dronon so far south. My name is Fenian, a trader from Rivers and Daub."

"I'm Theo, resident alchemist of this backwater mud pit," Theo said, smiling. "Hopefully, the road wasn't too dangerous."

Fenian waved a dismissive hand, his lilting voice coming back to grate against the alchemist's ears. "Any trader worth anything brings guards. Mine are outside."

"This guy is really haughty," Theo said. He could hear Tresk laughing in his mind.

"Can I interest you in anything? We've had a bit of a problem with wolves, so I'm afraid my selection is limited," Theo said.

Azrug was useless in the situation. He underplayed how intimidated he was by dealing with an outsider. It was one thing to sell something to a resident of Broken Tusk, but when it was an elf from another city, he was useless. Theo didn't fault him, seeing it as a learning opportunity for both of them.

"May I browse?" Fenian asked.

"Of course," Theo said, gesturing. "Oh, I have some more potions to put on shelf."

Fenian bowed his head, moving behind the counter and checking the offerings. He remained silent as Theo placed his Lesser Potions of Purification on an empty shelf. He only got fifty of them up before he felt the elf's eyes on him. His discerning gaze looked him up and down, an eyebrow cocked the entire time.

"Strange," Fenian said. "Don't worry, we can do business, I assure you, but I have a question, one that I hope you won't take offense to."

Theo shrugged. He was thrown so off-balance that he doubted anything could stumble him further. "Ask away."

"You're under Level 20, right? Perhaps even under 10... This is extremely strange," Fenian said.

"I am," Theo said, flushing.

Fenian thought for a moment, cupping his chin in his hand. "Outworlder. Recently transferred. Sent with a gift?"

He had thought wrong. It *was* possible to send him further off-balance. Fenian was clearly knowledgeable about more than just things regarding trade. He hit the nail on the head with little information. The alchemist tensed, unsure if he was in danger.

"Calm yourself," Fenian said, holding up a Lesser Healing Potion. "If it hasn't been explained to you, let me do so now. Distillation is a gift honed over years. It's reserved for alchemists who have done their time brewing potions the slow way. The first alchemy core ability to distill comes at Level 20. Anyone who attempts to distill this before then blows themselves up. Drogramath Dronon don't exist—not on this continent. You're too friendly and civilized to be one of his ilk. Therefore, you're an outworlder with an amazing gift."

Theo was overwhelmed by the information. He was sent to Broken Tusk with no explanation of his origins. People in the town told him about Dronon and how they weren't uncommon, but they wouldn't have known about the different lineages. He was left feeling both exposed and relieved.

"You have me at quite a disadvantage," Theo said, chuckling nervously. He wondered if the trader could hear his heart hammering in his chest.

"Maybe," Fenian said. "But only in deductive reasoning. *These* are truly amazing. The alchemists above Level 20 don't want to waste their time brewing Level 1 potions."

"They're valuable, then," Azrug blurted out, putting his hands over his mouth. "Sorry."

"An alchemist in Broken Tusk. I just had to see for myself. I expected someone flinging those vile salves that all Level 1 alchemists sell," Fenian said, letting out a wistful sigh. "No, this is a find indeed."

"Well. Now that you've exposed my entire origin, are you interested?" Theo asked, managing a smile.

"Yes," Fenian said, cocking his head and staring off into the middle distance.

Theo took the chance to update Tresk on the situation. She wasn't surprised that an elf from the fancy city had him pegged for an outworlder. *"Take him for all he's worth!"*

"The Cleansing Scrub is as impressive as the potions. You figured it out on your own, didn't you?" Fenian asked, letting out another sigh. "Gods, you're such a gem. Right, I'm interested in buying most of your stock."

Theo was glad that his Vigor attribute was so high; otherwise, he would have had a heart attack. "We're more than happy to sell them to you." He couldn't think of anything else to say.

"I'll pay 25 copper a flask of Lesser Healing Potion, the entire stock of seventy potions. Lesser Barkskin Potion, 30 copper each, twenty flasks. And finally, 15 copper per Lesser Potion of Purification, twenty of those," Fenian said, his eyes going glassy for a moment. "26 silver and 50 copper in total, if my offer is acceptable to you."

Azrug made a surprised sound, but clamped his mouth shut quickly. Theo mentally sent the totals to Tresk, and she responded by screaming into his mind. He took that as an affirmative, but he tempered his excitement for a moment. Traveling traders weren't just running around buying things; they also sold stuff.

"Very acceptable," Theo said, grinning. "I have a question for you, though. I assume you carry a stock of items with you."

Fenian grinned. "Ah, an alchemist in the middle of nowhere. Of course, you're short on supplies. I carry a vast array of items with me. Is there anything you're looking for?"

"An artifice that generates fire," Theo said. "I assume the standard use would be for cooking, but I'd like it to heat my stills."

Fenian's grin grew wider. He held his hand out, and an item appeared. The elf gestured for him to inspect it, which he did.

[Flame Artifice]
[Specialty Artifice]
Rare
Created by: Melgar
Feed the artifice motes to produce a steady flame. Each mote can sustain six hours of fire. The intensity of the flames is determined by the dial on the side. Setting the artifice's power to zero preserves the mote's stored energy.

"As you assumed, it is a very common item for cooking," Fenian said. "I'm willing to part with it for 5 silver."

"Do you have two?" Theo asked, grinning.

Fenian produced another Flame Artifice in his other hand and smiled. "Since you're new and this is the start of a very profitable relationship, I'll give you a discount on the equipment. Don't think for a moment that it isn't a selfish motivation. 8 silver for the two, and you agree to take work orders from me."

Theo thought for a moment. He couldn't think of a better arrangement than to produce a specific number of potions for the trader. Having someone show up in town randomly was nice, but if he had had time to prepare, he could have made more of the precious Lesser Healing Potions. He reached out a hand for the elf to shake, which he did.

"18 silver, 50 copper," Fenian said, producing the coins and setting them on the counter with the two pieces of equipment. Then he began collecting his goods.

Theo placed the coins and the Flame Artifices in his inventory, surprised when his copper rolled over 100 and was added to his silver. He had been wondering if he would have to see someone to exchange his copper for silver, so he was glad the system could take care of it for him. He was also pleased that Fenian was happy with his order. The permanent smile on his face said that he was going to resell the goods at a premium, but it was a massive sum of money by Broken Tusk standards. He now had 23 silver and 39 copper.

"I look forward to working with you," Theo said as Fenian stored the last of the potions in his inventory.

"This is going to be an *extremely* profitable relationship," Fenian said. "Not just because you're in Broken Tusk, and I say this honestly. You get little honesty from merchants, but I won't squander this opportunity. You fill a very specific niche in the market, and people are going to fall over themselves to get your goods. This lab is a money-making machine."

"I appreciate your candor," Theo said. "I'm aware of the prices in Qavell, and I don't feel that you were unfair in what you offered."

"Naturally," Fenian said. "I'll be in town for the day and part of tomorrow. I'll stop by the shop with a work order before leaving. You'll get a list of the potions I want, how much I'll pay you, and a deadline. Sounds good?"

"Sounds perfect," Theo said.

Fenian shook his hand again and made for the door. "I look forward to working with you."

The elf was only a few paces from the store when Azrug erupted. He shouted, pumping his fist in the air and losing his mind. Theo watched the boy's outburst for a while, finally unable to contain the pressure that was building inside him and joining him. They jumped in the middle of the shop, screaming.

"We just made 18 silver," Theo said.

"You what?" Tresk shouted into his mind.

Chapter 22
The Gracious Lord Administrator

It took Azrug a long time to stop celebrating. The advantages of youth saw him rolling on the floor long after Theo calmed down. The excitement he felt mounting in his chest didn't relent, though. With the first out-of-town trader stopping by, he made absurd headway toward paying off his debt. Getting the Flame Artifices was just another thing that would make his life easier. Managing the small fires under his stills was tiresome, and the devices would provide six hours of steady fire.

"I've never seen that much silver," Azrug said, shaking his head.

"We'll put it to good use," Theo said. "I'll spend most of it paying off my debt to Miana."

"That sucks. Thought you'd buy something nice for yourself."

"I got the Flame Artifices. That's good enough for me," Theo said. "Anyway, aren't you done for the day?"

Midday had come in the time they spent celebrating. The sun shone brightly overhead, flooding the small shop with its light. Tresk told Theo about her day out in the swamp, and the improvements the adventurers were making. They might have been making progress, but one of them caught the [Creeping Rot] and would need a potion. She said they were depositing the cores into the town before returning to the shop.

"Right," Azrug said. "As soon as my taskmaster pays me."

Theo fished five copper coins from his inventory, placing them in the wide-eyed boy's hands. "To celebrate a big sale. Don't get used to it."

"Thank you," Azrug said, his eyes focused on the coins in his hand. "Do you think some of this coin will flow to the rest of the town?"

"I hope so," Theo said. "My goal has never been to be selfish with my alchemy."

Azrug nodded, making his way to the door. He stopped before leaving, flashing the alchemist a wide grin. "See you tomorrow, boss."

Theo took stock of his potions before moving back to the lab. He had more Lesser Potions of Purification than he knew what to do with, but no restoration potions. The merchant didn't end up buying any Cleansing Scrub, leaving him with fifty vials of it. His Lesser Barkskin Potion stock was down to nine units. That left him with a mostly empty shop and no materials to distill new potions with. He climbed the stairs and took stock of the lab, finding a scattering of half-empty essence flasks, but nothing worth making a reaction with.

Tresk arrived with Luras shortly after, jumping with excitement. "Let's see it."

Theo produced his 23 silver, cupping his hands as they appeared in midair. The jangling sound they made when they appeared was incredibly satisfying. He put them back in his inventory after his friends got a good look.

"This is the real prize," Theo said, bringing the Flame Artifices out of his inventory. The small disc-shaped contraptions were lighter than they appeared, completely flat on top with a slot on the side for motes. A turn-style dial sat on the side with a small picture of an increasingly larger flame.

"You found your fire source," Luras said.

"This is good. No more tending the flame for hours on end," Tresk said, letting out a sign. "That was my least favorite part."

"Mine too," Theo said, nodding. "I should have bought more, but they were 5 silver each. Well, I got a deal for the pair, but still."

Luras took the contraption and inspected it, nodding his approval. "The hunt went well. We're seeing the same number of wolves, so that's a good sign."

Theo produced a Lesser Potion of Purification from his inventory and held it out. "You said someone had the rot?"

"Well, I didn't want to break your excitement... Miana is calling for a meeting regarding the rot," Luras said. "She told us when we were dumping the monster cores."

"Right now?"

"Right now."

Theo grumbled, stuffing the potion back into his inventory and letting out a heavy sigh. "Off we go, then."

When they arrived at Miana's office, Theo was surprised to see they were the only ones in attendance. He knew this was a special meeting meant for the Newt and Demon, a fact that he wasn't happy about. The half-ogre woman sat behind her desk, scowling around the room the way she always did, while Luras stood in the back with his arms folded. He was important enough to get the invite, whereas the others on the mercantile board were not.

"We've got an epidemic," Miana said.

"The Creeping Rot?" Theo asked. "I have a cure for that."

"I *know* you have a cure," Miana said, scoffing, "but as the mayor, *I* need to provide the cure. I'm bound by some nonsense law of the kingdom to provide care for my citizens."

"Doesn't sound like a nonsense law to me," Theo said, shrugging. "Sounds like your duty to the people of Broken Tusk."

Miana scowled even harder, trying to pierce the alchemist with her gaze. "I know you've made more money in a day than the rest of the town has in a year, combined, but try to level with me here."

Theo shrugged. He was feeling bold after his massive sale. The merchant only promised more riches in the future, and he was feeling full of himself. If there was ever a time for him to assert his position as the architect of the town's success, it was now.

"I'll donate Lesser Potions of Purification to the town, for free," Theo said.

"Ah, yes. I can smell the catch in your words," Miana said, groaning.

"I'm not content with my mercantile seat," Theo said.

"What are you doing?" Tresk asked. She cast him a concerned look, even if the words were between them.

"Trust me."

"You want to be the mayor?" Miana said, scoffing.

"Not yet," Theo said. "I want a position in the town that affords me decision-making ability without the need to run the politics."

"Maybe 'Lord Administrator'?" Luras asked, shrugging.

"This isn't Qavell," Miana growled, "or Rivers and Daub, or Farstretch, or any of those other haughty cities. We're a tiny town in the middle of nowhere—I can't afford your services."

"I see what you're doing," Tresk said. *"You want to determine the town's growth, like the walls. Miana could pick some stupid option in the upgrade menu. Lord Administrator is your best bet, she can give you that title."*

"Give us a year," Theo said, spurred on by his companion's words. "We'll overshadow any other town in the south. Have you seen how many cores we've already added to Broken Tusk?"

"I have," Miana said.

"I don't want a salary. I don't need a salary," Theo said. "Broken Tusk's development, the way it's shaped, is the only thing I want control over."

Miana pressed her fingers into her temples and groaned. "Gods, you're so annoying. Technically, you're already Lord Theo Spencer based on your holdings."

"He's what?" Tresk blurted out.

"Everyone who holds core property in the city has the 'Lordship' title, even if it's meaningless in a small town like this," Miana said. "Fine. So, you're dangling the potions over my head so you can have sole control over the town's upgrade system. Seems like an ultimatum to me."

"No, it's a functional relationship between the two of us," Theo said. "How much tax does Broken Tusk owe this year?"

"Five silver, and we're four short. Again," Miana said.

The spiky edges of her personality were softening. Theo didn't know if it was his annoying persistence wearing her down, or that glimmer of hope he was offering. He summoned his inventory screen and withdrew five silver, slapping the sum down on the table with a wide grin. Her eyes went wide.

"Here's the agreement. I'll cover the difference in taxes from here on out. The Newt and Demon will provide provisional potions for the town for free. You make me the Lord Administrator of Broken Tusk," Theo said.

"Very impressive." Tresk smiled while looking at her Tara'hek. *"We'll tie ourselves directly to the success of Broken Tusk. It's bold. I approve."*

Miana sat there for some time, staring down at the silver with hungry eyes. The taxes that Theo paid to the kingdom were minimal, but it was still a gamble.

"How many potions can you provide for the current epidemic?" Miana asked.

A broad grin spread across the alchemist's face. "We can spare 100 potions."

Miana's mouth fell open, and she stared at Theo for a moment. "You've got me against a wall here. How am I supposed to decline?"

"Take the deal, Miana," Luras said, his voice growling from behind. "Before he comes to his senses."

"Done," Miana said, reaching out her hand for Theo to shake. Her expression went blank for a moment before a notification appeared in the alchemist's vision.

Miana Kell has granted you a title in **[Small Town]**

Broken Tusk. You are now the **[Lord Administrator]**.

[Lord Administrator Theo Spencer]
The responsibilities of the Lord Administrator relate to the design, planning, and advancement of the core settlement. This specialized role has been customized by Miana Kell to include covering taxes lost because of the delinquency of the town's members. The Lord Administrator of Broken Tusk handles all upgrade slots for Broken Tusk.

Miana designated a place for Theo to bring the potions, but she didn't expect him to produce them from his inventory immediately, causing her to sputter in surprise. The thought of hoarding all the Lesser Potions of Purification didn't sit well with him, and the allure of making more with his new Flame Artifices was strong. The alchemist left with Tresk and Luras, finding themselves standing in the muddy square with stupid grins on their faces.

"Bold move, Theo," Luras said. "You gave her the one thing she needs more than anything. Coin."

"This way we don't have to worry about her picking something stupid for the Level 5 upgrade," Tresk said, bouncing on the spot. "The potions you gave her will be put to good use. A half-ogre adventurer got bit on our outing today; he's resting in Miana's house."

"So she exaggerated that it was an epidemic," Theo said, scoffing.

"That's just how she is," Luras said.

Theo didn't know if forcing himself into the position was the right thing to do. If being thrust into this new world taught him anything, it was the value of seizing every opportunity. He was on sure footing now that he had made his first big sale, and the merchant was going to place a big order. Someone who threw that amount of silver around wouldn't be looking for anything small.

Fenian would place an order for an absurd number of potions, pushing the lab's production capacity to its limits.

The alchemist pushed down a feeling of guilt that came from a sense of greed. He had never been one to desire power, but that was what he needed. This was a first step for him—a step toward a direction he didn't know if he wanted. Miana didn't want the mayor's seat. How long would she hold on to it out of a sense of duty? No, she would relinquish the seat when she was rendered obsolete—that was the source of his guilt. Mayor Theo was inevitable, but that didn't stop the pang in his chest. With what he had accomplished so far, it was a simple thing to push aside.

Adapt and move forward.

The companions stood in the square for a while, watching as people passed by. The alchemist was left with his thoughts, mostly centered on strategizing a large-scale order. He regretted not asking for dimensional storage items while Fenian was in the shop, but the excitement had been too much at that moment. He would need money for more storage, and more potions for that money. The bottleneck in his operation was the gathering of herbs. While it was incredibly important to level his herbalism core, he considered hiring outside help.

Tresk picked up on his wandering thoughts, staring a hole through him with her inquisitive gaze. "What's the plan?"

"I need reagents," Theo said, nodding to himself. "Spiny Swamp Thistle Roots, Moss Nettles, and Manashrooms. Lots of them."

"Hire some laborers," Luras grunted. "You're rich now."

"Not a bad idea," Tresk said. "I bet Perg would hire her tannery staff out."

Theo nodded. The tannery workers were already familiar with gathering the Ogre Cypress Bark and would take to the other ingredients easily. "All right. I'm going to go pay her a visit."

"Sounds like a plan," Tresk said, smiling.

Theo's companions accompanied him as far as the shop before waving him off. The town seemed to be more active than normal, even in the southern section. The foul stench that made the tannery so characteristic of that part of Broken Tusk was completely gone. A hard breeze drove from the south, washing over the alchemist with only the scent of the swamp. It wasn't an entirely pleasant smell, but it was better than rotting hides. Perg wasn't standing in her normal spot, and Theo began searching. The warehouse was devoid of leather and the woman, but he finally found her in the yard where the hides normally sat.

"Perg," Theo said, waving.

She turned around suddenly, a wistful smile playing across her face. "Two hundred hides, Theo. That elven trader bought all 200 of our hides for 40 copper apiece. I've never seen this much silver."

Theo fully rounded the corner, spotting what she was talking about. A bucket sat on the ground, mostly filled with silver coins. He remembered the amount of leather that sat piled high in the now-empty warehouse. Perg said it was a year's worth of work she planned to sell. By his estimation, it was significantly over double what she would normally work in a year. Since the adventurers were slaying wolves by the score, she had been buying up all their hides. The tannery's small processing area only allowed them to treat a small number of leathers at a time.

"You're rich," Theo said.

Perg shook her head, digging eight silver coins out of the bucket. "And this is your cut."

Theo took it. The thought of refusing never crossed his mind. This was the cycle of money he wanted to create. The constant push and pull against investment and profit that would make everyone in Broken Tusk rich. Perg would have significantly more than just 200 hides ready to go the next time the merchant stopped by. She wasn't someone who rested while the good times came around. She would push harder to make even more money.

"I appreciate it. This gives you the head seat of the mercantile chairs," Theo said.

"Does that offend you?" Perg said, flashing a devious grin.

"Not at all," Theo said, waving a haughty hand and smiling.

"I've taken a higher position in the town's leadership. You'll refer to me as 'Your Gracious Lord Administrator' from here on out."

Perg burst out laughing, slapping her knees and wheezing before gaining control of herself. "Oh, I can think of a few names I'd like to call you. You must've conned Miana to get the title."

"Basically," Theo said, shrugging. "Congratulations on the riches. Now, I'd like to rent your laborers."

"They're yours," Perg said. "How many do you need?"

Theo didn't think she'd be so quick to offer her people's services to him. He didn't know how many laborers he needed to accomplish his goals. Perhaps five would do the job. "Five," Theo said after a moment. "To collect reagents, of course."

"Done," Perg said, withdrawing a notebook from her satchel and writing something down. "What are they going to collect?"

Theo detailed the reagents and where to find them. Perg dutifully scrawled on the pages, nodding as the alchemist gave more detail. Her brow knitted tight when he described the Manashrooms, but shrugged shortly after. He was glad to see that other people hated the vile insectoid creatures in the cave as much as he did.

"They're hard workers, and they're getting good at harvesting your ingredients," Perg said. "Speaking of, I'll need another run of your potions in a week."

"No problem," Theo said. "I assume they'll start collecting tomorrow?"

"They will," Perg said, nodding.

"All right. I'll see you around. Take it easy," Theo said, turning on the spot and waving.

"You too."

Theo returned to the shop to find the sign flipped to "Open". When he opened the door, Tresk was standing behind the counter, beaming at him. "Welcome to the Newt and Demon! Can I interest you in our potions?"

The alchemist leaned against the counter and laughed. "Giving up the life of adventure to run our shop?"

Tresk scoffed. "Just filling in for my Tara'hek while he runs off doing alchemist stuff."

"Sounds like a cool demon to me," Theo said.

"He's an idiot. But he's my idiot," Tresk said.

Theo shook his head, coming behind the counter to look at their plundered stock. He applied some Cleansing Scrub to himself before he got too far, dropping a few drops on the ground to scour the mud away. The afternoon was fading quickly, his stamina bar drained along with it. It was too late to go out and pick herbs, but too early to go to bed.

"Want to go sit in our fancy new chairs?" Theo asked.

Tresk nodded, bounding behind him up the stairs and into the lab. They left the door unlocked for when Luras inevitably came by to steal their soup. The pair took a seat in their fancy new chairs and let out a synchronized sigh, letting the silence between them grow. It had been a busy day, and Theo was feeling it in his bones. The excitement left him feeling drained, unable to strategize for the day to come.

"Let's see your new magical fire," Tresk said.

Theo retrieved one of the Flame Artifices and set it down on the table. He inserted an Earth Mote into the side and stood back, but nothing happened. The dial on the side was set as far left as it would go. He turned it clockwise, gaining a faint click for his efforts. A small flame danced from the center of the mechanism. He clicked it again, and the flame grew larger. When the dial was set to the highest setting, it raged from the artifice, threatening to burn the roof of their lab.

"Better not use that setting," Theo said, clicking it to the lowest setting and sitting with his companion.

They watched the flame for a while before they got hungry. Theo produced the hot cauldron of soup from his inventory and dished out a bowl for each of them. Tresk would turn her head toward the door occasionally, waiting for Luras to show up. The fourth time she did so was in response to the tinkling of the bell downstairs. Sure enough, the half-ogre came into the room with a sheepish grin.

"I smelled the food," Luras said, shrugging.

Theo gestured for the man to take a seat and chuckled. "I have a question. Are you just sitting outside, waiting for me to get the soup prepared?"

"I was passing by," Luras said.

"Uh-huh." Tresk mocked the half-ogre's poor excuse.

The group ate their traditional meal together, talking about the events of the day and enjoying each other's company. Theo was craving bread with the soup, but he wouldn't complain. On Earth, he was eating the same army rations every day, which was more than a lot of the citizens were getting. Mass starvation was a distant memory by now. This new world had plenty to give, he just had to take it. The alchemist let these thoughts wash out of his mind, enjoying the soup too much to entertain the desolation of his home planet. He didn't even know if the planet he was on was in the same universe, and he didn't care.

Luras excused himself after finishing his soup. Neither Tresk nor Theo would wait for dusk to come before heading to bed. They locked up the shop, turned off the artifice, and settled down in the bedroom.

"Now that we're rich, I'm going to buy you a bed," Theo said.

"That'd be nice."

Sleep came quickly that night. Earth was a distant memory, and Broken Tusk was his home. He wouldn't have it any other way.

Chapter 23
Fenian's Request

The morning came early for Theo. Darkness still blanketed Broken Tusk, the depth of the gloom telling him it was well before dawn. Tresk snored away on the far end of the room, and he left her to her dreams. The alchemist spent those early hours reviewing his notes and making new ones in the margins of his books. He was already beyond anything they could teach him, but he grasped at their words, looking for hidden things that he might have overlooked. Frustrating hours passed by with no hint as to what lay beyond the base-level distillation. The irritation he felt vanished when he considered the endless possibilities of experimentation.

Tresk rose as dawn drew closer, bounding from the bedroom with an excitement Theo couldn't help but match. The day that sat before them was filled with excitement, not just because of his Lord Administrator title, but the return of the merchant. Fenian was more honest than the image Theo had in his mind of a traveling merchant. It was a relationship of convenience, he realized, but the elf's coin spoke volumes.

Theo removed the pot of soup from his inventory, serving out the last scoops into two bowls before placing the kettle on the Flame Artifice. He cranked it to the lowest setting and stared as the small flame danced to life. A smile spread across his face as he dug into his soup, no longer needing to tend the wood fire.

"I'll never get over that," Tresk said, giggling.

"My thoughts, exactly. No more smoke in my eyes," Theo said. "You're training the adventurers again, right?"

"Luras thinks they'll be ready after today," Tresk said. "I should hit Level 10, and then we're going to attempt the dungeon."

Theo felt his heart jump in his chest. To venture into the swamp was one thing, but delving into the dungeon was another. He let out a heavy sigh, steadying himself before responding. "You're going to need more potions."

Tresk took a mouthful of her soup before talking, gnashing her teeth noisily as she spoke. "We'll be fine. The first floors are easy."

"If you say so," Theo said, nodding. "I need to ask Fenian if he has dimensional bags for the shop."

The alchemist had a few crates of reagents that needed to be thrown out. Some of his early collections were rotting in the corners of the lab, unable to hold out without the stasis of his inventory. He didn't lament their loss but wanted to prevent it from happening again. Fenian would demand an absurd number of potions when he stopped by today. Space would become a premium within the lab.

The pair sat there, drinking their tea and eating their food. They talked about the town, and how he could leverage his new title for its betterment. The only authority he had was regarding the upgrade system, but the northern mine was looking more reasonable. He was certain that the new title gave him the right to strike a claim for the city, hire laborers, and excavate the stones required to pave the muddy streets. The sensation of mud in his moccasins was still unnerving.

A knock came from the front before dawn. Theo lit the candles downstairs, opening it to find a fresh-faced Azrug beaming from the early morning gloom.

"You're early," Theo said.

"I was too excited," Azrug said, dancing in place. "Barely slept."

"We're having tea upstairs, if you're interested."

The boy followed Theo upstairs, finding a chair next to Tresk and taking a cup of the Moss Nettle tea. Theo seemed at home among people from Broken Tusk. Even if the alchemist wasn't truly from here, the citizens considered him one of their own.

"We're getting walls, soon," Azrug said, nodding to himself. He sipped gingerly on the tea, making a sour face every time. "Someone saw a wolf in town last night."

Tresk set her tea down and knitted her brow. "Seriously?"

Azrug nodded vigorously. "Xam told me about it. A mean-looking marsh wolf just trotting down the main road. An adventurer drove it off, but it got away."

"That's incredibly dangerous, Theo. Don't tell Azrug, but that's a sign of a monster that's been out of the dungeon too long. It lost its fear of people," Tresk said, keeping the words from Azrug.

Theo cupped his chin in his hand, weighing his options. The only solution he saw was to get the walls up sooner. If they couldn't do that, he'd stretch his authority to create a militia. He put his thoughts into words, saying, "Broken Tusk doesn't have any guards, does it?"

"None," Azrug blurted. "No night watch, no militia, no irregular army—nothing."

"That has to change," Theo said.

The group fell into a somber silence as the alchemist went back into his thoughts. Broken Tusk had too many problems to fix them all at once. It was easy for him to solve an issue that was directly related to alchemy, such as the water or the tannery. But solving a logistical problem related to the defense of a small town, cut off from greater civilization, was another. He thought back to the media he consumed back on Earth, and the depictions of medieval towns. There always seemed to be a night watch, patrolling the streets after hours, but standing in a *real* medieval town was another story. The guards would need wages, lodging, and a command structure.

"Broken Tusk doesn't have military people. That's the problem," Tresk said with a shrug.

Theo tilted his head. That wasn't entirely true. He recalled Aarok, the new adventurer who had come to buy potions from his shop a few days earlier. He was well-prepared and claimed to have had some experience training for the Qavelli Irregulars, whatever that was. A plan was forming in his head, but it needed time to stew.

They let those thoughts fade away in favor of Azrug's hopes. He was excited to get a job out of the fields. The boy had imagined himself working the land for the rest of his life, never able to realize his dreams, although he admitted that no grand schemes had formed in his head yet. Breakfast soon ended, dawn breaking outside, and the boy took up his station downstairs. Tresk departed soon after, pressing her forehead against Theo's before she left.

The alchemist joined Azrug downstairs, not willing to start any projects before Fenian delivered his demands. He wanted to pick the boy's brain about the former Qavelli trainee.

"Have you met Aarok?" Theo asked, leaning against the counter.

"Now that's a question. He's worked the fields with the other laborers before. Silent guy," Azrug said, kicking his feet up on the counter and reclining. "Why?"

"Did he ever talk about his days as a soldier?"

"You'll have to ask Luras about that," Azrug said. "I like a bit of gossip as much as the next person in Broken Tusk, but he's silent—like I said."

Theo sighed. "If we want a town guard, we need soldiers."

"Oh. I'm finally picking up on the annoyingly vague way you're speaking," Azrug said. "That's an expensive venture, I think."

"Five full-time guards, maybe. Two copper a day in wages," Theo said. "We'd bleed nearly a silver a week just in defense."

"I mean, why not just get volunteers?"

"Volunteers would work as hard as volunteers work," Theo said. "When you're young, you can ask your friends to help you move for pizza and beer. But when you get older, you're better off hiring a moving company."

"I understood half of that," Azrug said.

"People in Broken Tusk are poor. Safety is one thing, but they deserve a wage," Theo said.

Azrug shrugged, pulling the book from his satchel. He was only a few words in when the bell on the door rang, the elf merchant stepping in with a wide grin on his face. "Good morning."

Azrug's face flushed, and he quickly pulled his feet off of the counter, stowing his book away and standing at attention. "Good morning, sir."

"How is your stay in our town?" Theo asked.

Fenian managed a weak smile. "What did you call this place? A mud pit. Yes, it's like staying in a mud pit."

"I'm working on the mud problem," Theo said.

"Lord Administrator. Yes, I've heard the rumors at the tavern," Fenian said, chuckling. "You're destined for great things."

Theo didn't know if he was being sarcastic, and he didn't care. "Before we get to business, I have a few items I'd like."

"I won't refuse a sale."

"I need a placeable dimensional storage container, something like—" Theo said, cut off as Fenian produced an item from his inventory.

"Like a dimensional storage crate," Fenian said. He smiled, holding a wooden crate in his left hand. "A hundred slots. Here's the catch. Once you place an item inside the crate, it cannot be moved or added to your inventory. Ah, the quirks of the system."

"How much?" Theo asked.

Fenian smiled. "I love the people in Broken Tusk. There's no dancing around the trees with you folks. Right to the point. In Qavell, I'd get 10 silver for this, but you can have it for 5."

"Why would you take a loss?" Azrug asked, blurting the words out.

"If you're interested in how the art of trade works, young half-ogre, I'll be happy to instruct you."

Azrug froze under the man's gaze. Theo stepped in. "The boy is eager to learn. Please do instruct him."

"I won't take a loss on this item. If the alchemist buys it for 5 silver, I'll still make a silver. That doesn't make it worth the trip this far south, but it does something else entirely. Do you know what that is?" Fenian asked.

Azrug got over his shyness, the eagerness to learn about trading burning bright in his eyes. "To establish a relationship. Theo is a new, untapped market, and you want to exploit it. You want him to remember that you were generous so that he'll work with you."

"He's a natural," Fenian said. "Do you have your cores yet, boy?"

"Not yet," Azrug said, shuffling his feet.

"Hold me to my word on this, but you'll make an excellent trader when the day comes," Fenian said. "I'll turn a massive profit on the potions I bought from the alchemist, a fact he knows, and giving him a break on smaller items does indeed establish a better relationship. Here's a tip for you, young Azrug. Never give your items away for free. You'll be tempted to think that you're sweetening your clients up, but it does the opposite. They'll think you're cheap. They'll think your merchandise is not worth paying for, and you'll lose your reputation."

Theo didn't know what he thought about being used as an example in this exchange. If it helped Azrug achieve his dreams, then he was all right with it. The boy had a way with people, and he had a feeling that Fenian was a bigger deal back north than he let on. Free advice from a master trader was something he couldn't deprive the boy of.

"Understood, sir," Azrug said, nodding. He knitted his brow, distilling the information that Fenian gave down to a concise point and regurgitating it. "Set expectations with clients for the future and deliver."

"That's a good lad," Fenian said. "You have a mind for this kind of work."

Theo produced five silver pieces and placed them on the counter. He couldn't help but laugh at the merchant's directness. "Sold."

Fenian placed the crate on the counter and scooped up the coins. "Now, are you ready for my order? Do you need some parchment?"

Theo tapped his temple with his finger. "It goes right up here. No worries."

"High Wisdom and all that... Of course. I need to return to Qavell to secure funds for this transaction, but I'll need the following from you in a week's time. Five hundred of each of the lesser restoration potions at 20 copper apiece," Fenian said, grinning. "Do you need to sit down? No? Can you produce attribute-enhancing potions?"

Theo needed to sit down. He swayed on the spot for a moment, trying to process the absurd number of potions the elf already wanted. And he wanted more. "I've made Lesser Vigor Potions."

"Do you have a sample?" Fenian asked.

Theo still had three of the potions in his inventory. He produced one and handed it over to the trader. Fenian rolled the potion over in his hands, humming for a moment before returning it to the alchemist. "As I've said before, you're a gem. A bonus of 5 Vigor for an hour is absurd for low-level people. Those who are rich enough to afford this kind of potion give it to their kids to train their combat cores. The ingredients are absurdly hard to find in the north, but I'm guessing..."

"The swamp provides," Theo said, managing a weak smile.

"This one is a tall order, so I'll only ask for 50 for each attribute —or whatever you can manage in the time I've allotted; 50 copper each," Fenian said. "How does that—Oh my, look at that. It generated a quest."

[Fenian's Request]
Quest
Fenian Feintleaf has requested that you produce the following for an order.
Objectives:
500x [Lesser Healing Potion]
500x [Lesser Stamina Potion]
500x [Lesser Mana Potion]
50x [Lesser Strength Potion] **(Optional)**
50x [Lesser Dexterity Potion] **(Optional)**
50x [Lesser Vigor Potion] **(Optional)**
50x [Lesser Intelligence Potion] **(Optional)**
50x [Lesser Wisdom Potion] **(Optional)**
Time Remaining:
7 days
Reward:
Random Epic Alchemist Tool

"You really are blessed," Fenian said, laughing. "I think I need to revise my theory about your gift... It's much more potent than I thought before."

"We'll do it," Theo said, nodding. "A week is plenty of time and that's... That's a lot of money. I do have a request, though."

"Oh? Let's hear it, then."

"Coin is fine for the restoration potions, but I'd like to be paid in monster cores for the attribute potions," Theo said.

"I can do that," Fenian said, reaching out to shake Theo's hand. It was a symbolic gesture, seeing as the system already made him accept the quest. "I'll bring my stock of Level 30 monster cores when I return. We can also do coin if you change your mind."

"Honestly, Fenian," Theo said, letting out a heavy sigh. "I don't want to sound weird, but you've been a huge blessing to my shop."

Fenian smiled, shrugging. "Think of it as the start of a very profitable relationship. I'm headed north now. I'll return in a week."

Fenian bowed before turning on the spot and leaving the shop. Azrug was counting on his fingers, muttering to himself. "Boss. That's 3 gold for just the restoration potions." His face flushed.

"We'll need it," Theo said. "This town is going to get very expensive."

The shock of the massive order left Azrug unable to celebrate. He sat back down in his chair, releasing a heavy sigh. Theo left him there, marching upstairs to deposit his new storage item. He placed the Large Dimensional Crate in the room's corner, snatching up the junk and stowing it away. The crate had an inventory screen like his inventory system. He could even transfer items directly into the crate from his inventory. The top of the wooden crate was just a black void. When he went to reach inside, the screen simply popped up.

"Care for an errand?" Theo said, emerging into the shop.

Azrug was still in shock. "I could use the air."

Theo gave him twenty copper coins to retrieve a bed from the carpenter. As the boy left, the alchemist remembered he didn't ask the trader about rogue cores for Tresk. It seemed like she was a back-burner item for him, something that made him sick to his stomach. She was happy with their arrangement, but he wanted to see her become someone great. His goal was to become the best distillation expert in the world, and the marshling would walk the path to greatness alongside him.

The alchemist left the front door unlocked, finding his way to the lab and casting his gaze over it. While it was a temporary fix, the clutter was gone. Fifty of the crate's slots were now occupied thanks to the random garbage that sat around his lab, but it wasn't out in the open. He rearranged the tables, shoving his weight against them to create a line of two tables near the stills, and a block of tables in the center of the lab. The table that he had pushed against the window earlier stayed there, and he moved the four chairs around it. He would much prefer looking out the window while he took his meals.

The gentle tinkle of the bell downstairs drifted through the lab.

Newt and Demon

When Theo went to see if it was a customer, he found a burly half-ogre scratching his head at the threshold. "It won't fit."

"Allow me," Theo said, pressing his hand against the bed. It vanished into his inventory.

The man shrugged, turning and leaving. Azrug came in after, laughing. "I used all your coin to hire that man and get the bed. They said it was the softest they had—goose feathers or something."

"Thank you, Azrug," Theo said, smiling. "Man the shop, I'm going to rearrange my bedroom."

Azrug plopped into his seat, pulling his book out as Theo went back upstairs. He rolled the bedroll up and set it in the corner, pulling the new bed from his inventory and arranging it in the room. There was enough space for them to sleep foot-to-foot with a wide walkway in between. Upon laying on the bed, he found it to be incredibly soft. Compared to his straw-stuffed mattress, this was a luxury. He popped his head downstairs and smiled at his shopkeeper.

"Go buy another one," Theo said, throwing twenty more copper coins with an underhand toss. They clattered on the ground.

Azrug groaned, rising to his feet and disappearing out the door again. Theo would have felt bad, but the business was slow, and he wanted a bed for himself. He returned upstairs while he waited for the boy to return, lying on Tresk's bed and letting out a heavy sigh. He accepted the straw bed as a fact of life, something that was standard in Broken Tusk. If someone had told him there were decent beds in this town, he would have snatched one up. The bell rang downstairs, and the annoyed half-ogre stared inside and waited for Theo to add the bed to his inventory.

"Thank you," Theo said, chuckling.

The alchemist swapped the straw bed for his fancy bed and smiled at the scene. When he returned downstairs, Azrug groaned. "Do you need a third bed for some weird reason?"

"No, I'm off to pay my laborers," Theo said. "Watch the shop."

Chapter 24
Third-Best Adventurer

Theo left the Newt and Demon before midday, feeling as though dusk was around the corner. His deal with Fenian took a toll on him, even if the news was good. He successfully predicted what the merchant wanted, not that it was a difficult thing to guess. The restoration potions he made were extremely useful and often the difference between life and death for adventurers. He mentally informed Tresk of the deal he made, and she screamed into his mind with excitement.

"*Three gold? Are you kidding me?*" Tresk said. Her words came labored, as though she were exerting herself at that moment.

"*And monster cores for the attribute potions,*" Theo reminded her. "*It's a lot of work, but obviously worth it.*"

"*No kidding. Now you just need to collect a whole lot of stuff,*" Tresk said. Theo wasn't happy that she could laugh into his mind while using Tara'hek Communication.

"*Stay safe out there,*" Theo said.

"*Of course.*"

Instead of taking the road directly south, he headed toward the river. Theo harvested Spiny Swamp Thistle Root along his ambling path, eager to take advantage of the early hour of the day.

It was unlikely that Perg's laborers were back from their task, but he wanted to instruct them to bring it to the lab. The Spiny Swamp Thistle he harvested the other day had returned. The alchemist didn't understand what made the precious plant grow, and he didn't care. It was an endless supply of reagents provided by the swamp.

Theo arrived at the river, clearing every plant he found along the way. He inspected the flora he had seen before but found it to be common weeds and other plants. The goal wasn't to fill his entire 500-unit requirement for the Lesser Healing Potions, but to get more experience in his Drogramath Herbalist Core. It was at 15% of Level 6, whereas his alchemy core was ready to level to 7. The obvious imbalance in the way he hired others to harvest his ingredients was showing, and he made a mental note to make more of these trips. The prize for his trouble was a thick patch of Widow Lily near the river. He carefully harvested the poisonous flowers and stowed them away in his inventory, not willing to risk exposing himself to the deadly things.

When he finally looped around to the tannery, Perg was standing around the back, where the hides used to start their journey. She dug into her satchel and produced a fist-sized object that looked like a giant seed. "Guess who spent their life savings?"

Theo inspected the object, knitting his brow.

[Tannery Building Core]
[Building Core]
A seed-shaped core that can be planted in the ground. When fed monster cores, this building will grow into an upgradeable tannery. When using a building core inside a core town, permission from the king, governor, mayor, or appropriate functionary is required.

"Fenian had a building core?" Theo asked. "I don't even know how you get these."

"Dungeons," Perg said. "He stopped by before leaving town. We're going to demolish this tannery and replace it with a core building."

"That's amazing," Theo said, shaking his head. "The upgrades for my lab were great."

"That's what I'm hoping for," Perg said. "Seeing as you're the Lord Administrator, I have to ask for your approval."

"You have it," Theo said without hesitation.

The alchemist had thought about replacing all the buildings in town with core buildings, but it was the last item on his long list of tasks. Planting the seeds of core buildings would cause growing pains, but it would be worth it in the long run. From his small sample size, he saw the power they had. Upon giving Perg his mental acceptance for the building, he felt something tingle inside him. He assumed it was the system giving her permission.

"I sent the laborers out this morning," Perg said. "They'll be back sometime mid-afternoon."

"Perfect," Theo said. "Have them stop by the shop when they return."

"Works for me," Perg said.

Theo swept his gaze over the tannery. When he first saw the building, it was revolting. The smell alone was enough to mark it in his mind as a place worth demolishing. Now that it operated with alchemy and the smell was gone, he would miss it. The building that would go up in its place would be better in every way, but that week-old nostalgia returned. He settled the matter in his mind with the conclusion that if Perg was the one running the tannery, he would be happy.

"Hey, want to come to the shop for dinner tonight?" Theo asked. "And do you have any idea where we can get some bread?"

A smile spread across Perg's face. "I can bring some bread. The farmers mill the Zee Kernel down to a grain and bake it into bread."

"Sounds like cornbread," Theo said, nodding.

"What's corn?"

"Corn is like small Zee. It grows a lot like Zee, but the fruit of the plant is tiny," Theo said, gesturing with his fingers to approximate the size of a corn kernel.

"That's really weird," Perg said. "I'd be happy to come. Who else is going to be there?"

"Well, if I crack my window as I'm making the soup, Luras shows up," Theo said. "So, me, Tresk, Luras, and you."

"Sounds like a party," Perg said.

"Hey, it's free soup. My soup is a lot better than Xam's," Theo said.

"Don't let Xam ever hear you say that," Perg said, looking over her shoulder. "She thinks that perpetual stew is the best thing in the realm."

Theo scrunched up his nose. If the mystery meat didn't put someone off the soup, the bland flavor would. At a copper per bowl of soup, it was also robbery. The alchemist bid farewell to Perg and made his way back to the shop. Azrug didn't even glance up from his book when he entered, simply waving and issuing a grunt. With his new Custom Copper Stills, Theo could make massive runs of potions. A full load in either would produce enough essence for 200 potions, the reaction for base-level potions being a one-to-one mix of Purified Water and essence, resulting in a two-unit solution.

With everything cleared away, Theo judged the amount of Spiny Swamp Thistle Root by eye. It was enough to make forty units of essence, resulting in forty Lesser Healing Potions. His goal was to create healing potions to sell to locals, as the shop downstairs was mostly barren. The alchemist processed the roots he harvested, cutting them into manageable sizes before mashing them. After dumping them into a still, he rubbed his hands together. The excitement for the new Flame Artifices was too much, and he wanted to get started. He leveled the still off with Purified Water, clamped the lid shut, and placed the small disc underneath.

Theo retrieved a piece of parchment from his inventory, the one that contained the bulk of his notes, and drew a table documenting the inputs, outputs, and heat level for this run. As with most things in alchemy, he started at the lowest setting on the artifice. The flame licked the bottom of the copper still, barely reaching it. He nodded to himself and took a seat.

"I'm thinking of writing a book," Theo said to Tresk.

"On alchemy?" she asked.

"All the basics of distillation from a Drogramath Dronon's perspective," Theo said.

"Your handwriting looks like a child's."

"There has to be a writing artifice for this very reason," Theo said. "For now, I'm taking notes."

"We're wrapping up out here. More cores for the town," Tresk said.

"Perfect. Perg is coming over for soup tonight," Theo said.

"Sounds fun."

Theo ended the conversation there. He knew Tresk was nice about it, but she was usually fighting monsters out there. The condenser started its slow drip into a flask. Even when he used the smallest flame possible with actual fire, there was a lot of sputtering in this phase. The unchanging flame of the artifice heated the still evenly, creating a smooth extraction. The alchemist made a note of it on his parchment, underlining the need for an artifice in distillation. He made a short list of his recipes so far, detailing the brewing process and the exact quantities. This was especially useful for the tannery materials, as fractions of a unit in error caused explosive consequences.

The artifice issued a faint click, and the flame disappeared. Theo inspected his flask of essence, surprised at the upgrade in quality.

[Healing Essence]
[Essence]
Common
Created by: Belgar
Quality: Excellent

40 units (liquid)
Concentrated essence of healing, used to create healing potions.

A wide grin painted his face as he stared at the rose-hued liquid. It wasn't perfect, but the flame bumped up the quality of the extraction process. He prepared to set off a large reaction, finding one of his ridiculously sized flasks and hoisting it onto the table. It slipped halfway, slamming against the side of the table with a resounding gong. To his surprise, the glass didn't show any cracks. Theo wondered if the glass couldn't break and realized that he hadn't bothered to test it yet. He scooped up an unused vial and stomped on it without leaving a mark. His low Strength attribute might have something to do with the glass's amazing durability. He would need to ask Tresk to step on some glass later.

Azrug poked his head up the stairs, waving at Theo. "I'm heading out for the day, boss."

Theo retrieved two copper coins from his inventory and tossed them to the boy. He caught the money in the air and ran down the stairs without another word. The alchemist turned his attention back to the synthesizing process. It was the easiest reaction he knew, and he kicked off the eighty-unit recipe without a problem. He propped the window, wafting the smoke outside and inspecting his new creation.

[Lesser Healing Potion]
[Potion]
Common
Created by: Belgar
Quality: Excellent
A lesser healing potion. Drink to restore health.
Effect:
Instantly restores 35 health points.

The increase in quality resulted in restoring an additional 5 health. It wasn't the biggest jump in power, but the effort involved was minimal. Keeping the fire at a certain temperature was an arduous task. His new method was not only easier, but it also made better potions. His intuition had told him that the catalyst for the reactions should influence their quality, but that wasn't the case, according to his observations. He made a note of his findings on the parchment and let his thoughts take natural paths to the reason. It was likely because these were Level 1 potions, still branded with the "lesser" tag. There was no information in his books on how to produce more potent potions.

Theo worked the Glassware Artifice to produce forty flat-bottomed vials. He was curious about his new distribution method and the effects it had on the stability of the potions. The alchemist measured out a unit of the potion and placed it in a vial. He waited for a moment, swirling the liquid around until it exploded in his hand. Black smoke rose from the top of the vial with force, getting ripped from his hand and slamming against the floor. He confirmed the vials were mostly indestructible and that an odd quantity of a potion's solution had a violent reaction when left alone.

The system allowed for a reaction to happen in a large vessel before being transferred, which sped up bottling, but it didn't appreciate it if he tried to cheat it by splitting the potion into strange quantities. He quickly scooped a unit from the flask and tossed it out the window to avoid his entire eighty-unit solution from exploding in the lab. With the crisis averted, he filled the remaining vials with the potion, ending up with thirty-nine Lesser Healing Potions of excellent quality.

Theo stuffed the potions in his inventory, bringing along his parchment, and headed down to the shop. He placed the items on the shelf and took more notes, categorizing them as theories instead of facts. The Drogramath Alchemy Core was his prime suspect as to the strange way he could make large potion reactions, but it was just an idea. He long suspected that his legendary core granted him more effects than it let on. The hours of the day passed by as he sat at the front counter, and the shop spent the day devoid of customers.

Perg's laborers arrived in the afternoon. There were five of the half-ogres as she had promised, each with a heavy satchel at their side. Theo greeted them and beckoned them upstairs to offload their items directly into the Large Dimensional Crate. The first thing that surprised him was that they had harvested Manashrooms. Next was exactly how much of each reagent they had harvested. Without herbalism cores, they gathered 200 Spiny Swamp Thistle Roots, 150 Moss Nettles, and 200 Manashrooms. At this pace, they would finish gathering everything he needed for his order in no time. He pulled back from the crate's inventory menu and gave them a surprised look.

"You guys don't mess around," Theo said.

"We've been collecting ingredients for the tannery for years," one said. "We don't have gathering cores, but we get by."

"Well, you've done a good job," Theo said, summoning his inventory screen. If he broke down what they gathered into how much he'd sell it for, they brought him at least one gold's worth of materials. It seemed like a jerk move to pay them standard laborer wages. He produced five copper coins for each of the laborers, distributing the twenty-five coins among them.

"We agreed to a coin for the labor, sir," the lead laborer said. "What's this for?"

"Money makes money," Theo said. "This is the rate you'll work at when you do dangerous work for me. I can't stand those insects in the Manashroom caves."

"I won't refuse the coin," a half-ogre at the back grunted. The others nodded their agreement.

"Two more days of this, and we'll have enough for my current order," Theo said. "As long as Perg is all right with you guys working for me."

"She's waiting to do a new batch of hides. Won't have work for us for a few days," the lead half-ogre said.

"What's your name?" Theo asked.

"Ziz Rotgut, sir," he said, looking sheepish. "It's a family name."

Theo looked him over for a moment. He didn't know if Ziz was a common name or not. If he had to guess, the man had combat or farming cores—perhaps even a specialized laborer core. He would have dumped all his points into Strength and Vigor. The perfect person to run his stone mine. "I have a proposition."

"Does it mean more coin?" Ziz asked.

"It always means more coin," Theo said, grinning. "We're not starting this project now—I need more coin before we do—but I want to start a stone mine to the north."

"Aye. The northern reaches near the Manashroom caves are granite," Ziz said.

"They're marble." Another half-ogre chimed in.

"I heard they're shale."

"Whatever they're made of, I want to establish a quarry," Theo said. "It would be a chance for you to fill the gap between doing labor work for Perg."

"Yeah, we can make that work, I have the Stonecutter's Core," Ziz said, "and we're all familiar with the process."

"Perfect," Theo said. "I don't have anything ready, but keep it in mind. When the tannery is slow, we can work the stone. I'm tired of the dirt roads in this place."

"Depends on the value of the stone, sir. Exporting might be worth your time," Ziz said.

"Perfect fallback plan. If the upgrades to the town give us paved roads, we can always sell the stone to some faraway cities," Theo said. "Fine. That's all for today. Thank you for your hard work."

The half-ogres bowed slightly, stomping out of the shop with wide grins on their faces. Greasing the wheels worked best in every world. It didn't matter if this wasn't Earth. People loved money. Theo decided against running the stills tonight; he locked the store and returned to the lab. He focused on reorganizing his notes before Tresk came home. Somewhere buried in those bits of information was the key to approaching the next level of alchemy. He just needed to find it. The bell jingled downstairs, signaling Tresk's arrival. He ran down the stairs to press his forehead against hers, their Tara'hek cores hitting Level 3.

"Long day," Tresk said, letting out a heavy sigh. "I hit Level 10 and got a new core slot."

Theo's eyes went wide. He didn't know she had been so close to getting Level 10. He forced his surprise away and smiled. "That's amazing!"

"I know," Tresk said, posing heroically. "Third best adventurer in Broken Tusk. I got a new skill and an empty core slot."

"Any idea what you're going to get?" Theo asked.

"No idea. I'm putting it off," Tresk said, striking a pose again.

"Come upstairs," Theo said. "I'll start the stew, and you can tell me about it."

The pair left the door unlocked and went up to the lab. Tresk appreciated the new layout and took a seat by the window. She produced more Swamp Onions and wolf parts for him to cook before recounting the day. Theo chopped the onions as she told him about their encounter with a goblin outside of the dungeon that roamed the swamp. The onions produced a pungent aroma that filled the room, sizzling away over a slick of wolf fat. He was stepping up his game tonight, removing the onions and setting them aside as he seared the wolf meat.

"We're seeing goblins on the surface, which means the first few levels of the dungeon are growing in power," Tresk said.

Theo prodded at the wolf meat, carefully flipping it over to avoid burning. "We need to rush the development of the town." The Flame Artifice was set to the middle setting, putting a nice sear on the bits of wolf meat quickly. He removed them from the hot cauldron after only a few moments, deglazing the bottom of the pot with water and adding the bones. He left it to simmer before returning to the conversation. "I had an idea for establishing a town guard, but I haven't thought of any specifics."

Tresk worked a knot out of her shoulders, rolling her neck and groaning. The bell downstairs tinkled, and two pairs of feet ascended to the lab. Luras and Perg waved, finding seats with the marshling near the window. "Let me guess, you smelled the soup?" Theo asked.

"Perg found me," Luras said.

"That smells so good," Perg said.

"About your town guard idea, Theo," Tresk said, nodding to the alchemist. "Not a horrible idea, but..."

"An adventurer's guild would be better," Luras said, finishing her thought. "That might be tricky, though."

"You'll have to explain the difference," Theo said, stirring the soup. Steam rose off the liquid, and he turned the dial up a notch on the Flame Artifice.

"There are a few problems, but basically, they give out quests. If we have an adventurer's guild, it'll take over the quest that Miana gave. The guild can still pay out wolf bounties from the royal fund," Tresk said.

"Rivers and Daub has an adventurer's guild," Luras said. "It started out as an unofficial branch but was incorporated later on. The problem Tresk mentioned is that we'd need someone to be the guild master. We can use the guild members to defend the town, though. Take that royal fund and use it on watch duty wages."

"That doesn't sound like a problem," Theo said. "That sounds like what we need."

"Well, there's paperwork... Right?" Perg asked.

"To become incorporated, yeah. They'd have a lot of rules that the guild master would have to follow," Luras said. "The good news is that Miana unknowingly gave you the authority to make an adventurer's guild in Broken Tusk."

The soup had been bubbling since the start of the conversation. Theo took a spoonful and tasted it. It needed more time for the flavor of the bones to really seep into the stew.

"If I can divert funds from the kingdom to pay people to stand watch, that sounds perfect," Theo said. "Less money out of my pocket."

Newt and Demon

"You should figure out how Miana is communicating with the crown," Luras said. "She gets information with magic."

Theo hadn't considered that fact before. As a core town on the outskirts of the kingdom, the mayor would need a way to easily send and receive information. In a world of magic, it made sense that she would have some kind of magic mirror, or something. He dismissed the thought for a later date, settling his mind on the problem at hand. An adventurer's guild sounded like what they needed, not just for the defense of the town. If there was some larger guild that managed all adventurers, it would make sense to have a branch in a place where they could check in.

"Adventurer's guild it is," Theo said. "Who wants to lead it?"

"Sure, sign me up," Perg said sarcastically.

"Don't look at me," Tresk said, holding her hands up defensively.

"I'm not opposed to the idea," Luras said.

"It's between Luras and Aarok," Theo said. "If you could talk it over with him tomorrow, that'd be helpful."

"Of course," Luras said.

Theo added the onions and wolf meat to the soup, dropping the heat and letting it simmer for a while. The conversation shifted away from business and back to the adventures happening outside the town. Luras was concerned about a goblin showing up, seeing it as a sign that the dungeon would level once again. The only good news concerned the adventurers. They were forming small parties of their own, easily contending with the wolves out in the swamp. The sun was getting low by the time the soup was ready.

"This is good," Tresk said, shoveling large hunks of wolf meat into her mouth.

Theo sampled his creation, satisfied with the depth of flavor. Searing the wolf meat and separating out the onions was the missing step. The stock was richer and the meat was more tender. The group ate until they couldn't anymore, saying their farewells for the night. Tresk and Theo locked the shop up, and the female marshling let out a shriek of joy when they entered the room.

"Is that one of those fancy goose feather beds?" she asked, yelling and jumping on the spot.

"It is," Theo said, climbing into his own. It was impossibly soft, and he could hardly maintain consciousness as Tresk shouted her thanks at him. She was saying something about him being the best Tara'hek in the realms when he fell asleep, absorbed by his impossibly comfortable bed.

Chapter 25
The Order of the Burning Eye

Tresk and Theo ate more of the leftover soup the next morning. They shared ideas on establishing the new adventurer's guild while slurping soup and sipping on steaming cups of tea. The alchemist wished Perg had held true to her promise to bring bread to their gathering, but the soup was extremely good. Tresk helped him clean his stills out to prepare for today's run of potions. Dried chunks of root stuck to the side of one, requiring intense scrubbing. It was an effortless task for his companion's superior Strength, and she made quick work of it.

"I'm going to come with you before the adventurers head out for the day," Theo said. "Assuming you gather before running off to murder monsters."

"We do," Tresk said, dumping the last of the water from the copper still. "They'll be excited to hear the news."

A knock came from the door downstairs. Theo went to answer it, letting his young shopkeeper inside. He barely said a word, assuming his traditional seat and kicking his feet up. The alchemist assessed the potions currently on display. His short run of Lesser Healing Potions would have to be enough for now, thirty-nine of them now sitting on the shelves. There was also a scattering of other potions, but his focus was on Fenian's job.

Tresk came downstairs, greeting Azrug and nudging Theo. "Ready?"

"I am," Theo said. "Hold down the fort, Azrug. I have to meet with the adventurers."

"Sounds good to me," Azrug said.

Theo and Tresk left the shop, making their way up the muddy road to find a gathering of townspeople. The alchemist didn't expect to see so many of them—at least twenty—preparing to head into the swamp. He spotted Luras and Aarok near the back talking to each other. They were arguing about something likely related to who would run the adventurer's guild, and it was getting heated.

"Can I have your attention, please?" Theo said, trying to raise his voice above the chatter. "Over here. No, pay attention to me. Guys?"

"Listen up!" Tresk shrieked, immediately gaining the attention of the crowd. She gave Theo a sly grin.

"Thank you. As the Lord Administrator of Broken Tusk, I declare the establishment of this town's first adventurer's guild," Theo said. He felt something swirl within him—some hidden power he didn't know he had. The power burst from within him, snaking from his chest in ribbons of light that gathered in the air above the adventurers before dispersing to all corners of the town.

[Small Town] Broken Tusk has gained a feature: [Adventurer's Guild].
This adventurer's guild is informal and not affiliated with any guilds currently existing. The creator of this guild may apply for membership in a larger guild but may become subject to their laws.
The quest **[Clear the Swamp]** assigned by **Miana Kell** has been transferred to the authority of the Lord Administrator. Funds will still be paid out automatically at the end of every day.
The guild has automatically been assigned to **Marsh Wolf Tavern**, the current location of the quest notice

board. The Lord Administrator can move the guild's headquarters.

Lord Administrator Theo Spencer may now elect a guild master.

A murmur of conversation spread across the crowd. Luras and Aarok shared a glance before nodding to each other. "Aarok is going to run the guild," Luras shouted over the crowd.

"Then that's it," Theo said. He focused his mind for a moment, mentally electing Aarok for the role.

Aarok Thane is now the guild master of the **Broken Tusk Adventurer's Guild.**

Theo expected the man to smile, but instead, a grimace appeared on the soldier's face. It was a lot of responsibility, but the alchemist couldn't run around town filling every role. If Luras was to be believed, the half-ogre had the most experience in both military tactics and adventuring.

"Thank you," Aarok said, collecting himself. "It's not a role that I was fighting for, but I'll do it for Broken Tusk. May I have a word before we depart, Lord Administrator?"

Theo nodded, crossing through the gathering and following Aarok out of earshot of everyone else. Luras stayed behind, while Tresk joined them.

"You alone, Theo," Aarok said, leveling his gaze at Tresk pointedly.

"You know we're Tara'hek, right?" Theo asked.

"What he knows, I know," Tresk said, scowling.

"Fine. I'm just worried," Aarok said. "The true reason I accepted the role is because something is wrong with the dungeon. It's gaining power too fast."

"I'm not an expert on dungeons," Theo said. "What determines the rate of a dungeon's growth?"

"Whatever core was used to seed the dungeon," Tresk said.

"The Swamp Dungeon was here before the ogres settled. It took hundreds of years to get to Level 20, and now its level has gone from 22 to 25 in just a few months."

"Then, how do we stop it?" Theo asked.

"Maybe a wizard?" Aarok said, shrugging. "Someone who specializes in dungeon cores."

"Here's my suggestion for now," Theo said, knitting his brow. He spoke before his thoughts formed, giving himself a moment to create a simple plan for Aarok to follow. The dungeon was growing and would likely continue to grow. "Induct all the adventurers gathered here into the guild. Require them to donate all of their cores to the town as an emergency measure."

"That's a lot of money in cores," Tresk said.

"Just until Level 5," Theo said. "Once we have our walls, they can keep them."

"That's your plan?" Aarok said.

"That's the start," Theo said. "We have a government stipend for adventurers. People just need to learn about it. Build our wall, strengthen our adventurers, invite foreign adventurers... That's my plan."

Aarok knitted his brow, falling into thought. He shrugged after a while, unable to poke holes in the short-term plan. "Fine. This works for now, but I assume I have full authority over the guild?"

"I think so," Theo said with a shrug. "I don't know how any of this works."

Aarok let out a groan, rubbing his hand over his face.

"He's doing his best," Tresk said, scowling.

"Fine. I'm going to address the *troops* before they head out for the day," Aarok said. "Xam is going to be mad when she learns the tavern is an adventurer's guild."

"One step at a time," Theo said, waving him off.

"Talk to you... Uh, whenever. Since we can, you know... Talk whenever," Tresk said, pulling Theo down to press her forehead against his.

"Stay safe out there," Theo said.

"I will."

Theo made his way to the Marsh Wolf Tavern, having no interest in the rousing speech Aarok planned to give. He wanted to leave the military aspect of things to those with knowledge in the realm. Xam needed smoothing over if peace was to reign over Broken Tusk. He found her tidying up the tables. When she spotted him, she grimaced.

"Why don't you come in anymore?" she asked.

"Busy," Theo said, lying. "So, your tavern is going to house the quests for the adventurer's guild."

"The what now?" Xam said, throwing her filthy rag down and stomping her foot. "We don't have one of those."

Theo managed a sheepish smile. "We do now. It's temporary."

"Well, I didn't approve of this," Xam said. "I won't have a bunch of rowdy adventurers messing up my tavern."

"The 'rowdy adventurers' are your current patrons," Theo said. "Listen, it's temporary. If you want to grab a knife and head out to kill these wolves, go for it. Until we get the walls up and a permanent structure for the guild, this is what we've got."

Xam folded her arms and stared at the alchemist. Maybe if she bore a hole through him, he would relent. But he returned the gaze, matching her intensity with his violet eyes, his tail swishing back and forth. She relented after a while, picking her rag back up.

"Aarok is heading the guild, so expect more of him," Theo said.

"Aarok? Really? Alchemist, you should have led with that!" Xam shouted. She went into a frenzy of cleaning, putting more effort into the task than when Theo entered the tavern.

Theo left her there, shaking his head. He wanted nothing to do with whatever romantic drama was playing out. His preference was to let those things work themselves out, even back on Earth. He idled around Throk's smithy for a while, striking up idle conversation with the marshling before departing. The blacksmith was working on a few projects, some related to the farmers and others to the new adventurers.

The alchemist found a lazy path toward the river before

returning to the shop. He collected reagents along the way, feeling the tension in his body subside now that the adventurer situation was sorted. Aarok was the best person to put in charge of it, he was sure of it. Luras was a close second, but the man had wanderlust, Theo could tell. The half-ogre was a better hunter than he was a military man.

Theo sat at the river for a while, listening to the sound of the river and relaxing. The marshling fishermen he saw so often passed by, giving their greetings and moving downriver toward the ocean. The alchemist was enjoying his time alone up until Tresk's voice shrieked into his mind, "*Run!*"

The sudden outburst startled him, and he rose to his feet, scanning the surrounding area in confusion. "*What? What's going on? Wolves?*" Theo asked.

"*Not wolves—shoot! Head north—North? Yeah, go north, Theo. Run!*"

Theo had learned to trust the woman with his life. She knew more than him about this world, and if she said run, he ran. He sprinted as fast as he could along the river, finding the terrain difficult underfoot. The rocks on the beaches gave way, causing him to stumble onto the wet ground.

"*What am I running from?*" Theo asked, unable to keep his panting breath from his mental message.

"*The Order of the Burning Eye,*" Tresk whispered. She was following someone. *Oh crap, he's too fast. He's coming for you, Theo —get ready.*

Theo's potions were back at the shop, and he didn't have any combat cores. Whatever this order was, he wanted nothing to do with it. He drew his dagger and scanned the forest but saw nothing. His heart hammered in his ears as he waited. The bushes rustled, then exploded with a rush of wind, sending the alchemist flat on the ground. A man stood over him, taller than any human he had ever seen but baring the features of the race. He wore full plate armor and a long sword at his hip. His hair was cut short, and his facial hair was freshly shaven. The man's face was a track of ruddy scars and pits, falling mostly over his left eye, which was missing.

"Theo Spencer. Belgar," the man said, scowling. Something in his voice struck terror in Theo's heart, and he held the dagger aloft.

"I don't know you," Theo said, swiping the dagger through the air. "Leave me alone!"

The man snatched Theo's arm and hoisted him high into the air. He wasn't just taller than a normal human; he was three heads taller than the alchemist. "Stand," he said.

Theo obeyed, his dagger falling to the ground in a clatter.

The man narrowed his eyes, looking Theo up and down before speaking again. "Drogramath Dronon in the southlands. Not as fearsome as the last one I purged."

"Please don't purge me," Theo said weakly.

The man's face twisted in surprise, sending the many scars on his face into deeper tracks. He relaxed after a moment and nodded. "I am Sulvan Flametouched, High Inquisitor of the Order of the Burning Eye. I'm in charge of destroying the line of Drogramath."

"Stop!" Tresk shouted from the forest. She heaved a breath and came to stand next to Theo. "He's not a real Dronon."

Luras and Aarok burst from the forest shortly after, joined by a mob of adventurers. Sulvan looked over his shoulder; a wave of energy washed over the group and caused them to cower. He turned his attention back to Theo and Tresk after a moment and performed a shallow bow, placing his hand on his chest.

"Forgive me," Sulvan said. "I've been hunting the *true* demons for centuries, and often forget my manners. For a Dronon to take the Tara'hek is impossible. Has he transitioned?"

"He has," Tresk said, scowling, "so don't kill him."

Sulvan's face went blank for a moment before nodding. "Noted. Theo Spencer, you're the first being transitioned into a Drogramath Dronon in recorded history. Congratulations for sending my blood pumping for the hunt only to find a harmless whelp."

The words seemed to calm the mob of adventurers. Theo

wasn't sure what they could have done against this man, though. He had a feeling that the inquisitor's powers were beyond anything they could muster and that the human could easily wipe the village off the map with little effort. Sulvan turned his attention back to the alchemist after a while, reaching his hand out. A rush of energy flowed through him, stinging every nerve in his body.

"What are you doing?" Tresk said, resting her hands on the pommels of her daggers.

"Calm yourself, marshling," Sulvan said. "I found your Tara'hek by following a trail of taint. Drogramath is aware of him, and I thought one of his true children was in the southlands. I'm extremely excited that I was wrong."

Theo didn't notice any excitement on the man's face. A permanent scowl rested on his visage. "Drogramath? This really sucks—what does that mean?"

Sulvan gestured. "Remove your shirt."

Theo wasn't about to disobey the man. He pulled off his black robe and lifted his shirt. Sulvan placed his massive hand on the alchemist's chest and closed his eyes. A light tingle played over the place he touched for a moment, and then burning pain followed. Theo shouted, grabbing the giant man's hand and struggling without avail. He collapsed to the ground after a moment, gasping for breath. The crowd of adventurers moved forward a little but kept their distance.

Tresk attacked the inquisitor, jabbing her daggers into the gaps of his armor and finding flesh; however, the points of her weapons didn't penetrate it, simply bouncing off as though his skin were iron. As she struggled, a window appeared in Theo's vision.

Sulvan Flametouched has branded you with [Grandmaster Exalted Extra-Dimensional Tracking Blocker].

Sulvan produced a potion from nowhere and handed it to the marshling. "The pain is temporary. I've solved a problem you didn't know you had, Theo."

Newt and Demon

Theo looked down to find a brand on his chest. It was an intricate webwork of lines and symbols that seemed impossibly precise to be a brand. It glowed with a faint red energy.

"What is that?" Tresk shouted, snatching the potion and forcing Theo to drink it.

"It prevents Drogramath from tracking him," Sulvan said. "A problem he didn't know he had."

"Calm down, Tresk," Theo said, groaning to a seated position. "I got a message from the system. It looks like a good thing."

"Again, I apologize for my fervor," Sulvan said.

"What would have happened if you didn't find me?" Theo asked.

"Drogramath has agents in the physical realm," Sulvan said. "They would have organized to find you once they realized you were linked. You are a very rare thing, Theo Spencer. Reincarnating into a Dronon is possible, although extremely rare, but it's never happened for Drogramath's line. Someone gave you a powerful gift for this to happen—I'd wager you have some extremely rare gifts."

"He does," Tresk said, her mood changing suddenly. She wrapped her arms around Theo and hugged him tight.

"To accept the Tara'hek is another thing," Sulvan said. "When I saw the marshling, I knew I was wrong."

Sulvan suddenly cocked his head and turned, staring at the crowd and causing them to flinch. All but Aarok withered under his gaze, and Theo could see that the inquisitor was smiling when he turned back. He produced a small medallion from nowhere and held it out for Theo to take. The alchemist accepted it, too awestruck by the man to inspect it.

"This went better than it could have," Sulvan said. "I've caused a disturbance in your town, and I apologize."

Theo rose to his feet, dusting himself off and reaching out a hand for the inquisitor to shake. "I'm not dead. That's what matters."

Sulvan shook his hand and nodded. Whatever guilt that man

could feel was long gone. Theo wondered if that sense of distance from other people came with being alive for that long, but he dismissed the thoughts. The encounter was just too strange for him to comprehend.

"Please inspect the necklace. I'm going to depart now," Sulvan said, vanishing on the spot in a gust of wind.

Aarok was the first to sprint over to Theo, his eyes wide. "Did you inspect him?"

"Inspect him?" Theo asked. "I was trying not to crap my pants."

"That guy was Level 135," Aarok said.

"What?" Tresk said, her jaw dropping.

Luras joined them, voicing similar concerns.

"You must have not noticed," Aarok said, shaking his head. "He didn't teleport away. He ran."

Theo shook his head, sputtering. "That's absurd... What's going on?"

"Demons are a serious thing," Aarok said. "Most Dronon are fine, but the Order of the Burning Eye keeps the bad ones in check. They banish the demon lords when they awaken."

"He mentioned Theo getting a gift to get the body," Luras said, knitting his brows. "I don't even know any other alchemists. How powerful are your abilities, Theo?"

"I really don't know," Theo said, shrugging. "I'm just thrilled I'm not dead."

Theo pulled his shirt and robe back on, and the group moved back to the town to regroup. Today was the day that Luras and Tresk were going to take on a few floors of the dungeon. The marshling hugged his arm the entire way back to town, shaking her head occasionally. When they were back in town, she reluctantly departed, and he finally inspected the necklace.

[Mark of the Burning Eye]
[Necklace]
Legendary

[Scaling]
A talisman created by a High Inquisitor of the Order of the Burning Eye. Wearing this necklace will protect the wearer from demon lords.

Effect:
Alerts Sulvan Flametouched when demon lords are near or watching you through magical means.
Grants the wearer significant damage reduction against demon lords.
+5 Strength
Item will scale with the wearer's level.

Theo pulled it over his head without hesitation. Any bonus to attributes was good in his book, and the item increased his Strength to 12. He felt his muscles bulge, his noodle arms filling out significantly. The necklace hung from a comfortable leather string. The medallion was made of silver and depicted an eye on fire.

The alchemist returned to the shop, shaken but relieved. Azrug had the door propped open, looking up and down the street in confusion. "Did a storm blow through?"

"Something like that," Theo said, laughing. "Come inside. I'll tell you about it."

Chapter 26
Business As Usual

"A High Inquisitor of the Burning Eye?" Azrug asked, shouting and jumping in place. "How are you not dead, man? You're a demon!"

Theo just got done explaining the situation to the boy. In his normal fashion, he was overly excited and extremely animated. Watching the boy's reaction made the alchemist feel even more relieved, giving him a better grasp on how dangerous of a situation it was. Tresk constantly spoke into his mind, reassuring him that this was a good thing. He wanted her to stop focusing on him and get on with her task.

"Tresk attacked him," Theo said.

"She what?" Azrug said, groaning. "By the Gods—all of them at once—what on earth was that woman thinking? He could have thrown her into the sea. Into the sea!"

"She's almost as excitable as you," Theo said, smiling.

The door opened, the bell jingling noisily, and Perg stepped inside. "Are you okay?"

"Small town, huh?" Theo asked. He gave her the short version, but she seemed more understanding of the situation.

"Right. Dangerous, but good. If what he said was true, you would be in far greater danger without his help," Perg said. "If

Drogramath took an interest in you, it'd be over. He's banished right now, but still has agents."

Theo placed his hand on the half-ogre's shoulder and nodded. "I appreciate the concern. I'm fine, and I got a fancy scaling necklace for my trouble."

"What? Those are rare," Perg said. "They grow with you as you level."

"Speaking of. I'd really like to get some alchemy done," Theo said. "Azrug, embellish the tale if anyone comes looking for me. Make it sound like Tresk and Sulvan had an epic duel by the river."

"Oh, I was going to do that anyway," Azrug said, laughing.

"Let me know if you need anything," Perg said.

"Thanks," Theo said, smiling.

The alchemist wanted nothing more than to put this behind him. He knew it was a good thing and that Sulvan understood his situation, but he didn't care. His only desire was to craft potions and protect the town, and he couldn't do that while worrying about what some dormant demon lord had planned for him. He closed the door to the lab for once and left the windows closed.

"Still better than Earth," he said, latching onto the thought for reassurance.

Sulvan's sudden appearance was comforting. While the townsfolk of Broken Tusk constantly reassured him that being a Dronon didn't matter down south, it clearly mattered elsewhere. As far as Theo was concerned, the necklace was the Order of the Burning Eye's endorsement. If anyone had a problem with his horns, he could flash the necklace or show his brand. The alchemist understood how disturbing the situation would be to another person, but he was content.

Theo focused on the task at hand. Fenian had placed a ridiculously large order and would return in a week to collect it. As he prepared the mash for his first run of Healing Essence, he lamented the manual process. The Spiny Swamp Thistle Root was the hardest of the restoration essences to process in the initial stages. The hard root required cutting before mashing, so more time had to be spent with the heavy stick and bucket to get it ground fine enough. Theo's increased strength from the necklace was a boon, making the mashing significantly easier.

Theo transferred the root in stages, making a mental note to get a larger bucket, and filled the first still. He leveled it off with Purified Water and started the Flame Artifice on its lowest setting underneath. The running list of notes wouldn't receive additional entries this time. For his delivery to Fenian, he wanted to keep everything as even as possible and get 500 excellent-quality potions for each type. Essence began dripping from the condenser not long after the fire started. The alchemist prepared his next batch.

Manashrooms were easier to prepare than the hard root. Theo barely smacked his stick against the bulbous mushrooms before they fell apart. He placed a flask under the second still's condenser and added the mash in steps before topping it off. With a mote stuffed inside his second Flame Artifice, he set it under the second still and watched the fire burn away.

"*How are you holding up?*" Tresk asked.

Theo smiled to himself. "*I should ask you that. I'm not the one delving into a dungeon today.*"

"*The first floors are fine. The monsters here practically crumple at a light touch,*" Tresk said. "*I was just worried that the Paladin shook you up.*"

"*Not really,*" Theo said. "*The necklace he gave me is awesome. It makes smashing up all my reagents easy. It's a scaling item, which Perg said is rare.*"

"*They are sooo rare,*" Tresk said, sounding surprised.

The bell jingled downstairs, and for the first time in a few days, he heard Azrug's boisterous voice. Theo suspected that there was actually a customer; his suspicions realized when the boy cracked the door to the lab and said, "We've got an outsider adventurer."

Theo looked at his flasks before descending the stairs. The massive glassware he put under the condensers would be fine for a while, and he could attend to the customer. He emerged into the shop to find a cat-person standing behind the counter, drumming his fingers on the surface. He was slightly shorter than the alchemist, with a leopard's pattern on his visible fur, the rest of his body covered by chain mail armor. His pointed ears perked up upon seeing the alchemist.

"Ah, the sign makes sense now. The Newt and *Demon*, I get it," the man said. "I am called Zan'kir, and I have come for potions."

"I'm Theo, and this is Azrug, my shopkeeper," Theo said. "Are you here for the Swamp Dungeon?"

"Not today," Zan'kir said. "I'm going to raid the River Dungeon."

"Well, a trader cleaned most of my stock out, but I still have a few potions," Theo said, gesturing to the back shelf. "You're welcome to browse."

Zan'kir nodded and went to the shelves. He found the Lesser Healing Potions immediately and gave Theo a confused look. "You created excellent-quality potions in this town? That's impressive."

"Only the best for our customers," Theo said, smiling.

"I'll take five healing potions, two barkskin, and the purifying one," Zan'kir said. "I hope you're not expecting Qavelli prices."

Theo waved a dismissive hand. "Of course not. I'll take 30 copper for each potion."

Something about the cat-person, whatever their race was called, screamed bargaining. His discerning eye told Theo that much, and he intended on throwing him a price that was absurd to start with.

Zan'kir shook his head, grimacing. "I'll give you 15 copper each, and not a coin more."

Theo grinned. "Twenty copper each, and I'll throw in Cleansing Scrub. You'll need it in this mud pit."

Zan'kir reached out his hand for Theo to shake, beaming from ear to ear. "Simple negotiation is the pleasure of life, is it not?"

Azrug was standing near the back of the room, mentally taking notes on the exchange, although he was still too timid to strike a deal with an outsider.

"Couldn't agree more," Theo said, shrugging.

Zan'kir brought his potions to the front counter and withdrew the coins from a satchel at his side. Theo noticed it wasn't a dimensional bag. He placed 1 silver and 60 copper on the counter, gesturing for the alchemist to count it. His alchemical sense for measuring units didn't extend to loose coins, and he quickly counted them out before adding the lump sum to his inventory.

"A discerning man like you knows the price these potions fetch in the capital," Zan'kir said. "Your reasonable prices will make it possible for up-and-coming adventurers to delve."

"That's my plan," Theo said.

Zan'kir let out a heavy sigh. "The laid-back attitude of this place... It reminds me of home."

Theo raised an eyebrow. He didn't even know what the man's race was called in this world, let alone where they called home. "Where is home, exactly?"

"Across the great sea to the east is a land called Khahan," Zan'kir said. "It's mostly desert, but the Khahari have called it home for eons. We have Dronon there, but none of your lineage. Where do you hail from?"

"My home was destroyed," Theo said.

"I'm sorry to hear that."

"Don't be," Theo said, waving a dismissive hand. "We were doomed long before the sun sought to swallow us."

"So, a second chance. An outworlder," Zan'kir said. There was something wistful on his face, a longing for something else. "Broken Tusk is a delightful place to settle. I wonder, could I buy property here?"

"I think so," Theo said. Upon thinking about the topic, a screen appeared, displaying a detailed map of the town and the available properties. Only now could he see the amount of land assigned to the Newt and Demon. It stretched far to the east, encompassing most of the area between the town and the river. He dismissed the screen and nodded. "Yes, we have a lot of property. I'm the local administrator, so you can find me if you want to settle down."

"A decision for a later time," Zan'kir said. "My family will have a say, and I'll have to sort my holdings in the north."

"No rush."

"Well, until next time," Zan'kir said, waving and departing.

When the Khahari was out the door, Azrug let out a heavy sigh. "You should have told him about the stipend provided by the kingdom."

Theo waved him off, running upstairs to swap the flasks out under the condensers before returning.

"We won't convince him. He's going to have to decide," Theo said. "I'll pay you an extra copper coin today if you stick around to help me with the stills."

"You know what motivates me," Azrug said.

The boy stayed downstairs while Theo tended to his stills upstairs. Sometime during the distillation process, Theo gained a level in his Drogramath Alchemy Core.

Drogramath Alchemy Core gained experience (5%).
Drogramath Alchemy Core reached Level 7!
Theo Spencer gained experience (2%).

The rest of the run went as expected, with 200 units of Healing Essence and Mana Essence, both of excellent quality. He summoned Azrug upstairs and explained how he dumped the stills out the window. The half-ogre boy burst out laughing, slapping his knees and pointing at the alchemist. Theo waited for him to get it out of his system.

"You're the dumbest alchemist I know," Azrug said, shaking his head. "You've got all this alchemical knowledge in your brain, but no common sense."

"I'm the only alchemist you know," Theo said.

The boy disappeared down the stairs, returning with a bottle of Cleansing Scrub in his hand and grinning. He placed a drop of the solution inside the first still, the powerful reaction bathing the room in a bright white glow. When it was done, the massive pot was completely clean.

"I'm an idiot," Theo said, nodding.

"I'm still getting paid more, right?" Azrug asked.

Theo produced three copper coins, as promised, and handed it over to the boy.

"See you tomorrow," Azrug said, bounding down the stairs and out the front door.

The alchemist left the stills for now, stowing the essences in his inventory and making for the front door. Before he could leave to harvest more herbs, the five burly laborers appeared. He directed them to deposit their hard work into the dimensional crate upstairs and took stock of the herbs before paying them. Their haul was 200 roots, 200 mushrooms, and 300 units of the moss. They must have figured out how to climb the trees properly to harvest the moss.

"Another day of hard work, guys," Theo said, shaking his head. "You're really doing a good job."

Ziz grunted, holding his hand out and smiling. Theo produced 25 copper and placed the coins in the half-ogre's hand, who said, "Same for tomorrow?"

"Yes, after that, I'll have new reagents for you to harvest," Theo said.

Ziz waved and departed, taking his band of laborers with him. Theo left, locking up the shop and swinging around the side into the gravel yard. He let out a groan, suddenly remembering that he had wanted to talk to Miana. Any conversation with the woman ended with her scowling a hole through his forehead. He changed course, heading up the main street and into the square. Before entering her house, he checked the monolith in the square.

[Small Town]
Name: Broken Tusk
Owner: Kingdom of Qavell

Mayor: Miana Kell
Administrator: Theo Spencer
Faction: Qavell
Level: 4 (25%)
Features:
Alchemy Lab
Blacksmith
Large Farm
Tannery
Tradesmen
Adventurer's Guild
Upgrades:
None

The adventurers were doing a great job feeding the town cores. It would be Level 5 soon. Theo knocked on Miana's door, and the woman emerged, glowering down at him. "What?"

"Business," Theo said.

She reluctantly held the door open, allowing him to enter. She snapped it shut once he was inside and regarded him, shaking her head. "Well?"

"How do you communicate with the capital?"

Miana simply gestured for him to follow, leading him down the hall and into the office where the town's mercantile seats held their meetings. She retrieved a small pink crystal from a locked chest and set it down on the table. "Just grasp it and you'll be connected with some annoying functionary."

"All right," Theo said. "I just wanted to know if you had a line directly to them."

"I do. And now you do too," Miana said. Her expression softened for a moment, and she sighed. "Why have you taken to this like an Ogre Snapper to mud? Should've figured you'd be good at this."

"I'm not," Theo said, waving her off. "I'm so good at thinking about myself that my self-interest encompasses the entire town."

Miana laughed, maybe for the first time since he had met her. "That alchemy shop has been empty for as long as I can remember. You show up, and suddenly the town is buzzing."

"It's a confluence of events," Theo said. "The dungeon gaining levels rapidly has more to do with it than me. Have you considered the idea that we're seeing more success because *you* have more support?"

"See? You even know the right words to say," Miana said, letting out another sigh. "Keep it up. Use the crystal whenever you need."

"All right. I need to gather my thoughts on that one. It boils down to getting more financial aid from the crown," Theo said.

"They seem willing," Miana said, shrugging.

Theo bid farewell to the woman, not willing to commit to contacting whoever was on the other end of the crystal. He wandered toward the river, gaining updates from Tresk along the way. They had gone down to the tenth floor of the dungeon before turning back, and they were currently making their way back up. She found new gear and even a few reagents she thought were alchemical. Without an herbalism core, she wouldn't be able to tell. He wished her a safe journey back.

The area between the shop and the river was picked over, but there were still hidden roots that were invisible to the laborers. Theo knew the plants would grow back within a day but spent his time gathering the more difficult ones. He hadn't considered *why* they came back so quickly, but dismissed the thought as soon as it came. The herbs in the area behind his shop were locked in his mind, their locations stored away by his high Wisdom attribute. While he knew those well, the plants that grew along the river were unknown.

According to the information detailed in his book, elemental flowers were related to their equivalent attribute. Water Lilies grew in thick patches along the muddy bank and would produce potions that enhanced Wisdom. He stowed them away in his inventory and worked his way north until Tresk informed him she had arrived back at the shop. A massive wooden bridge spanned the river at one point. He noted its location and turned back around, the journey back to the Newt and Demon resulting in fifty of the Water Lilies in his inventory.

Tresk looked exhausted, sitting in Azrug's chair with her head resting on the front desk. Theo dripped a few drops of Cleansing Scrub on her head, and she laughed. It washed away the layers of grime and blood covering her body, sending flashes of light through the shop.

"I got this new shiny dagger," Tresk said, pulling a wicked-looking blade from her belt and grinning. "Finally picked my Level 10 ability too. It's called [Blades from Shadow] and enhances the damage of my first attack after leaving stealth."

"You're a sneaky one," Theo said, patting her on the head. "Not much to say about my day. Got Level 7 in my alchemy core and made some potions."

"Ah, the life of an alchemist," she said, laughing. "I'm going to take a few potions from the shelf, if that's okay."

"They're your potions, too," Theo said.

Tresk shrugged, groaning as she stood up, and stowed five Lesser Healing Potions in her dimensional bag. "You're working on the elf's job, right?"

"Yeah, I'm getting there," Theo said. "I also owe Perg some tanning potions, so I want to get this job done soon. Is Luras stopping by for dinner?"

"He is. Perg will invite herself, too," Tresk said.

Theo and Tresk went upstairs, propped the windows open, and made a new batch of soup. The reagents she found in the dungeon turned out to be common plants, a fact that annoyed her. As if on cue, Luras knocked on the front door. Perg was with him, and they joined as a group upstairs. The soup was as delicious as the last time they had made it, and the conversation switched around aimlessly. It finally landed on the inquisitor, Sulvan.

"That's the thing!" Perg shouted. "We sit here in some backwater town, knowing that there are high-level people out there. It's absurd to think about."

"It's scary," Tresk said. "He didn't even flinch when I stabbed him."

"You shouldn't have stabbed him." Luras groaned.

"I thought he was going to kill my Tara'hek." Tresk shrugged.

"Theo is just lucky that the guy was one of the good ones," Perg said. "Imagine if he was just a jerk that killed all the unknown Dronon."

"Well, demon lords are the least of our worries," Luras said. "The Swamp Dungeon is still leveling, and we don't have walls."

"Has Aarok organized a night watch?" Theo asked.

"Have you sorted the night watch's wages?" Luras shot back, grinning.

Theo shifted uncomfortably in his seat. He had the chance to talk to the capital earlier but didn't want to get ahead of himself. "No."

"Well, he's organized it anyway. Two people will patrol the streets in shifts," Luras said. "It's horrible work, but they're doing it for free until we get that sorted."

Everyone at the table but Perg was exhausted from the day. She babbled on for longer than was acceptable and was eventually dragged out of the shop by Luras's powerful grip. Theo and Tresk locked the shop up and headed for bed, pressing their foreheads together before saying goodnight.

Tresk's loud snores filled the room immediately. Despite the softness of the bed and his exhaustion, Theo was awake for quite a while. Although twilight had already enveloped the town, he still wasn't tired. He replayed the events of the day in his mind, appreciating how lucky he was. There were still things he couldn't change in this world, but Broken Tusk wasn't one of them. He could alter the fate of the town for the better, sending it into an era of prosperity it could have only dreamed of. Only after embracing the dreams of his new home did he find rest that night.

Chapter 27
The Master Negotiator

Theo and Tresk ate breakfast together the next morning, cursing Perg's betrayal. She once again failed to bring the bread she promised, but neither of them knew how to make it. With things being so hectic lately, they had little time to spare to pursue it. Fortunately, the soup hadn't lost its luster. Back on Earth, the alchemist wasn't picky about his meals. When food came after the collapse started, he was content eating whatever protein bars they threw at him. Compared to those tightly packed "chocolate"-flavored cubes, the soup was a delicacy. The delicious, orange-flavored tea didn't hurt either, making their time staring out the window into darkness enjoyable.

"I used to sleep in a lot," Theo said. "Whenever I could, really."

"People in the big city sleep a lot," Tresk said, slurping her soup. "That's what I hear, anyway. Can't afford to do that out in the middle of nowhere."

"No, we have to make the daylight count," Theo said.

The thought that he had to contact the capital hung over his head that morning. Tresk sensed it and tried to motivate him.

"You can't put it off forever," Tresk said. She didn't even need to ask to know what he was worried about.

"It's easy to be in Broken Tusk," Theo said, "but now I have to talk to someone in Qavell?"

"We need those guards," Tresk said, shrugging. "It's not fair to expect them to patrol the town without a wage."

Theo let out a long sigh and finished his soup. The adventurer's guild was a step forward, but it would take even more effort to have the town properly defended. The dungeon provided enough problems, not to mention talks of war in the north. If the rumors were true, they would have bandits fleeing south. The alchemist thought about his customer yesterday, Zan'kir the Khahari, and wondered if he had good intentions. He explained the encounter to Tresk, aiming to get her opinion of the man.

"Are the Khahari good people?" Theo asked.

"As good as any other people." Tresk shrugged. "Bandits wouldn't say they wanted to settle down here, though. They'd come to pillage, hiding out in the forest and raiding towns for loot."

"He might buy some property in town," Theo said, nodding. "Seemed like a guy who just missed home."

"That's good," Tresk said. "We need more adventurers here."

The pair cleaned their breakfast away before Theo showed the cleaning technique Azrug came up with. She laughed at the alchemist for a while, slapping herself in the forehead. "How did we miss that?" she asked.

The sun was creeping over the horizon when they left the shop. Azrug was leaning up against the wall outside. He flipped the sign and entered the shop without a word. Tresk shrugged it off, and they made their way to the monolith in the town square. The adventurers were already gathered, receiving a speech from Aarok. Theo's mind drifted in and out of listening. The man was talking about keeping the swamp secure and how they were so close to getting the walls they desperately needed. The alchemist was too worried about what he would say to the people in the capital. All the expectant eyes of the adventurers fell on him, and he snapped back to reality.

"What?" Theo asked.

"He asked if you made progress on negotiating with the big guys," Tresk said, punching Theo in the arm.

"I have—kind of—I'll contact them today and negotiate a salary," Theo said, swallowing hard. "They gave us the wolf quest, so why wouldn't they give us more money to defend the town?"

"More adventurers hitting the dungeons means more in taxes," Aarok said, nodding. "We're putting our faith in you, Alchemist."

"That's 'Lord Administrator' to you, Aarok," Tresk said, blowing raspberries.

"Calm down," Aarok said, laughing. "Anyway, concerning the monster cores, we're donating until it hits Level 5, and then..."

Theo's mind wandered again, leaving the half-ogre's words behind. He knew too little about the way the kingdom distributed funds and felt uneasy going into negotiations without that knowledge. He set a simple plan in his mind, the same plan he used on Zan'kir, aim high and accept low. Broken Tusk would request 10 copper a day, with guards working in four shifts, two for the day and two for the night. Realistically, he'd be happy if they offered two copper coins per person.

"We're going," Tresk said, nudging Theo. She beckoned for him to lean over, and pressed her forehead against his. "You'll do fine."

The adventuring party filed out of the square, leaving two people who left in opposite directions to patrol the town. Theo took a deep breath and knocked on Miana's door. She emerged quickly, narrowing her eyes at him and grumbling. "What?"

"Need to use your fancy crystal," Theo said, managing a weak smile.

"Fine. You know where it is," she said, holding the door open.

Theo found his way to her office and retrieved the crystal from the unlocked chest. He sat down in a chair and looked at the curious object, rolling it over in his hands. Without defined instructions on how to use it, he just sat there for a while. After a few frustrating attempts, he closed his eyes and focused on what he wanted. The alchemist fell through the air, plummeting from the room into a sheet of inky blackness. When he tried to shout, nothing came out, and he was suddenly standing on a stone platform, illuminated from an unknown source.

"Hello?" he shouted, his eyes refusing to focus. His voice echoed over the platform.

A figure appeared in front of him, seemingly out of nowhere. It was the vague shape of another person, possibly a woman, but cloaked in darkness. "Hello, thanks for reaching out to the Qavell City Administration Services. How can I help you?"

Theo had flashbacks to customer support people back on Earth. Her tone was far too cheery for the darkness surrounding them. "Yes, I have a question about Broken Tusk's defensive... fund."

She took a moment and tilted her head before exclaiming. "Oh! You're the new administrator for Broken Tusk. Theo Spencer. Yes, I got you right here. Miana has a lot of good things to say about you, and the town has been growing rapidly since you took over. All good marks," she said, barely taking a breath. "I'm Lauris, by the way. Do you have any specific requests at this time?"

"We're having a bit of a wolf problem. It's because the nearby dungeon is growing rapidly," Theo said. Despite his initial fears about this conversation, he was getting more comfortable.

"Right. Wolves. Let's see," Lauris said, pausing for a moment. "We assigned a quest to take care of the wolves. Is the dungeon still growing in strength?"

"Yes, we're seeing more wolves in the swamp and some goblins," Theo said. "I created an adventurer's guild, but we still need people to run patrols through the town."

"An adventurer's guild? Smart move," Lauris said, chuckling. "I can provide another quest for you. How many patrols is your guild master running?"

"Two for the day, two for the night," Theo said.

"Four adventurer subsidies—your adventuring guild master can assign whoever they want—5 copper a day per person," Lauris said. "Does that sound good?"

Theo blinked, unable to understand why this went so well. "That's perfect."

"Any other questions?"

Theo thought for a moment. The situation was extremely easy, and he wasn't expecting it to go off so well. He had to think for a moment before responding. "That's it. Can I use this crystal at any time?"

"During business hours."

"That's it, then," Theo said. "Thank you."

"Bye."

The connection was cut without warning, and Theo was sent hurtling upward through nothingness. He was back in the chair, with Miana staring daggers at him.

"Did it work?" she asked. "They're usually jerks."

Theo blinked, unable to process the sudden change. He stammered for a moment before collecting himself. "Oh, yeah. Real tough lady, Lauris. I had to threaten her life, but she gave me what I wanted."

Miana narrowed her eyes. "I *hate* Lauris."

Theo left Miana's home, shocked at how easy it was to get what he needed.

"Aarok said he got a notification about a new quest," Tresk said, speaking into Theo's mind. *"How did you seal the deal so quickly?"*

"Ah, you know. I'm just an extremely good negotiator," Theo said, beaming. It felt silly to smile while you were talking to someone through telepathy.

"You didn't have to do anything, did you?"

"Nope. Some nice shadowy figure sorted it out for me," Theo said. "Which makes me mildly suspicious. Why are they so interested in Broken Tusk doing well? I understand the tax angle, but a few silver will not tip the scales."

"A broader mystery?" Tresk asked. *"Maybe. I'm sorry, Theo. I'm just a country marshling, so I don't understand all this stuff."*

"Right. Stay safe out there," Theo said.

Relief flooded through Theo's body. He took his time walking back to the shop, picking an ambling path out into the forest to the east. Things were going better than he expected. Leading a life that led from one bad thing to another hardened him against such things, though. He constantly flung himself into motion to prevent those bad things, preparing for an eventuality that never came. The alchemist returned to the shop, finding Azrug with his feet kicked up and reading his book.

"I've secured funding for the guard patrols," Theo said.

"That's good," Azrug said. "Someone said they saw a wolf up near the tavern last night."

"We'll get the walls today," Theo said. "As long as they find enough cores."

"Well, I made a sale," Azrug said. "10 copper's worth."

"Good. Keep it up," Theo said. "I'll be in the lab."

Azrug grunted a response without looking up from his book. Theo took stock of his dimensional crate, deciding that he wanted to make batches of Stamina Essence and Healing Essence today. That would put him 100 potions shy of his order for healing potions, and 300 short on the other two. His process was simplified once more, increasing his production capacity significantly. Cleaning the stills had been a task that he hated, and now he didn't have to worry about it. The Cleansing Scrub took care of the caked-on reagents that had given him so much trouble in the past.

Theo prepared the Moss Nettle first, mashing 200 units fairly quickly and transferring them to the first still. He leveled it off with water and prepared the Spiny Swamp Thistle Roots, cutting them into small pieces and smashing them down. His increased Strength was paying off, and he completed the task in half the time it normally took. The Flame Artifices burned away on the lowest setting, slowly heating both stills. The alchemist had this process down to perfection, allowing him to leave the shop and search for herbs while the stills did their work.

Between his cores, the Drogramath Herbalism Core was the one that needed more experience. While his alchemy core hit Level

7, the herbalism core was still at Level 6, and he wanted them to be in a similar range. Theo made his way to the river, mentally keeping time while he picked Water Lilies. He knew the locations of the flowers that enhanced Wisdom and Vigor but didn't have a lead on any other attributes. The attribute-enhancement potions that Fenian requested were optional, but the alchemist wanted to make the most money possible from the request.

Tresk updated him on the day's journey so far as he was heading back to the shop. The adventurers were at a point where they didn't need help taking on the swamps' wolves. A few of them were even venturing to other areas to check on the local dungeons. The closest one after the Swamp Dungeon was the River Dungeon. Next was the Hills Dungeon, to the north, which Theo had heard nothing about. He reasoned it was an extremely low-level dungeon—not worth mentioning. His marshling companion took all of this as good news, as she could now focus on herself more. Luras became her adventuring partner for the time being, until the wanderlust took him.

Azrug hadn't made another sale by the time he got back and didn't acknowledge him when he returned. Theo swapped the flasks under his dual condensers and planned his next run. The next batch would be Mana Essence and Stamina Essence, which should end around midday. There would even be enough time to do another batch if his stamina held out, but he had his doubts.

He took out the finished essences and added them to his inventory, pulling out a bottle of Cleansing Scrub. He dripped it in either still, and started the mashing process again. Thankfully, this run would be Manashrooms and Moss Nettle, the two easiest reagents to grind down. When he fired up the first still after leveling it off with Purified Water, the Flame Artifice sputtered to life, then suddenly died. It was the first time his new tools ran out of power, but he crammed an Earth Mote into them, causing the machinery to fire back up in an instant.

Midday came with Theo staring out the window. It was the

second half of his last run of the day when a prompt suddenly crowded his vision.

[Small Town] Broken Tusk has advanced to Level 5!
[Small Town] Broken Tusk is eligible for an upgrade. As the Administrator, you may make a selection from the following:

[Stone Walls and Gates]
Your town will gain stone walls around its borders, complete with gates. The walls will adjust if your borders expand. One gate will be placed in each cardinal direction, aligned with the road exiting your town.

[Stone Roads]
Your town will gain stone roads that cover all interior roads within your borders. The roads will expand as you expand your town.

[Watchtowers]
Your town will gain watchtowers placed along the border. Should you expand, the watchtowers will move to match the edge of your borders. Twelve watchtowers will be placed.

Theo was tempted for a moment to select the roads, but the walls were a clear winner. Roads would only prevent people from getting their feet wet in the mud, and he couldn't see much use for the watchtowers. He mentally selected the walls and felt the ground rumble beneath his feet. The alchemist steadied his flasks as the rumbling continued, almost losing his footing to the sudden shift. Azrug bolted up the stairs moments later, his eyes wide with fear.

"What happened?"

"We just got an upgrade," Theo said. "We'll go check it out once I'm done with the distillation process."

Azrug stayed with Theo upstairs, bouncing up and down from excitement. The alchemist somehow kept him calm enough to wait for the last of the essences to finish. They departed the store and made their way to the town square. A group of people were already there, babbling to one another with excitement. Thanks to the clearing to the west, he could see the sizable stone wall and gate. It was a portcullis-style gate with a cranking mechanism nearby. The gate was currently down.

Theo addressed the crowd, spotting Miana popping her head out of her house. "We have walls," he said, keeping it simple.

Those few words were enough to send the group into a frenzy. Azrug joined them, jumping some more and hooting as loud as he could. The alchemist couldn't help but smile and add a few excited shouts of his own. The adventurer who fed the last core to the town stood nearby, sheepishly smiling as the group praised him. Theo inspected the monolith.

[Small Town]
Name: Broken Tusk
Owner: Kingdom of Qavell
Mayor: Miana Kell
Administrator: Theo Spencer
Faction: Qavell
Level: 5 (1%)
Features:
Alchemy Lab
Blacksmith
Large Farm
Tannery
Tradesmen
Adventurer's Guild
Upgrades:
Stone Walls and Gates

Theo knew that the climb to Level 10 would be arduous. His plan was to use his alchemy earnings to buy powerful cores from the traders and upgrade quickly. He hoped that a new set of upgrades would be available at Level 10, because he couldn't stomach getting the towers. While he'd been thinking of the reduction of muck brought by the roads, the walls were too good. Everything else would need to wait. The townsfolk were safe, for now. He raised his hands to get the attention of those gathered.

"I'm sure Aarok will spread the word, but we'll have two adventurers on patrol in the city at all times," Theo said. The crowd roared, and he waited for them to settle down. "I think we can all agree that the gates should be closed at night, but I want to run it by Aarok first and hear what he thinks."

"Speaking of," Azrug said, pointing toward the western gate.

Theo could faintly see the adventurers standing outside the gate. They were waving their hands and shouting something he couldn't hear. The group moved through the mud to the gate, taking a while to figure out how the mechanism worked, and slowly raising the portcullis. The alchemist spotted the mechanism that would release the gate, causing it to come crashing down, and hoped that the entire assembly was magical. He didn't want to see his new gate rusted out.

"I see you selected the *correct* upgrade," Aarok said, beaming.

"The other options were terrible," Theo said. "Do you know if we get different options at Level 10?"

"You're already planning for Level 10?" Luras said, creeping from behind Aarok.

"I have a plan, yeah."

"Theo always has a plan," Tresk said.

"Yeah. We should see new stuff at Level 10, but you can pick the old stuff too," Aarok said.

Theo joined the adventurers as they walked the length of the wall. As the description promised, it followed the border of Broken Tusk. It even wrapped all the way around the farmland, putting the alchemist's mind at ease. He was worried that the farms weren't considered part of the town, but he remembered seeing them on the town's map when he inspected the plots. He pulled up that same map again, finding that the wall traced an outline around the town. When they finally finished their circuit back to the western gate, Theo was exhausted, and the day was getting late.

"We should head to the tavern and get some food to celebrate," Tresk said, giggling with excitement.

"I don't think that's much of a celebration, but I'll go," Theo said, grimacing.

Chapter 28
Flowers

It was strange returning to the Marsh Wolf Tavern after spending so many nights eating dinner in the lab. Theo had never seen the crowds inside as boisterous as they were now. They raised toasts to everyone involved and sucked down the slop that Xam served. The alchemist had to agree that the soup was better today, but his good spirits were likely the cause. He sat with Tresk, Luras, Aarok, and Perg near the window.

Theo sat with his friends, taking in the sights and sounds of an overexcited group of townspeople. He was too tired to join them, his stamina bar almost depleted, and just sat.

Broken Tusk had walls now. Thick walls that would give a small army a hard time, with ever-strengthening adventurers standing ready within. The fortune that they poured into the project was only possible because of the adventurers themselves.

"Interesting time to live in the southlands," Aarok said, smiling. "What's next for our people, Alchemist?"

"You're as much of a leader as I am," Theo said, shrugging. "I want you to decide the fate of the adventurers. I don't know a thing about adventuring or monsters."

"I think Perg is onto something," Luras said, his usual somber self. "We need to replace these crummy wood buildings with strong core buildings."

Perg flushed, busying herself with her soup.

"Even Miana's place, the mayor's house, isn't a core building," Tresk said. "Imagine coming here and seeing all the rotting wood. It's an awful sight if you're used to the grandeur of the capital."

"That will be expensive," Perg said, not looking up from her soup. "Fenian gave me a deal on the seed core. 80 silver."

"An amount you'll make back in a week with Theo's help," Tresk said.

"Yeah. He's a bit too sweet, that elf," Perg said, staring off into the middle distance.

Theo held his hand out to bring the conversation back on track. The marshling was too excitable at the best of times, and doubly so when she was tired. "We'll work on production buildings first. Then we can replace all the rickety houses. But that's a long-term plan."

"What's happening in the short term?" Aarok asked, tilting his head.

Theo had been thinking about his finances. The job for Fenian would earn him three gold coins at a minimum. If he shifted into high gear, he could have the special attribute potions ready for him as well. Those potions would earn him high-level monster cores, and lots of them. He was considering a plan that would see less profit in the short term but more expansion of the town and its export channels. The alchemist summoned his administration map of the town and traced his eyes along the northern section near the farms. The town ended where the farms did, leaving the stretch of rocky lowlands unincorporated.

An option popped up when he focused on the parcel to the north, which included most of the hills.

[Small Town] Broken Tusk can be expanded to the **Northern Parcel** for 1 gold. Funds will be removed

directly from your inventory or the nearest dimensional container in your possession.
You do not possess the required funds.

The plan was simple. He would expand the town north, establish a quarry and a stonecutter workshop with seed cores. Theo would hire the laborers, especially the one with a Stonecutter Core, to work the quarry and hew the stone. It was an expensive operation that might cost him all his gold coins, but it would be worth it. He was tired of using Cleansing Scrub every time he entered a building after trudging through the muck of the roads. The idea was to get his stonecutter good enough to export blocks, inviting bulk traders to come and whisk the heavy goods away.

"I'm going to fund a quarry," Theo said. "I'll purchase the land to the north and seed a few core buildings."

"Wow. That's bold," Tresk said.

"Expanding Broken Tusk?" Luras said, laughing. "By the gods. This place has been the same old core town since my grandfather was here."

"Theo has a habit of transforming everything he touches," Perg said. "The guy just can't sit still."

Tresk giggled, finishing her soup with a loud burp.

"How are the adventurers liking their wage for patrol duty?" Theo asked, nodding at Aarok.

"They're fighting for the spots," Aarok said, grunting. "Five copper a day... How did you manage that?"

Theo averted his gaze for a moment, rolling the situation over in his head. It was incredibly easy to convince Lauris to contribute the funds. He expected to fight for a single copper a day, but the woman offered five without hesitation. While he knew little about how kingdoms operated, the alchemist knew that when war was on the horizon, fists got tight. Either Qavell was swimming in coin or he was missing something.

"Keen negotiation skills," Theo said. "If the system had the Charisma attribute, I'd be sitting at 50 points."

The group laughed, shaking their heads in disbelief.

"I couldn't agree less," Luras said.

They stayed for some time, chatting about nonsense until dusk threatened outside. Theo was ready for bed hours ago, but the excitement of the past few days was getting to him. Perg pulled him aside as he went to leave, informing him that her laborers stored the day's worth of reagents at her place. With the town's upgrade, he completely forgot about them and promised to give them their pay the next day, along with new instructions. She agreed to send them over in the morning so that they could be briefed on their new foraging targets.

Tresk and Theo found their way back to the shop, locking it up before retreating upstairs. They both fell asleep as night settled in outside, trying and failing to keep their eyes open for even a moment longer.

Breakfast the next morning was a pleasant reprieve. Despite Theo's high spirits at dinner last night, he understood with hindsight that it was awful soup. Tresk had plans to delve back into the dungeon today, driven by her desire to get more gear. The adventurers didn't need instruction anymore and would be fine to run off on their own.

Slurping the last of his tea, Theo went downstairs to wait for Perg's laborers. As he sat in the shop, twiddling his thumbs, he couldn't help but think he was stealing them from her. The only comfort he took was that she was an assertive person and would complain if he overstepped his bounds. The laborers showed up, and he invited them into the lab to deposit what they had collected the preceding day. They brought approximately 200 of each reagent, which was more than he needed for this current run.

Theo led them to a table, where he produced a parchment. "I'll sketch these reagents out for you, but they're easy to spot. Stone Flowers and Water Lilies are what you're looking for. They're the only attribute-based reagents I found so far."

"What are the other ones?" Ziz asked. He seemed to become their default leader.

"Not sure. They should be related to fire, wind, and lightning," Theo said. "The Stone Flowers are for Vigor and the Water Lilies are for Wisdom."

The alchemist sketched out the flowers, providing a written description of how they looked and where to find them. He paid them for the work they had done the day before and sent them on their way. Azrug showed up as they left, holding his hand out and scowling. "Didn't pay me yesterday too."

Theo fished two copper coins out of his inventory and handed it to the boy. A smile spread across his face as he sauntered over to his chair, plopping down and pulling out his book. Tresk left for her adventures soon after, leaving the alchemist to his work.

Theo hatched a plan to run exact quantities for his batches today. He had 400 of each essence and only needed 100 more to fulfill the minimum order for Fenian. The plan to send the laborers off to collect the rare flowers would sweeten the deal, allowing him to get monster cores instead of cash, although he rethought that strategy. The alchemist pushed his doubts away, cleaning his stills and preparing for the first run. He created a mash using the Spiny Swamp Thistle Root, lamenting the arduous process of cutting the roots up and started the Flame Artifice. With the 100-unit Healing Essence distillation started, he set his sights on the next batch.

The shop was out of both Lesser Stamina Potions and Lesser Mana Potions. Theo mashed 200 Moss Nettles, which were significantly easier to prepare than the roots, and clicked the second Flame Artifice into life. He watched as the flasks filled with essence, and wondered whether he should buy another still. Proper equipment was something that paid for itself, and he made a mental note to talk to Throk.

The bell rang downstairs, Azrug's voice revealing that it was a local. After a few minutes, he made a sale, and the bell rang again. Theo waited for the customer to leave before heading out for more herbs. Once again, he set a timer in his mind and headed out. The half-ogre laborers passed him near the river, giving their greetings before moving on. That group was all business. He finally saw a level-up in his herbalism core, bringing it up to match his alchemy core at Level 7. It also tipped him over the edge in his personal level, bringing it to match at 7. He dumped his point into Wisdom without a second thought.

> **Drogramath Herbalist Core** gained experience (2%).
> **Drogramath Herbalist Core** reached Level 7!
> **Theo Spencer** gained experience (2%).
> **Theo Spencer** reached Level 7!
> **Theo Spencer** received one free point!

Theo felt something twinge in his mind, signaling that he needed to swap a flask back at the lab. He rushed back with a few new Water Lilies in his inventory. Azrug grunted as he rushed upstairs in time to swap the almost-overflowing flasks out. The first still, the one containing the Spiny Swamp Thistle Root, was done running. The alchemist cleaned it with Cleansing Scrub and set it up for the next run.

The Manashrooms smashed easily enough, even without his enhanced strength, and he had the mash prepared quickly. Theo leveled off the water, fed the Flame Artifice a new mote, and placed a fresh flask under the condenser. He propped a window open and wiped the sweat from his brow, noticing his dwindling stamina points. With 500 units of Stamina Essence in reserve, he decided it was time to abuse his supply of potions.

Theo's supply of Copper Shavings wasn't even dented after he set up ten fifty-unit reactions on a table. He poured Purified Water into each, going down the line of flasks and kicking off ten reactions in a row. The lab was filled with a pleasant-smelling smoke that choked him. He frantically waved it out the window, inspecting the resulting stamina potions and nodding to himself. They were all of excellent quality, which he had expected. The alchemist began the tedious process of distributing the potions into individual flat-bottomed vials, finding that he would need more motes if he wanted to finish this entire batch.

The table was filled with an endless crowd of vials that were slowly filled with the yellow potion. The only potion Theo had drunk in recent memory was a Lesser Health Potion, the one tipped into his mouth after the inquisitor had branded him. As he downed a Lesser Stamina Potion, he remembered the strange citrus flavor from before, a rush of energy flooding through his body. His stamina bar was restored to full, and he went back to work with reinvigorated muscles. The still containing the Moss Nettle finished, and he set off a reaction for the 100 units of essence it produced, quickly bottling those as well.

Apparently, 600 Lesser Stamina Potions could fit in a single slot in his inventory. Theo approached his Large Dimensional Crate and split the stack, mentally taking 500 when a message popped up.

> **[Inventory Transfer]** Do you want to transfer 500 Lesser Stamina Potions into your Large Dimensional Crate?
> **[YES/NO]**

Theo gave his mental confirmation, and the potions vanished from his inventory. This was a welcome feature, but one he wasn't aware of. Azrug came upstairs during his frenzied crafting, holding his hand out expectantly. The alchemist furrowed his brow, moving to the window to see the sun hanging in its midday position. He chuckled, not having noticed that the time had flown by him so fast, and handed the boy his two copper coins for the day.

Before he could leave, Theo stopped him. "How are you liking the job?"

"Are you kidding? This is the easiest thing I've ever done. I made a few sales today, by the way. Coppers under the counter. More local adventurers looking for potions."

"Did they ask about any other potions?" Theo asked. He

wanted to know if people were interested in the things he was currently working on, namely Lesser Stamina Potions.

"Not really. They just buy whatever they see," Azrug said, shrugging. "Can I go?"

"Of course," Theo said, waving him off.

The boy left, and Theo went downstairs to inspect what he sold today. Azrug had sold ten Lesser Healing Potions, netting the shop 50 copper. It would hardly pay the bills, but the money would keep the laborers working for another two days. The Newt and Demon would live and die by the big jobs for people like Fenian. The alchemist needed more people like him to come into the shop to make massive purchases.

Theo updated Tresk, learning that she had more than enough motes stashed away in her dimensional bag to finish the job. During her dungeon run, she had promised to return with something she was certain could be used in alchemy, but he had his doubts. His herbalism core granted him the ability to see what was useful for alchemy, a trait others lacked. With everything cooked down for the day and the stills completely cleaned, Theo found himself with nothing to do. He had written as much as he wanted about the process of distillation the other day and had no desire to work on his book.

The alchemist was doubting any book he could create and its usefulness to other alchemists. It was possible that the way he made potions was unique to the descendants of Drogramath. He pulled his shirt down to look at the brand on his chest. The webwork of lines was impossible to understand with symbols, which even the translation function of the system couldn't resolve. After pacing back and forth in the lab for a while, he threw his hands up in exasperation and left the shop. The moment his feet hit the muddy road, the laborers he had hired arrived.

"Got some good stuff for you, boss," Ziz said, grinning.

"To the lab," Theo said, unlocking the door and leading them upstairs.

The group unloaded their satchels into the dimensional storage crate, and Theo assessed their findings. He was immediately shocked by what they found—115 Stone Flowers, 100 Water Lilies, and 122 Flame Roses. He had never seen the roses before, so he inspected one from the crate.

[Flame Rose]
[Alchemy Ingredient]
Common
Rose enchanted with elemental fire. Grows near sources of fire or ignitable materials.
Properties:
[Increase Strength] [???] [???]

"Flame Rose... Where did you find this?" Theo asked. "It says it needs to be near a source of fire."

"There's a peat bog in the swamp. With the wolves under control, it's pretty easy to get there now," Ziz said, grinning. "Did we do good, boss?"

"Beyond good. This is an absurd amount of materials," Theo said. He wanted to tell them how much money it was worth but stopped himself. He didn't know if flaunting his potential wealth would anger people, and he wasn't about to test it. "Stop by the shop tomorrow morning, I need to decide if I have a new task for you."

"Well," Ziz said, shuffling his feet. "Miss Grott—Perg Grott—told us to poke you in the butt about the tannery materials."

"Right," Theo said, nodding. He accessed his memory, instantly remembering the requirements for his potions. He had plenty of Ogre Cypress Bark for the Stripping Solution but needed a lot of Marsh Tubers and Swamplight Spider Silk for the Alchemic Tannin. "Do you remember the tubers and the spider silk?"

"I do," Ziz said, nodding.

"I'll need as much of that as you can get tomorrow. And you're on Perg's dime for that job," Theo said, withdrawing 25 copper from his inventory and handing the sum over.

"Sounds like you're trying to steal us away," Ziz said, grinning.

"I am," Theo said. "I doubt Perg really needs you guys anymore—no offense meant."

"Nah, it's true. She takes pity on us because we're just laborers," Ziz said, shrugging. "You replaced our jobs with alchemy. Not that I blame you."

"Well, there are a few things alchemy can't solve," Theo said, chuckling. "We're going to go ahead with the quarry when Fenian comes to collect his potions. You *do* know how to quarry and shape stone, right?"

Ziz shrugged, his companions joining with him. "Well enough. Give us a few weeks, and we'll be very good at it."

"Sounds good to me," Theo said. "I'll employ you full time when that happens. It might be at a lower or higher rate. I won't know until we get rolling."

"Well, I'd like to negotiate my part in that," Ziz said, "seeing as I'm somehow the leader of this group of idiots."

One laborer voiced his objections to being called an idiot, but his complaints were silenced by a stare from Ziz. "Anything in mind?"

"Ownership of the quarry and the stonecutter's shop," Ziz said.

Theo wouldn't give up full ownership of his investments so easily. He would be lucky if the seeds for the two core buildings cost anything less than a gold coin. The alchemist had a mind for charity with the people of Broken Tusk, but this was asking too much. He pushed his anger at the outrageous request down, his mind snapping back to his negotiating tactic. Aim high and settle for the middle ground.

"You get the land on a lease, paid for with your work," Theo said. "You start at zero percent and work your way up to full ownership."

Ziz's eyes brightened, and Theo knew that the man had been

aiming for far less. "They're going to be core buildings, aren't they?"

A grin spread across Theo's face. "With any luck."

Ziz reached his hand out, shaking Theo's with a broad smile on his face. "We live and die by our success. I like it."

"I'll figure out a way to make the arrangement official," Theo said.

The laborers departed in better spirits than when they arrived. Theo inspected the storage crate again. The reagents they brought him were worth a gold coin, according to Fenian's deal. A half day's work for years' worth of wages, by Broken Tusk standards. The entire situation seemed too absurd for him to understand. Tresk arrived shortly after, and they departed with Aarok and Luras close behind.

"Aarok has invited us over for dinner," Tresk said, pressing her forehead against Theo's. "I accepted for you."

"Well, I took a Lesser Stamina Potion earlier. Drop your motes off in the lab before we go. Oh, and use some Cleansing Scrub—you smell like the swamp," Theo said.

Tresk giggled, running upstairs to deposit her haul before returning. "Let's go!"

Chapter 29
Salt

Theo never gave any consideration to the cluster of houses at the north end of town, at the bottom of the farmer's hill. He had seen it on his administrator's map but never put the information together to understand that it was where most of the people in the town lived. Aarok led them there, up through the square and past the tavern. They walked quickly past the Marsh Wolf Tavern, not wanting to draw Xam's eye. She seemed to think everyone should take three meals a day from her establishment.

"It's not much," Aarok said, shrugging.

Theo didn't want to agree, but he was right. The house sat off a side road, nestled among boulders and trees. It was the same rotting wood construction that the rest of the town was made of—shoddy foundation miraculously holding the frame up. The inside was more inviting than the outside, although the alchemist spotted some holes in the roof. It had the clean smell of a place just doused with Cleansing Scrub, the walls adorned with hunting trophies. They entered a living area with a bedroom off to their right, the door barely holding onto the frame.

"It's nice!" Tresk shouted, overshadowing Theo's mental response.

She was right. It wasn't a core house, but it was cozy.

Compared to what was left on Earth, this place was delightful. Theo felt himself lifted by the marshling's positive attitude, and he started searching for the good in the place. The living area held a hearth on the far side made of stone, the remnants of a cooking fire still smoldering. There was plenty of seating in the main area and a window looking out the front.

"It's a Broken Tusk hovel," Luras said, plopping down in a chair and glaring at Theo. "What more could you expect?"

"It's nice," Theo said, nodding. "No, really, it is. If you went to my planet, before it was destroyed, and found a swamp... It was far worse than this. Bombed-out houses, radiation everywhere. It was bad."

"What's radiation?" Tresk asked.

"Like poison, but it gets into your body by just existing in your vicinity," Theo said.

"We have something like that," Aarok said, shivering. "Wizards can cast nasty magic."

Aarok busied himself with the fire before digging a pan from a crate near the hearth. He withdrew something from his dimensional bag and set it aside, waiting for the newly lit fire to burn to coals. Theo found a seat and reclined, watching as a group of people passed by the window. He noticed significantly more people on this side of town and realized that the reason for that was his alchemy lab's placement near the tannery—a place no one wanted to go near.

"Hey!" Tresk shouted, jumping from her seat and crossing the room. "Is that *butter*? How the heck did you get Karatan butter?"

A smile crept across the half-ogre's face. "It's been in my bag for a *long* time. I've been saving it for a special occasion, and this seemed fitting."

"With the adventurer's guild and new walls..." Luras said, grunting. "Seems appropriate."

While Luras tried to hide his excitement, Theo could see it. He leaned forward in his chair a little more and licked his lips. The alchemist tried not to laugh, but then Aarok pulled a loaf of bread from the bag.

"No way," Theo said, his stomach suddenly grumbling. "Bread? Where did you get bread?"

Aarok laughed. "I pull out Karatan butter, and you drool over the bread? I can't believe I'm going to say this, but I can show you how to mill Zee Kernels and make bread. I'll get to instruct an alchemist on something."

"I'd really appreciate it," Theo said. "Why don't the farmers mill it themselves?"

"They used to, a while back," Tresk said, shrugging. "No idea why they stopped."

"Because townsfolk won't pay premium prices for bread," Luras said. "They had to use querns to mill it by hand—can't keep Karatans this far south."

"What the heck is a quern?" Theo asked.

"Two big slabs of rock that crush the grain," Luras said, shrugging. "I worked the farm for a few summers when I was a kid."

Aarok placed the pan on the coals, satisfied that the fire had died down enough. He put a bit of the butter in, the group watching as it danced across the surface. It sizzled and filled the room with a nutty aroma that sent Theo's stomach growling louder. The group watched without speaking as the half-ogre produced four fat wolf steaks from his dimensional bag, setting them on a wooden cutting board and pulling a smaller bag out. He sprinkled something on top of the steaks.

"Salt!" Tresk shouted. "Who are you, Aarok?"

Aarok couldn't help but laugh. "Just a half-ogre who likes his wolf steaks."

Theo hadn't considered a lot of things about his new world, but the availability of spices suddenly became high on his list of things he needed to know about. Even the soup he made in his house was bland when compared to the foods on Earth before the fall. The scent of the four steaks cooking in the pan made him realize how flavorless his food had been. The group sat, hushed and listening to the sizzling meat, while they awaited their meal.

"This is a meal for celebration," Luras said, nodding to himself. "For all we've accomplished."

"It pays to have an alchemist, I guess," Tresk said.

Theo still wasn't certain about that idea. Any old alchemist wouldn't have accomplished what he had. The gifts given by the Harbinger were the defining factor, putting him in a tier of master alchemists in faraway cities. He was overpowered by every measure. He could produce more types of potions than a low-level alchemist, and the potions he created were more powerful.

"There might be consequences for my skills," Theo said.

Luras cast him a knowing look, nodding in agreement.

"What? All I see is free potions and money," Tresk said.

"That inquisitor was the first sign," Aarok said, flipping the steaks and returning to his seat. "Theo's abilities will draw some attention. We need to be prepared to make sure that attention is positive."

"The walls," Theo said, shrugging. "I wanted the walls to keep more than wolves out. Prying eyes and bandits."

"With the way the adventurers are leveling, I'd like to see someone try something," Tresk said. "We're all shooting up in level so fast."

"Let's keep away from the gloomy topics," Aarok said. He moved about the room, finding plates for everyone and dishing out the steaks.

The half-ogre's command for silence was unnecessary. The group fell into hushed silence as they were handed their food. Theo inspected his steak, a thick slab of meat seared perfectly on both sides with globules of butter and fat running over the surface. He withdrew his Copper Alchemy Knife and cut it down the middle, finding it to be perfectly medium. He cut a small chunk and put it in his mouth, an explosion of flavor dancing over his tongue. It was almost *too* flavorful compared to the food he had been eating. He closed his eyes, savoring the way the meat melted in his mouth as he chewed..

"Why have we been eating slop every night?" Theo asked.

"Can we buy your salt?" Tresk said, foregoing the knife and taking large chunks out of her steak with her teeth.

"Shouldn't there be an alchemical solution for that?" Aarok asked mockingly.

Theo knew he was joking, but there might be a way he could make salt. His extremely high Wisdom skill told him that the extraction of base materials should be possible, but he couldn't put it together yet. It was too advanced for his alchemy core, but he suspected that Level 10 would reveal a lot of new abilities.

"I know that look!" Tresk shouted, pointing at Theo. "There *is* an alchemical way to make salt!"

"Hold your horses—hold your Karatans. I have an idea, but who knows. Seems like advanced stuff," Theo said.

"You can buy salt. Just ask the trader when he comes around," Luras said. He was eating like Tresk, taking bites out of the steak instead of cutting it. "It's pretty cheap too."

"Yeah, I was messing around. I paid 10 copper for this bag," Aarok said, laughing.

Luras and Aarok shared war stories for a while, recalling their time as young men with aspirations for soldiery. After a while, it was clear why they hadn't been accepted into the irregular army. The pair of them were always messing around, walking their own path while neglecting the core discipline of the Qavelli army. Theo understood how their hopes to become soldiers would be crushed by their desire for freedom. He didn't envy anyone serving in a fighting force, not even his old self. Being told where to go and what to do was too much for him.

The group chatted until the sun hung low in the sky, giving way to twilight. Tresk was falling asleep in her chair, barely able to keep her head up to nod in response to the conversation. Luras helped Theo carry her back to the shop when she finally fell asleep. He must have had a massive Vigor attribute, as he didn't seem tired. The alchemist, having downed a Lesser Stamina Potion earlier, wasn't tired at all. He could feel the day wearing on him, but he was a long way from being sleepy. The pair put the marshling to bed and retreated down to the shop.

"You've come a long way, Theo," Luras said. "From a wide-eyed outworlder to who you are now. It's impressive. I can't imagine falling into a world I don't know, then hitting the ground running like you did."

Theo sighed, moving around the shop to light the candles. He leaned against the front counter and smiled at the half-ogre. "People can do some crazy things when they have no other choice. This was a second chance for me, though."

"A way to atone," Luras said, nodding. "I can relate."

"You've done some stuff, huh?" Theo asked. "I'm not surprised."

Luras reached into his satchel and brought something out. It was a core, but not like the other cores the alchemist had seen before. The energy that radiated off the object was powerful, whipping ribbons of power across the room and buffeting Theo. The half-ogre gestured for him to inspect the object.

[Mastercraft Leatherworker's Core]
Epic
Leatherworker's Core
Unbound
2 Slots
Level 1 (0%)
Mastercraft core created by combining many lower-grade cores.
Effect:
Increase the effect of leatherworking efforts.
+1 Wisdom

Theo looked at the core in awe. He could see now that it reflected the sensibilities of a leatherworker. The core was a web of metal surrounding a glowing leather interior, exuding a pale brown light. He couldn't even guess how much the thing cost.

"My life's savings," Luras said, almost as if reading Theo's mind. "To give up the life of adventure and start a leatherworker's shop."

"You made these, didn't you?" Theo said, gesturing at his moccasins.

"I did," Luras said. "Not with the power of a skill, though. The items I'd make with this core would be a lot more powerful."

Luras had done more for Theo than he could ever repay. The half-ogre dropped everything to help the alchemist. Even if there was money involved, that was a powerful thing. He summoned his administrator's map of Broken Tusk without hesitation, finding a large plot of land next to Perg's tannery.

[Broken Tusk Parcel #52] can be purchased for **10 silver coins.**
Buy Parcel? [YES/NO]

Theo bought it without hesitation, mentally transferring ownership to his friend.

[Broken Tusk Parcel #52] has been transferred to Luras Trinner.

Luras narrowed his eyes at the alchemist. "Theo... You didn't have to do that."

"I wanted to," Theo said, smiling. "I'll buy you a core seed, too. Enough to get you started."

Luras was moved, even if his stony expression wouldn't show it. He placed his hand on the alchemist's shoulder and nodded.

"It's not free," Theo said. "In case you forgot, my Tara'hek is a rogue. She needs gear."

Luras laughed, unable to find the words to thank his companion. They left the shop, heading out into the darkness to inspect the new parcel. Theo couldn't remember if he had been out in town after nightfall, but it was lovely. A pale-yellow moon hung overhead, almost full and illuminating their path. They found the parcel next to Perg's tannery and walked the length of it. Like most parcels on the southern side of the town, it was massive.

The pair returned to the main road, finding an adventurer performing his night patrol. He held a lantern high and greeted them before moving on. The sight was comforting, mostly because of the baying of wolves outside the walls. Theo gestured for Luras to follow him. They found their way to the western gate, ascending the battlements and looking out over the swamp.

"That's a dangerous place at night," Luras said, shaking his head.

Theo didn't need him to say that to understand. Quadrupedal figures danced in the distance, darting between shadows and lying in wait. The alchemist wanted nothing to do with the life people led outside of the walls, preferring a solid curtain of stone between him and the horrors of the dungeon-spawned things. He couldn't understand Tresk's lust for adventure but resigned himself to that fact. She did her thing, and he did his.

"Steak... Need more steak. Stop hogging! Mine!" Tresk's voice came into his mind.

Theo laughed, incurring a curious look from the half-ogre. "Tresk and I normally sleep at the same time, so this hasn't happened yet. She's projecting her dreams into my mind."

"I didn't know that was a thing," Luras said, narrowing his eyes on the swamp. "What is she dreaming about?"

"Steak," Theo said, squinting to get a better look through the gloom.

A cloud moved out from over the moon, bathing the swamp in its light. Theo spotted the massive form of a wolf darting between trees. It coiled on the spot and made a run for the wall, sloshing through the mud and leaping against the stone. Its jump fell short, only making it about a quarter of the way up the wall. The alchemist still fell back, startled. "Do they normally do that?"

"The big, mean ones do," Luras said. "Maybe he's testing it. We might have to put a special bounty out on him."

The wolf growled at the base of the wall, baring its teeth up at the pair before slinking off. Once Theo got a better look at it, he saw how large it really was—twice the size of a normal wolf—and foamed at the mouth, snapping at the air even as it joined back with the shadows of the marsh.

"*Now* I'm going to have trouble sleeping," Theo said. "That thing was as big as a cow."

"What's a cow?"

"They're livestock. Kinda like Karatan. I think," Theo said. He didn't know what a Karatan looked like, only that it tasted delicious.

"Yeah, maybe smaller. The wolves have a lot fewer legs, anyway," Luras said.

Theo didn't want to know if he was joking or not and left it at that. They dismounted the battlements and walked around town for a little while longer. Lights extinguished from people's windows, signaling the town's slumber in full. At the town's square, the alchemist bid Luras farewell and made his way back to the shop, tiredness finally setting in. The Lesser Stamina Potion did wonders to perk him up earlier in the day, but his stamina bar had finally drained past half-empty. He crept into the shop, locking the door behind him, and ascended the stairs to the bedroom.

As he settled down in his bed, he heard Tresk snort loudly. *"More steak, please."*

Theo drifted off, eager to take part in the dream-steak.

Chapter 30
Rain and Steak

Theo rose near dawn the next morning, his late-night excursion with Luras clearly taking its toll. Tresk was waiting in the lab, sipping on her tea and smiling when he emerged. The alchemist withdrew the days-old pot of soup from his inventory. Steam rose from the cauldron, having lost none of its heat while in dimensional storage.

"You had quite a night, huh?" Tresk asked, laughing.

Theo assumed his seat near the window, shaking his head. He explained how he bought the parcel of land for Luras, and the Half-Ogre's intentions to become a leatherworker. He dished out two bowls of soup, passing one to his companion.

"That's just a smart move," Tresk said. "The town is going to do a lot better with more crafters."

That was just a fact. Theo's recent progress in putting Broken Tusk on the map would see their population explode. It would be a gold rush of people seeking to exploit the swamp's natural resources. Luras would put himself in a fantastic position with an endless supply of leather to work on. It wasn't just good leather, it was impossibly supple, durable leather brought directly from the swamp itself.

"He's going to make a killing," Theo said.

"No doubt."

"Did you get anything good from the dungeon yesterday?" Theo asked.

Tresk shrugged, slurping noisily on her soup. "Lots of cores. No gear."

"What about that thing you thought was a reagent?" Theo asked.

Tresk's face brightened. "Oh! I almost forgot." She withdrew something that looked suspiciously like a skull fragment and handed it over.

[Reanimated Skeleton Fragment]
[Alchemy Ingredient]
Common
Skull fragment of a skeleton reanimated by necromantic powers.
Properties:
[Withering] [???] [???]

"It's a skull fragment," Theo said, grimacing. "Of a magic skeleton. This is gross, but it has the [Withering] property."

"Hah! I knew it," Tresk said. "I tried to eat one, and it gave me a bad cramp. Drained my stamina a bit."

Theo closed his eyes, pressing his fingers into his temples. "Tresk. Why would you eat a skull fragment?"

"To see if it was an alchemy thing," Tresk said, shrugging. "I saw you do it."

The alchemist had to wonder why she wasn't dead yet, with that kind of recklessness. "And the motes?"

"Oh yeah," Tresk said, withdrawing some motes from her bag. Then she withdrew some more. Theo couldn't scoop them up fast enough, and the floor was soon littered by rolling balls of pulsating energy.

"Thanks," Theo said, scooping the absurd amount of motes

from the ground. Along with his dwindling stores, it would be enough to make Fenian's potions.

A knock at the door brought Theo downstairs, Tresk close behind. Ziz stood with his laborers, waving and smiling. "Morning, boss. Perg is mad that she has to pay us again, but I wanted to see if you needed anything while we're scouring the land."

Theo produced 10 copper coins from his inventory and handed them over. "As many motes as you can find. Those coins are a *tip*."

Ziz grinned, distributing the money among his companions and turning on the spot. As soon as they departed, Azrug showed up. He didn't say a word to either Tresk or Theo, closing the door behind him.

"Well, I guess I should get going," Tresk said, shrugging. Theo bent down to press his forehead against hers, and she departed, waving as she went.

Theo retreated to his laboratory, taking stock of what he had to brew for the day. The entire base order for Fenian was done. The alchemist was guaranteed to get his three gold coins at the end, but he wanted the additional pay. After cleaning the stills with Cleansing Scrub, Theo prepared to make the largest run of attribute-enhancing potions he had ever done. Fortunately, it ran off of the same basic recipe as the lesser restoration potions and wouldn't cause him any problems. The flowers were effortless to mash, and he had both stills running within half-hour of starting.

Theo's Drogramath Alchemy Core was almost Level 8, and his Drogramath Herbalist Core trailed behind by a significant margin. The first still he set up ran 200 units of the Water Lily, while the second only ran 100 units of the Stone Flower. He also had 122 Flame Roses in his inventory, and he would use them once he got back from gathering herbs. The thought of heading out into the swamp crossed his mind, but quickly left as the image of the giant wolf made him uncomfortable. He set his mental timer and left the shop, waving at Azrug as he went.

Unlike during most of his jaunts across his parcel, the sun was obstructed by a thick layer of clouds. It was the first time he had seen a storm loom over Broken Tusk, but the dark clouds blowing from the southern sea meant rain. By the time he made it to the river, a light drizzle fell on his head. It washed over him, the soft patter of the raindrops cleansing his mind and sharpening his focus. The alchemist stood by the river with a Water Lily in hand, gazing out over the turbid rush of water with hooded eyes. A chill ran up his back as the rain soaked through his clothes, matting them down on his body.

Theo sat on the pebbled shore of the river, breathing in the wet smell. Something swelled in his chest, the deluge stirring something in his soul. He used to love the rain back on Earth. Before the fall of civilization, he would stand on his balcony and listen to the raindrops for hours. It took every bit of his willpower to stand up and return to the lab when his mental timer went off. He entered the shop, dripping from the rain, which gained Azrug's attention.

"The rain is finally here," Azrug said, grunting and returning his gaze to the book.

Theo withdrew two copper coins and slapped them down on the counter. "In case I forget to pay you."

"Again."

Theo ignored the comment. "Does it normally rain like this in the Season of Blooms?"

"It's usually worse," Azrug said, glancing up to look out the window. "Mid-morning storms like this were my childhood. It used to rain every day until the season ended, but not so much anymore."

Theo nodded, ascending the stairs with his sloshing moccasins and swapping the fresh flask in the still brewing Wisdom Essence. The still processing Vigor Essence was done. He cleaned it out with Cleansing Scrub and prepared the Flame Roses by mashing them, adding the paste to the still and leveling it off with Purified Water. Then, he brought the Flame Artifices back to life.

The alchemist fed motes into the Glassware Artifice, generating an absurd number of flat-bottomed vials for the attribute-enhancing potions. He cleared away some junk for a table and distributed the restoration essences he had made earlier. Like the Lesser Stamina Potions, the other restoration potions stacked to at least 500. He noticed that Fenian's quest's objectives weren't marked as done and reasoned that only when he handed the potions over would they finish. Theo kicked off the simple reaction for the Lesser Potion of Vigor, holding back on the Lesser Potion of Wisdom until the remaining 100 units had distilled. He distributed it into vials while he waited for both batches to finish, then repeated the process.

It was midday by the time he cleared out his stills, causing the reaction on the remaining essences and taking stock of his creations. He had 500 of mana and health potions, 600 of the stamina potions, 200 Lesser Potions of Wisdom, 100 Lesser Potions of Strength, and 100 Lesser Potions of Vigor. According to the quest, it was two gold coins' worth of potions, assuming he didn't exchange them for monster cores. It was a quantity of money that seemed absurd—an absolute embarrassment of riches. He had to wonder if Fenian's deal was too good to be true.

Theo pulled up his quest menu, found [Fenian's Request], and knitted his brow. He was great at losing track of the days, but he was certain more than one day remained on the order. And yet the quest claimed he had one day before Fenian returned. It seemed the elf was returning a day early. It would be nice to clear the quest out of his log, but that was too soon. The elf must have hastened his pace back to Broken Tusk, and the alchemist didn't doubt the merchant's ability to cover long distances quickly. It made sense that a merchant would have a magical means of transportation.

The shop was empty when Theo went to check on his shopkeeper. It was past midday, though the rain still obfuscated the sun above, and he was still soaking wet. He cleaned the place up, organizing the potions on the shelves and adding new ones. His stock was pathetic, but he had no time to distill anything else today. Perg's order had to take priority. He withdrew a parchment from his inventory and scrawled batch quantities on it. She was expecting a 200-unit solution of Stripping Solution and Alchemic Tannin. With his improved knowledge and skills, he would instead produce 500 units of each. The reactions were incredibly forgiving at a 0.1 to 5 ratio of essence to Stabilized Water.

Theo would need to prepare 50 units of Ogre Cypress Bark, Swamplight Spider Silk, and Marsh Tubers each, but would run as large a batch as he could and store the essences. If the laborers brought an absurd amount of reagents, he would process them all. The plan was to hold the essences in reserve, without telling Perg, allowing him to produce the solutions quickly upon request. His math checked out on paper, solidifying the knowledge he gained from experience.

Shortly after finishing his plan, the laborers showed up. They were all drenched from the rain but had wide smiles on their faces. Theo led them upstairs, everyone's shoes sloshing as they went, and had them deposit the materials in his dimensional crate. They had gone crazy out in the marsh. Over 200 units of Swamplight Spider Silk and Marsh Tubers were now in his possession, along with a bounty of motes. He couldn't even imagine how they had found so much silk, but knew that the adventurers' efforts to clear the wolves had something to do with it.

"Did we do good, boss?" Ziz asked.

"You did great," Theo said. "You're on regular reagent duty starting tomorrow. Thistle root, mushrooms, moss—you know the deal."

"How about the quarry?"

Theo managed a wry smile. He would hate to lose his laborers, but he also understood that their work wasn't good for his herbalism core. "We'll talk about it tomorrow. The elven trader should be here. We'll see what seed cores he has in his wares."

"Understood, boss," Ziz said. He turned and left the lab, his companions' boots sloshing behind him.

Theo downed a Lesser Stamina Potion, cleared out the stills, and got to work. The surge of energy allowed him to chop the Marsh Tubers up quickly, but he knew his enhanced Strength attribute did the heavy lifting. The Swamplight Spider Silk didn't need more than a light tapping of his pestle and was the first to be tossed into the still. With fresh motes in the Flame Artifices, he started the slow distillation process. Tresk updated him about her adventures again, letting him know she was safe and returning home. Fortunately, she didn't say she had any more dubious alchemy ingredients this time, but she sounded tired.

The alchemist could only imagine what happened in those dungeons. The fitful battles between life and death that played out daily beyond the walls of Broken Tusk were beyond him. He listened to the slow drip of the condensers filling the dual flasks. The rain outside played against his window, and he opened it to let the sound in. Theo breathed in the wet air, letting out a heavy sigh. There was something about the smell of falling rain that roused something within him.

Tresk arrived home when the first two flasks were full with 100 units of each essence that he needed. He stowed them away and greeted his companion, pressing his forehead against hers and gaining another level in his Tara'hek Core. The special core was now Level 4, and he was curious about how the unalterable core would provide them with new abilities at the threshold of Level 5. As they sat together at the table, Tresk closed her eyes and smiled, listening to the sound of the rain pouring outside.

"That's a lovely sound," Tresk said. Her skin was still slick from the rain, but she didn't seem to care.

"It really is," Theo said. "Azrug said there are seasonal rains during the springtime."

"Springtime? Ah, the Season of Blooms," Tresk said, nodding. "I guess 'spring' makes sense. But, yeah. We have a lot of rain down south during the spring."

"I bet it's good for the alchemy reagents," Theo said.

Tresk shrugged, pulling random junk out of her dimensional bag. "We didn't make it to the first boss. Again. Luras just doesn't have his heart in it, I think."

"He wants to live the life of a crafter," Theo said, gesturing to the lab. "Who could blame him? Look at this place. It's nice."

"You're a homebody," Tresk said, giggling.

"I won't argue with that," Theo said. "I traveled all over Earth. Despite the nature of the job, it was still nice."

"The job being murder," Tresk asked, grinning.

Theo frowned. He knew his assignments boiled down to that, but he preferred to think of them as assignments and marks. Not missions and people. Nonetheless, the marshling was right. Whatever he wanted to call it in his head, he'd be lying to himself if it was anything but murder. "Much like an assassin here, I guess."

"Some people need to die," Tresk said, shrugging. "Best way to remove a despot here is with a high-level assassin."

"That's morbid," Theo said, chuckling. "True, but morbid."

"Don't worry," Tresk said, retrieving one last item from her inventory. It was a wide copper pan. She brandished it like a weapon and grinned. "I'll protect you."

Theo shook his head. "With that?"

"This is for the wolf steak," Tresk said. "Once you're done with the magic fire, I'm making us some steak."

Theo doubted that the steak would be as good as the ones made by Aarok, but he wouldn't object. He wondered for a moment about how healthy it would be to eat steak every day but couldn't speculate on how cholesterol worked in this strange world. There might even be a potion he could use to cure people of their bad eating habits. He would need to look into it.

"So, the salt problem," Theo said, withdrawing a scroll and laying it down on the table.

"I knew you'd crack this," Tresk said, bounding over with a wide smile on her face.

"No progress... yet," Theo said. "My Wisdom tells me there's something I can do beyond Level 10, but I only have theories right now. Maybe transmutation, or the separation of base elements from more complex compounds. I don't really know."

"So, what's the theory?" Tresk asked, bouncing up and down.

Theo shrugged. "Exactly what I said. I think I can do something to matter once I level up a bit more. It only makes sense if you think about everything in the world having a bunch of properties, like my alchemy reagents. I can separate out those properties into essences, so why not base materials?"

"I'm excited for free salt," Tresk said, nodding to herself.

"Not just salt." Theo shrugged. "Technically, everything is made up of small amounts of a lot of precious things. I remember hearing back on Earth that the human body had gold in it. Other stuff probably has random junk in it, I just have to figure out how to extract it."

"Well, I'm mostly useless for that kinda stuff. I'm *really* good at stabbing things. Let me know if you need something stabbed," Tresk said.

"Your stabbing prowess has been noted."

The essences finished cooking, and Theo stowed them away into his inventory before cleaning the stills. Tresk stole a Flame Artifice and placed the large copper pot on top. She waited a moment for it to get hot before placing four thick strips of wolf meat, the steaks sizzling instantly.

"Four steaks?" Theo asked. "Are you really that hungry?"

Tresk cast him a devious look, wiggling her eyebrows. "Wait for it."

Theo only had to wait a few tense moments for the knock at the door to come. He blustered, throwing his hands up in exasperation. "How can he even smell it with the rain?" he asked.

The alchemist marched downstairs, finding both Luras and Perg standing expectantly on the other side of the door. He folded his arms and waited there for a moment. "Do you guys wait outside of my house every afternoon? Waiting for handouts?"

Luras and Perg shared a look, then said "Yes" in unison.

Theo led them upstairs, maintaining the farce that he was upset only for so long. By the time they reached the stairs' landing, he was laughing about the situation. The group sat down at the table by the window, the sounds of the storm washing over the room in turbid waves. The scent of the cooking meat filled the room. Tresk sat dutifully by the skillet, licking her lips without even looking up to greet the guests.

"Almost done with my stuff?" Perg asked, smiling.

"No business over dinner!" Tresk shouted, waving her wooden spoon.

"It's fine. Yeah, I'll be done tomorrow," Theo said.

"Good, because I almost need to take out a loan. That seed core drained my funds," Perg said.

"No one wants to hear about your funds," Luras groaned.

"Hey! I don't have an alchemist benefactor supporting my business," Perg said.

"Yes, you do," Luras said.

Perg went to speak, but stopped before any words came out. She folded her arms in front of her chest and focused her attention on the cooking steaks. "I guess we're all becoming dependent on Theo."

"Not for long," the alchemist said. "I'm trying to be mindful of that. Made a deal with Ziz to start a stone-cutting business—I'll give him ownership after a time."

"Still," Luras said, shrugging, "we depend on you now."

"Yeah! You have to defend him. He's too precious," Tresk said, flipping the steaks one last time. "Now shut up! No business over dinner."

A small marshling brandishing a wooden spoon was enough to silence the group. They moved on to small talk as they ate their meal. As Theo predicted, it wasn't as good as the cuts that Aarok had made for them, but it was still great. He made a mental note to switch between the soup and steak for dinner, perhaps combining them. The conversation went on until dusk, when Luras and Perg departed for the night. Tresk turned in before Theo, who was still under the effect of a Lesser Stamina Potion. He spent the alone time with his thoughts, correcting old notes and listening to the storm that raged until after nightfall.

After a short while, he finally fell asleep, thankful that none of Tresk's dreams invaded his thoughts.

Chapter 31
Fenian Feintleaf

Theo vowed never to rely on the stimulating properties of his Lesser Stamina Potions unless absolutely necessary, but he made an exception in his mind regarding the tea he brewed from the moss. Rising from his soft bed, he stretched. The storm was over, and he sat on the edge of his bed for a long time before getting up. Light filtered through the window, pale orange sun shafts cutting through the bedroom and signaling the coming of dawn. The sound of clanging cookware echoed from the lab.

The alchemist emerged to find Tresk cooking more wolf steaks on her new pan. She must have just plopped the considerable strips of meat down on the hot copper as the smell wafted his way. He made his way to the table, sitting down and sipping on the tea she provided. A long moment passed before he said anything to his companion.

"No more stamina potions," he said, shaking his head. "Feels like I have a hangover."

"You just need to be tired like the rest of us. Or put some points in Vigor," Tresk said.

"Find anything in your dungeon with Vigor? Maybe a ring?" Theo asked, grinning.

Tresk waved him off, flipping the steaks with another satisfying sizzle. "That necklace of yours is high-level stuff. We won't find anything like that in the first few floors of the dungeon."

Theo leaned back in his chair, looking out the window at their impressive backyard. He would have to confront the reality of establishing his masonry venture today and feared that it might be too much for him to take on. With the town leveled-up enough for a wall, he saw no need to feed monster cores into it anymore. He hoped Fenian would pay him in coin along with the cores he requested. If he was lucky, the elven trader would have seed cores for the quarry and a workshop.

There was also the promise he had made to Tresk to find more rogue cores, so she could upgrade her crummy one to a better quality. Theo often forgot that not everyone was running around with two legendary cores inside them. He also didn't know how to remove a core from himself—not that he wanted to. They seemed like rare things that cost a lot of money, and he was already up to his eyeballs with investments and debt.

"Fenian should be here today," Theo said. "The quest claims that I have zero days left until he returns. I'm guessing he has a magical way of transportation now."

"Or some mount," Tresk said, shrugging. "It takes seven days to get to Qavell—or so I've been told, I've never been there myself. I've heard of magic carriages that can zip across the countryside. If he's rich enough, he could have one of those."

"Well, I'm thinking of changing my deal with him. We don't need as many monster cores, and I was going to get you some rogue cores," Theo said.

"That would be lovely," Tresk said, nodding to herself and smiling. She flipped the steaks one last time, moving to prepare some plates. "How much money do you still owe?"

"Well, I've promised a few gold in investments," Theo said, shrugging. "I owe 2 gold to Miana for this place, maybe another 2 gold for the stone operation, and another for Luras's leatherworking operation."

"So, you're going to spend all your money as soon as you get it," Tresk said, nodding. "Gotcha."

"Honestly, I'm going to work out a deal with Fenian," Theo said. "Buy a bulk of things from him, hoping for a discount."

"What's your budget, and what's on your shopping list?"

"I'll get 5 gold from Fenian for his order. I need a seed core for a stonecutter workshop, a quarry seed core, and a leatherworker's seed core. If I can get those seed cores for around a gold, I'll be in good shape. Then I need your rogue cores, some artifices, and monster cores," Theo said. "How many rogue cores do you need to get a legendary one?"

Tresk pushed the steaks onto their respective plates, squinting her eyes and staring up at the ceiling for a moment. "Maybe... 36? 24? 16?" she asked, screwing up her face. "I really don't know."

"Well, how does it work?"

"You feed your current core like a building core," Tresk said, taking a seat at the table and handing a plate over to Theo. "So, I don't really know the experience drop-off."

"It's problematic to go into a negotiation without knowing what you need," Theo said, grimacing. "Well, I'll do my best."

Theo learned that morning that steak was an excellent option for breakfast. With the swamp filled to the brim with wolves, it was a viable option. It wasn't as tender as the Karatan steak, but it was still delicious. By the time he finished his tea, he was feeling much more like himself. The grogginess faded away, and he found himself ready to complete Perg's order. The companions talked as he prepared the stills, aiming to run a double batch of Ogre Cypress Bark for the essences required to make Stripping Solution.

Tresk tried to hide her excitement but failed. She chomped at her steak with abandon, tearing large chunks off and talking with her mouth full. "That's the thing. These traders can be a real boon to small people in trades. Fenian likely wants something from you. A long-term deal."

Theo had the stills prepared, and the Ogre Cypress Bark already mashed. He planned to run 400 units total, 200 in each still, focusing the first on the [Cure Ailment] property, and the other on the [Cleanse] property. He dumped the last of the mash in and thought about it, unable to find where he landed on the subject. A deal with Fenian would be great. He didn't mind the absurd production quotas, and the gold was good.

"Is this a bad thing?" Theo asked. "Should I be cautious?"

"You should always watch your coin purse around a trader, but I think I know this guy's angle," Tresk said, wiping her mouth off with the sleeve of her leather jacket.

"What's that?" Theo asked, starting the Flame Artifices and stepping back.

"Imagine you're an upstart trader in the northlands. Most of the trade routes are claimed, and every alchemist in Qavell has century-long deals with the established merchants. You find a diamond in the middle of the swamp. Do you milk him for all he's worth, or do you entice him to strike a pact?" Tresk asked.

"You think he wants to be *my* merchant?" Theo asked.

"Yep. He wants you to keep bulk orders with him," Tresk said, "before the big trade guilds pick up on it. They're usually slow to respond—or so I hear."

"I see absolutely no downside for us," Theo said, shrugging. "That would be an enormous win."

"Agreed. In this case, it works well for us because he's desperate," Tresk said. "But my bet is that he took those potions to the big city and blew everyone's minds. He didn't tell them where this new alchemist was, and made a hefty profit. You sell him a potion for 20 copper, and he resells it for 50. Maybe more."

"And he can do it because he's a traveling merchant with all the connections," Theo said. The marshling's logic made sense, and he wondered why he hadn't thought of it. He knew that Fenian was reselling the potions but didn't think that the elf thought of him as a resource rather than a simple supplier.

Theo looked over his lab, the glaring flaws of inefficiency fouling the scene. What he needed was better equipment that cut out the grunt work of the process.

Newt and Demon

"So, my point is that Fenian is going to make you a deal. You'll agree to take his bulk orders over everyone else, and he'll give you a break on supplies."

"That sounds like a sweet deal to me," Theo said.

"I agree. I think you should take it," Tresk said.

A knock came from the door downstairs. It was Azrug, waiting to do his shift at the shop. Theo got his attention before the boy sat down. "Fenian is going to be here today. Let me know when he arrives."

Azrug went pale, swallowing hard. "Yes, sir."

Theo returned to the lab, leaving the half-ogre boy to deal with his fear of outsiders. Tresk passed him on the stairs, pressing her forehead against his before departing for the day. She planned on prodding Luras into action, trying to get his head back in the adventuring game. The alchemist suggested that she find another adventuring partner, a suggestion that only drew exasperated sputtering from the marshling.

The condensers were doing their job, slowly filling the flasks up. Theo's nerves were getting to him while he waited for the elven trader. If Tresk was right, the deal he had to offer would be irresistible. He took stock of the equipment he had, focusing with his high Wisdom attribute and determining what the best artifice would be. The mashing process took far too long, and something that could grind the reagents for him would be amazing. He had a feeling that the stills weren't as optimal as they could be, either in production volume or capacity. There were no simple solutions for that problem, though. The distillation process was delicate.

Just as he was swapping out the flasks for the second step of the run, the bell on the door tinkled downstairs. Azrug's hurried steps up the stairs came next, followed by the boy poking his head into the lab. "He's here!"

Theo calmed himself for a moment, taking a few steadying breaths. He double-checked that all the required potions were in his inventory before going downstairs with the half-ogre boy. As expected, Fenian stood behind the counter with a massive grin on his face. His clothes were just like the ones he had worn before, with more ruffles than seemingly possible, and a new wide-brimmed hat on his head. The feather was still sticking out, long and ostentatious, like a peacock's tail feather.

"Theo," Fenian said, holding his arms wide. "Let me tell you something. Your potions were a hit in Qavell. The wholesalers could hardly contain themselves."

Theo approached the counter, reaching his hand out for the elf to shake, which he did. "Glad to hear."

"They paid *more* than what I planned to ask. Low-level potion distillation is usually left to the apprentices, resulting in shoddy quality. Your stuff is top-shelf," Fenian said, punctuating his statement with something that looked suspiciously like a chef's kiss.

"I'm glad to hear it, Fenian," Theo said, nodding. "If you thought the old stuff was good, wait until you see this."

Theo withdrew a single Lesser Healing Potion from his inventory. Unlike the old, great-quality batch, this one was marked as "excellent." Fenian sputtered, dramatically swaying on the spot and exclaiming. "You never cease to amaze me, sir. Was it the Flame Artifice that did the trick?"

"It was. The low-temperature heating was the key," Theo said.

"Glad to hear it. Before we get started, I have a few gifts to establish our new relationship," Fenian said, gesturing to reveal a book from his inventory. The cover was bound in some kind of leather, and the words on the front weren't in the standard language he had been reading. The characters were sharp, dagger-like things that ran together in a jagged script.

"*Basic Drogramathi Alchemy*. Where did you find this?" Theo asked, pressing his fingers into the cover and feeling the grain of the leather.

"Hah! I knew you'd be able to read it," Fenian said, beaming. "Your outworlder powers, or your heritage of the demon lord, allow you to read the text. A trader promised me it was related to Drogramath's art."

Theo wanted nothing more than to thumb through the pages,

discovering the secrets of his art. He held himself back, trying to put up a strong front against the elf's overt advances toward an exclusivity deal. The alchemist wanted the deal, but negotiations were about subterfuge. "Shall we get down to business?" Theo asked, smiling.

"Ah, yes. Business," Fenian said, waving a dismissive hand. "I have a few more gifts for you, but we'll take care of the transaction first."

"First things first," Theo said. "If you have the coin on you, I'd like to exchange half of the attribute potions for coin or other goods."

"Well, let's settle up. What goods are you interested in?"

"Seed cores first," Theo said.

"My specialty," Fenian said, raising an eyebrow. "That tannery woman, Perg, must have told you I sold her a seed core. You may be unaware, but those with legendary trader cores get a generous inventory. I have almost every production building available."

"I need a leatherworker's shop, a stone-cutter's shop, and a quarry," Theo said.

"I have them," Fenian said, nodding with a smile. "I have regular house seed cores, too, if you're interested."

"I might be," Theo said, trying not to sound too eager.

"I normally sell the seed cores for a gold coin," Fenian said.

"What about your favorite alchemist? Does he get a deal?" Theo asked, grinning.

Azrug let out an audible gasp behind them, quickly covering his mouth.

Fenian leaned in, placing his elbows on the counter. He gestured, producing a piece of parchment before placing it on the counter. Theo glanced over it, finding the entire thing to be a fairly concise contract between the two parties. As Tresk predicted, it gave the elf rights over everyone else to commission batches of potions, within reason. It promised better rates than the alchemist was currently getting from their arrangement, and access to the merchant's stock at a discount. It was incredibly generous.

"Enter into this contract with me, and I'll give you a *generous* discount on all my wares. Within reason," Fenian said.

Theo hesitated for a moment, even after reading and agreeing with everything it said. He tilted his head, mentally informing Tresk that she was right. After pretending to consider the deal for a while longer, he rose and smiled.

"I can agree to these terms," Theo said, nodding.

Fenian Faintleaf is attempting to enter **The Newt and Demon** into a contract.
You have already read the contract. Do you agree to its terms? **[YES/NO]**

Theo mentally accepted, feeling a rush flow through his chest.

"A wise decision," Fenian said. "I'm altering our current deal. I have no intention of bleeding you dry out here in the swamp, and I have a very specific clientele—namely noble-born whelps—interested in excellent-quality potions. Twenty-five copper a potion for the restoration ones, and 60 for the attribute-enhancing potions."

"That's very generous," Theo said.

"Right. So, you're the first person I'm testing this new ability with, so bear with me. You should see something pop up here in a moment," Fenian said.

[Trade with Fenian Feintleaf?] [YES/NO]

Theo accepted, and a window appeared in the middle of his vision. It had two sections on either side, with each person's name above the areas. At the bottom, there was a section for coins. Both were currently empty.

"Mentally add all your potions. I'll do the math in my head. This ability only works if the other person has an inventory. I'm very glad you chose that power—I'm not interested in shoving thousands of potions into my inventory myself."

Theo mentally added all the potions. 500 Lesser Healing

Potions, 500 Lesser Stamina Potions, 500 Lesser Mana Potions, 100 Lesser Potions of Vigor, 200 Lesser Potions of Wisdom, and 100 Lesser Potions of Strength appeared on the alchemist's side.

Fenian let out a long whistle. "You've been a busy little demon."

After a moment, a number appeared under the gold counter on Fenian's side that almost stopped Theo's heart. A sum of 6 gold and 15 silver appeared, flashing with a glowing golden border. The alchemist clicked the small green "Accept" box and waited for the trader to do the same. The window made a satisfying beeping sound before disappearing.

[Fenian's Request] Completed.

Theo would check what rewards he got from the quest later, focusing on the trade at hand.

"We'll just do it this way, and you can buy however many other things you want," Fenian said. "For the seed cores, I'll give you the three you want for 1 gold, 50 silver."

"That sounds like a deal to me," Theo said, nodding. "What do you have in terms of rogue cores? I need 30 of them, or something like that."

"Looking to upgrade your Tara'hek's core? Smart move," Fenian said. A grin spread across his face as he withdrew something from his inventory, holding it out for the alchemist to inspect.

[Assassin's Core]
Legendary
Assassin Core
Unbound
2 Slots
Level 1 (0%)
A specialized core that focuses on assassination techniques. Can slot either Rogue or Assassin skills. Equipping this core unlocks the Assassin class. Equipping this core over an

existing rogue core will consume it, setting this core to its current level.

Effect:
Increases the effect of all Rogue and Assassin skills
+2 Dexterity

Theo's eyes glittered. It was an absurdly nice core, but he had a feeling that it was unapproachable in terms of cost. He narrowed his eyes on the elf and feigned a smile. "How much?"

"Oh, about 10 gold on the open market," Fenian said, shrugging. "But for your Tara'hek, and the strength of our relationship, a gift at 1 gold, 50 silver."

Azrug let out a yelp, clasping his hands over his mouth again. Fenian smiled at the young half-ogre's reaction.

"Done," Theo said. "That's not even a question."

"You owe me 3 gold so far," Fenian said. "Anything else?"

"What kind of monster cores do you have?"

"Level 30, mostly," Fenian said. "Four for 1 gold—they should give you five levels apiece at your alchemy lab's current level."

"I'll take four," Theo said. "Any interesting alchemy artifices?"

"Ah, my other gifts," Fenian said, withdrawing four items from his inventory. The first three items were the same—large discs with clasps on the sides. There was a slot on the side to feed motes and an ominous-looking grinder on top. The other item was another Flame Artifice. "Alchemical Grinder Artifice. This will allow you to grind your reagents directly into your stills."

Fenian gestured again, withdrawing a small mote from his inventory. "But wait, there's more."

Theo inspected the mote, shocked at what he saw.

[Glassware Artifice Upgrade Mote]
[Upgrade Mote]
Uncommon
Feed this into a Glassware Artifice to expand its features.

Allows for the production of multiple glassware items at a reduced cost directly into your inventory.

The alchemist was at a loss for words. Fenian must have been making a killing off of the potions if he would part with so much valuable stuff.

"This is *incredibly* generous," Theo said.

"Everything I've provided will increase your output," Fenian said, shrugging. "It's self-interest that drives me. Ah, one more thing."

Fenian produced one last item from his inventory. It was a small, purple communication crystal like the one in Miana's house.

"So we can stay in contact?" Theo asked.

"Exactly," Fenian said. "If I'm honest, you're my one hope for greatness. Well, is there anything else?"

"How much for the house seeds?" Theo asked.

Fenian waved a dismissive hand. "Six for 1 gold."

"Then that's the last thing I'll buy. Six of those," Theo said. A plan centered around selling or renting houses was emerging in his mind. It wasn't fully formed yet, but it was getting there.

"Right. The Assassin's Core, the workshop seed cores, four Level 30 monster cores, and six house seed cores," Fenian said, opening the trade window and placing the items inside. "The total is 5 gold."

Theo happily put the gold into the window, accepting the trade and flooding his inventory with new things. The excitement was overwhelming and exhausting. He was left with 1 gold, 23 silver, and 31 copper after the deal.

"Now, if you'll excuse me, I need to head back to Qavell," Fenian said, straightening the ruffles on his coat. "I'll contact you with a new order when I arrive."

The elven trader turned on the spot and departed, leaving the pile of articles on the counter. As soon as the bell jingled, Azrug shouted, jumping on the spot repeatedly, "You just made more money than I've ever seen in my entire life—and then spent it!"

Chapter 32
Fire Salamander Eggs

Theo inspected his inventory, finding the reward from Fenian's quest sitting there. He removed the knife from his inventory, grimacing at its appearance. It was a short, ceremonial blade with too many jagged points leading up the length. It was made of a dark metal that he didn't recognize. He inspected it before leaving Azrug to his celebrations.

[Drogramath Alchemy Knife]
[Alchemy Equipment]
Epic
Ornate knife used by the disciples of Drogramath.
Effect:
Using this knife to harvest herbs will reveal nearby reagents.

The knife would streamline his harvesting process, allowing him to find those plants that hid from his sight. He wondered if the blade could detect something underground, but left that for another time.

Theo left Azrug to his excited dances downstairs, stuffing his new artifices in his inventory and running upstairs. He noticed

Fenian had given him three Alchemical Grinder Artifices and an additional Flame Artifice, no doubt encouraging him to expand his distillation setup. The stills were finished with their batches by the time he went upstairs and cleared everything away. With the essences in his inventory, he checked to see if they fit on the grinders. The artifice he pulled from his inventory seemed too large to fit on his stills, but as he brought the item near, it magically shrank to fit the rim.

"I have some really cool stuff to show you," Theo said, communicating his thoughts to Tresk.

"I hope it's some rogue cores," she said.

"You're gonna freak out," Theo said.

"Can't wait. I'm making Luras cut this run short so I can come see," Tresk said.

Theo converted a barrel of Purified Water into Stabilized Water and stowed it away in his inventory. He gathered the rest of his reagents to perform the explosive reaction but stopped at his Glassware Artifice before heading down. He stuffed the Glassware Artifice Upgrade Mote in the slot and watched as the machine dazzled with a bright blue light. It blinded him for a moment, but when the light faded, it seemed unchanged.

[Glassware Artifice] has been upgraded. New features added.

It was a simple-enough system message, not explaining exactly what had happened. He inserted an Earth Mote into the slot and thought about a large, 100-unit flask. The artifice wobbled on the spot for a moment before another message appeared.

[Glassware Artifice] has 4 more charges left.

Not only did the artifice now directly deposit the flasks into his inventory, but it could create five times as many pieces of glassware per mote. He focused his mind, touching the machine and imagining four of the same 100-unit flasks. The artifice hummed, wobbling again, before the message appeared.

[Glassware Artifice] is out of charges.

Theo inspected his inventory, finding five flasks inside. He whistled, shaking his head at the improvement. This would streamline his process, removing the need to feed the thing motes constantly. He set his mind on obtaining better upgrades for his equipment, something that would increase the charges again. He pushed these goals aside and left for the gravel yard out back. Azrug held his hand out as he left, and Theo tossed him two copper coins.

Without Theo's high Wisdom, he wouldn't have been able to remember the exact recipe for the leather-processing potions. He worked with methodical precision, laying out his flasks and measuring everything down to the tenth of a unit before introducing the Stabilized Water. A stream of smoke shot from the first 100-unit reaction, the one that smelled of shoe polish, then the next. The reaction was absurdly efficient but costly in terms of the water. For every unit of essence, the alchemist needed fifty units of Stabilized Water. The result was him snatching more barrels from the lab and making a run down to the river to create the solution. He realized he had an absurd amount of essence left over and returned to the lab to stow it away in the Large Dimensional Storage Crate.

Theo now had 500 units of Stripping Solution and Alchemic Tannin for Perg. As he was leaving to deliver the items, he found Ziz and his group of laborers waiting. The alchemist invited them to join him at the tannery, and they obliged. The group seemed excited about what was next in store for them, but he didn't want to get their hopes up. His plan was to dump the last of his gold to lay claim to the northern section of the parcels and establish the stone block production facility, but there would be stipulations.

"Finally," Perg said. She was standing in a mostly demolished building, the rotting wood lying in messy piles on the ground. "I assume this is the delivery of my potions?"

Theo withdrew ten flasks from his inventory, each containing 100 units of their respective solutions. He set them on the ground and nodded. "This should hold you over, right?"

"Eager to keep me out of your hair?" she asked. "Yes, it will. For now. I've been buying up every hide I could, but I'm almost broke."

"Me too," Theo said.

The alchemist turned on the spot, beckoning for the laborers to follow him. They reached the farm before he spoke. "I have the seed cores, but we're going to need to specify our terms."

"Getting down to business, huh?" Ziz asked, ascending the farmer's hill with the alchemist. "We just want a fair shake."

"This is an *enormous* investment for me," Theo said. "I need 3 gold in return, over time, if this is going to be worth it."

Ziz sputtered. "That's obscene, isn't it?"

"The cost of the land and the seed cores," Theo said. "Plus something so I can make a profit. Also, I want to renegotiate our original deal."

"What do you have in mind?"

The group approached the northernmost section of the farms, affording them a view of the hilly land that stretched in all directions. The town's wall stopped twenty paces from where the farms ended. According to his administrator map, everything he could see from this spot would be incorporated into the town, giving him full ownership of the parcels. At the foot of the crags was where he wanted to establish the stone-cutting area. It seemed stupid, looking back on it, to assume this would be profitable, but ridding the town of its muddy roads would be worth it.

"Your first step is to cut enough stone to pave the town. Get someone to tell you the quality of the stone and how we can export it. Do people even buy stone?" Theo asked.

"They do," Ziz said. "Not everything in a city relates to them being core towns. Roads that go from town to town also need to be paved by hand."

"Well, it's better than nothing," Theo said, descending the farmer's hill and leaving through the northern gate with his laborers close behind. "As far as ownership of the land, you can't have it. Not all of it, anyway. You're working as laborers until the debt is paid. You owe me three gold coins. Once I get that money from the sale of the stone, I'll section off a parcel that includes the quarry and the stonecutter's workshop."

"That's steep," Ziz said.

"Who knows," Theo said, shrugging. "How much do you think a trader would pay for blocks in bulk? Well, that's for you guys to figure out."

He opened his administrator's map, bidding farewell to the last of his gold coins.

[Small Town] Broken Tusk can be expanded to the **Northern Parcel** for 1 Gold. Funds will be removed directly from your inventory or the nearest dimensional container in your possession.
Expand Broken Tusk? [YES/NO]

Theo gave his consent, and the ground rumbled beneath their feet. The stone wall appeared around them, snaking its way up the hills before looping back around toward the main part of town.

"I'm broke again," Theo said, shrugging.

The group approached the foot of the rocky hills. A small section of land, flat enough to hold the first building, was the perfect spot for the workshop. Theo withdrew the Stonecutter's Seed Core from his inventory, relying on his superior intuition to see him through the process, and jammed it into the ground.

"We'll want to take a step back," Theo said.

The core was charged already and didn't require additional monster cores. The group watched as a building grew from the ground. Stone blocks pushed their way through the earth, joining with a sloped, shingled roof to create the squat building. The process took only a few moments, but the result was amazing. A small workshop was attached to the side, reminding Theo of Throk's smithy. The laborers stood in awe.

Theo repeated the process for the quarry core, this time simply setting it near the jutting crags and stepping back. The hills flattened out for 100 paces in every direction, the ground shifting under their feet. A small, wooden booth jumped up from the ground and settled in amid the stone. The alchemist inspected the quarry first.

[Quarry]
Owner: Belgar (Theo Spencer)
Faction: Broken Tusk
Level: 1 (0%)
Rent Due: 7 days
Stone Quality: Perfect
Expansions:
None

"If the stone quality is anything like my potion quality, that's an amazing sign," Theo said. "'Perfect' stone quality."

He inspected the workshop next.

[Stonecutter's Workshop]
Owner: Belgar (Theo Spencer)
Faction: Broken Tusk
Level: 1 (0%)
Rent Due: 7 days
Expansions:
None

The workshop was nothing special, but it was a start. Theo

added all five laborers as workers to the two core buildings and turned to them. Ziz was thinking about something, the gears in his big head turning rapidly.

"So we're not leasing this from you?" Ziz asked. "We're workers until we pay it off?"

"Right. I need you to show me that this place wasn't a mistake," Theo said. "You have the Stonecutter's Core, right?"

"Yeah, I've hewn blocks for a living. I have a few skills," Ziz said.

Theo couldn't tell if the half-ogre was mad about the arrangement or not. He felt more like a taskmaster than a generous benefactor, but he wouldn't give the people of Broken Tusk handouts, not when he needed money as much as them. He wouldn't hand them a business, counting on them to fail for whatever reason. They would be forced to make it profitable through blood, sweat, and hard labor. Once they paid for the cost of the buildings and his time, he would hand the two buildings over to Ziz.

"Just a moment," Theo said, taking Fenian's crystal out of his inventory. "I'll settle the question of cost."

The alchemist held the crystal tight in his hand, focusing his mind. Unlike Miana's crystal, he didn't fall into a strange void to communicate. Fenian's voice simply entered his mind. *"Yes?"*

"Fenian, I have a question about stone," Theo said.

"I'm friends with a dealer in the northlands. I'm surprised you contacted me so quickly, though. Ask away," Fenian said.

The group of laborers were busy inspecting the new buildings, leaving Theo to chat in peace.

"I started a quarry. Hired someone with the Stonecutter's Core. How much can we get for blocks?" Theo asked.

"It all depends on the quality of the stone. If you planted that Quarry Seed Core of mine, you should be able to see the quality," Fenian said.

"The quarry says 'Perfect Quality.'"

"Perfect? Are you sure? Perfect stone is rare. I assume you own the land this stone is on?"

Newt and Demon

"I do. How much would people pay for perfect stone blocks?" Theo asked.

"Assuming your man can cut them properly, I've seen them sell for 15 copper a block. Wholesale, which is how you'll sell them. A stone merchant would also offer you 15 copper per block," Fenian said. "A decent stonecutter can do 50 blocks in a day. Nothing to sneeze at."

"Seems like I just invested in a cash cow," Theo said, laughing. The laugh came out, not transmitting through the crystal.

"What's a cow?"

"Nevermind. Thanks for the information, I appreciate it," Theo said.

"Consider me your insider for all things trade. Until next time," Fenian said.

The elf cut the connection. Theo stowed the crystal away and approached the quarry, where the laborers were standing. He cleared his throat, gaining their attention again. The alchemist looked up at the midday sun, nodding to himself before speaking.

"Figure out how to work the stone," Theo said. "Stop by the Newt and Demon tomorrow and let me know if you find a way."

"I know how to work the stone, Theo," Ziz said, narrowing his eyes. "We can start now if needed."

"All right, then. I want you to work the quarry tomorrow. Craft as many blocks as you can. I'll stop by at the end of the day," Theo said. He didn't want to reveal the cost of the blocks if they couldn't produce them. "My merchant friend will judge the quality. He'll tell us a fair price."

It was a lie, but Theo didn't feel bad. He didn't want the laborers to get it into their heads that they were sitting on a gold mine. Ziz seemed to agree with this proposal. The half-ogres were always eager to prove themselves.

"We'll show you, boss," Ziz said. "You'll see what we can do when you set us loose."

Theo produced a single silver coin from his inventory and

handed it to Ziz. "A few day's wages, and whatever you need to commission from Throk."

"We won't disappoint," Ziz said.

"I know."

Theo turned on the spot and left them there, rolling the numbers over in his head. The venture would turn a profit in a month if they kept a decent pace. If the half-ogre team went beyond the pace of fifty blocks a day, it would make even more money. The alchemist wasn't focused solely on profit, though. His mind stayed with the idea that the people of Broken Tusk needed to stand on their own, although his alchemical intervention had put them on their feet. The stone-cutting business was a test of Ziz's abilities.

Tresk returned to the shop before Theo, mentally telling him she had arrived. Luras was waiting with her, equally excited to see what the alchemist had bought for his Tara'hek. He took the long way back, following a path along the river, then up through the gravel yard in the back of the shop. The marshling pestered him the entire way, but he dismissed it. She was bouncing up and down when he entered the shop, with Luras standing nearby with a grin on his face.

"Show me!" she shouted, grabbing his robes with both hands. "The suspense is killing me!"

"Now, you need to know the backstory before I hand this over," Theo said.

Tresk screamed, "Show us the core!"

Theo withdrew the Assassin's Core from his inventory, a grin spreading across his face. The orb was made of metal mesh, concealing a pulsating black swirl of energy in the center. The power it gave off was both sinister and alluring. Tresk took it in her hands and gasped. Luras strode over, inspecting the core, and his eyes went wide.

"A legendary core? Did you sell the entire town for this?" Luras asked.

"Not quite," Theo said, grinning.

Tresk held the core in front of herself. It stirred, rocking for a moment before darting inside her chest. Wreaths of black smoke consumed her, swirling for a long moment before vanishing. "This is amazing." She gasped, vanishing from sight.

The marshling reappeared at the foot of the stairs, a stupid grin on her face. "All my abilities are stronger. And I get a bonus to Dexterity!"

"I'm full of gifts today, apparently," Theo said, taking out the Leatherworker's Workshop Seed Core from his inventory. He held it out in front of Luras.

"Seriously? I thought you were joking," Luras said. "The land was enough, but this?"

Theo never thought the big half-ogre could get emotional, but he looked to be on the verge of tears. The alchemist clasped his hand on his shoulder and smiled. "I made a deal with Fenian. He gave me a great discount on all this stuff, but I spent all the gold I made."

"You what?" Tresk asked. "*Please* tell me you at least got to hold it before you gave it away. I've never seen a gold coin, let alone four of them."

"It was 6 gold, actually," Theo said with a shrug.

"Six!" she shouted, stumbling dramatically, her hand on her chest. "You spent 6 gold today? I'm gonna faint."

"You're not very good with money," Luras said, shaking his head. "You're giving it away as quickly as you make it."

"Nonsense," Theo said. "Come upstairs, look at my new toys."

Tresk and Luras followed him upstairs. Tresk whistled, then shrugged. She pointed at the artifices sitting atop the stills. "I have no idea what those are."

Theo explained how the grinders would improve his efficiency, removing the tedious mashing process from distillation. He had to explain it a few times for the marshling to understand, and he suspected that her excitement for the new core was too much.

Tresk stared into the distance for a moment before jumping with excitement. "Oh! You don't need the mashing stick anymore!"

"Very nice, Theo," Luras said, nodding. "You're getting good at this."

"Oh! You also got monster cores from him, right? We should use those," Tresk said.

"I have a feeling it's going to send the place over Level 10, so I want to wait until I'm not so tired," Theo said. "It's a big decision, especially if it gives me new options."

"It might not," Luras said.

"We'll wait. There's just too much excitement for one day," Tresk said, peering out the window. "I say we get dinner started."

"That's where *we* have the surprise," Luras said, grinning. "Nothing worth even a single gold coin, but I think you'll like it."

Luras produced a handful of small red pods and held them out. They looked like scaly cherry tomatoes. Theo inspected them.

[Fire Salamander Egg]
[Alchemy Ingredient] [Food]
Common
The egg of a fire salamander is said to contain its raw potential
Properties:
[Flame] [???] [???]

Theo grimaced. "I don't think I've ever had lizard eggs. Isn't there some moral quandary here?"

Tresk bristled. "I'm *not* a salamander. Anyway, they're super spicy."

Theo perked up at that. He loved spicy food back on Earth. Any chance he got, he would stuff his face until he was sweating and crying at the same time. "I assume one of you knows how to prepare it."

Luras nodded, holding his hand out to Tresk. She handed him her copper skillet and retrieved a Flame Artifice. Theo took a seat and watched as he seared a few wolf steaks, flipping them once before setting them aside. The half-ogre retrieved water from the Purified Water barrel, deglazing the bottom of the pan and adding something the alchemist didn't recognize.

"Zee flour," Luras said, noticing Theo's confused look.

"Yet no bread," Theo said, his shoulders slumping. The comment went unanswered.

Tresk chopped a large portion of Swamp Onions off to the side. The liquid within the pan came to a boil and bubbled away for some time. Luras dutifully adjusted the heat, bringing it down before chopping the wolf steak into chunks and introducing it into the mix. The marshling plopped the onions in when she was done chopping, staring at the mixture with hungry eyes. They worked as an efficient team, something Theo imagined was common in the dungeon.

"Now for the best part," Tresk said, tossing five Fire Salamander Eggs in with the shell intact.

Luras broke the eggs with his wooden spoon, small gouts of fire shooting up to lick the ceiling. The liquid inside the pan turned a vivid red and resumed bubbling away. The half-ogre stirred it occasionally, each motion filling the air with a spice that stung Theo's eyes.

"Have some water nearby," Luras said, nodding. "This is a bit of a delicacy, but not everyone can handle the spice."

Luras dished out three plates, handing Theo his portion and grinning. The first thing that came through in the smell was the spice. Before the fall on Earth, there were places that would ask you for a spice level. It usually went from 1 to 10, but this was a 15. Because of the Zee flour, the salamander eggs resulted in a sauce thickened into a kind of spicy gravy.

"Here goes nothing," Theo said.

Spicy food usually took a moment to coat his mouth, leaving room for the flavors to take hold. The spiciness created by the Fire Salamander Egg held nothing back. It was as though fire spread across Theo's tongue, moving instantly to cover every part of his mouth with its burning heat. His eyes watered immediately, sweat forming on his brow, and he gave the thumbs-up to his friends.

"It's good." He wheezed.

Tresk and Luras laughed, taking the first bite of their food. They both experienced similar effects, crying, sweating, and laughing their way through the first few bites. By the time they had eaten a few pieces of wolf meat, they were in the thick of it. Every concern in the world washed away, their thoughts dominated by the impossibly spicy food. The meal went on in relative silence. The only sounds coming out of the group were wheezing, coughing, and laughing. None of them went for the water.

"That was so good," Tresk said, wiping the tears from the corners of her eyes. She mopped her brow and let out a contented sigh.

The group dripped Cleansing Scrub over themselves and every surface that the food touched, preventing the spread of the spice to their skin. Theo couldn't remember the last time he had food this hot. It would have been before the nukes dropped, but that was a distant memory, driven further by the salamander's egg.

"We need to do this more often," Theo said, falling into a fit of coughing.

"I never took you for a masochist," Luras said, beaming. The spice seemed to affect him less, but the results were present.

Theo finished coughing, smiling at his companions. "It's like all your worries wash away. You can't think of anything but the spice."

"I love it!" Tresk shouted. "Once a week, at least!"

Their conversation moved away from the meal briefly before Luras excused himself. Theo and Tresk spent time in the lab, talking about nonsense for a while before they pressed their foreheads together. Their Tara'hek Cores were on the verge of hitting Level 5. It would be exciting to see what strange ability they would get once they hit the threshold.

"Time to go to bed," Tresk said, yawning. "I can't wait to test this new core out."

Theo went with her to the bedroom, lying in his impossibly

comfortable bed. He was tired after the meal, and he was happy to see that it was sitting well in his stomach. It was a good thing that Dronon physiology was agreeable to spicy food. It was even better that having spicy things was an option. He lay there for some time, Tresk's loud snores filling the room, before he fell asleep. When he finally drifted off, it was with a feeling of contentment.

Chapter 33
Marble

Theo woke well before Tresk the next morning. His sleep became restless in the early hours, with visions of things left undone playing through his mind. The alchemist couldn't tell what time it was outside, only able to conclude that the inky blackness of twilight still hung over Broken Tusk. The visions that brought him awake were those regarding his new book. *Basic Drogramathi Alchemy* sat in his inventory, unread. More than anything, he wanted to explore its secrets, but something told him they weren't so easily discovered. He snuck out of the bedroom and settled in at the shop, lighting a candle and moving Azrug's chair.

The first quarter of the book described the illustrious history of Drogramath. Theo ignored most of this, finding it impossible to understand. The book seemed to be a jumble of Drogramathi words. At points they made a story, but even the content there was hard to grasp. He discerned no alchemical knowledge from it. He let out a heavy sigh as he turned to the chapter regarding distillation. It was as bad, if not worse, than the introduction section. Where he expected to find details on his craft, he found more nonsense. His ability to read the book brought him no closer to understanding it. Despite this, he went through the entire section on distillation, committing it to memory.

Buried deep in a description of Drogramath's mastery over a realm Theo wouldn't attempt to pronounce, there were a few gems. While most of it eluded him, a small section concerning the demon lord's persistent fire, whatever that meant, related to temperature control. It said that Drogramath tempered his enemies with a flame, like a blacksmith heated a blade, and that constant heat wasn't always the solution. Theo took this confusing message to mean that distillation wasn't only about keeping the fire at a constant temperature. Some essences might extract better if he changed the intensity of the fire.

The alchemist withdrew some parchment from his inventory and started scrawling. He labeled it "Drogramath Decrypted" at the top, referring to the page numbers and his interpretation. At the end of a few hours' work, he was left with more contradicting information than information that agreed. Letting out a frustrated sigh, he leaned back in the chair and stared at the ceiling. When he first cracked the book open, he expected all of Drogramath's secrets to reveal themselves to him. Theo wanted one brilliant flash of inspiration to fill the gaps in his knowledge, but the only thing he got was confusion and disappointment.

Theo shrugged, standing up and stretching on the spot. Fenian thought the book was a gift, holding that coveted secret knowledge, so it was worth investigating. For now, he put it on the back burner and planned to do something different for the day. The alchemist wanted to take the day off from distillation to spend his time working on the town. He planned to use his four Level 30 monster cores when Tresk woke up, eager to see if there were any new enhancement options to pick from. Then there was the matter of the stonecutter's endeavor. If he knew Ziz as well as he thought, the half-ogre would go nuts and cut as much stone as possible.

Theo felt something tap his shoulder. He spun around, heart hammering hard in his chest, and spotted the grinning face of Tresk standing there. "Didn't even hear me, did you?"

The alchemist clutched his chest, letting out a sigh of relief.

"No, I didn't," he said, letting out a few calming breaths. "You scared the crap out of me."

Tresk chuckled, picking up the book and looking it over. "You can read this?"

"Yeah, but it's not helpful," Theo said, waving her off. "Whatever cultist wrote it had more to say about Drogramath than his alchemy."

"That's demons for ya," Tresk said. "Cults, in general, like to guard their knowledge."

"Well, on to exciting things," Theo said, groaning as he rose to his feet. "Let's use our monster cores."

Tresk bounced with excitement. Theo withdrew a monster core from his inventory and held it high, willing it to go into the shop. It disappeared, and two messages crowded his vision.

[Alchemy Lab] has advanced to Level 8!
Select a direction you wish to expand the lab into (north/south/east/west).
[Alchemy Lab] has advanced to Level 9!
Select a direction you wish to expand the lab into (north/south/east/west).

Theo frowned, expecting a lot more levels from each Level 30 core. He selected east for both, preferring that the building expand toward the river, where he owned property. The shop rumbled under their feet, the floorboards creaking as the shop visibly expanded to the back. It was a good five paces of new space.

"Didn't get Level 10? Shame," Tresk said, tutting.

Theo held another core in the air, watching it disappear and receiving another barrage of messages.

[Alchemy Lab] has advanced to Level 10!
Select a direction you wish to expand the lab into (north/south/east/west).
[Alchemy Lab] has advanced to Level 11!

Select a direction you wish to expand the lab into (north/south/east/west).

[Select Upgrade Option]
[Root Cellar]
A cellar for preserving reagents housed under the lab. Reagents placed inside of the cellar decay at a slower rate.
[Experimentation Room]
A reinforced room placed behind the lab, creating a safe place to conduct explosive experiments.
[Drogramath Distillation Specialty]
Specialize your lab in Drogramath Distillation. This option is only available to owners of the Dronon race and Drogramath's heritage.
Effect:
Reduces the likelihood that essences will explode when interacting.
Increases the rate of distillation in all stills.
Increases the Wisdom bonus for all alchemists within the Alchemy Lab.
Provides the Alchemy Lab with a Drogramath Still.

"Well, that's not fair," Theo said, laughing. "There's an obvious winner."

Theo expanded the shop east again, the building rumbling under his feet as he read over [Drogramath Distillation Specialty]. It was an option that only showed up because of his Drogramath Dronon heritage. Any of the effects alone would be worth it, but to get that many at once was absurd.

"That's an obvious pick," Tresk said, laughing.

Theo selected [Drogramath Distillation Speciality] and the building rumbled again. Dark, purple energy swirled around the building, consuming the duo for a moment before subsiding. The pair shared a look before sprinting upstairs to inspect the lab. The first thing they noticed was how much larger it was. Two Theos could lie down, feet to head, in the newly created space. The next thing that dominated the room was a wicked-looking still, looming near the copper stills created by Throk. It looked like a pot still decorated on every available surface with nasty spikes and blades. The condenser apparatus was incredibly complex, containing more loops and turns than should be possible. It was made of a purple-black metal that Theo had seen before—in his new knife.

"That looks like a torture device," Tresk said.

Theo inspected the new still.

[Drogramath Still]
[Alchemy Equipment]
Legendary
Created By: ????
A 500-unit-capacity Drogramathi still with an advanced condenser attached. The advanced condenser allows for more efficient cooling of essences, decreasing the time needed to distill. The Drogramathi metal increases the spread of heat, providing an even distribution across a run.
Effect:
Distillation time reduced.
Occasionally produces more essence per run.

"Five-hundred-unit capacity," Theo said, whistling. He checked the lid, putting a Alchemical Grinder Artifice on top. The artifice adjusted itself and latched on. "I wish it didn't look so demonic."

Tresk shrugged. "Looks like a fancy piece of gear to me."

Theo looked at the remaining three monster cores in his inventory, weighing his options. It was unlikely the three cores would bring the shop to Level 15, and he had enough upgrades to keep him happy for a long time. He had a feeling that the fancy equipment would outpace his skill, making it a bit of a waste. A plan formed in his mind, a plan aimed at extracting maximum profit from the stonecutter's operation.

"Tell me if this is stupid," Theo said, running his finger over the sharp edges of the still.

"If you have to ask..."

"What if we invest these cores into the town," Theo said. "Get it to Level 10 and take the [Stone Roads] upgrade. Then sell all the stone from the quarry and invest that back into cores."

Tresk thought for a moment, shrugging. "The problem with laying your own stone is that you have to keep laying new stone when we expand. I'd say put the monster cores into the town and see what the Level 10 upgrade is. Adventurers have been putting cores in anyway. We're almost at Level 8."

"Right," Theo said, nodding. "That's settled, then. I'm guessing your plans for the day involve stabbing things?"

"You guessed right," Tresk said. "We'll have some breakfast first."

The pair went back upstairs. Tresk handled the food, and Theo prepared their morning tea. The alchemist wanted more variety in their diet, but that was a task for another day. They settled on more wolf steaks, mostly because the marshling had more wolf steaks in her dimensional bag than she knew what to do with. She talked about how excited she was to test out her new core. While it didn't provide any world-breaking advantages, it was still a big step-up from her common-grade core. Theo couldn't imagine how big of a leap it was from common to legendary.

Azrug arrived earlier than normal, coming with the dawn. "Did this place get bigger?" he asked, craning his neck at the door. The boy normally didn't say a word, but the sudden expansion of the Newt and Demon left him wondering.

"We upgraded to Level 10," Theo said. "Got some fancy new features."

Tresk came down the stairs soon after, patting her stomach and grinning. "I'm off to the dungeon."

"Bye," Theo said, waving her off.

Azrug entered the shop as Tresk left, walking to the back and looking toward the front. "It's *a lot* bigger."

"On average, it gives two to four paces per level," Theo said.

Azrug spent some time walking around, admiring how large the space had become. Theo left him to it, heading off into the swamp to test his new knife. He decided against doing any distillation today, favoring a calm walk and gathering. The Drogramath Alchemy Knife was cumbersome to use. The alchemist dug a Spiny Swamp Thistle Root out of the ground and cut away the stem. A pulse spread out from him like a rolling wave of purple energy. When the wave subsided, he could see everything around him that was alchemical in nature. There were the Spiny Swamp Thistle Roots, which he knew of, but also something buried deep in the ground. The vague, glowing shape that the knife created wasn't enough to identify it, but Theo didn't feel like digging.

The alchemist picked a path along the eastern wall, passing by the gate and noting the fishermen outside. He didn't know what they caught or where they sold it, but they were out there every day. He cut a Water Lily near the wall, and the pulse spread out over the river. Glowing shapes danced near the shore. Theo investigated, getting as close to the water's edge as possible without getting wet. A green weed danced in the current, just below the surface. He knelt, getting his knees wet and muddy, and cut a piece off. Another wave of revealing magic pulsed out, but he ignored it. He inspected the reagent.

[River Kelp]
[Alchemy Ingredient] [Food]
Uncommon
River kelp is known for its medicinal properties.
Properties:
[Regeneration] [???] [???]

Theo already had a source of the [Regeneration] property, the Spiny Swamp Thistle Root, but hadn't created any essences for this property. He stuffed the item into his inventory and made his way further upriver. Mussels grew near the pebbled shore, but none of them were alchemy ingredients. Small crayfish scattered away from the shallows when he approached, but he doubted they were reagents. He found a small, rounder-shaped bivalve creature similar to a mussel, which reminded him of clams back on Earth. It was alone, and a pulse radiated from the alchemist when he pried the thing open. A small, misshapen white pearl sat near the meat of the thing. He picked it up and inspected it.

[River Clam Pearl]
[Alchemy Ingredient]
Rare
The pearl of a river clam.
Properties:
[Hone Edge] [???] [???]

Theo did not know what the [Hone Edge] property could be, but his intuition told him it was something similar to [Poison]. Not that it would apply any negative effects to a weapon, but that it would change them somehow. He wondered how he would get the hard thing down into a mash for the distillation process. The alchemist shrugged, placing the item in his inventory before moving on.

Tresk arrived at the dungeon, informing Theo how much she loved the new core. He didn't understand how combat cores worked or how they enhanced someone's abilities, but she explained it. The increase in core quality more than doubled her damage. It also made it impossible for equal-level monsters to detect her when she used her [Sneak] skill. She raved about being able to leap from the shadows, destroying anything with ease, and how they were making their way to the tenth floor's boss room. The alchemist told her to be careful and keep him updated.

"I stole a few more Lesser Healing Potions. Don't worry about me," Tresk said, cackling.

It was midday by the time Theo found his way to the quarry. His journey was winding, the knife sending him in a zig-zag pattern across the countryside. He found more reagents thanks to the knife than ever before, the glowing indicator revealing things he would have never seen with the naked eye. The quarry came into view, joined by the sounds of hammers and chisels on stone. Ziz spotted him, waving excitedly.

"Come look, boss," Ziz said, gesturing behind the workshop.

Theo joined him, his eyes going wide at the massive pile of shaped stone. There must have been fifty blocks the size of the alchemist's head piled up. They were all hewn expertly, and when he ran his fingers across the surface, he could find no imperfections. He inspected the block, confirming his suspicions.

[Marble Block]
[Building Material]
Quality: Perfect
A block of white marble.

Ziz must have lied about his Stonecutter's Core. The blocks had lost none of their quality, meaning that he was a noteworthy craftsman. Theo knew, from his time brewing potions, that messing up any step of the way would degrade the quality. The half-ogre knew his stuff, and his speed at processing the blocks was absurd. The laborers worked near the quarry, grunting and working a winch to crane the blocks out of the hills.

"You're a lot better at this than you let on," Theo said, running his fingers over the blocks again.

Ziz had a permanent grin on his face at this point. He slapped one of the blocks and shrugged. "What can I say?"

"Let's see what Fenian thinks," Theo said. He withdrew Fenian's crystal from his inventory and held it tight. His head rushed for a moment, as though the line were trilling on the other end, then it passed.

"Theo, how are you?" Fenian asked.

"Well, thank you. I have a question about stone—again."

"Let's hear it."

"My laborers are better than expected. I can expect 50 blocks a day. Marble, perfect quality," Theo said.

"Marble? Did you say marble? Sorry, I'm in a high-magic area right now, there must have been some interference. You couldn't have said marble," Fenian said.

"Yeah, it's marble. I inspected the finished product. About the size of my head," Theo said.

"I'm sending my friend to Broken Tusk," Fenian said. "They will want a deal for wholesale, but you're sitting on a goldmine. You can expect him to offer 25 copper a block."

Theo tried to do the mental math. His mind always worked in strange ways when doing mental arithmetic, and his low Intelligence attribute wasn't helping. After some effort, he determined that the blocks Ziz had crafted so far would fetch somewhere around 12 silver coins.

"My guys are going to lose it," Theo said. "Fenian, thanks for the information."

"No problem. I'm going to contact you with an order in a few days," Fenian said. "Take care."

The connection terminated, and Theo returned the crystal to his inventory. Ziz was looking at him expectantly, and the alchemist smiled. "Five percent off the top," Theo said.

"What?" Ziz asked.

"When you pay me back for the startup, 3 gold coins, all I want is five percent of sales," Theo said.

Ziz narrowed his eyes. Theo knew immediately that he should have said a higher number to start. "How much can I get for a block? 2 copper? Maybe 3? Come on, don't leave me hanging."

Theo laughed. The half-ogre laborers of Broken Tusk were underpaid. They sat on a goldmine of resources they had never exploited. "Fenian knows a stone trader. What you're cutting here is marble of perfect quality. The elf is going to send the stone merchant to confirm, but we can expect 25 copper coins per block."

"Per block!" Ziz shouted, grabbing his head with both hands. "Per block?"

"Yes, just like those blocks here," Theo said, grinning. "Over 12 silver a day. You'll pay off your debt in a month."

Ziz swayed on the spot, leaning against the pile of stone blocks and breathing hard.

"Do I need to give you a Lesser Health Potion?" Theo asked.

"Maybe," Ziz said, taking a few calming breaths. "By the Gods. Five percent? You'd really do that for me? You'd give me and these mud-slinging laborers a chance like that?"

"I would," Theo said. "There's no sense in me trying to run a quarry. I don't have the time or the skill core to do it. If I get my money back on my investment, I'll be happy."

"How am I supposed to say no?" Ziz said, reaching his hand out for Theo to shake.

The alchemist took his hand and shook it. "It's a deal."

"I'm guessing we have to reserve some stone and split it into cobbles to pave the town's roads," Ziz said.

"No, we'll sell everything here," Theo said. "I'm off to upgrade the town to Level 10. If the upgrade options suck, I'm going to pick [Stone Roads]."

"I'd better get back to work," Ziz said, his eyes going wide. He turned to the other four laborers and shouted, "Work faster! We're gonna be rich!"

Chapter 34
Upgrades

Theo made his way back to the square, feeling good about the day. Perg's order was filled, Ziz had his stoneworker's workshop, and Fenian was sending his contact to the town. As he passed through the farm, the well-trodden mud streets annoyed him even more. This new body had incredible resistance to infections, because even though his feet were soaked with mud for most of the day, they were fine. He inspected the monolith when he arrived at the square.

[Small Town]
Name: Broken Tusk
Owner: Kingdom of Qavell
Mayor: Miana Kell
Administrator: Theo Spencer
Faction: Qavell
Level: 8 (1%)
Features:
Alchemy Lab
Blacksmith
Large Farm
Tannery

Tradesmen
Adventurer's Guild
Small Quarry
Upgrades:
Stone Walls and Gates

Tresk was right. The town was teetering on the edge of a new upgrade. Theo withdrew a Level 30 monster core from his inventory and offered it to the slab of stone. It accepted the offering hungrily, the core vanishing from his hands as a message appeared in the alchemist's vision.

[Small Town] Broken Tusk has advanced to Level 9!

Broken Tusk was 20% into Level 9. Another core would send it over the edge and reveal the new upgrade features. Theo hoisted another core and watched as the monolith swirled with energy, snaking out over the town. Everything glittered, motes of white energy falling off the buildings and the walls. Another screen popped up.

[Small Town] Broken Tusk has advanced to Level 10!
[Small Town] Broken Tusk is eligible for an upgrade. As the Administrator, you may make a selection from the following:

[Stone Roads]
Your town will gain stone roads that cover all interior roads within your borders. The roads will expand as you expand your town.

[Watchtowers]
Your town will gain watchtowers placed along the border.

Should you expand, the watchtowers will move to match the edge of your borders. Twelve watchtowers will be placed.

[Water Tower]
Your town will gain a single 1,000-unit water tower at its center. The tower will not fill itself automatically.

The new option was hilariously bad. The town already had a water tower with a higher capacity. There was no way he would pick any other option. Theo mentally selected the [Stone Roads] and waited for them to appear underfoot. The ground shook ominously, the same white energy that danced across the town suddenly covering the muddy roads. Gray cobbles popped up from the ground, sending the alchemist high into the air before slamming down in a tight pattern. Theo fell on the hard stone and watched as mortar spread between the cobbles, forming a tight webwork of sealant.

The process happened like a wave centered on the monolith, crashing out from the center of town. Shouts of surprise came from all directions. Theo ran his hands over the stone. It wasn't as nice as the stuff Ziz was cutting, but it would do far more than the natural stone could. The roads would extend out when the town expanded, removing the need to lay more stone when the town grew. The alchemist brought himself to his feet and traveled south, to the shop.

Azrug was standing outside the Newt and Demon with Perg. They both had a look of confusion on their faces. As soon as they spotted Theo, they understood what had happened. "That was you, wasn't it?" Azrug asked, laughing.

"Gods. You can always count on the alchemist to upset things," Perg said. Despite her jab, her eyes were on the road.

"It's not as soft underfoot, but you won't get caught in sinkholes," Theo said, smiling. He withdrew Cleansing Scrub from his inventory and dropped it over his clothes. The light washed away the mud, leaving his moccasins fresh.

"I noticed your shop has gotten bigger," Perg said, shaking her head. "You stole my workers away."

"Did you have work for them?" Theo asked, smiling.

"Nope," Perg said. "I don't need anyone to work the pits because there are no pits. You have my gratitude for giving them a job."

"More than a job," Theo corrected. "I gave them a way to support themselves. After they pay me back for the cost of the seed cores, I'm giving Ziz the buildings."

"Absurdly generous of you," Perg said, shaking her head.

"Hardly," Theo said, waving her notion away. "I own the land they're working on. And I'm taking a percentage off the top."

Perg sauntered over to the alchemist and grinned. She placed her hand over his shoulder and smiled. "If anyone asks me, you were born here. Maybe not physically, but you have the spirit of a Broken Tusker. You help your neighbors without question. Everyone in town knows how much those potions cost in the big city."

Theo couldn't disagree with her. The moment he set foot in Broken Tusk, he knew he was home. He was even used to the humidity and the heat. Air conditioning would be nice, but once he spent a week in the oppressive soup they called air, it wasn't that bad. He placed his hand on her shoulder and smiled.

"Hey, you gonna pay me?" Azrug said, scowling.

Theo withdrew two copper coins from his inventory and handed them over to the boy. Azrug stuffed the coins in his pocket and continued to give the alchemist the stink eye.

"What about you, Azrug? Any opinion?" Perg asked.

"Well, the demon got me out of the fields," Azrug said, tapping his chin. "There's still many people working the farm, making crap for coin."

"One project at a time," Theo said. "Once I find reagents that promote crop growth, they'll be up to their eyeballs in Zee."

Azrug shrugged, turning to walk up the road. "Can't change the world overnight."

Perg and Theo watched the boy stomp off. He kicked at the cobblestone path and shouted, stumbling the rest of the way up the hill. The boy was spiky at the best of times.

"What a tender moment." A voice came from the shadows near the shop. It was a horrible impersonation of a villain, but an obvious culprit. Perg was startled, but Theo was not.

"Tresk is enjoying her new core," the alchemist said. He couldn't see her lurking there in broad daylight, but she dropped her voice about as well as he swung a sword.

"Don't ruin my fun," Tresk said, emerging with a grin on her face. She had a look of surprise on her face, as though she had just noticed the cobblestone below her feet. "Roads!"

"New core?" Perg asked.

Tresk explained, in excruciating detail, her new core. Her day in the dungeon went extremely well, the cloak hanging off her shoulders being the proof. It was made of an impossibly soft silk that seemed to have no weight. According to the marshling, it made her even more light on her feet, empowering her Sneak skill even more. She claimed to have walked up to the boss and waved her hand in front of his face before Luras charged, ruining her fun.

Perg departed after a while to plant her seed core. Luras was apparently doing the same thing next door. The half-ogre was already in talks about leather supplies, striking a deal to get some of Perg's stock at a discount. Theo appreciated the gesture of paying it forward, letting some profits remain inside Broken Tusk. His entire plan from the start was to create that cycle of coin, those production chains that exploited the natural resources of the land—and the swamp had a lot of resources to provide.

Theo and Tresk made their way into the shop. She noticed the lab was mostly untouched from the morning and raised a brow. "You brewed nothing today?"

"I took it easy," Theo said. "It's still pretty early, anyway."

"I thought you'd be all over the new still," Tresk said. "Did you check on the stone boys?"

Theo laughed, explaining their situation. "They'll turn a profit within a month. Then they will be on their own."

"Well, I finally have something nice for you," Tresk said. "The 10th floor boss was some horrid troll, but he had a few additional friends. Spriggans. They're these weird little tree creatures that shamble around and throw vines at you."

Tresk withdrew something that looked like a wooden heart from her bag, holding it out for the alchemist to inspect.

[Spriggan Heart]
[Alchemy Ingredient]
Rare
The animated heart of a Spriggan; contains the creature's ability to influence nature.
Properties:
[Growth] [???] [???]

Theo suddenly found the solution to the farmers' problem. The only issue was that his intuition told him this was a volatile ingredient, something he couldn't handle at his current level. Even the power that flowed from the reagent gave him a bad feeling, his instincts telling him not to handle it. He stowed it away in his inventory and smiled at his companion.

"My marshling investment is finally paying off," Theo said.

Tresk bristled for a moment, then stuck her tongue out. She beckoned for him to bend down to her level, pressing her forehead against his. A rush flowed through his body, and a new status box appeared near his own, showing another set of health, mana, and stamina bars. Another message popped up on his screen to explain it.

Tara'hek Core gained experience (5%).
Tara'hek Core reached Level 5!

Tara'hek Communication has evolved, gaining a new effect.

[Tara'hek Communication]
Marshling Bond Skill
Rare
The first step to a Tara'hek is communication.
Effect:
Allows you to communicate with Tresk, no matter how far away they are. Others cannot hear your conversation.
Allows you to know the current state of your Tara'hek. Their health, mana, and stamina will appear near yours at all times.

"Woah!" Tresk said. "Your stamina bar is almost empty."
"So is yours," Theo said.
A knock from the front door broke Theo's excitement, but only fueled Tresk's. She squealed with glee, answering it and cocking her head. The bulky frame of Ziz stood at the door, scratching his head and grinning sheepishly.
"I saw the roads," Ziz said, managing a weak chuckle. He held something behind his back. "Makes me think you never intended to do anything but give me and my sorry lot jobs."
Theo waved the statement away, shaking his head. "It's an investment."
Tresk punched his arm playfully. "Come on. You're all kinds of nice."
Ziz moved inside over the threshold, revealing what he concealed behind his back. Three fat steaks, far too fatty to be wolf steaks, glistened in the fading light of the day. "Karatan steaks," he said, grinning. "I assume you haven't eaten dinner yet?"
Tresk's eyes went wide. Whatever playful mode she was in vanished at the sight of the steaks. Theo found it impossible not to be interested as well. The memory of the steaks at the Marsh Wolf Tavern lingered in his mind. The marshling bounced up and

down, the frills on the side of her head wiggling along with her movements.

"No way!" Tresk shouted. "Let's eat!"

Tresk darted upstairs, with Theo and Ziz close behind. She had one of the Flame Artifices going before they even reached the lab, muttering something to herself and licking her lips.

"We're really having a good time working the quarry," Ziz said, smiling.

Theo took stock of the man, noticing how exhausted he looked. They had gone all out today, trying to produce as many stone blocks as possible. He took a seat by the window, happy to let the marshling do all the preparation. The scent of the cooking steaks filled the lab, a smell that sent a wave of excitement through the alchemist's body.

"Hopefully we can keep this momentum up," Theo said, sighing. "I was lucky to get enough cores to level the town to 10, but it's going to be slow from here on out."

"The walls do more than you know," Ziz said, shrugging. "Everyone feels safer. Gods... Not to mention the roads."

Theo let that thought swirl around in his mind for a while as Tresk cooked the steaks. He had done a lot of good for the town, but it wasn't just him. He was the catalyst, like the unassuming shavings of copper in his potions that set off a chain reaction. The townspeople of Broken Tusk just needed a firm prod to get into it and a clear path forward. He was more than happy to be their lodestone.

The pair watched, chatting idly, as Tresk finished the steaks. When they finally dug into the meal, it was everything Theo expected. Even without butter, it was beyond the wolf steaks in flavor. Something about the fat that laced through the meat elevated it beyond anything the swamp could provide. The alchemist made a mental note to explore alchemical flavor enhancements.

The group ate slowly, heads nodding as tiredness set in. Everyone seated at the table by the window was exhausted, but the company was good. Ziz was in as good of spirits as Theo had ever seen him. Tresk was constantly talking about her new core, but the alchemist doubted it was as much of an improvement as she said. He didn't have any frame of reference for combat cores, though, and thought about learning more about them. The chance never came to ask her about it that night.

As the sun dipped below the horizon, Ziz bid the two farewell. The moment he left, Tresk let her shoulders slump. "I didn't want to be rude, but I'm *so* tired."

"Me too," Theo said, struggling to keep his eyes open. "It's been a busy day."

"Let's sleep."

The pair made their way to the bedroom, snuggling into their impossibly comfortable beds and leaving the worries of the day for tomorrow.

Chapter 35
Cores and the Khahari

Theo woke the next morning to the delightful smell of moss tea and wolf steaks. He lingered in bed for a while, blinking away the sleep and preparing for the day. Sometimes he had to brace himself for Tresk's level of excitement. She elevated his mood every time he saw her. He departed the bedroom, dawn still not showing itself outside, and found her in the lab. She was humming something to herself, prodding at her pan with a wooden spoon.

"Morning," Theo said, stretching.

"Theo! I had a dream that I killed a *dragon*," Tresk said, casting a devious glance at the alchemist.

Theo couldn't help but laugh. He didn't even know if dragons were a real thing in this world, or if the excited marshling was making things up. "Are assassins good at killing dragons?"

"Nope," Tresk said. "No one kills dragons—not really. They're giant, intelligent monsters that can level whole towns."

Theo laughed, taking his spot at the table and pouring two cups of the brewing tea. The citrus smell flooded his nose, sending a wave of energizing warmth through his body. Their morning ritual had a way of calming him like nothing else.

"What's your plan for the day?" Tresk asked, serving him a

wolf steak on a plate. She didn't even bother putting hers on a plate, simply grabbing it with both hands and tearing large chunks out of the still-hot thing.

Theo thought for a moment, cupping his chin in his hand and shrugging. "I need to take stock of our materials and potions. I have a feeling that I need to make a push for Level 10."

"Good idea," Tresk said, nodding and chomping. "Luras is gonna be busy with his new project, so I'm going solo for the first time."

"Can you handle it?" Theo asked, feeling a flash of concern ripple through his heart.

"With my new core? Yeah," Tresk said, spitting a little steak out onto the table when she snorted. "It basically doubled my damage. If I get the drop on the monsters, anyway."

"Good," Theo said. "It helps that I can see your health bar."

Theo cast his eyes out the window, idly taking bites of his food. Dawn broke over the eastern horizon, painting the area behind the Newt and Demon in a brilliant orange-purple light. The pair talked about idle things while the sun was rising, until Tresk finally decided to head off for the dungeon. She promised to take it easy, but the alchemist was still worried. He understood so little about the way dungeons worked; even her class was a bit of a mystery to him. Therefore, he made her promise to take extra healing potions.

"You worry too much," Tresk said, pressing her forehead against his before departing.

Theo watched her go, wincing at the sight of it. She couldn't have been better prepared, but it was still hard. He made a mental note to keep an eye out for gear for her. The thought made him realize that his experience with adventurer gear was lacking. He checked the dimensional crate upstairs, finding a healthy supply of essences related to the tannery process. He also had a small number of Moss Nettles and Spiny Swamp Thistle Roots, as well as a few Widow Lilies. Downstairs in the shop, there were a few potions, but nothing in bulk. Fifteen Lesser Healing Potions, seven Lesser Barkskin Potions, fifty units of Cleansing Scrub, a hundred

Lesser Stamina Potions, and a handful of Lesser Potions of Purification.

He stayed there for some time, planning a route through the town to collect more ingredients. The longer he stayed, the more he felt like something was missing. The alchemist poked his head out of the door, peering up and down the street, before finally putting his finger on what was wrong. Azrug hadn't shown up, even though the boy had been arriving at the store early lately. Theo locked the shop up, ensuring the sign was set to "Closed", and walked down to Perg's tannery. He couldn't help but marvel at how nice the new road was, grinning to himself as he arrived.

The town's tannery had also changed considerably. It was no longer a roving workshop, open to the air and falling apart. It was now a squat stone building with a wooden roof, several chimney stacks visible on top. Theo whistled in approval, approaching the thick oaken door and knocking twice. He realized it was the first time he didn't find the half-ogre woman simply standing outside as though she were waiting for him.

"Theo!" Perg said, arriving at the door with a grin on her face. "Get in here."

The alchemist was dragged inside by the arm, stumbling over himself as the woman gestured broadly. The interior of the new tannery was clean and organized. Shallow recesses in the floorboards sat under the things he thought were chimneys. Those were vents to whisk away the foul air, sending it skyward. A small bed sat in the corner, as did a modest eating area.

"This is great," Theo said, taking in the place. "This is really streamlined."

"Just wait until I get some upgrades," Perg said, beaming.

"Well, I'm sure people in town are going to be happy."

"Why's that?" Theo asked.

"Well, have you ever noticed how the southern section of Broken Tusk doesn't have any houses?" Perg asked. "That's because the tannery stunk so bad. People are going to buy property here now."

"I guess it's my job to sell that property to them," Theo said with a laugh. "Yeah, I don't know anyone who wants the scent of death in their house all day."

"That's a thing of the past," Perg said, waving her hand dismissively. "Not that I have to tell you, but this is a proper tannery now."

Theo walked around the interior. It was bare, but then again, it was a Level 1 core building. It would only grow as she fed it monster cores, and if the alchemist's intuition was right, their business would boom in the coming months.

"Did Luras plant his building yet?" Theo asked.

"Yeah, it's taking time," Perg said. "I talked to Ziz yesterday. He's excited about the quarry. Says he's gonna be rich."

"By Broken Tusk standards, yeah," Theo said, laughing. "He lucked out. The place we picked for the quarry has some rare stone. Fenian is sending a merchant to check it out."

"Trade routes," Perg said, nodding. "That Fenian elf bought all my hides the last time he was here."

"He's a nice guy," Theo said, shrugging. He almost forgot the reason he had come down this way to begin with. "Hey, have you heard anything about Azrug?"

"I've been too busy with this," Perg said, gesturing vaguely at the tannery. "His house is up by the farm."

"Yeah, I think I remember," Theo said, knitting his brow. "Hold on—what was his surname?"

"Slug," Perg said.

Theo shook his head, summoning his administrator map and locating a parcel labeled "The Slug Family."

"There it is," Theo said. "I'm going to check on him... Make sure everything is okay."

"Are you worried?" Perg asked, cocking an eyebrow.

"Yeah. I'm always worried," Theo said.

"You're like everyone's mother."

Theo waved her off, shaking his head. "See ya."

He made his way north to the town square. He wondered if

Miana had a core that let her know every time he was near, because she popped her head out of her house and scowled at him. "Theo! A word," she said.

The alchemist went over and sighed. "What is it, Miana?"

"Good work," she said, giving him an approving nod. "I need to have a word with you later, but you look busy."

"Okay," Theo said. "Hopefully it's nothing bad."

"Of course not," Miana said, scowling. She snapped the door shut before he could get another word in.

"Rude," Theo muttered under his nose, continuing on his way.

He found his way up to the base of the farmer's hill, ducking east into the tangle of rotting homes. He spotted Xam, the proprietor of the Marsh Wolf Tavern, standing outside of a home. Theo double-checked his administrator map, confirming that she was standing outside of the Slug residence. The moment she spotted him, she had a pained look on her face. As he approached, she managed a weak smile that dropped Theo's heart into the pit of his stomach.

"What's wrong?" Theo asked. His mind reeled with possibilities. If Azrug was sick, he could distill a potion to help him. The Purifying Essence could have a lot of uses that he hadn't explored yet. However, the soft smile that spread across Xam's face dismissed all the panic. She placed her hand on his shoulder and laughed.

"You're funny," she said. "He's not sick or hurt. I was going to send someone to tell you, but... well, here you are."

"What happened?"

"He's getting his cores," Xam said, smiling. "It's a painful process, but it usually happens when someone comes of age. Azrug is still too young, but... we think working in your shop pushed him along."

A pang of guilt spread through Theo's gut. "I'm so sorry," he said, grimacing. "I thought giving him a job would help—"

Xam held out a silencing hand, shaking her head. "No, it's a good thing. It was going to happen eventually. When a transformation happens early, it usually means someone has found what they really want to do."

Theo breathed a sigh of relief. The moment Azrug didn't show up to the shop, he had a horrible feeling in his stomach that the boy was injured. The alchemist didn't even consider that people would get their cores in adolescence—there was just too much about this world that he didn't know. As long as Azrug was safe, he was happy.

"Can I see him?" Theo asked.

"No," Xam said, shaking her head. A pained smile played across her face. "If he sees you, he's going to want to run the shop. I already lied and told him that Tresk was working the shop today."

Theo nodded. "Yeah, that makes sense. Listen, if he needs anything, just let me know."

"I will," Xam said. "He should be fine tomorrow... Well, he's going to be insufferable. Bragging about whatever special cores he gets."

Theo opened his inventory, withdrawing a single silver coin. He didn't know what kind of celebration people in Broken Tusk would have for a kid getting their cores, but he knew the best present. Money. He handed the coin over to Xam, which she refused to take.

"For his ascension to a core user," Theo said. "I'll hand it to him personally if you don't take it."

Xam snatched the coin out of his hand and grinned. "You're too nice to this kid."

"I know," Theo said, turning on the spot. "See you, Xam."

Theo made his way north from the farmer's hill, tracking a path through the forest. He couldn't get his mind off the excitement of Azrug getting his cores, but he did his best to focus on his herbalism. His Drogramath Alchemy Knife significantly increased the rate at which he could harvest reagents. The gentle ping of energy that washed over the ground revealed things he would have missed before. Those things growing deep underground were tempting to dig up, but there was no way for him to access them easily.

The alchemist focused on reagents that he could sell in his shop and bolster his Tara'hek's prowess. He spent the morning collecting Spiny Swamp Thistle Root, Widow Lily, and Water Lily. The effort earned him a sizeable chunk of experience in his Drogramath Herbalism Core, but it still lagged behind his alchemy core. The advantage the new knife gave him was in volume. Compared to his gathering life before the new tool, he was collecting twice as many ingredients in the same amount of time.

Theo noticed Tresk's health bar shoot down by a quarter, hover there for a while, then rocket back up to full. He breathed a sigh of relief, resisting the urge to send a panic message into her mind. Any break in her concentration might spell disaster, and he didn't want to interrupt her.

"I'm fine," Tresk said after a moment. "In case you're freaking out back in town."

"I was," Theo said, laughing. "What happened?"

"That troll got the drop on me—well, he's dead now," Tresk said, giggling. "They're just so big and stupid!"

The early morning gave way to the blistering sun, burning away the low-hanging fog of the swamp. Theo made his way back to the shop, intent on brewing potions and tending to any customers. He rounded the corner, dripping some Cleansing Scrub on himself before stepping foot on the stone path. He spotted someone standing patiently outside of the store, his arms folded and tail swishing. After a moment, he recognized the man as Zan'kir, the Khahari adventurer who had inquired about a house a few days earlier.

"Zan'kir," Theo said, waving at the man. He relied on his high Wisdom attributeto remember the name, a feat he could have never achieved on Earth. "What brings you back to Broken Tusk?"

Zan'kir grinned, gesturing toward the shop. "I have a tale to tell."

Chapter 36
Confluence

Zan'kir groaned as he sat at the table by the window upstairs. Theo brewed some tea for him, feeling sorry for how worn the Khahari looked. His fur was matted down in spots, and the glitter of ambition behind his eyes had dimmed slightly. The alchemist would have offered him a healing potion, but he knew it was the kind of exhaustion that couldn't be remedied by alchemy.

"This place is a confluence, alchemist," Zan'kir said after a while. "I thought it impossible for a place to have so many resources. Three dungeons within a half-day's walk are a lot, but now a Drogramathi alchemist?"

"I try not to think about it," Theo said with a shrug. "Things were so bad back on Earth... I just figured I had some good luck coming my way."

"I think that's exactly it," Zan'kir said. Some of the tiredness in his eyes had faded, revealing a glimmer of that ambition. "Well, I didn't mean to sound ominous. A confluence can be a good thing. Broken Tusk was unremarkable before you came. Now look at it."

"It's not just me, though." Theo shrugged. "I'm giving these people the tools."

"Just so," Zan'kir said, nodding and grinning. "The reason I came here today is to buy property. When I was in the north, I heard that merchants are taking an interest in this place."

"Ah, I can help you with that," Theo said. "We have a lot of land for sale, actually."

"Care to give me a tour?"

"Gladly."

Theo waited for Zan'kir to finish his tea. They chatted idly about other things while he drank. The Khahari told him about the River Dungeon to the east. It was an incredibly tough place to clear, as most of it was underwater. It was also only at Level 8, making it more attractive than the Level 25 dungeon in the swamp. Zan'kir had no information on the Hills Dungeon. They departed the shop, locking up, and began the tour of the town.

"So, let's go north first," Theo said, leading toward the town square.

They arrived at the monolith, and Theo could tell by the look on Zan'kir's face that he wasn't interested. The space was tight, and the roads were busy. "This is a bit of a cluster," he said.

"Yeah, this is where most of the people live," Theo said. "We have roads now, which is good, and walls."

"I noticed," Zan'kir said. "Very impressive for what little you have down here. Shall we?"

Theo nodded, leading him further north. They passed through the farm and out onto the sloping plain heading toward the quarry. Zan'kir seemed more interested in this plot of land. The alchemist noted that the road had extended north on its own. He reasoned that it was connecting the main part of town to the quarry. Since the walls expanded on their own, it made sense.

"You'd be all alone out here," Theo said, shrugging. "And you'd have to pass through the farm to get to town."

"That's fine," Zan'kir said, smiling. "How large of a parcel can you offer me?"

Theo accessed his administrator map, tilting his head. He owned every bit of land in the northern stretch of town. His intuition said he could split the parcel up and sell the land outright or rent it to Zan'kir.

"As much as you'd like," Theo said, shrugging. "My preference is that you don't buy the entire tract of land, though."

Zan'kir laughed. "Nothing like that. Just enough space for me to build a decent home."

"Well, if you're interested, I have core seeds for a house," Theo said.

Zan'kir raised an eyebrow. "How did you come across those?"

"I know a guy," Theo said, grinning.

"You truly are blessed," Zan'kir said. He positioned himself on the road and began walking in a large rectangle, beckoning Theo to follow. The alchemist's superior Wisdom allowed him to estimate the size of the plot as they went. "How much would this cost me?"

Theo had to think about the question for a moment. He tilted his head and did the mental math on the land and the house core. It was hard to find the desire to bleed the man dry, as every adventurer added to the town was another point of prosperity. The parcel that Zan'kir drew out was small compared to the size of the tract, not even a hundredth of its total size.

"I'm horrible at negotiations," Theo said, managing a sheepish smile. "I'll be honest with you—I'm no merchant. The land is worth, perhaps, a silver coin. The seed core is about 20 silver coins for me to make a profit."

"You're *too* honest, alchemist," Zan'kir groaned. "I was prepared to part with at least 1 gold."

"If you're willing to give up 1 gold so easily, then you must be a pretty high-level adventurer," Theo said. The urge to inspect the man was strong, but he resisted. Luras had told him it was rude, and he didn't want to ruin their relationship. "How does 50 silver sound?"

"For the seed core and the land?" Zan'kir asked. "That's an absurdly good deal."

"I know," Theo said. "Consider this an invitation to make your home here, in the open arms of Broken Tusk. You're like a settler, populating a new land."

Zan'kir reached his hand out. Theo grasped and shook it, beaming. Without waiting for the adventurer to give him the coin, he opened his administrator map, sectioned off the parcel, and assigned it to the Khahari.

"All yours," Theo said.

Zan'kir withdrew 50 silver coins from a dimensional bag and handed them over. Theo took out the House Seed Core, which looked like a wire mesh sphere with swirling timber inside, and handed it over. The adventurer marched to the middle of the field and buried it in the ground. The alchemist watched as he withdrew monster cores from his inventory and shoved them into the ground. After a moment, the earth rumbled, and the adventurer retreated.

"Laying down some roots," Theo said, watching in awe.

An *actual* root sprung from the ground, swirling around and forming a box. Boards appeared on the outside of the gnarled root, snapping into place to form a beautifully boarded exterior. The roof sprung from nowhere, flying into the air and landing gracefully on top of the structure. When it was done forming, the building was a single-story home with two neat windows in the front. The road snaked to connect to the doorstep.

"Beautiful," Zan'kir said, beaming. Without another word, the adventurer disappeared inside. The house rumbled after a moment, expanding in either direction before shaking violently. The roof jumped again, boards springing to create a second floor.

"That was cool," Theo said, nodding at Zan'kir as he emerged.

"It's *very* satisfying," Zan'kir said, admiring his new home. "I have a question."

"Yes?"

"I'm going to depart to retrieve my family from the northlands," Zan'kir said. "Could you keep an eye on the house?"

"No problem," Theo said, shrugging.

"With this matter sorted, I'll depart in the morning," Zan'kir said. "If you'll excuse me, I have some decorating to do."

"All right. See ya," Theo said, waving.

Theo departed, heading north to the quarry to check on Ziz. A massive pile of blocks sat near the workshop. The half-ogre was working a slab of marble, cutting it into smaller blocks, when he spotted the alchemist. They exchanged pleasantries, but his real reason for being there was to see if the merchant Fenian sent had stopped by. He hadn't. Theo stayed for as long as was polite before leaving, letting the men do their work.

When he passed by the farm, his mind went back to the Spriggan Heart Tresk had found in the dungeon. Theo's mind reeled at the possibilities of enhancing the growth rate of the crops, enabling the farmers to make more money on their hard work. Something in his gut told him they would be less accepting of his alchemical solutions, but as with all things in Broken Tusk, results mattered more than promises. He would come up with a potion to grow the crops before pitching the idea.

Theo stopped at the square, reluctantly finding his way to Miana's house. She poked her head out, flashing an uncharacteristic smile and beckoning for him to come inside. He followed her inside, taking a seat in her office. There was something she was hiding from him, but he couldn't figure it out. Her mood was far better than any time he had ever seen her, which never bode well for the half-ogre mayor.

"You wanted to see me?" Theo asked.

"I'm quitting," Miana said, grinning wider.

Theo felt his heart stop in his chest for a moment. "You're what?"

"You've made me useless, Alchemist," Miana said. "Gods do I feel useless!"

"Come on," Theo said. "You're not useless."

"I do nothing here," Miana said. "Truth be told, I never wanted to be the mayor. When I got the appointment, it was a punishment. Felt like it, anyway."

"Well, who's going to run the town?" Theo asked. "Is Qavell going to send a replacement?"

"They already have," Miana said.

"Who are they?" Theo asked.

He couldn't stand the thought of Broken Tusk falling into the hands of someone who didn't care about it, some bureaucrat sent from the north to make their town something it wasn't.

"What has two horns and is now the mayor of Broken Tusk?" Miana asked, pointing dramatically at Theo. "You do!"

The blood in Theo's veins turned to ice. The feeling subsided quickly, as he realized he had already been running the town anyway. The only thing Miana did was collect taxes and glower from her house.

"What are you going to do?" Theo asked.

"I'm staying here," Miana said. "I'll live out my life doing whatever. I'm not exactly young, you know."

Theo felt a rush throughout his body. The message that popped up sent a chill down his spine.

[Mayoral Transfer]
Miana Kell has transferred the mayorship of **[Small Town] Broken Tusk** to you! Your Lord Administrator role has been revoked.

"Just like that?" Theo asked.

"Just like that. This was actually Lauris's idea—our handler in Qavell. They're impressed with the way you're running the town," Miana said.

"I feel bad," Theo said, knitting his brow. "It's like I just came in here and took your spot."

"Make it up to me," Miana said. "Someone told me you bought some house seed cores from that merchant. Sell me one along with a plot of land and we're square."

Theo thought for a moment. He felt so bad about taking the mayor's position that he didn't even want to consider it. Luras's advice about him giving things away for free came into his mind, but this was Miana. He withdrew a seed core from his inventory and set it down on the table.

"For free," Theo said. "Just let me know what plot of land you want, and it's yours."

"Thank you, Theo," Miana said.

It was hard to get used to this new side of her. The weight of the mayor's position must have weighed heavily on her. It was a yoke that brought her mood down every day, turning her into that moody person. By contrast, Theo felt none of that weight. Running the town had been a joy, and he would gladly do it forever if he could.

"What about my debt?" Theo asked.

"You still owe me," Miana said, flashing a grin. "Can't get away that easily."

The pair departed Miana's home, walking out onto the well-cobbled streets.

"You're the mayor!" Tresk said into Theo's mind. *"I'm coming home—I gotta get the story in person."*

Theo smiled, following Miana's lead. She went south, much to his surprise. They moved past the tannery and Luras's new building to the edge of town, near the wall. She gestured to a small plot of land that was already sectioned off. The alchemist bought it without hesitation, happily spending the 5 silver his new mayor's map interface requested. He transferred the property rights to Miana.

"Thanks, Theo," Miana said. "I'll plant the seed and feed it cores—don't worry, I have a couple stashed away. When I move all my junk out, you can have my old house."

"I don't think I'll use it," Theo said with a shrug. "I'm going to miss your scowls."

"Just come down here. I'll be happy to hurl curses at you from my front porch," Miana said.

"I'm going to call a meeting with the mercantile chairs tomorrow," Theo said. "I think you should have an advisor seat."

"Does it pay?"

"Nope."

The half-ogre woman scowled, then brightened up. "Bah. I'll come anyway," Miana said. "Goodbye."

Theo turned on the spot and left, having strange feelings about the entire encounter. He returned to the Newt and Demon to inspect his new interfaces. There were several new screens he could access when thinking about the concept of Broken Tusk. The screens popped up, displaying detailed information about the town. He saw things like population, resources, and the town's current level and upgrades.

Tresk arrived sometime later to find Theo sitting in the shop, staring off into the distance. He relayed the story to her, laughing at the sight of her being just as surprised as he had been. They settled down upstairs so that the marshling could tell him about her day.

"I was fighting some big, hairy goblin when you got promoted," Tresk said. "I think everyone in town saw it."

"I guess it makes sense, but I feel bad," Theo said. "I hope her new situation makes her happy."

"Miana will do whatever she wants, that's not your concern," Tresk said. "You're the *mayor* of Broken Tusk. Think of the things we can do!"

"Yeah, we don't have to run around asking for permission to do stuff," Theo said. "We just do it."

The afternoon sun blazed outside, but neither of them wanted to do anything else today. The shock of becoming mayor was too much to handle. Theo inspected the facets of the mayor's interface. From the map that detailed property ownership to demographics, he probed through more menus than he cared to have. The financial tab broke down the distribution of taxes and what influenced them. Everyone who owned property had to pay a weekly tax to the mayor, who then paid that money to the capital. Then there were the businesses. The town was smart enough to know when coin exchanged hands and tax them based on a fixed rate. He couldn't set the tax rates himself. It must have been something Qavell did on their end.

Theo found himself in a daze, flicking through those menus idly as he waited for the day to end. Suddenly, a loud knock from the door downstairs broke his concentration. Tresk scampered downstairs, answering it and letting out a squeal. Theo went to investigate the commotion.

In the door stood Perg and Luras, both of them grinning.

"So, when were you going to tell us Miana made you the mayor?" Luras asked, chuckling.

"When it suited him, I imagine," Perg said.

"I'm still processing it," Theo said.

Luras strode across the shop, snatching Theo by the arm and dragging him to the threshold.

"What's going on?" Theo asked.

"What do you think?" Luras asked. "We're throwing a party."

Chapter 37
Party

Theo had never seen the entire town of Broken Tusk assembled in one place. How they had assembled everyone on such short notice was beyond him. The town gathered in the square, smiling and greeting their new mayor when he arrived. Fires were built around the monolith, holding massive cooking pots and pans. A torrent of scents washed over him as they approached.

"How did you manage this?" Theo asked.

Luras just smiled, clapping his hand over the alchemist's back.

"This is great," Tresk said.

Perg came to stand by Theo, placing her arm around his shoulder. "This is the first step for us," she said, taking a deep breath. "You're the mayor now, but once the city upgrades, you'll get a new title."

"And more authority," Luras said. "That's the important part. Once we get bigger, we'll have more autonomy."

"I mean, the capital has left us alone," Theo said with a shrug.

"For now," Perg said. "Give it time. You don't know them yet. The crown has an interest in their investments. A greater interest when their investments rise above them." "Good to know," Theo said.

"For now, we party!" Tresk said, pumping her fist.

Theo went around shaking hands and receiving well-wishes from the citizens of Broken Tusk. They were all excited to let him know how much of a natural fit he was for the position, but he had his doubts. He knew his heart was in the right place, but he doubted his ability to lead them to greatness. As a few of them said, though, it was hard to argue with the results. In a few short weeks, the town had grown more than it had in an entire century before his arrival.

The alchemist sampled a bit of every dish on offer, making the rounds with Tresk to sample what the townsfolk had come up with. Both of them favored the spicy dishes made with the Fire Salamander Eggs. There were incredibly inventive pots of spicy noodles with tender wolf meat. Theo couldn't get over how good that dish was and made a point to get the recipe from the farmer who made it. He vowed to learn the secret of creating Zee noodles from scratch.

It was a shame Azrug couldn't attend. The boy was still bedridden, as far as Theo knew. Still, it was easy enough to move on from the thought—the food was just that delicious.

"We need a mill," Theo said, returning to Perg and Luras.

"Here he goes again," the female half-ogre said, feigning annoyance.

Theo shrugged, flashing a sheepish grin. "I can't help it. There are too many opportunities."

Theo spotted Aarok, flanked by a pair of adventurers, approaching through the crowd. He wordlessly beckoned the alchemist to follow him, shrugging when Tresk padded closely behind. The guild master knew it was pointless to keep her out of the loop because of Tara'hek Communication. They ascended the battlements of the wall, looking out over the swamp. The setting sun cast the marsh in a dim, orange light.

"I suppose I have to call you 'mayor,'" Aarok said, chuckling.

"I don't care what you call me."

Aarok waved him off, shaking his head. "I'm nervous, Theo."

"About what?" Theo asked, knitting his brow. Something in the half-ogre's eyes sent a chill down his spine.

Aarok patted the crenulations of the wall, nodding his head. Something was running through the man's mind that Theo couldn't figure out, and he just waited for him to speak. "The walls are a good measure. Recruiting more adventurers helps, too. But I have a bad feeling about the Swamp Dungeon."

"What's the issue?" Tresk asked. She brought a fat piece of meat with her the whole way and was currently gnawing on it.

"I have a theory, but I need to request some resources from the capital," Aarok said.

"Which is where I come in," Theo said. "What's the theory?"

"I think the dungeon is growing in strength because of something else," Aarok said. "We haven't seen the core in ages—it's simply too deep—but it's getting power from outside of the swamp."

"Is that possible?" Tresk asked through a mouthful of meat.

"That's where the resources come in," Aarok said. "I need some books—records of monster waves."

"You think it's a monster wave?" Tresk asked, gawking. "The southlands have never seen a monster wave. We're just too small—not enough magic."

"Until you consider a *confluence* of events," Theo said, trailing off. His mind snapped back to what Zan'kir said about the dungeons and his rebirth in Broken Tusk. "The Harbinger... The entity that reincarnated me here... That had to be some powerful magic."

"Exactly," Aarok said. "Look, I don't think this is anything to worry about right now. We're two steps ahead of the problem already."

Theo suddenly wished he hadn't dumped all his money into things like seed cores. Upgrading the town to Level 20 would have been a boon against whatever threat they faced, but he couldn't worry about what had already been done. They had taken the right precautions to protect the people—Aarok was right. Between the walls and the adventurer's guild, they were ahead of the curve. His intuition told him there was more he could do to defend the town.

"I'll contact Fenian and the capital tomorrow," Theo said. "My handler, Lauris, will get you the information you need."

"Why contact the merchant?" Aarok asked.

"Merchants know things," Tresk said, waggling the bit of meat knowingly. "They've always got an ear to the ground and a hand in your pocket."

Aarok snorted a laugh. "I just wanted to make sure you were properly worried about the situation."

"Hah! Theo is always worried about something," Tresk said, striking a pose, "but I'm not. I'm never worried about anything."

Aarok sighed. "That's a problem, too. You owe some dues to the guild, Tresk."

"You need a guild hall," Tresk said, sneering. "I won't recognize your authority until you have a proper hall."

"How much does she owe?" Theo asked.

"A silver for the month," Aarok said.

Theo produced a silver coin from his inventory and handed it over, preferring to avoid any issues with the guild. If they were truly the first line of defense, he wanted to make sure they were funded. His mind wandered to that realm of the town.

"Speaking of," Theo said, thinking out loud. "Is the guild properly funded?"

"For now," Aarok said. "The capital is footing the bill for my quests, and almost everyone is paying their dues."

"Everyone except Tresk," Theo said, casting a glare at his companion. "You need to pay the man next time."

"I'll pay when he has a hall," Tresk said, turning up her nose.

Theo ran his hand over his face, letting out a groan. "Fine. Aarok, let me know if you're ever having issues with funding. Talk with Miana—when she clears out her old house at the square, you can use it as a hall. When Fenian gets in town, I'll buy a seed core for a guild hall."

"Wow. That works," Aarok said. "Don't you need a place to do mayor stuff?"

"No. I've been doing my Lord Administrator stuff from the Newt and Demon," Theo said.

The group fell into silence for a while. Then a group of marsh wolves howled in the distance, causing the two adventurers standing with Aarok to nod at each other. They descended the stairs and left the safety of the gates. Theo appreciated how much they did to keep the town safe and had to make sure he was on top of keeping the guild happy. The adventurers down below battled the wolves with trained precision, no longer displaying the novice styles they had shown at the start of their training. The alchemist understood nothing about close-quarters combat, but it was clear they were good.

The shining jewel of Broken Tusk was its alchemist, Theo. The key to his strategy was to reinvest his wealth into the town. He could hoard the money or invest it into alchemy supplies, but that wouldn't have as big of an impact. Building his town would give the highest return in the long term, and it would make people's lives better. It was a win-win.

"Back to the party," Tresk said, tugging on Theo's sleeve.

"Right," the alchemist said. "Aarok, I want to have a town meeting tomorrow. I'll summon all the relevant people once I've spoken to Fenian and Lauris."

"Sounds good," Aarok said.

Tresk and Theo returned to the town square, finding the fires burning higher as the sun dropped lower on the horizon. The alchemist looked but didn't spot Azrug among the townsfolk. He would need to check on the boy tomorrow to make sure he was all right. He cast those thoughts of worry out of his mind and enjoyed the company, making his rounds once again. Perg led some townsfolk in a dance on the northern end of the square. It barely looked like a dance from his point of view and was more like a war ritual performed before a battle.

"Looks more like fighting than dancing," Theo said, watching.

"Marshlings don't dance," Tresk said, waving her hand.

"Yeah, I'm a horrible dancer," Theo said.

"This is my best one," Tresk said. She bobbed up and down awkwardly, a stupid grin playing across her face.

Theo joined her, bending at the knees and keeping his arms straight at his side. Other townsfolk joined in with them, laughing at how stupid the dance was. Before long, everyone was bobbing up and down, trying to keep a straight face.

"Well, that was awkward," Theo said. Everyone suddenly stopped dancing, trying to contain their laughter.

The party went on after dusk. Theo ate more food than he'd ever had in his life, finding himself waddling around to talk to people. He even spotted Zan'kir among the crowd, awkwardly grabbing food and talking to the other members of the town. The alchemist made introductions for him, especially to Aarok, who returned sometime later. The half-ogre was excited about having a new adventurer in town.

"I'll be departing tomorrow to fetch my family," Zan'kir said.

"Not a problem," Aarok said. "Just remember to check in with me when you get back. We'll get your membership sorted."

"Yeah, just watch out for the *hidden fees*," Tresk said, scowling.

Theo and Tresk left when their stamina bars were drained low. After the marshling deposited some materials she got from the dungeon into their dimensional crate, the pair lingered in the lab section of their home for a while. While the alchemist had put on a brave face for Aarok, he wanted to do everything in his power to protect Broken Tusk.

"What is a monster wave?" Theo asked, jotting down some notes on a piece of parchment.

"A whole bunch of monsters," Tresk said with a shrug. "I don't know much about them, though. Like Aarok said, they don't happen in the southlands."

Theo considered the idea before responding. It was easy to think of a "monster wave" as a bunch of monsters, but what did that mean for Broken Tusk? Would the monsters engulf the town, besieging it for prolonged period of time? He found it hard to imagine the town surviving any prolonged battle. The walls were sturdy, but he needed to explore other options.

"What are you writing?" Tresk asked.

"I'm trying to keep ahead of the game," Theo said, tilting the parchment to catch enough candlelight. "I don't want to respond to problems when they come. I want to be prepared."

Tresk grabbed some parchment, tearing some from a roll and scrawling. She made a crude representation of the town, detailing which sections were the weakest. "So, attacks are coming from the west right now. That's not a surprise, because that's the direction where the Swamp Dungeon is. If Aarok is right and something else is giving these monsters power, they'll start coming from other directions."

Theo pointed to the north, then south. "They shouldn't be coming from these. The hills to the north turn into mountains, and the south is even worse."

"Right, so whatever we do, we need to focus our attention on the east," Tresk said. "Do you have anything in mind?"

Theo thought for a moment. Something itched in the back of his mind, like a long-gone memory. Something he should have known about that just wouldn't surface. "Whatever it is, it needs to be automated," Theo said. "Maybe a defensive artifice."

"That's Fenian's domain," Tresk said.

The alchemist let out a heavy sigh, finally nodding to himself. "Right. All this means is that I need money."

"Lots of it," Tresk said.

Theo stood and marched to the bedroom, putting out the candles with Tresk close behind. "It's back to the grind tomorrow. Making potions that sell for big coin."

The pair settled into their beds, Tresk snoring almost immediately. Theo was left with his thoughts on the matter. Getting to

Newt and Demon

Level 10 would change everything. He knew that through his intuition. He could only imagine the price a higher-tier potion would fetch and was eager to find out. During his strategizing for the next day, sleep got the better of him. He drifted off with the sound of Tresk's dreams playing through his mind. She was dreaming about steak again.

Chapter 38
Fenian's Other Request

Theo rose before Tresk the next morning. He found his way into the lab and prepared breakfast, a simple meal of wolf soup and moss tea. The tasks he needed to accomplish today were many, as a sudden realization that the mayor's position would add more work to his daily routine hit him. The alchemist banished the thoughts away, smiling to himself as he cooked the soup. His position within the town gave him autonomy to steer its direction in the way he wanted, ensuring the safety of everyone inside. He would turn the town into a fortress if he could.

"Morning," Tresk said, stretching at the threshold of the lab. "Soup for breakfast? Yes, please."

The marshling came to sit next to Theo, pawing at his shoulder. "What's the plan for today?" she asked.

"I need more reagents—that's my first goal. Then I need to call a meeting with the mercantile chairs, talk to Fenian, and call my contact in Qavell."

"Busy boy," Tresk said, letting out a breath. "I have mandatory patrol duty for the guild tomorrow. Yuck."

"At least I paid your dues," Theo said, glaring at her.

"I refuse to recognize Aarok's authority until he has a proper guild hall," Tresk said, folding her arms.

"Well, he's going to have Miana's old house when she moves all her stuff out," Theo said.

"That's fine."

They ate as fast as they could, slurping down the hot soup and burning their tongues. Theo gave Tresk a Lesser Stamina Potion to take with her, knowing the day would be too busy for either of them to spare a moment for rest. He had no intention of waiting for Azrug to come to the shop—he would march directly to Xam's place and check in on the boy. The alchemist didn't spot him at the party last night and was worried. He plotted a course in his mind to loop through his massive property to the east, collecting as many healing roots as he could before following the river for the lilies. He would then check on Azrug before contacting Fenian and Lauris.

"Stay safe," Theo said, patting Tresk on the head. "Keep me updated, and... keep an eye out for new clothes." Theo gestured to his simple attire. The only piece of clothing he owned that wasn't torn were the gloves Luras gave him. Everything else had enormous holes or tears.

"Of course," Tresk said. "We might need to get those from a merchant, though."

Theo nodded, bidding farewell to his companion and heading out the door. Tresk followed close behind, locking the shop up before scampering off into the swamp to the west. The alchemist followed his planned course, intent on getting as many reagents as possible. As expected, the Spiny Swamp Thistles had all grown back overnight. He harvested them, following a roving path toward the river. By the time he made it there, his inventory had 200 more Spiny Swamp Thistle Roots, and following the river north netted him 100 Water Lilies.

Theo found Xam inside the Marsh Wolf Tavern, cleaning up the place from the celebration last night. Apparently, some revelers took the action inside, making quite a mess. She brightened upon spotting him, waving and smiling. "Hey, Mayor."

"How is he?" Theo asked, cutting to the core of his worries.

"He's good. Azrug will be able to work tomorrow," Xam said.

"I'm forcing him to rest today, but he's extremely excited to tell you about his new cores."

"What did he get?" Theo asked.

"That's for him to reveal," Xam said.

Theo didn't want to pry into the issue. It always seemed like such a personal matter to inspect someone else's class and cores. He bid her farewell and made his way to Miana's old house. The half-ogre woman had cleared it out sometime last night. The alchemist found himself in empty halls he hardly recognized. It was a shell of its former self without all that junk of hers scattered around. The only thing that remained was the furniture in her office, in which he settled to talk to his contacts.

The communication crystal was in the same spot she always left it, waiting for him to dive back into that strange shadow place. Theo grasped it in his hands and leaned back, tumbling into that strange place to await Lauris.

"Good morning, Mayor." The familiar voice came from the gloom. A shadowy figure resolved, sanding in the void and waving. "Miana Kell sent word that you'd taken the position. Congratulations."

"Thanks," Theo said.

"Most of us here at the administration unit were hoping you'd take the job," Lauris said. "You're proving to be a valuable asset."

"Well, I appreciate the sentiment. What I really need is some information," Theo said.

"Oh? What about?" Lauris asked.

"The guild master of the adventurer's guild here in Broken Tusk needs to see any research regarding monster waves," Theo said.

"Monster waves? In the southlands?" Lauris said. It was hard to tell through the strange void, but there was a tinge of worry in those words.

"It's just a suspicion," Theo said. "We're experiencing a lot of growth in our dungeons—too much to chalk it up to coincidence."

"Right. Okay, your guild master should get a notification about an increase in his budget," Lauris said. "Let's see... Your communication crystal locator beacon is still active. I'll send you copies of what we have in Qavell."

"Thank you," Theo said. "I appreciate it."

"Also, I see your town is currently at the [Small Town] status. I recommend you try to expand and upgrade that status to [Town]," Lauris said. "For now, just leave the crystal somewhere in the open. We'll teleport the materials sometime today."

"You can teleport?" Theo asked, laughing.

"It's complicated. Most of our mages who can do such things are busy with other things, but I'll push you to the front of the line," Lauris said. "Do you need anything else?"

"That's it," Theo said.

"All right, thanks. Have a good day," Lauris said.

Theo felt himself jerked backward by the navel, sent hurtling upward into a yawning maw of light. He snapped back into his body, feeling a shiver run down his spine. The implications of Lauris's words resonated in his mind. He couldn't help but think that the reason Miana stepped down was because of the administration in Qavell. The alchemist suddenly felt even worse about the situation, like he didn't deserve the position. All those thoughts vanished when he remembered his tasks for the day. He withdrew Fenian's crystal from his inventory and held it tightly.

"Theo? How are you doing?" Fenian asked.

"I'm well. I have a few questions," Theo said.

"All right, that's fine. I have an order request, if you'll hear it," Fenian said. *"Remember those snot-nosed nobles I was talking about? A particularly annoying house is rearing whelps. They've heard of your prowess from me and want a lot of restoration potions."*

"How many?" Theo asked.

"I wouldn't come back to them with anything less than a thousand of each," Fenian said.

Theo felt his heart stop for a moment. Creating 500 of each

potion was hard enough, but Fenian wanted 1,000 of each restoration potion now.

"That's 7 gold, 50 silver worth of potions, Theo," Fenian said. The man always knew how to motivate him. "And as many attribute potions as you can make. Vigor and Strength being the preference."

"So, standard rate... Would you accept anything over the requested amount?" Theo asked.

"Absolutely," Fenian said. "Make the potions and contact me when you have them. I'll be in Rivers and Daub for a few days, then I'm heading west. Easily a day's travel from Broken Tusk. Now, what was your question?"

"We have a bad feeling about an incoming monster wave," Theo said.

"Me too," Fenian said.

It was hard to tell the elf's motives at the best of times. If Fenian had a bad feeling, what did that mean for Broken Tusk? He was their lifeline to the outside world. Perhaps he had *other* means to defend the town.

"I'm interested in defenses. Something that doesn't require a person to be in danger," Theo said.

"Ah. Expensive artifacts would be the key... Well, there are also core attachments for your walls, but you'd need to get your [Small Town] to [Town] and level it up to 15."

"I can do that," Theo said, nodding to himself. "How do these attachments work?"

"You'll get an upgrade on the town. Basically, turret slots for your walls. Every gate will get two slots, and also a slot every fifty paces of wall," Fenian said.

"And how much are these special attachments going to cost?"

"It's been a while since I sourced them," Fenian said. "I know a woman who farms them up north, so it'll take me a while to get them. Assume they'll cost you between 5 and 10 gold each."

That was an absurd amount of money for a defensive structure.

But if it meant Broken Tusk adventurers could stay safe behind the walls, it would be worth it.

"*All right. I'll work on your potions,*" Theo said.

"*If you discover any new potions, let me know. The family has a long list of stuff that they want, and it's impossible to source the lesser potions up north right now. The army is buying them all up,*" Fenian said.

"*Thanks, Fenian,*" Theo said.

"*Any time, my friend,*" Fenian said. The connection was severed, and Theo was left feeling raw for a moment. He gave himself some time to recover before standing, wiping the sweat from his brow.

Theo wouldn't be able to collect the ingredients on his own in a reasonable timeframe. He would need to outsource the work to hirelings, but he feared Ziz and his laborers would be too concerned with their stone-cutting project. The alchemist left Miana's old home, collecting all the mercantile chairs for a short meeting. He found Luras, Aarok, Perg, Throk, Miana, and Banu-rub. He hadn't seen Banu in a few days, but the farmers typically stuck to their farms, so it wasn't surprising. The group crammed into the small meeting room in Miana's house, the place destined to be the new base of the adventurer's guild.

"I promise, this is going to be a short meeting," Theo said.

"Take your time, Mayor," Perg said, grinning.

"The capital approved your request, Aarok," Theo said. He had a nose for this matter, understanding that the guild master wanted to keep it quiet. "The materials you requested and an increased budget for the guild."

"I got the notification earlier," Aarok said, nodding.

"Good. If anyone is unaware, we have a new citizen. I think he left today, but an adventurer named Zan'kir moved in north of the farms."

Theo received a series of nods, but no verbal responses. "I'm holding off on projects for a while until I can get more to upgrade the town. I'd rather be prepared for events before they happen."

"Do you expect something to happen?" Banu asked, knitting his brow.

Theo didn't know Banu well, but he knew enough about farmers. They were always scared of something. Perhaps it was the way the changes of weather affected their crops, but they seemed skittish about most things.

"Always expect something bad to come." Luras cut in.

"Agreed," Miana said. "We don't want to get caught with our pants down."

"So, if you see adventurers in town, send them my way," Theo said. "They need to know about the stipend to live here, and I'll give them a great deal on property."

"What about people who already live here?" Throk asked.

"You already own property, Throk," Theo said, shaking his head. "I'll offer land at cost to anyone who wants it, though. One per person, of course. Don't want anyone here turning into a land baron."

"You're kind of a land baron," Luras said, grinning.

"Not yet," Theo said. "Don't tempt me—I'll buy every step of land in this town."

Everyone in the group besides Banu laughed. The farmer just didn't understand the joke. The group calmed down, and Theo continued. "That's all for today, though. I just wanted to set the stage for my plans as the town's mayor."

Throk held his hand up before everyone left their chairs. "Have you considered buying the rights to the land from Qavell?"

Theo looked at the reactions around the room. Luras tilted his head, considering it a workable option. Banu had a look of horror on his face.

"What would that do for us?" Theo asked.

"It would be a long-term thing," Luras said. "Technically, the town core is on loan from the king. That means we all owe the crown for our property and sales."

"Would we still get their support? That seems kind of important," Theo said.

"I think so," Throk said, beaming.

"How much would it cost?" Theo asked.

Miana laughed. "You know that coin that's bigger than gold? The one no one around these parts has ever seen? A few of those."

Theo couldn't even imagine that much money. He filed it away for something to take care of later. "Right. Oh, one more thing. If anyone knows laborers for hire, send them to my shop. Otherwise, that's it for the day."

The group filed out of Miana's old, tiny office. A buzz of chatter spread through the group, with Luras joining Theo on the road south. His leatherworking building was up and running, but he had yet to produce anything to sell. Something in the half-ogre's expression said he was happier than before. Theo was just happy to have helped him get to a better place. They stopped by the Newt and Demon, saying their farewells and parting ways.

"Right. Time to cook some potions," Theo said.

Chapter 39
Stone Merchant

Theo cracked his knuckles, swishing his tail happily as he looked over his alchemy equipment. It hadn't been that long since he distilled anything, but it felt like forever. There, in the stuffy second-floor lab, was where he felt most at home. He updated Tresk on his situation and got her report for the morning. She was working her way through the dungeon again with a pair of Broken Tusk adventurers. They were already past the tenth floor, moving as deep as they could for the day. She found a few more Spriggan Hearts and some gear that wasn't useful for either of them.

The Alchemical Grinder Artifice resized itself, clicking onto the Drogramath Still with a satisfying sound. Theo stepped back to inspect the machine before withdrawing a Spiny Swamp Thistle Root from his inventory to test it. The moment the root touched the top of the artifice, it whirred into action, grinding it down into the perfect paste. The alchemist wanted to test the limits of the device, pulling as many roots from his inventory as he could carry and dumping them in the machine. It ate through them like a knife through paper, grinding 500 units of the root in no time. He pumped his fist, doing the silly little squad dance that Tresk had invented.

Newt and Demon

After patting himself on the back for a while, the alchemist got back to work. He topped the high-capacity still off with water and placed the Flame Artifice underneath. Clicking the knob on the side to the lowest setting, he stepped back to inspect his materials. He placed his two grinders over the other stills and prepared to distill a 200-unit batch of Widow Lily to make poison for Tresk and a 200-unit batch of Water Lily because he had a lot of those. The grinder whirred over both stills, mashing up the flowers into the perfect size. He stowed the grinders in his inventory and latched the lids on both stills.

Theo sat there, waiting for his essences to distill, thinking about how easy the rest of the process would be with his new equipment. The grinder cut down the time significantly, and the magic fire made it even easier. His job for Fenian would be decided by volume, he realized. The problem was that he just couldn't get enough reagents to distill down, forcing his mind to reach out for more solutions. Nothing came in the short time it took the Drogramath Still to extract the essences. It felt like less than half an hour was enough for the advanced still to do its work, a fact that boggled his mind.

"Now *that* was fast," he said, chuckling to himself.

With the upgrade to the Glassware Artifice, Theo could generate bulk glassware. He could shove five motes into the thing and get five identical vials deposited directly into his inventory. The artifice didn't seem to have a cooldown, so he could just repeatedly shove the motes inside to get his glassware. The process took him no time at all, leaving him idle while he waited for the other two stills to finish. When they completed their run, he cleaned everything out with Cleansing Scrub and went to set up the distribution of the potions. A knock at the door downstairs interrupted him.

Theo made his way to the front door of the Newt and Demon, finding a short man standing at the threshold. He had a surly expression on his face, a bald head, and a braided brown beard. The alchemist took him for a dwarf even before he spoke.

"Hello, do you need potions?" Theo asked.

"Potions? No. I need *stone,* lad," the man said. "Fenian sent me. I'm Thistum Stonebreaker and I hear you're sitting on a gold mine."

"Oh! I didn't expect you so soon," Theo said.

"Aye, well, you don't hear about perfect-quality marble every day. None that's not claimed by some royal, anyway," Thistum said, spitting on the ground.

Theo exited, stepping around the dwarf after locking the front door. He beckoned for the man to follow him north, to the quarry.

"I don't remember such a pleasant town lying so far south," the dwarf said. "The stories I heard were that Broken Tusk was a glob of mud."

"Well, I've made a few changes," Theo said.

"I should have figured a Dronon would have such ambitions," Thistum said. "Half-ogres are content to do what they've been doing for centuries."

"You'll love the stone," Theo said, wanting to change the subject.

"Fenian doesn't send me unless he finds something nice," Thistum said. "Now, you aren't expecting the big city prices, are you?"

"Of course not," Theo said, grinning.

They made their way through the square and up the farmer's hill. Thistum seemed amazed at the progress Broken Tusk had made, constantly saying how it should be impossible. The alchemist knew better than to mention the strange confluence of circumstances that saw the small town burgeon as it had in the past few weeks. Instead, he gave a tour of the place as though the dwarf were looking for real estate.

"Quaint little quarry," Thistum said in a low voice.

Theo waved Ziz over, marveling at the massive pile of stone blocks they had processed so far.

"Ziz, this is Thistum. He's a stone merchant," Theo said.

"Nice to meet you," Ziz said.

Thistum waved him off, pushing past the half-ogre to inspect the stone.

"Let me do the talking," Theo whispered, nudging Ziz with his elbow.

"Sure."

Thistum pulled something out of his inventory that looked like a spyglass. He placed it against the stone blocks and tried to hide his excitement. He let out a few yelps before clapping his hand over his mouth and clearing his throat.

"It's middling by my standards," Thistum said, shrugging.

"That's not what the other merchant said," Theo said. "I have contact with the Khahari out east—they were going back to check about logistics."

Thistum bristled. "Was it that muck-mouthed dwarf Azmuil? Gods, if he steals another client from me because of those cat-people…"

The dwarf regained his composure, straightening his tunic and setting his stone-gray eyes on Theo. "Right. So, you know what you have."

Theo couldn't stop smiling. It was too easy to get the dwarf to take the bait. "I'm an alchemist," he said, shrugging. "I've got my methods. Let's make a deal; 40 copper a block. My laborers can produce 50 a day."

Thistum sputtered. "I wouldn't pay a coin over 25 copper a block."

"Give us 30, and we'll supply you exclusively. You won't have to worry about *Azmuil*," Theo said.

Thistum reached out his hand, and Theo shook it. "Deal. What other sort of treasures are you sitting on here, Dronon?"

"More than you know," Theo said.

"Right. I'll be by weekly to collect," Thistum said, looking at the pile for a moment, then turning to the alchemist. "Looks like 140 blocks today. Comes to 42 silver."

The dwarf produced the silver out of thin air and handed it over to Theo before making the pile vanish. He had some kind of inventory power, which made sense for a stone merchant. Thistum turned to Ziz for a moment, clapping his hand over the half-ogre's shoulder. "Fine work, lad."

"What?!" Ziz said, once the dwarf was out of earshot. "You said we'd only get 25 copper a block."

"Negotiation, my friend," Theo said, beaming. "I figured he gave Fenian a low number when they talked."

Theo withdrew two silver coins from his inventory and handed them over to Ziz. The half-ogre took it with glittering eyes, jumping up and down shortly after. The alchemist noticed that when he added the coins to his inventory, the silver rolled over into the gold. He now had 1 gold, 5 silver, and 27 copper.

"That's 40 silver off your debt," Theo said. "You'll have this paid off in no time."

Ziz looked like he couldn't come up with the words to express his gratitude. Instead, he pulled Theo into a hug and held him there for a long time. After releasing him, he rushed off to show the coins to his companions.

Theo departed, smiling the entire way back to his shop. It seemed cruel to leave them with two coins out of forty-two, but it was for their own good. His investment in the quarry represented a deficit in his ability to defend the town, something he was still kicking himself over. He still felt good about the situation, though. These laborers were nothing more than porters a few days ago. Now, they could provide for themselves and then some. One day, Ziz's quarry would be the stuff of legends.

Tresk reported in, stating she was almost done running the dungeon for the day. Theo didn't mind, as he had planned to do some minor experimentation before she came home. The alchemist discovered a few properties that he hadn't tested the effects of and wanted to judge if they would make good potions to sell to Fenian. He made his way to the lab to run two extremely small batches of about ten units each.

His stamina bar was being drained, but not low enough to use his Lesser Stamina Potion yet. Theo was driven to experiment, feeling himself getting back into the swing of things. It was effortless to run two stills at the ten-unit capacity. He filled one still with Spiny Swamp Thistle Root and another with Moss Nettle. When he snapped the lid on the first one, he concentrated on the [Regeneration] property. Attending the second, he focused on the [Stamina Surge] property and set both to cook. It only took a few minutes to distill the essences down, and the alchemist inspected the results.

[Stamina Surge Essence]
[Essence]
Uncommon
Created by: Belgar
Quality: Excellent
10 units (liquid)
Concentrated essence of stamina surge.

[Regeneration Essence]
[Essence]
Uncommon
Created by: Belgar
Quality: Excellent
10 units (liquid)
Concentrated essence of regeneration.

Theo knew that the essences never gave away what they did and set out some flat-bottomed vials. His intuition told him they would react with the standard restoration recipe, pegging them squarely as "lesser" potions. The [Stamina Surge] reaction kicked off explosively, sending tiny bolts of lightning from the top of the vial. The plume of yellow smoke it gave off smelled like dirty laundry. He inspected the result.

[Lesser Sprinting Potion]
[Potion]

Uncommon
Created by: Belgar
Quality: Excellent
Drink to run faster and use less stamina.
Effect:
-50% stamina use while running.
+15% movement speed while running.
Effect lasts 15 minutes.

This was one of the most curious potions he had ever made. It was incredibly specific, and he did not know how useful it would be. He could imagine that someone running longer and faster was a good thing, but he didn't see any practical use for this effect himself. He would ask Fenian about it later. The next potion kicked off with a similar reaction, this time shining with a green hue before letting out a cloud smelling of dirt. He inspected the new creation.

[Lesser Regeneration Potion]
[Potion]
Uncommon
Created by: Belgar
Quality: Excellent
Slowly regenerates health.
Effect:
Restores 75% of the imbiber's health over 5 minutes.

The Lesser Regeneration Potion would be useful to have in effect during combat. An adventurer wouldn't have to worry about popping potions constantly, but he could tell it wasn't as useful as a regular health potion. He added it to his mental list of things to ask Fenian about before moving on and taking stock of his reagents. The scattering of random plants wasn't enough to make a good run. He stood in the lab, tapping his foot as though some great idea would wash over him.

Newt and Demon

There simply wasn't enough time left in the day, leaving him waiting awkwardly for Tresk to return home. He saw her stamina bar jump up earlier, meaning she had drunk her Lesser Stamina Potion. Even after taking the powerful elixir, her stamina was draining away by the second. He concluded, without needing to communicate with her, that she was running back to the lab.

He found no laborers pounding on his door, looking for work. Despite his words to the mercantile council, they didn't find anyone to run his errands. Theo concluded it was a good thing since his herbalism core had been trailing behind his alchemy core for some time. If he wanted to make a serious push to Level 10, he would need the experience from both of his cores. The alchemist reclined in a chair, staring up at the ceiling and wondering what cores Azrug would get.

A short time later, Tresk returned. He met her downstairs, grimacing as she reached into her bag and presented him with more of the sappy Spriggan Hearts.

"No new gear today," Tresk said. "Tons of monster cores, though."

Theo smiled, leading her upstairs so they could have dinner. "I've been pretty productive myself. Ziz is going to be a rich man before long."

"You handed him something great," Tresk said. "Also, I think there's some logic to Aarok's idea about the monster wave. There's this sense I can't shake the deeper I get in the dungeon."

Theo withdrew the still-hot cauldron of soup from breakfast, setting it down on the table and serving out two bowls. Tresk sat down, staring out the window and into the fading light of day.

"More reason to prepare proper defenses," Theo said. "Should we dump our cores into the town?"

"Maybe," Tresk said, gnawing on a piece of gristle. "We're a long way from Level 15."

"The town is far off, too," Theo said. "Either one seems like a good choice."

"You need to worry about one thing at a time. Speaking of..."

She belched loudly before continuing. "Upgrading the town, defending the town, creating jobs for the people. When does it end?"

Theo hadn't considered the thought before. He didn't see a stopping point in the immediate future, nor did he care to entertain one. "It doesn't end," he said, nodding to himself. "It just keeps going on until I can't do it anymore."

"As long as we're on the same page," Tresk said, grinning. "We both have that kind of personality. Go until you die."

"Let's avoid the *dying* part, all right?" Theo asked, grimacing.

"Naturally."

The pair finished their meal, and, once again, Tresk's bravado was a facade. She was shambling by the time they went to the bedroom, dragging her feet across the floor and groaning. Theo tucked her into bed before retreating to his own impossibly soft resting spot. He laid his head on the pillow and stayed there for some time. The echoes of the marshling's words rang in his mind. There wasn't an end to the path he traveled. It stretched on forever, encircling Broken Tusk and protecting it until he couldn't do it anymore.

He fell asleep with that sense of hope in his heart, joining Tresk in her dragon-slaying dreams. He didn't take part in the slaying and simply cheered her on from the side.

Chapter 40
A Million Potions

"So the elf wants like a million potions?" Tresk asked.

The pair assumed their regular seats near the window in the lab, the sun barely a glimmer on the eastern horizon. Tresk was going through the random junk she had found in the dungeon yesterday and cursed her patrol duty with the adventurer's guild that awaited her today. She wanted to get more cores and more strange ingredients for Theo, but the guild took priority.

"He's offering very good money," Theo said, "but I think my next project is going to be expensive."

"Maybe," Tresk said, idly sipping her tea. "You're already rolling in money. You just have to make more."

Theo idly ate his soup, remembering his lack of laborers. "Hey, could you harvest reagents while you're on patrol?"

"Sure, what do you need?"

"Moss Nettle and Manashrooms mostly," Theo said.

"Perfect," Tresk said. "We usually clear out that horrid cave, anyway."

Theo filled her in on the details of the dwarven merchant, Thistum, that had come the day before. She was surprised he would pay so much for stone blocks, but most of the houses in Broken Tusk were wooden. They wouldn't know about the difference in stones or what a higher quality meant. The alchemist didn't pretend to be an expert, but he trusted Fenian's judgment. Ziz and his laborers could pay off their debts in a few short weeks if they kept at it, but they had to be careful not to burn out.

"Well, I'm off," Tresk said, pressing her forehead against Theo's.

The marshling departed, leaving the alchemist in the lab, free to organize his thoughts. The problem with today was the long list of things he needed to get done. The potions for Fenian were one thing, but he needed to sort out Aarok's research that the capital promised to teleport in and find some laborers. If he kept giving everyone better jobs, there would be no one to collect his herbs.

Theo pulled his threadbare robe close and left the Newt and Demon. The sun had risen, casting the stone streets in streaks of long shadows. He found his way to the square, greeting a few townsfolk before inspecting the monolith.

[Small Town]
Name: Broken Tusk
Owner: Kingdom of Qavell
Mayor: Theo Spencer
Faction: Qavell
Level: 10 (1%)
Features:
Alchemy Lab
Blacksmith
Large Farm
Tannery
Tradesmen
Adventurer's Guild
Upgrades:
[Stone Walls and Gates]
[Stone Roads]

He knitted his brow, disappointed that they hadn't reached the

[Town] status. Theo summoned his mayoral interface and scrolled through a few menus. It was mostly statistics and information about taxes, but he found a section on expansion.

> **Broken Tusk** can be upgraded to a **[Town]** when the following conditions are met:
> **Small Population: COMPLETE**
> **Expanded Land Ownership: INCOMPLETE**

Theo tilted his head. Since he became mayor, he hadn't gone into these menus. He urged the system to drill down on the concept of land ownership and what it meant. A box appeared, defining it for him.

> **[Primary Land Ownership]:** Land owned directly by the settlement. This land is directly incorporated into the land and receives all the benefits of the settlement's upgrades.
> **[Expanded Land Ownership]:** Expanded land is not incorporated into the settlement, but still falls under its ownership. An example of Expanded Land Ownership is a forest outside of a city designated for hunting. Expanded land cannot contain another settlement, but may contain dungeons, towers, and so on.

Theo summoned his mayor's map and zoomed out, mentally clicking on the swamp to the west. The tag of [Expanded Land Ownership] popped up, detailing the cost of the land and the benefits of obtaining it. From what he understood, it was something that prevented others from settling on your land. The other advantage of owning the land was that Broken Tusk would have the first right to delve into a dungeon on its land, including the destruction of its core. This sent a chill down his spine. Someone could have come along and simply destroyed their dungeon.

The price of the land was ridiculously cheap compared to

other sections of land. The system informed him that houses couldn't be built on the land, and it was only meant as a management area for the Swamp Dungeon. It cost just 50 silver to own the land, so Theo bought it without hesitation. The wall to the west didn't move out to incorporate the swamp, as he expected, but a sense of accomplishment tingled in his mind. A new screen he had never seen popped up in the middle of his vision, complete with a goofy fireworks effect.

[Small Town] Broken Tusk has grown into a **[Town]**!

Theo patted himself on the back for a moment before delving deeper into the mayoral screens. Qavell technically owned most of the property in the surrounding area. When he bought the parcels from the interface, he was paying them for the right to own them. Currently, he had over 50% ownership of Broken Tusk, but that was just the land. The seed core for the town itself was available for purchase on the screen for 5 spiritstone, which must have been the next tier of currency.

"Do you ever rest?" Aarok shouted from across the way.

"Not really," Theo said, smiling.

"You're going to make Miana feel bad," Aarok said, beaming as he approached the alchemist. He clasped a hand over his shoulder.

"Miana isn't a demon alchemist; you can't blame her," Theo said with a wry grin. "Right, let's see if the capital came through on their promise."

Aarok followed him inside Miana's old building and into her office. Sitting on the old desk was a stack of scrolls and tomes, arranged neatly next to the communication crystal. Theo stuffed the crystal in his inventory and gestured for the half-ogre to take the papers.

"This is what they sent, I guess," Theo said.

"By the gods, this is a lot of material," Aarok said, scowling at the papers.

"Yeah, they like me. So, this is now your building," Theo said, gesturing vaguely to the adventurer's guild. "It's not a core building, so I don't need to transfer the rights to you."

"Thanks, Theo," Aarok said. "One day, I'd like to get a proper core building for the guild."

"Well, I'm sure we can work on that... What time do you think it is? Do you think Fenian is awake?" Theo asked.

"Morning? I don't know," Aarok said.

Theo withdrew Fenian's crystal from his inventory and held it tight. He felt the familiar trilling sensation for a moment before the elf's voice rushed through his mind.

"Good morning, Theo," Fenian said.

"Morning. I have a question about some potions. I created a Lesser Sprinting Potion and a Lesser Regeneration Potion. Are they useful to you?" Theo asked.

"The sprinting potion is, but not the regeneration one. Honestly, neither are useful for my current order," Fenian said.

"Understandable. Another question; do you have any seed cores for adventurer's guilds?"

"Sure. They're a bit pricey compared to workshops and such. Three gold," Fenian said.

"What are you doing?" Aarok asked, cocking an eyebrow.

"Talking to Fenian," Theo said. "He can bring a seed core for an adventurer's guild around—for three gold."

Aarok nodded. "The guild can afford that."

Theo tilted his head, raising an eyebrow. Since when could the guild afford anything?

"All right, bring it around next time. Aarok wants to buy it," Theo said.

"Sounds good. Listen, I've got to go. Talk to you later."

The connection was severed before Theo could say another word. He didn't mind and was surprised that Fenian answered to begin with.

"So, the adventurer's guild is rich?" Theo asked, laughing.

"Luras has a contact in Rivers and Daub. He got us in with the network of adventurer's guilds in the northlands," Aarok said. "We're getting a few coins to help us get started."

Theo couldn't have been happier to have someone other than himself fund something. He was worried about ownership of the guild falling outside of the hands of Broken Tusk, but it was nice not having to manage it. A thought suddenly struck him about the guild.

"Hey, can I post a contract with the guild?" Theo asked.

"Sure, what do you need?"

"Reagents, mostly," Theo said, shrugging.

Aarok nodded, pulling a stone tablet from nowhere. He punched his finger on the surface, and a screen appeared in Theo's vision.

"The guild has a template for this kind of quest," Aarok said. "Just put in your request, how long you want it to run for, and payment."

Theo inspected the screen and filled it out. He reviewed it before pressing the submit button.

[Supply Run]
Quest

The proprietor of the Newt and Demon is requesting all adventurers to collect reagents for his potion empire.

Objectives:

Collect [Spiny Swamp Thistle Root] (1 silver per 500, a maximum of 1000)

Collect [Moss Nettle] (1 silver per 500, a maximum of 1000)

Collect [Manashroom] (1 silver per 500, a maximum of 1000)

"Seems like more money than they'd normally make," Theo said with a shrug.

"People will snatch this up right away," Aarok said, submitting the quest. "You were smart to put a maximum number on the reagents—they'd have cleaned you out."

"Will they be able to see if they're harvesting the right stuff?" Theo asked.

"They'll get quest notifications when they collect the right item," Aarok said, nodding. "So, there's normally a deposit fee for the quest, but you're the mayor."

Theo frowned. He hated when people did stuff for free. "How much is it?"

Aarok laughed. "Don't worry about it, Theo. Everyone in town owes you more than you know. Just leave it at that."

Theo narrowed his eyes at the half-ogre. "Fine, but I'm gonna get you something nice. You can't stop me."

The pair shared a laugh, then spent some time talking about smaller things before Theo departed. Aarok had to get the old building in working order for the guild. Xam would be happy to hear that the adventurers wouldn't be crammed into her tavern all the time.

Theo left the square, running his regular route through the forest to collect reagents. His Drogramath Alchemy Knife sent out the familiar ping, the strange shape revealing itself underground once again. This time, the alchemist's curiosity got the better of him, and he started to dig. He removed his gloves, digging into the earth with clawed hands. Several fat roots were in the way, but he cut through them easily with the knife. Before long, he removed the gigantic, lumpy ball, hefting it out of the hole and inspecting it.

[Swamp Truffle]
[Alchemy Ingredient] [Food]
Epic
These extremely rare truffles, typically found in swamp-lands, are prized for their flavor and properties.
Properties:
[Experience Boost] [???] [???]

Theo's heart skipped a beat as he read the property on the truffle. If a noble house was training up their low-level people, what could be better than [Experience Boost]? He knew Fenian would pay a lot of money for any potions that gave increased experience, and stuffed the item in his inventory. He judged it to be five units by weight, which was absurd for a single reagent. It also helped that he could see the truffles scattered underground, clustered here and there.

It was too good to be true, but his intuition told him there were some drawbacks to using any potion derived from the truffle. He returned to the lab immediately, intent on running a tiny batch to determine what kind of potion the truffle could make. Theo washed it off with Purified Water before putting it through the grinder and into the Drogramath Still. He topped the water off and set the Flame Artifice to work, mentally informing Tresk about his discovery.

"That sounds too good to be true," Tresk said.

"I figure there's going to be some restrictions," Theo said, watching as the silvery liquid dripped into the flask.

"Isn't that always the way?"

Theo did nothing else while he cooked down the five-unit batch. He inspected the essence before moving on, sensing that there was something odd about it.

[Experience Boost Essence]
[Essence]
Epic
Created by: Belgar
Quality: Great
5 units (liquid)
Concentrated essence of experience

The thing that tipped him off about this essence was its quality. He had used the same technique he always used to make the most potent extracts, usually getting excellent quality, but this was only at "great." Theo ran his fingers along the side of the flask, trying to figure out what made him so uneasy. Something swelled in his chest, radiating a warmth that sent his heart beating. His Drogramath Alchemy Core wanted him to do something, and he obeyed.

Theo cleaned the Drogramath Still out with Cleansing Scrub and dumped the five units back in. When the still was done running, he was left with one unit of the same essence at excellent quality. As the alchemist stood there, looking at the flask, he understood what had happened. The Experience Boost Essence was incredibly unstable. Anything below excellent quality would simply explode when he tried to introduce a catalyst. His core practically screamed at him when he went to add the new essence to a vial of Purified Water. Instead, he introduced it to a solution of 1 unit of Stabilized Water and the standard two units of Copper Shavings. The reaction was still violent.

Theo learned enough about the Glassware Artifice to know it could produce vials of different durability. The glassware he used for this experiment was stronger than most, otherwise, it would have shattered. The two-unit reaction sent ribbons of light and electricity dancing through the lab, almost striking him in the process. The smell it put off was like cotton candy, and the solution had a rainbow color when the reaction was done. Theo inspected the new dangerous potion.

[Lesser Experience Boost Potion]
[Potion]
Epic
Created by: Belgar
Quality: Excellent
Drink to receive bonus experience.
Effect:
The imbiber will receive 25% bonus experience for 5 hours. This effect doesn't work above personal Level 10 and may have deleterious effects if used over time.

"Yeah, I'm not drinking that," Theo said, laughing.

Chapter 41
Hallowed Ground

The holding pattern of evening rain for the Season of Blooms came back. Theo sat in his lab, looking over his new creation with mixed feelings. He knew that some potions might have negative effects, his books told him as much, but for the item's description to give a specific warning was frightening. The rain outside brought the scent of renewal. Only the pattering sound of the driving wind awakened him from his stupor. The alchemist withdrew Fenian's crystal and squeezed it tightly.

Theo only felt the trilling sensation a few times before the elf answered. *"Theo! How are you?"*

"I'm well, thanks. I think I have something you might be interested in," Theo said.

"What is it, my dear alchemist?"

"I've been experimenting around a bit, and I came up with a Lesser Experience Boost Potion," Theo said.

"You what? Hold on a moment..."

Fenian went silent for some time. Theo simply sat there, holding the crystal, while he waited. It was strange to be put on hold while communicating through the crystals, but after a few long moments, the elf was back.

"A real one?" Fenian asked.

"As far as I know," Theo said. *"I brewed it myself."*

"All right, listen to me carefully," Fenian said. *"Don't put it in your shop for sale. Keep it under your hat. Make sure your Tara'hek knows this, too."*

"What's going on?" Theo asked. He felt vindicated after having such a bad feeling about the potion.

"Experience potions are rare. Sourcing the ingredients is a nightmare. I recommend you brew them in as small a batch as possible and sell them to me. I'll sell them to a fence—not my usual contact, but someone who understands discretion," Fenian said.

"Why the secrecy? We deal in gold coins' worth of potions, why is this different?" Theo asked.

"It's the implication, really. Restoration potions and attribute potions are one thing, but an experience potion? That's a line we don't want to cross, yet," Fenian said. *"The rarity is one thing, but the effect they have on people is another. Noble born people use them very often, but the effect is bad. They produce weak-hearted adventurers unable to slay rats, let alone monsters."*

"All right. I had a bad feeling about them," Theo said.

"Right. I'll take any off your hands, but keep it under ten potions," Fenian said.

Theo let out a sigh of relief. He felt like he had something illegal in his lab, quickly stowing it away into his inventory before anyone found it.

"I appreciate the warning," Theo said. *"Perhaps I can find another use for the reagent."*

"Please do. I'll talk to you later."

"Bye."

Theo informed Tresk about the experience potion problem. He made sure she knew not to tell anyone about it, and the marshling promised secrecy. She was returning home, intent on making more of the spicy wolf stew. The alchemist was excited to have something other than the ordinary. He departed the shop to check out Luras's new place and invite him to dinner. The rain seemed to come in waves, ebbing and flowing by some unseen force. He was soaked by the time he arrived.

The new leatherworking shop was fairly small, but maintained the wood-paneled wall aesthetic of Broken Tusk. Theo knocked on the door, standing back to admire the humble beginnings of Luras's new business. The alchemist knew the half-ogre would make something of himself. The man was simply too driven to do anything less. After a moment, the big half-ogre appeared at the door with a smile on his face.

"I thought you'd never come by," Luras said.

"It's been busy, as always," Theo said.

Luras gestured, beckoning him inside the small building. It looked a lot like Perg's building, only ten paces in either direction. The seed core had created a gorgeous interior, but it was still bare. A small workbench sat on the far side of the room, with a bedroll on the other. None of these sparse features seemed to dim the half-ogre's enthusiasm for his new place.

"What do you think?" Luras asked.

"I think this is the start of something big," Theo said. "Where did all this drive come from?"

"I've always wanted to do it," Luras said. "Something happened—I don't want to talk about it—but it pushed me to go through with it."

Theo didn't care if his friend wanted to have secrets. Some things just weren't ready to come out in the open, and he knew that all too well.

"You couldn't have picked a better spot to set up shop," Theo said. "Right next to Perg's tannery. Perfect."

"Agreed," Luras said, walking over to the only storage area in the room. He withdrew a simple pair of leather slacks and held them up. "I'm just crafting whatever to get my core leveled up."

"Well, if I need some leather chaps, I'll ask you," Theo said, grinning.

He trusted Luras as much as anyone in this new world. His problem was that he was often too trusting of people, even his close friends. The issue with the Swamp Truffle was something he didn't want to bring up with the leatherworker. It seemed like too much of a burden to place on another person, and he had learned to heed Fenian's warnings. If the elf said it was dangerous information to spread around town, he would keep it under wraps for now.

"Need any funding?" Theo asked.

"Gods, you just throw money around, don't you?" Luras said, groaning.

"It's a defense mechanism," Theo said.

"No, I'm funded for quite a while," Luras said. "I appreciate the gesture, but it just seems like another ploy to get your hands in my pockets."

"I'm managing an entire town now. I need all the money I can get," Theo said.

"How is that going?"

"It's going well. I've been doing it since I got here, anyway. I just don't want to get caught unawares," Theo said. "If Aarok is right about a monster wave, we could be in some trouble. The good news is that I expanded our territory out into the swamp, so Broken Tusk owns the dungeon outright."

Luras seemed to accept the answer. He talked about his business and how he would leverage the fine wolf leather to become well known. Theo didn't doubt him for a moment, his mind going back to the confluence of events that bred greatness within the townsfolk. Until the half-ogre leveled his leatherworking core up, he would be making simple things for a few coins. Before departing, the alchemist invited him over for some spicy wolf stew that night, to which the half-ogre agreed.

Theo couldn't help himself. While he distilled the Swamp Truffle down to its base property's essence, he still wanted to see what secondary properties it had. With Tresk nearing the shop, he ran off into the eastern reaches of his property and searched for another buried mushroom. The range on his Drogramath Alchemy Knife was excellent, allowing him to find one quickly. He dug it out of the muddy ground, stowing it away in his inventory and burying the hole before his companion returned to the shop.

The alchemist returned to the shop, finding Tresk upstairs preparing the meal for the night. "That's it?" Tresk asked as Theo produced the truffle from his inventory.

"The thing Fenian warned me about, yeah," Theo said. "Its experience-boosting property are dangerous, so we'll avoid it as much as possible. I want to see the other properties."

"You're gonna eat it?" Tresk said, grimacing.

The truffle was roughly the size of Theo's head. It was black as night and lumpy all over. He took his knife and cut into the fungus, revealing a lace of black and silver inside. A strange scent filled the room, like a mixture of cut oaken boards and olives. The alchemist took the smallest piece he could and popped it into his mouth. That nutty, oaken flavor spread across his tongue, followed by an intense sensation that flooded his mind. His stomach churned in objection, but he managed to not vomit. The familiar window filled his vision, explaining the new property.

[Properties Discovery!]
You've discovered an additional effect of the Swamp
Truffle by eating it.
[Hallowed Ground] discovered.

"It's called [Hallowed Ground]," Theo said, tilting his head to the side. "I wonder what it does."

"Can you distill it before our guests arrive?" Tresk asked, stirring her copper pan and smiling. The smell of the cooking wolf meat hadn't yet been infused with the extremely spicy aroma of the Fire Salamander Eggs.

"With my new still, yeah," Theo said, immediately attending to the process.

With the Drogramath Still, he could easily cook the five-unit mash down in a few minutes. He had the first distillation done before Tresk even introduced the eggs to her dish. The special effect of his new still kicked in on the first run, producing double the amount of essence. It seemed absurd, but Theo ran the second distillation to purify the unstable mixture. The Hallowed Ground Essence was as unstable as the Experience Boost Essence, meaning that he would have to be careful when working with it. He had a feeling that the Drogramath Distillation Specialty in his lab made it more stable, but he couldn't be too careful.

The [Hallowed Ground] property was as temperamental as [Experience Boost] and required a second distillation. Unlike the first batch, this one failed to produce more essence than he put in. At the end of the run, Theo had two and a half units of Hallowed Ground Essence. Inspecting it, he found it to be much like the experience-boosting version.

[Hallowed Ground Essence]
[Essence]
Excellent
Created by: Belgar
Quality: Great
2.5 units (liquid)
Concentrated essence of ground hallowing.

Theo kicked off a single-unit reaction with Stabilized Water, exactly the way he handled the experience-boosting essence, and inspected the potion as Tresk was finishing the meal.

[Lesser Hallowed Ground Potion]
[Potion]
Epic
Created by: Belgar
Quality: Excellent
Drink to create a zone of banishment.
Effect:
The imbiber creates a twenty-pace circle around themselves with the [Hallowed Ground] effect. The undead,

ghosts, and other similar creatures may cross into the circle but will be banished once they do so.

The completion of the potion got him Level 8 in his Drogramath Alchemy Core. He wasn't doing the same volume of potions as in his previous order, so his leveling had slowed. The good news was that his Drogramath Herbalism Core was catching up and was almost at Level 8. Theo showed the potion to Tresk. Her eyes lit up when she saw it, her mouth agape as she read the description.

"That sounds really useful," Tresk said.

A knock downstairs turned the conversation silent. Theo made sure his companion knew not to talk about this with anyone. He went downstairs to let Luras in, but as expected, he was joined by Perg. The allure of the spicy food was too much for her. He led them upstairs, where the meal waited, already served out on four plates. Everyone took a chair and shared greetings before digging into the meal.

Theo's tastebuds were once again assailed by the absurdly spicy flavor of the Fire Salamander Eggs, making his eyes water immediately. Sweat formed beads on his forehead, but the food was just too good.

"Aarok is afraid of a monster wave," Perg said, taking healthy mouthfuls of the food. She swallowed and continued, "There hasn't been a monster wave in the southlands since the ogres ran the show."

"I'm not really worried," Theo said. "My focus is getting funding to upgrade the town, just in case."

"I imagine that's easier for you to do than most," Luras said. His eyes were watering, but he didn't bother to clear them away.

"What I'd really like is to own Broken Tusk completely," Theo said. "But that's a far-off dream."

"How far?" Tresk asked.

"Qavell will sell me the town for 5 spiritstone," Theo said.

"All right. I don't know what spiritstone is," Perg said.

"It's the currency above gold," Theo said. "But I don't know how many gold coins go into a spiritstone coin."

"Hopefully 100," Luras said. "But 500 gold is still a lot of money."

"No kidding," Tresk said. She had already finished her food. The marshling fanned her face with her hand, keeping her mouth open. "What do you two think about Theo's mayorship? Isn't he just the best mayor?"

"He said it earlier, but he was the mayor even before he officially took the position. From the second he came into town, he had a vision for us," Luras said.

"You'd be hard-pressed to find someone who did more for this ball of mud than him," Perg said. "I mean, we have *roads* now."

Theo waved the compliments away. "I have a theory that this is none of my doing."

Tresk chuckled, punching him playfully in the arm. He remembered the playful hits stinging a lot more when he had first met the marshling. "Just look at this place, Theo. You're doing great."

"He might have a point," Perg said.

"Sadly, I do," Theo said. "The entity that brought me here might have messed with the balance of the southlands. That guy that bought property in Broken Tusk, Zan'kir, described it as a 'confluence of events.'"

"We've only had good things happen so far," Tresk said, "and that's because we're all proactive about it. If we keep it up, we'll be fine!"

"Your endless optimism is extremely useful, Tresk," Theo said, patting her on the head. "We can't slouch. We need to keep expanding. Get Broken Tusk to Level 15 and put some automated defenses on the walls."

"They have those in Qavell," Luras said. "Very expensive stuff."

"Extremely expensive, but I'm already sourcing some from Fenian," Theo said. "This place will be a fortress before long."

The group's conversation shifted for a while. Theo could finish his soup while the others discussed smaller matters. Perg and Luras came up with interesting leather items he could craft for sale. They had insights into the market, specifically what merchants might want to buy. According to the rumors they had heard, high-level leatherworkers could make dimensional bags.

The conversation died down as dusk threatened outside. Theo was getting too tired to hang on to their every word, a fact that the two half-ogres picked up on. The pair said their farewells before departing for the day. The alchemist sat there with Tresk for some time, which got them another level—sixth—in their Tara'hek Core. Happy at their progress, they set off to go to bed.

Theo fell onto his comfortable mattress and fought off sleep. His mind darted in every direction, unable to maintain focus without sleep. He fell asleep with a contented smile on his face, his plans for the next day falling apart in the face of exhaustion.

Chapter 42
Rent

Theo always enjoyed his morning ritual of food and tea. As he sat there with Tresk, gazing out into the darkness of early morning, he felt content. The marshling went over the loot she had found in the dungeon so far, which was mostly junk. In the alchemist's eyes, it wasn't a waste of time. The stronger she got, the better. He had no way of defending himself if anything were to happen and would rely on her for that.

"I still don't have anyone making good on the quest I posted at the adventurer's guild," Theo said.

Tresk swallowed a mouthful of leftover spicy wolf meat stew. "Cause you gotta go to the guild."

"What?" Theo asked, knitting his brow. "Really?"

"Yeah, if you issue a collection quest, they'll deliver it to the guild," Tresk said, giggling.

A tingle in Theo's mind drew his attention away from something that should have been obvious to him. The Newt and Demon was trying to say something to him, or so he thought. It was like an itch at the back of his mind that he could only scratch by bringing up the building's information screen.

[Alchemy Lab] [Alchemy Shop]

Newt and Demon

Name: The Newt and Demon
Owners: Belgar (Theo Spencer), Tresk
Faction: Broken Tusk
Level: 11 (31%)
Rent Due: Today
Expansions:
[Alchemy Shop]
[Drogramath Distillation Specialty]

"We have to pay rent today," Theo said, the furrow of his brow deepening. "Wait, who do I pay rent to?"

Tresk laughed, slapping her knobbly knees. "Sorry, the image of you paying rent to yourself was too much."

Theo poked around at the interface for a while before giving up. He summoned his mayor screen instead, cycling through the core buildings in town before finding the Newt and Demon. The weekly rent on his Level 10 building was somewhere around 1 silver, 50 copper and was to be paid to... himself. He manually clicked the button, and his rent timer reset.

"Okay," Theo said, the creases in his horned forehead growing deeper by the moment. "I told the town that I paid rent to myself. What does that mean?"

"I don't know," Tresk said, slurping her tea. "The rent is for the land, right? Maybe we have to pay it to Qavell. Try poking around some more."

Theo obeyed. Despite his high Wisdom, Tresk had a natural way of thinking about how this world worked. Despite his previous experience with the screen, it was too cluttered for him to remember where everything was. He browsed the finance screens for some time before finding owed rents, nodding to himself. It was obvious now, but everyone paid rent to Miana when she was mayor, and she sent the money off to the capital every month. The town calculated the rent of each building, aggregating it based on the current tax rate. Broken Tusk's flat rate was 10 silver a month, plus a rate based on citizens, owned land, the number of seed core buildings, and the town's level. It was all too confusing for the alchemist. He made a mental note to pay the tax in ten days.

"Found it," Theo said, explaining how the system works.

"That makes sense," Tresk said. "Didn't you offer to cover the excess taxes people couldn't pay?"

"Yeah, and I'm going to hold on to some coins after we sell this next batch to Fenian," Theo said. "I want some cash on hand just in case."

"You should ask him about that new potion," Tresk said. "Assuming it's not *forbidden*." She wiggled her fingers ominously.

Tresk stood up, putting on her best evil voice and saying, "Forbiiiidden." She vanished right in front of Theo's eyes, using the superior effect of her Assassin's Core before reappearing right behind him.

"Forbidden," Tresk repeated.

Theo tried to snatch her arm, but she was too fast. "You're slippery," he said. "Come here."

The alchemist did his best to catch the marshling. He never considered how dexterous she was, but it felt like trying to grab the wind itself. Tresk was disappointed when he gave up, pouting for a moment before getting over the entire ordeal.

"You're slower than a Swamp Turtle," Tresk said.

"A lot slower," Theo said, heaving a sigh. "What's your plan for today?"

"Grinding in the dungeon," Tresk said. "I'm getting garbage for gear, but that's not the point. Gotta get stronger. Gonna go deeper."

"Take the Lesser Hallowed Ground Potion with you. Here." He handed her the potion. "Let me craft some poison before you go."

"Oh good, I need more," Tresk said, following the alchemist as he made the potions.

Theo had already extracted the Widow Lilies' essence the other day. He withdrew the poison essence from the dimensional crate and set off the reactions. The alchemist made ten units of

Basic Poison for her, each coming out at excellent quality. Tresk was beyond excited to get more poison, but he wished she would speak up when she was out of supplies. She didn't want to speak up because she thought he was too busy, which he understood, but her safety was the most important thing to him.

The sun had peeked over the eastern horizon by the time he was done crafting. Tresk took the vials and departed before he could object. Her excitement for the day was infectious. Theo wasn't sure if he needed to drink the moss tea with her around, but he wanted to keep the tradition alive. His plan for the day was still forming in his mind. He went downstairs, peering up and down the street. In the distance, north toward the center of town, he spotted a familiar face skipping down the road.

"Azrug," Theo said, a broad smile painting his face.

The boy came up, flashing a devious grin. "Guess who got their cores?"

Theo pointed at the boy. "Is it that guy?"

"It is!"

"Come up and have some tea," Theo said, holding the door open for Azrug. "I want to hear what you got."

Theo and Azrug settled in upstairs, putting another pot on the Flame Artifice and propping the window open. A pleasant breeze flowed into the lab, washing away some of the funk that clung to the work area.

"They're *nothing* compared to your legendary cores, but I started with the Mercantile Core and the Shopkeeper's Core," Azrug said. "One ability each. The first one lets me judge the relative price of something within a certain distance. The other tells me how much stock is in a store."

"Wow. So, I guess you really wanted to be a shopkeeper," Theo said.

"Are you kidding? This is the best job I've ever had," Azrug said.

Theo poured two cups of tea, blowing on his cup to dull some of the heat. It was his second tea of the day, but this was a monumental achievement for the young boy. The alchemist wanted to change the way he thought about Azrug. He wasn't a boy anymore, not with two cores. He was a young man now.

"We should hammer out a better deal for you," Theo said.

Azrug waved him off. "Our current deal is fine. I'll get a lot of experience running the shop."

Theo let out a breath. "Two copper coins a day? That's not really fair."

"You must be rolling in coins if you're willing to give me a raise," Azrug said.

"Well, I'm just glad that you're all right. The Newt and Demon is at a point where we make most of our money from orders. Specifically from Fenian. I think you should get a cut of what sells from the shelves," Theo said. "What do you think?"

"How can I say no to more money?" Azrug asked.

"You'll be the face of the shop from here on out," Theo said. "I don't have the time to make potions and run the town, so people are going to expect to see your face in here every day. I mean, they already do. Let's say you get ten percent of all *sales*. That's not from my merchant contracts, just sales made in the shop."

Azrug screwed up his face for a moment, then brightened. "Ten copper on each silver?"

"Yeah, exactly," Theo said.

"Deal," Azrug said, reaching out his hand for Theo to shake.

The pair finished their tea, talking about the transformation process. Azrug detailed how he got incredibly sick for a few days. He couldn't even get out of bed while the cores took root in him. Theo listened, thinking about the confluence of events the entire time. The quality of his cores was rare, not just common. From what Tresk said, cores usually started at the common grade. He dismissed the thought for now, taking his shopkeeper downstairs.

"We're low on almost everything," Azrug said, scowling. "How am I supposed to run a shop with low stock?"

"I'll work on that today, boss," Theo said. "I need to check with the adventurer's guild to see if anyone has completed my quest."

A knock came from the door, and a smile spread across Azrug's face. He bounded across the shop, swinging the door open and taking a deep bow. "Welcome to the Newt and Demon. Home of every potion you could ever want."

The woman standing at the door had a shocked look on her face. Theo didn't recognize her race, but shrugged it off. Her attire painted her as an adventurer, likely from the northlands. He simply smiled and patted Azrug on the back. "I'm off to check on my quest. Good luck."

Theo could still hear Azrug's boisterous voice some ways up the road. The shop couldn't have been in better hands. The alchemist was reminded of his "Lord Administrator" position within Broken Tusk. He had been acting as the mayor for so long without the tools to succeed. The situation was a mirror of what happened to the shopkeeper. He made his way to the square, intent on inspecting the new adventurer's guild building.

"Theo!" Aarok shouted, scowling from the entrance of Miana's old house. It reminded him of the old mayor. "Come collect your crap."

Theo entered the newly repurposed building, finding a massive pile of reagents on the ground. He scooped them up with his inventory power, checking the quantities to find 1,000 of each restoration reagent. "They actually did it."

"Yeah, and you owe the guild money," Aarok said.

Aarok led him to the old office and sat behind the desk. He rifled through a pile of parchments, snatching one up and reading it over. "Right. Six silver coins for the completion of the quest. Gods, I'm going to ask for that in advance next time."

Theo withdrew the coins from his inventory and gave them to the half-ogre. "That's fine by me. Do you mind if I make another quest?"

Aarok shrugged, handing the stone device over. "Fine by me. Adventurers like simple work."

The alchemist filled the form out idly, creating a significantly bigger list this time. He included the restoration reagents as well as the attribute-enhancing ones. "How is the wolf population doing?"

"Increasing," Aarok said. "Although at a steady pace, it's still going up. We saw some goblins in the swamp too."

Theo blinked hard, turning his gaze back to the guild master. "The swamp is getting more dangerous, huh?"

"Nothing we can't handle, for now," Aarok said. "The research you got me has been helpful. It was obvious once I had the books. I'm going to send some scouts to confirm my suspicions, but I think we have a new dungeon."

Theo's mouth fell open. He had just finished fiddling with the interface, excited to see that he could put a generic entry for any reagent that enhanced attributes. "What? Where?"

"Near the ocean, I think. They align with the cardinal directions. Some kind of magic I don't understand. It's not dangerous, not if we know about it," Aarok said.

"We just have to be prepared," Theo said, nodding in agreement. "Can you make this quest urgent?"

"I'd normally charge a fee, but for the mayor? I'll do it for free," Aarok said. "You're hoarding money to buy defenses, aren't you?"

"Yeah."

"Fine. Just give me a 6-silver deposit for this new quest," Aarok said. "The guild will foot the bill until the adventurers collect."

Theo withdrew another six silver coins from his inventory and handed them over. This brought him down to 43 silver, 27 copper. He reviewed the quest before submitting it.

[Supply Run]
Quest
The proprietor of the Newt and Demon is requesting all adventurers to collect reagents for his potion empire.
Objectives:
Collect [Spiny Swamp Thistle Root] (1 silver per 500, a maximum of 1000)

Collect [Moss Nettle] (1 silver per 500, a maximum of 1000)
Collect [Manashroom] (1 silver per 500, a maximum of 1000)
Collect Attribute-Bearing Reagents (1 silver per 500, a maximum of 1000)

"Right. I need to brew some potions for the shop. Azrug got his cores," Theo said. "Now he's telling me I don't have enough stock."

"I was talking to Xam," Aarok said, finally flashing a smile. "*Rare* cores from a Broken Tusker? Very exciting news."

Theo grunted a response before bidding the guild master farewell. On his way back to the lab, Fenian's crystal gave off a slight buzz in his mind. He didn't want to consider how he knew it was buzzing from within his inventory, but he withdrew it and held it in his hand anyway.

"Theo. How is the order coming along?" Fenian asked.

"Extremely well—I'll be done in a few days if all goes according to plan," Theo said.

"Good. I'm still in the area, so let me know," Fenian said.

"While I have you here, I have another potion question," Theo said.

"More questionable potions? Let's hear it."

"The truffle produced another effect. [Hallowed Ground]," Theo said.

"Really? Now that's interesting. The [Experience Boost] property is dangerous, but that one is fine. I haven't really seen that potion floating around—no idea what it would fetch. I'll research it and inform you when I find out," Fenian said.

"Okay. Anything else?"

"That's it," Fenian said, hanging up before Theo could respond.

The alchemist shrugged, pushing his way into the shop. He found Azrug there, alone and beaming.

"I made a very nice sale. We need more potions, though," Azrug said.

"Don't worry," Theo said. "I'm going to brew an absurd number of potions today."

Theo went upstairs with the thought of a noble family going through *thousands* of potions. There wasn't a cooldown for lesser potions, and chugging them constantly didn't seem to have any negative effects. He imagined adventurers using the potions, pausing in combat to drink a few before going back to battle. The Lesser Mana Potions made sense for this, but he couldn't get his head around the others. It was a fact he hadn't considered until this point, the effect of the coin blinding his reasoning.

"Why do these people need so many potions?" Theo asked Tresk through Tara'hek Communication.

"Depends. I don't use many because I skip all the dungeon floors that don't have bosses. I've heard of front-liners who down potions like water—they're afraid of dying. Some Dexterity-based classes do fancy moves that take a lot of stamina. I guess that's where they're chugging the Lesser Stamina Potions," Tresk said.

"Thanks," Theo said, falling into his thoughts again.

As a crafting class, Theo had 42 health. His healing potions could restore between 20 and 40, but that seemed like a drop in the bucket for a front-line class. His intuition told him they would be closer to 200 health at levels between 10 and 20. It made sense that they would be drinking so many potions if they were getting only ten percent of their health restored. This led him to the conclusion that the next tier of restoration potions would have a significantly higher rate of resource replenishment, as well as a bigger price tag.

It was all academic, at this point. His interest in how people chugged away his hard work faded when he faced down the order Fenian placed. It was time to get to work.

Chapter 43
Everyone Likes Money

This was Theo's first big distillation run since he had filled Fenian's original order. He looked at the 3,000 reagents in his inventory and smiled. He improved the process, thanks to the artifices and his new still, to a point where he was confident he could process 2,000 units in a single day. The labor that he removed was the grinding of reagents, a step in the brewing process that he would never miss. The Alchemical Grinder Artifices removed that stage entirely, easily chewing through hundreds of units of reagents in a heartbeat.

Theo positioned his grinder over the Drogramath Still, feeding 500 units of the Spiny Swamp Thistle Root in and listening to the satisfying whirring sound. He topped it off with Purified Water, set the Flame Artifice to the lowest setting, and moved on to his two smaller stills. The alchemist repeated the same process on the 200-unit stills, setting them all to the lowest setting on the artifice and turning his attention to the Healing Essence he had stored in his inventory.

The bell rang downstairs, followed closely by Azrug's booming voice. His new confidence was an inspiration, spurring Theo on to synthesize as many Lesser Healing Potions as he could. He noted another step of inefficiency in his process as he generated several hundred flat-bottomed vials. His Glassware Artifice would deposit the vials directly into his inventory, but he had to remove them and set up the reaction by hand. The part of the reaction that he cheated on was the reaction itself. His intuition told him this was something specific to Drogramath Alchemy, where he could set off a large-scale reaction in a big flask.

Theo set off a series of 100-unit reactions, creating five flasks of bubbling red healing potions. He dispensed all 500 units of the excellent-quality Lesser Healing Potions into individual vials. During the process, which the alchemist estimated to have taken half an hour, the bell rang several times downstairs. Each time, Azrug's voice carried up the stairs for a few minutes before the bell rang again. He swapped the flasks from the still's condenser before going downstairs to hand over the new potions.

"I've made a few more sales," Azrug said, beaming from behind the counter.

Theo noticed that the young man didn't have his book out today. There was an aura around him that exuded excitement.

"Out-of-towners?" Theo asked.

"Yeah, adventurers," Azrug said. "They're mostly interested in restoration potions—they're all very surprised we have lesser potions."

"Right. I have a few more to add to your stock," Theo said, crowding the shelves with the 500 Lesser Healing Potions.

"Just a few," Azrug said.

Theo took a moment to think about the flood of new adventurers. Looking back, he found that at least four of them had come to the shop today. It was a good thing he bought the rights to the Swamp Dungeon. He was uncertain about the implications of someone coming in and buying it from under his nose, although he suspected they needed to be the mayor of an adjoining town to do that. His thoughts on the matter concluded with the inevitability of it all. Broken Tusk had at least three dungeons nearby. The information was finally spreading wide enough to see the flood of adventurers they expected.

"How long should I run the shop each day?" Azrug asked, breaking Theo out of his thoughts.

"That's up to you now," Theo said. The alchemist summoned the interface for the Newt and Demon, flicking through the menus until he found something he had missed before. Buried in the ownership tab, he found a section where he could assign a shopkeeper. He mentally gave Azrug that position, and the building shifted under their feet. A small key appeared in the half-ogre's hands and the door at the top of the stairs rattled. When he went to inspect the upstairs door, it now had a lock and key.

"That works," Azrug said. "You're giving a kid a lot of responsibility."

"Is it a responsibility you don't want?" Theo asked, cocking an eyebrow.

"It's a bit much," Azrug said. The excited sheen on his face faded a little.

Theo clapped his hand over the shopkeeper's shoulder and smiled. His tail swept the floor, the excitement of possibility building. "I'm here to support you, but the shop is yours to run. You're already better at dealing with customers, so it just makes sense. The cores you got seal the deal—I was told you only get specific cores if you're really driven to do something."

"That's true," Azrug said, brightening up.

"Keep your old hours or change them depending on how busy things are," Theo said. "You'll get inventory skill eventually. Carry some potions around with you and go looking for the adventurers. Just play it by ear and know there's no wrong move."

Azrug smiled sheepishly. "Thanks, Theo."

"What? No more 'boss'?" Theo asked.

"Maybe 'mayor,'" Azrug said, "but not 'boss.'"

Theo nodded, but then something tingled in his mind. He waved to the shopkeeper and darted upstairs in time to find his flasks almost overflowing. He swapped them out and took a seat near the window, withdrawing a parchment he hadn't looked at in a while. It was the book on the basics of alchemy he intended to write, something to distill the confusing Drogramathi book that Fenian had given him. His concentration broke after the bell rang downstairs, accompanied by no boisterous speeches from Azrug. The half-ogre came up the stairs, poking his head up and grimacing.

"People are lined up outside," Azrug said. "Coming to pay rent."

"Well, I should have expected that," Theo said, joining his shopkeeper downstairs. "We need a better system for this."

A line stretched out the door and up the road. Theo instructed Azrug to collect the money, keeping no formal list of what everyone actually owed. The alchemist didn't care if they could pay their "rent," whatever that actually meant. It was money that went straight to the capital, money that the alchemist would prefer to stay within the confines of Broken Tusk's walls. Half the citizens were short on their rent, and further half of that number had come empty-handed. The two to five copper coins they owed were nothing. He waved them away without accepting any apologies.

Theo urged the crowd to stick around before leaving, addressing them all on the street outside. "I want to make something clear," Theo said. "I bear no ill will toward Qavell or the administration in the capital. Broken Tusk owes them for the planting of the seed town core. That being said, I don't expect anyone to pay rent if they can't. If you can't find the money for the week, you don't even have to tell me. I'll foot the bill. It's not a problem."

"Good, I'm broke," Miana said, garnering a wave of laughter from the group.

"For the sake of transparency, we owe less than a silver coin this week," Theo said, shrugging. It was an incredibly insignificant sum of money to him. He reflected, for a moment, how far he had come since his arrival in Broken Tusk. He summoned his mayoral interface and flagged every plot of land as paid.

"That's very selfless of you, Theo," Aarok said from the crowd.

"Not really," Theo said. He was being honest. "The only thing

I ask is the same charity for your neighbors. If someone is struggling, don't let them suffer in silence. Speak up, and we'll work together to solve their problem."

"We could really use better lodgings," a half-ogre named Oruk, a man who had labored for Theo in the past, said.

"Houses, right," Theo said. "Almost everything in Broken Tusk is manually built. I'll add it to my list. I'll purchase a few house seed cores when Fenian is back in town. I have five left, but I'm selling those to adventurers."

A murmur of approval washed through the crowd, smiles spreading across every face. Theo couldn't help but join them, watching with excitement as they dispersed. The alchemist and Azrug retreated into the Newt and Demon.

"What's the plan there?" Azrug asked.

Theo shrugged. It looked like a benevolent act, but it was a practical approach. The rents they owed were so small that it wasn't worth chasing them down for the money. Providing houses for free would reduce the chance of diseases spreading or people getting sick from shoddy, leaking roofs. "It's the most practical approach," Theo said, boiling it down to the core of his thoughts. "The rent is tiny, so who cares? The house seed cores are cheap enough—it seems like something we should have already."

"You can admit that you're just a nice guy. You know that, right?" Azrug asked.

"I won't deny it anyway," Theo said. "Think of it this way. The stronger Broken Tusk is, the stronger we are. We're all links in a chain. Part of a cycle that generates money."

"I like money," Azrug said, beaming.

"Me too."

Theo went back upstairs and consulted his mayoral interface to see how many occupied plots of land didn't have house seed cores. It looked like twenty houses needed to be replaced. That would cost him 4 gold, assuming Fenian would keep his old rate. This posed a serious problem for his current strategy, as it cut into his defense fund significantly. The alchemist looked over his stills, bubbling away, and nodded to himself. He would need to make a lot more potions if he wanted to fund the town.

The first prediction of the day was that he would distill around 2,000 units of essence, getting to the other 1,000 tomorrow. Theo's dire need for money pushed him beyond what he expected to accomplish, distilling every unit of restoration potions and bottling them all. It was an absurd amount of work to do in a day, forcing him to pop a Lesser Stamina Potion somewhere around midday and make a trip to the river to fill and purify his water barrels.

Theo wiped the sweat from his brow, going downstairs to check on Azrug. Another adventurer had just left the shop, and there was a pile of silver and copper coins sitting on the counter.

"I'm done for the day," Azrug said. "Here's the take."

Theo took the coins into his inventory. He raised an eyebrow when he saw the amount. Azrug made the shop 55 silver, 20 copper today. "Where did these adventurers come from?"

"I was talking to one of them," Azrug said, smiling. "They heard about the alchemy shop sometime last week, but it took them a while to organize. Once that other adventurer, Jarson, got back to Qavell, it spread like wildfire."

"That makes sense," Theo said. "It's a bit of a journey back to the capital."

Theo withdrew six silver coins from his inventory, handing them over to the shopkeeper. "Just a little more than your usual two copper, huh?"

Azrug's eyes lit up. He took the coins, the light in his eyes fading. "What am I going to do with all this money? This is more money than I've ever seen in one place at one time."

"Well, you have cores now," Theo said, "so you'll be trying to buy other cores to upgrade them. There's also your seed core house, which I'll buy the next time Fenian is in town. It would be nice if those who could afford to help did so."

"Right... more expenses," Azrug said.

Tresk returned shortly after Azrug departed for the day. She hit Level 11 in both her cores, something that surprised Theo. She explained that when she was sneaking through the dungeon, she employed her tracking core's abilities to find enemies. This constant use of her skill made it shoot up so much. Compared to the alchemist's herbalism core, it was very easy to get experience with.

"What are those?" Theo asked, pointing at her boots. They were new and carried a shimmer that he hadn't seen before.

"Oh, yeah!" Tresk said, posing with her new boots. "I got them from the dungeon. The tenth-floor boss finally dropped something decent. Leather boots that make me better at sneaking."

Theo inspected them closer, nodding in approval. He looked at his own tattered clothes, something he had put by the wayside for a long time. Every turn he took led him away from getting decent gear for himself, but he didn't mind. Whereas Tresk's life depended on decent gear, his didn't. He could brew potions all day in his underwear and it wouldn't matter.

[Marsh Stompers]
[Leather Boots]
Rare
Enchanted leather boots.
Effect:
Increases the effectiveness of stealth abilities.
[Effect Locked]
[Effect Locked]

"Why does it have two locked effects?" Theo asked.

"That happens sometimes," Tresk said, waving her hand. "Equipment generated by a dungeon can come with a locked effect. You need a loremaster to identify the effects—there's probably some story behind the boots that can be unlocked."

Theo scratched his chin, tilting his head. "That sounds like a business opportunity."

"Speaking of, I still need to figure out what my third core is going to be," Tresk said. "I need to talk with those foreign adventures. They'll know some good synergy."

They settled in for a quiet night, eating their food and discussing small topics. Tresk was confident she could solo the fifteenth floor, but Theo was unsure. He knew little about adventuring, but it seemed like a risky thing for a sneaking class to do solo. He would defer to her judgment, even if he complained about it.

Despite taking a Lesser Stamina Potion, Tresk fell asleep quickly. Theo was left with his thoughts for a while, replaying the day in his head and making plans for the future. His immediate goals were centered on upgrading the town to Level 15 and getting the new defenses, but he couldn't stop thinking about Level 10. Once he reached Level 10 in his Drogramath Alchemy Core, he knew things would change. He would have access to more powerful potions, but his superior intuition told him it would come at a cost. Recipes were going to be more complex than the simple mashes he had been making.

Sleep found him after a while, and he drifted off. The comfort of his absurdly luxurious bed helped a lot.

Chapter 44
Challenges Ahead

Theo groaned, the light filtering through his window stinging his eyes. He regretted taking the Lesser Stamina Potion yesterday. It always felt more like a hangover than it was worth, but the allure of producing more potions was too tempting. Lately, he felt more like a potion production machine than a living thing. There were many things he didn't understand about his place in the world of alchemy, but that was a big one. Fenian fell over himself to get his potions, signaling something deeply wrong with the world of standard alchemy. He didn't even know what skills regular alchemists had access to, furthering the mystery.

Theo sat in bed for some time, ruminating on the strange situation he found himself in. When he stopped to take a breath, it all seemed too ridiculous to be true. The image of the Harbinger flashed through his mind, joined by the words of Zan'kir. A confluence had taken place in Broken Tusk. What that meant was beyond him, but his sharp intuition told him it was a wholly good thing. Just like the strange entity stood at the end of the world, the alchemist stood at the start of something else—something made of goodwill and friendship; a community that he would never allow to shatter, no matter how big the pressure from outside might get.

The smell of sizzling wolf meat and tea brought him back to

the present, no matter how much he wanted to linger in his thoughts. A voice in the back of his mind begged for information about the other alchemists, but he reined in his thoughts and decided to join Tresk for breakfast. She had already poured herself a cup of tea and was barely chewing a wolf steak, swallowing large chunks whole.

"Morning, sleepy-head," Tresk said, sing-song.

"Morning," Theo said, grabbing his general alchemy book and plopping down in his seat. Tresk served him breakfast, which he accepted with a smile.

"Something on your mind?" Tresk asked.

Theo allowed his thoughts to gather for a moment, waiting for them to join before he spoke. "I've memorized this book, mostly," he started, tapping the tome on the table. "Even the sections that aren't useful. The gap in power between distillation and standard alchemy is astounding."

"How do you figure?" Tresk said, belching. She chugged her tea.

Theo sipped his moss tea, letting that rush run through his body. "Standard alchemy uses poultices—salves and such—but the further you get from that starting point, the more likely you are to do distillation."

"I've used salves before," Tresk said with a shrug. "I don't care for them. They sting when they work. Your potions don't sting."

"Well, that's my point," Theo said. "What if a Level 1 alchemist tried to distill using my equipment?"

Tresk thought for a moment, cupping her chin in her hand. She always scrunched up her face when she was deep in concentration. "It would explode, I think."

"Right," Theo said, nodding. He felt as though he was on the verge of something but couldn't put his finger on it. This was a train of thought related to a problem he had been facing for some time. "There are hidden ranks, I think. There's a layer of the system we can't see, but it's there. Perhaps we can see it if you break the leveling system into groups."

"What do you mean?" Tresk said. She eyed Theo's steak, forcing him to cut into it and take a bite.

"I technically crafted some processed leather with my potions," Theo said. "How does that differ from what Perg does?"

"Same thing that would happen if you tried to work my dad's forge," Tresk said. "You can *technically* craft a knife, but the quality of the object is significantly lower. Good old Throk has access to skills with his blacksmithing core, which raises the quality. It also makes other tasks easier, like hammering the metal. You could smack on the anvil for hours, reheating the metal over and over, but he has skills."

Theo thought for a moment, letting things he already knew solidify. Anyone could technically perform a low-level craft, but the quality would be different. That made sense, but it wasn't the complete story. The *process* was the most important part. He considered his current process, operating three stills to distill an absurd number of potions. Without his legendary cores, it would result in disaster. Everything joined in his mind, and he formed a logical line to what he was after.

"I think I understand," Theo said. "I've been putting a lot of thought into the next tier of potions. The difference is layers in process."

"I think it's too early for this," Tresk said, grimacing.

"Listen. When my Drogramath Alchemy Core reaches Level 10, something is going to happen," Theo said. "I don't know if it's automatic, but I'll understand that additional layer better."

"Maybe you should ask Perg," Tresk said. "Even Luras might know."

Theo took another bite of his breakfast and washed it down with a mouthful of tea. That sense of discovery was too enticing. It was right there, at the edge of his mind, but he couldn't reach out and grab it. He reasoned it was because he was edging closer to Level 10 in his Drogramath Alchemy Core, but couldn't be certain. Questions about his Drogramath Herbalism Core lingered in his mind, but he pushed them away. There was already too much to consider for the day.

"I'm going to check the adventurer's guild, then I'm going to the dungeon," Tresk said. "Again. That's sort of my thing now."

"If you get more loot like your boots, it'll be worth it," Theo said. "Or perhaps a third core?"

"I'm going to be picky with that," Tresk said, clearing away her plate and cup. "I've been toying with combinations in my mind, and I'm hoping a certain demon will help me fund one of them."

"Of course," Theo said, waving his hand dismissively. "I have a feeling my defense project is going to take time. Producing thousands of potions is draining. I need to break through to Level 10 in my alchemy core. That's where the money is at."

Tresk shrugged, pressing her forehead against his before departing for the day. Theo left after writing some thoughts on parchment. It was a futile thing since his memory was nearing eidetic, but there was a finality to it that he enjoyed. The alchemist locked the door before leaving, counting on his shopkeeper's new key to let him in. He left for Perg's place, enjoying the early morning and its lack of rain. Every step over those cobbles was a reminder of how far he had come, something that made his heart swell.

He didn't enjoy Perg's absence on the outside of the tannery building. He missed the days when she would stand there, waving him on as he approached the place. Still, a few deft knocks on her front door saw it swing open, revealing the smiling half-ogre woman within.

"Theo, how's it going?" Perg asked. She gestured for him to enter.

"Very good," Theo said, entering the tannery. The smell of shoe polish hung heavy in the air. "I have a few questions about the crafting cores."

"Oh? You've never taken an interest in them before," Perg said, taking a seat on the far end of the room. Theo joined her.

"Not until I got close to Level 10 in my alchemy core," Theo said. "My intuition tells me there are challenges ahead that I need information for."

"What do you need to know?"

"First, I want to understand the nature of the other crafts," Theo said. "I can dump a potion on a hide, but that doesn't make me a tanner."

"No, but I suspect that Drogramath Alchemy has something to do with that success," Perg said. "Since you came to town, I've thought of it like this. You're on a different level to begin with. It's like you came here as a Level 30, even if you were Level 1 on paper."

Theo thought about the separation between himself and other alchemists. Where they ground salves, he brewed potions. The gulf separating the two methods was vast; she was right. "That makes sense. If I were to use your old process to tan hides, how would that go?"

"Well, you lack the cores and the skills," Perg started, reclining in her chair. "My core has an important skill you don't have. [Process Hides] is an extremely generic skill, but it gives me a bonus to the quality of any processed hides."

"Does that work with the alchemical method?" Theo asked.

"It actually bumped me from excellent to perfect," Perg said. "The quality of the wolf hides I start with is pretty high, but without the skill, you'd likely destroy them. When you process the hides with the potion, it will be good or even great."

Theo nodded. "I understand now. Although, I think I already knew that. What happens when a tanner's core hits Level 10?"

"It wasn't even a skill, but a step in my process became available," Perg said. "I read about it before I hit Level 10, but I can make enchantable leather."

"Interesting," Theo said.

Theo dismissed the topic and asked how Perg was doing. They chatted for a while, and the tanner even offered him breakfast. He was too full from the wolf steak to partake and simply chatted. When the alchemist finally left, he set his eyes on Luras's workshop next door, feeling a flash of guilt that he hadn't been visiting more often. Fortunately, the half-ogre was marching up the street when he left the tannery.

"Theo," Luras said, nodding. "Good morning."

"Morning," Theo said. "Can I ask you a few questions?"

Luras snorted a laugh, shaking his head. "As if you have to ask my permission. Why are you so formal today?"

Theo thought for a moment, but couldn't come up with a good reason. He felt strange about everything that had been going on. Between the mayor position and Fenian's newest 7-gold order, things were certainly odd.

"Good question," Theo said. "Things have been moving fast, so I think I'm just caught up in the tide."

"How poetic," Luras said. "Join me, I'm heading up to the guild. Ask away."

Theo quickly explained what he learned from Perg, even if she didn't know what information she revealed. Between Tresk's information at breakfast, and the tanner's input, he determined that crafting was broken into three sections. Harvesting didn't need special cores. Anyone could run around and pick flowers, there were no restrictions. Production usually needed cores, except for the rare case of his Drogramathi potions and the leather. Artisans, like Throk and Luras, absolutely needed cores. Sure, he could hammer away on a piece of iron, but like Tresk said, it would be garbage.

"You determined that on your own?" Luras asked, shaking his head. "Must be that high Wisdom. Well, you basically got it. The only thing you got wrong is that there's specialized harvesting that can only be done by people with specific cores. You'll run across some such herbs in the future, I'm sure. Right, so that wasn't a question."

Theo laughed. They arrived at the monolith in the center of town next to which they stood for a while. The townsfolk were passing by, giving their greetings to the mayor.

"At Level 10, things change. I understand how the process

changed for Perg. She got a new step in her line, and I suspect she'll get more steps at Level 20," Theo said. "What steps does an *Artisan* get at Level 10? You, for example. A leatherworker."

"There are books for this kind of thing," Luras said, flashing a devious grin. "You don't have to riddle it out on your own."

"The book I was given is written in riddles," Theo said. "*Basic Drogramathi Alchemy* has more poems than usable information."

"I'm a way off from Level 10 still," Luras said, "but I've heard what you're telling me, basically. Once you cross that threshold, something opens up in your mind. The floodgates release knowledge into your mind, revealing different ways to approach a piece of leather. There's a purity in the grain that I can't detect, yet. The example I've seen in the books is that I'll be able to innately know where that perfect grain is."

Theo was rooted in place, his eyes glassy. Something itched in the back of his mind, but he couldn't scratch it. That single word, "purity," set off a chain reaction in his mind that revealed a secret of alchemy. He was viewing the process of distillation all wrong until this point. He made a mental note, filing it away for experimentation later.

"You there?" Luras asked.

"I think you just told me how to make potions above Level 10," Theo said, beaming.

Luras snorted. "Care to share?"

"When I extract essences from reagents, I've always viewed it as telling the still which property to extract, which it magically did," Theo said. "The thing is, I don't think that's how it works. I think the still simply creates the closest possible essence, but impurities remain. Those impurities are the *other* properties."

"You got that from my rant about leatherworking?" Luras asked, casting a confused look at the alchemist.

"Yeah, that was the last piece," Theo said. "I think I would have understood that after hitting Level 10, but this gives me some time to come up with a plan. I *think* I've already experienced this with another essence."

Theo left out the part about the truffle. He trusted his friends, but that wasn't something the citizens of Broken Tusk needed to worry about.

"Well, glad I could help," Luras said.

Theo snapped out of his own mind, mentally kicking himself for being so selfish. He had a habit of putting himself before others in conversation, constantly wrapped up with machinations that would take a long time to bear fruit. He smiled, patting the half-ogre's considerable shoulder.

"How is the business?" Theo asked. "Do you need anything?"

"I need more experience," Luras said, grinning. "A lot of it. But no, things are great. I've got a little money saved, and I know my mayor friend will waive my rent if I fall short, won't he?"

Theo laughed. "Absolutely. Let me know when you produce something that's worth wearing. Tresk could always use new armor."

"I'll keep that in mind," Luras said. "Her gear is decent, and I'm not that good."

"Not yet," Theo said. "I'm serious, Luras. There are three artisans in town, but we need more."

"I know," Luras said. "I want to make it on my own."

Theo nodded, saying farewell to his friend. He fell back into his thoughts, feeling a sense of the unknown creep up on him. The alchemist wondered for a moment if his constant pestering was annoying Fenian. He shrugged, trudging north toward the quarry to check on the stoneworkers, and clasped the crystal tightly in his hand.

"I've had a revelation," Theo said.

"Good morning to you too, Theo," Fenian said.

Theo explained his theory about the artisan's progression, which the elf confirmed to the best of his knowledge. While Fenian didn't take part in crafting himself, he had heard enough to support the idea.

"Certainly, you didn't buzz me for that," Fenian said.

"No, I have a question," Theo said. "Something that's been bothering me for a while."

Theo passed by the farm, feeling another pang of guilt for not sorting their situation out. They were next on his long list of things to do.

"Let's hear it. I'm still in Rivers and Daub, by the way," Fenian said. "Almost done with business... almost."

"Why do adventurers use so many potions?" Theo asked.

"What a question. Why would you complain? No matter, I'll explain it as I understand it. The whelps these nobles are training are at Level 1, which means they cannot use the second-tier potions—the stuff you're going to be crafting me soon—so they must use the first-tier ones," Fenian said, pausing for a moment. Listening to the elf, Theo was watching the farmers work. "At Level 1, your potions will restore all their health. By Level 5, for the fighters, perhaps half. These people train constantly. They do not rest. A single noble child will consume fifty of your potions a day, maybe more."

"Fifty?" Theo asked. "That seems absurd."

"Well, once they hit Level 10, they'll upgrade to the second-tier potions. They'll consume a lot less because of their potency," Fenian said.

"So, the cost of the second-tier potions is higher," Theo reasoned.

"Exactly."

"I may have more questions later," Theo said. "I hope this isn't a bother."

"You? Never."

With that, the connection was severed. Theo stood there for some time, considering the economy of it all. He pushed those thoughts away, fording a path past the farms and into the rocky terrain of the northern reaches.

Chapter 45
Stone and Gem

The sound of chisels chipping rock hit Theo's ears before the sight of the quarry. The last time he was here, the dwarf merchant bought Ziz's entire stock of stone. It was hard not to wonder how much progress they had made, even if it had only been three days. If he were in charge, he would schedule the dwarf to arrive every week, but the intentions of the half-ogres weren't clear. They were likely eager to pay out their debt and start making noticeable progress to upgrade their seed core building.

"Theo!" Ziz shouted. "What do you think?"

The half-ogre was covered in a thick layer of dust and was pointing at a massive pile of stone next to him. Theo didn't have the Intelligence to count them all, but his superior intuition told him they slowed down progress. It was a state of mind that he understood all too well. The initial burst of energy for a project faded over time, and he would never expect them to grind without a break. Let alone for three days straight.

"Good morning," Theo said, waving. "How are the north reaches treating you?"

"It's cooler up here," Ziz said, wincing slightly. "The boys are complaining about it. They're accustomed to the dampness of the swamp. We're making substantial progress, though."

Newt and Demon

Theo grunted a response, moving to inspect the pile of hewn stone. He didn't *really* know the difference between low- and high-quality stone, but as he ran his fingers along the blocks, he could feel that perfection. The alchemist would have regretted letting so much of this business slip through his fingers if not for his other responsibilities. Delegating things that were unrelated to alchemy had become normal for him.

"Honestly, I'm not here to check on the stone," Theo said, smiling. "I'm here to make sure you're doing well."

"Of course," Ziz said. "Far better than working the pits at Perg's, that's for certain."

Theo pointed at the gate to the north. The wall had a strange way of wrapping the incorporated parts of the town, ignoring physics on the slope in the north. It sat at a funny angle, jutting from the hills like a misplaced asset in a video game. "We're lucky the quarry is within the walls. I don't imagine many monsters come this far out, though."

"Not really," Ziz said. "We hear things outside the wall at night, but they haven't gotten over the wall, and the guard keeps the north gate closed permanently."

Theo nodded, making a note of that in his mind. "Stop by the Newt and Demon if you need anything, friend. Especially if you have money to hand over."

Ziz laughed. "We're stockpiling for a bit before we contact Thistum. He's been giving me advice on how to work the stone," he said, pointing to a particular stone on the pile. Seams of azure ran through the thing, wrapping it in tight bands.

"What is it?" Theo asked, running his fingers over the seams. It was cold to the touch.

"Thistum isn't certain. He needs to inspect it. Well, he knows it's a gem, but not exactly which one," Ziz said. "Unfortunately, he told me it doesn't fetch much more coin."

"Hold those back unless he gives you more than 2 silver," Theo said. "How many do you have?"

"Five or so," Ziz said.

"Set a few aside. See if you can figure out how to extract the gems on your own," Theo said. "I'll cover the cost if it's an issue."

Ziz waved him off. "No issue, Theo. I had the same idea, but wanted to run it by you. Some gems are worth good coin, but you need someone with the Gemcutter's Core."

"Noted," Theo said, nodding. "I want more artisans in Broken Tusk. We need to establish more trades routes for export, but my plate is full at the moment. I won't be able to spend much money until I take care of the town's defenses."

"Right," Ziz said, nodding.

Theo thought for a moment, considering the current seats occupied by the mercantile-oriented peoples of Broken Tusk. Perg, Throk, Ziz, and Luras were the only producers, excluding the alchemist. That put the weight of production on their shoulders, which caused him great discomfort. He might have raised their status in the town, but he was no closer to relieving that burden. Perg was his hope, if he was being practical about it. He had a feeling that her next run of hides would be massive, netting the town a bit of the action.

There was also the ten-percent tax he had coming up in eleven days. All sales within the town were due to be paid to the capital, which shouldn't be an issue. Theo would take care of their back taxes, which were somewhere in the realm of 5 silver if he remembered correctly, and the tax from his massive sales. He pushed those thoughts out of his mind for the moment, reserving himself to take care of this matter when it came.

"Perhaps you could accept donations, when the time comes," Ziz said, shrugging.

"Donations?" Theo asked, running his fingers along the length of his horns. "For the defensive structures?"

"Yeah, I'd be more than happy to donate," Ziz said. "If you consider where we were and where we're going with this business."

That didn't sit right with Theo, for a reason he couldn't determine. He felt like a mother hen defending her eggs.

"Fenian claims the defensive structures, which I still know

nothing about, will cost between 5 and 10 gold," Theo said. "I'm expecting to pay 15 gold each. My confidence in his current information is lacking."

"We've got about a gold coin's worth of stone here," Ziz said, gesturing to the mountainous pile. "Three days of work—not bad at all for three days. Give us a few weeks, and we'll have the debt cleared."

Theo smiled, a warm feeling blossoming through his chest at the gesture. "We'll hold a mercantile council when Fenian returns. Pooling our resources might become necessary."

"No worries," Ziz said. "It's going to work out."

With that, Theo bid his friend farewell. The real reason for his visit was companionship more than anything else. Ziz's project was something he was incredibly proud of. It showed the heart of the people in Broken Tusk. They had everything they needed to make their fortune, everything except the capital to start those ventures. When given a way to generate absurd amounts of money, they were ready to throw it right back into the town.

Theo picked an ambling path back to the Newt and Demon, using his Drogramath Alchemy Knife to find Stone Flowers that would have avoided his detection. That familiar pulse washed over the rocky terrain of the northern sections of the town, revealing hidden flowers. The alchemist passed by Zan'kir's house, noting that it was still empty, and moved on to trace a path along the river. When he saw the faint pulse of light from underground, he ignored it. The truffles were incredibly difficult to dig up, and they weren't on the list of items requested by Fenian.

The rate of regeneration that the plants had defied reason, but Theo wouldn't complain. Without that constant cycle, he wouldn't be able to perform these massive runs. He made his way back to the heart of town, thinking about that fact. The adventurer's guild was buzzing with people, checking the notice board out front and talking amongst themselves. The alchemist nodded at them, pushing inside. He spotted his pile of reagents in the place where Miana used to sleep.

"Please don't post another collection quest," Aarok said, emerging from Miana's old office. "Or get me a dimensional storage device. This is absurd."

"I'll make a note of it," Theo said. "You can take the quest down. This should be enough for my current order."

"Good," Aarok said, letting out a heavy sigh.

The half-ogre led him into the storage room, where Theo shoved everything into his inventory. The adventurers delivered on the request, netting 1,000 of each restoration ingredient and 500 Stone Flowers, Water Lilies, and Flame Roses each. He had easily exceeded Fenian's request and hoped that the elf had the money. Even with that absurd amount of gold, he would be short of what he needed to defend the town.

"This feels like the start of a new chapter," Theo said, smiling. "I want to call a meeting when Fenian returns to town to discuss the purchase of defensive equipment for the town."

"Sounds expensive," Aarok grunted.

"It is," Theo said. "I'm going to ask for some help with that."

"You?" Aarok asked. "Asking for help, well, that would be a first. The guild has funds. We can pitch in."

Theo nodded. He knew that the capital was sending Aarok money, although he didn't know how. Some manner of magical money teleportation, most likely. A portion of that money was meant for the defense of the town, but the alchemist was cautious about that fund. How reliant on the kingdom could he allow Broken Tusk to become?

"I appreciate it," Theo said, letting his worries wash away. "How prepared are we for a monster wave?"

Aarok shrugged. "It depends on what kind and how many. A pack of fifty wolves? We'd be fine. An organized army led by an intelligent monster? We'll struggle to survive."

"Is the second thing an option?" Theo asked.

Aarok leveled his gaze at the alchemist, managing a weak smile. "Far worse options are on the table. From what the records say, what we're experiencing has never happened. We're looking at an unprecedented organization in the dungeons—likely a reaction to your arrival and the magic behind it."

"Making the defense of the town even more important," Theo said, nodding. "I'll push everyone to pitch in."

"I'll contact my liaison at the capital," Aarok said. "They have a wizard that's interested in the coming monster wave."

"A wizard," Theo said, sighing, "but not the military?"

Aarok clapped a hand on Theo's shoulder. "They don't care. I'm not interested in giving the town over to Qavell's control, but we can ask for money."

"How much would they be willing to give?" Theo asked.

"That's anyone's guess," Aarok said. "A few silver coins, a hundred gold, who knows?"

Theo nodded, feeling somber about the entire thing. "We'll deal with things as they come."

"Don't stress about it," Aarok said. "The adventurers are gaining strength by the day. It'll work out."

Theo bid farewell to Aarok. He agreed with the half-ogre, even if he wanted to be grim about the situation. They were well-prepared for this scenario, despite the alchemist's worries. Tresk updated him on her dungeon adventure, claiming that she found something amazing for him. After her revelation, he understood how she was clearing the tenth-level boss so quickly. It was a sneaky thing to skip floors, but lined up with her personality.

Azrug was dutifully manning the counter downstairs. A smile crept across the boy's face. The pair exchanged pleasantries for a while, but Theo only had a mind for potions today. With the mysteries of the advancement system out of the way, for now, he wanted to make some progress on Fenian's order. He stood in the lab for a while, looking out the window, while he considered his approach. The lab would need to synthesize 3,000 restoration potions to eat through his stock, as well as 1,900 attribute-enhancing potions. It was a tall order.

Midday had already approached, ruling out his desire to knock it out today. Even with a Lesser Stamina Potion, the task was impossible. Instead, he decided to run the three stills at full capacity for the rest of the day. Experience told him it would chew through at least 2,000 potions in the Drogramath Still and close to 1,000 in the other two.

The day had a way of blurring past Theo when he set his mind to alchemy. The next thing he knew, Tresk was beaming from across the lab, and the sun hung low in the sky. He didn't even notice his Drogramath Alchemy core ticking up to Level 9, but there it was. The knowledge was unfurling in his mind like an old piece of parchment, cracking along the edges and bleeding into his thoughts.

"You're a sight for sore eyes," Theo said, wiping the sweat from his brow. He had neglected to open the window.

"And I come bearing gifts," Tresk said, giggling. She held out her hand, revealing a small silver ring studded with a ruby. Theo took it, inspecting the item.

[Refreshing Ring]
[Ring]
Rare
An enchanted silver ring, inlaid with rubies.
Effect:
The efforts of crafting are less taxing.
[Effect Locked]
[Effect Locked]

"This is amazing," Theo said, slipping the ring onto his finger. The exhaustion he felt over crafting all those potions didn't vanish, but he was eager to test the effects.

"You've been crafting up a storm," Tresk said. Her eyes swept over the lab as she laughed.

The lab was in a state of disarray. Discarded vials were strewn about, and splashes of water made the ground underfoot slick. Theo inspected his inventory, finding that he had crafted the bulk of the potions he needed for Fenian. He had 2,000 of each restoration potion and 700 Vigor-boosting elixirs. It was a good run by any measure, but it still didn't feel like enough.

"Time for a break," Tresk said, taking Theo by the arm and dragging him out the door.

"I'm not done," Theo said, whimpering.

"Too bad! We're gonna go have some fun," Tresk said.

Theo groaned. "I don't like fun."

Chapter 46
I Got Soup!

"Well, why not celebrate?" Azrug asked.

Tresk, Azrug, and Theo were walking to Xam's tavern, intent on taking part in her infamous soup. The marshling was in a good mood. She explained to the pair how her dungeon clearing had gone, including the ring she had gotten. More monster cores, with levels between 10 and 15, were added to the stockpile. Before long, they would have enough to upgrade the town to Level 15, giving them access to the defensive slots on the walls. That was the most important defensive measure in the alchemist's mind. It was an all-consuming need that he wanted to satisfy.

The Marsh Wolf Tavern was decently occupied when they arrived. Azrug scampered off to talk to his sister at the counter while they found a table. Theo was excited when he spotted Zan'kir sitting with another Khahari he didn't recognize. He asked for permission to sit at the table—the best table in the tavern, no less—and they accepted.

"Mayor. You're an interesting Dronon," Zan'kir said, grinning. He gestured widely to the woman sitting next to him. "My wife. Zan'sal."

"Nice to meet you!" Tresk said, holding out her hand for the woman to shake. Theo shook her hand as well.

"That was fast, Zan'kir," Theo said. "I thought you had to go further north."

"My wife, in her infinite wisdom, knew I'd find land here. She met me part-way," Zan'kir said, smiling.

"He's predictable," Zan'sal said, grinning. "I could tell the moment he left that his heart was already set."

Zan'kir shuffled his feet awkwardly, busying himself with his soup. "The children love it. I love the walls."

"Yes, walls. Very safe," Zan'sal said. "It's not what I expected."

"So, do all cat people have Zan at the beginning of their name?" Tresk asked, casting her eyes toward Azrug. She was hungry.

"Khahari," Theo corrected, poking Tresk in the arm. "Calling them 'cat people' is rude."

Tresk shrugged.

"It's a surname," Zan'sal said. "You combine a Khahari's given name with their surname to make their full name."

"I got soup!" Azrug shouted, coming in from behind. Whatever he was discussing with Xam was done.

Theo eyed the soup suspiciously. It didn't seem like the regular stuff that Xam made, a fact that brought him joy. Taking a sip of the broth, he found that the flavor had improved. He would have felt guilty about pushing her to improve her recipe, but the food really wasn't worth the price. Not that he would utter those thoughts out loud.

"Isn't this *fun*, Theo?" Tresk asked, beaming.

"She thinks you're working too much," Azrug blurted out. His eyes went wide as soon as he said it.

Tresk vanished from the spot, quickly reappearing behind the horrified half-ogre. She whispered something in his ear and then vanished again, reappearing in her seat as though nothing had happened.

"Fun, right?" Tresk asked.

Theo let out a heavy sigh. He had hit the ground running when he arrived in Broken Tusk, never taking time for himself.

There was just too much to do, and he didn't want to fall behind. The constant threat of the unknown loomed behind him like a tide, threatening to wash over everything he worked so hard to build. It wasn't something he wanted to face, but the concept of burnout lingered in his mind like a storm cloud. The rain began outside, punctuating his thoughts.

"You're right, Tresk," Theo said. "I've been going too hard. I haven't even worked on my alchemy book."

"You could write some memoirs!" Tresk said. "People love reading about outworlders."

Theo grunted, taking another bite of his soup. It might have been mystery meat, but it was good this time. Xam had spent a lot of time working on the broth, and it showed. He suspected that someone had brought up some concerns to her, likely someone who enjoyed nightly meals at the Newt and Demon.

"Let's try to take some time off," Theo said. "Every now and again."

"Our people keep two days for rest during the week," Zan'kir said, smiling.

"At least," Zan'sal said. "The desert is a different place, though. It's too hot to work, most days."

"Tresk, you're just as bad. You raid the dungeon every day. Azrug shouldn't even talk. The only time he took a break was when he got his cores," Theo said. "Maybe I'm not the only one with a problem."

Tresk narrowed her eyes at the alchemist, poking him in the ribs. "Because your work ethic is infectious."

"I've heard of the Tara'hek," Zan'sal said with a note of awe in her voice. "The best parts of your personality bleed over to each other. The stronger your core gets, the more powerful that bond is."

Theo nodded. He had already deduced something important about the way cores progressed but hadn't put it into words. The stronger a core got, the more of its *essence* bled into the user. With his Drogramath Alchemy Core, that was alchemical knowledge, and the processing of essences. Every step that he took toward

Level 10, he gained a new perspective on the way it worked. This was a feature of the system that wasn't explained. He noticed a similar effect with his Tara'hek Core, allowing him to get a better read on Tresk.

The Tara'hek wasn't just a bond, though. It was as though the core knew what was best for both people, pushing them in a direction that would enhance both of their lives. Thus, while the core might claim to be a bonding core, there were more hidden features sitting just under the surface. Theo suspected that the core's primary function was to elevate both users above their station and had more theories about core interaction that weren't in any documentation he had read.

These thoughts washed over him as the conversation turned to smaller things, mostly concerning the Khahari's children. The kids couldn't get over the plants in the swamplands and were already dazzled by the wide array of new things in Qavell. They had already made friends with some half-ogre children, cementing their place in the town. A thought for another project entered Theo's mind, but he banished it. He would take Tresk's not-so-subtle prodding to heart.

"I should summon Fenian," Theo said. "I have his order, but I wanted to make some more potions. I had an idea about funding the defenses."

Theo explained his idea about accepting "donations" for the cause.

"Why wouldn't they have an interest in defending the town?" Zan'kir said. "Adventurers can make a lot of money—I make a lot of money."

"You make decent money," Zan'sal corrected. "Don't go spending our savings."

"It would strictly be voluntary," Theo said, waving a dismissive hand. He held up his hand with the ring, running his thumb over the length of the band. "How much would this fetch?"

"Don't sell my ring!" Tresk shouted.

Azrug rubbed his hands together, pulling Theo's hand close for inspection. "Without a loremaster to unlock the additional effects? Hard to say. I've been talking with the adventurers who come into the store a lot. Magical items like this go between 20 silver and 1 gold, depending on the effects."

"So the adventurers are loaded," Theo said.

"I'm not rich," Tresk said, scowling.

"Because you don't sell your loot," Azrug said. "I bet you have 10 gold's worth of junk in your bag."

Tresk narrowed her eyes, staring at the half-ogre boy. "Maybe."

Theo waved them away. That wasn't the point, of course. His point was that the adventurers were making money, and would likely be fine parting with their money. Those who held houses in the town had an interest in its defense, even if their expenses were many. An adventurer would burn through potions to keep themselves alive and cores to upgrade their current cores.

Tresk and Azrug bickered while Theo withdrew Fenian's crystal. The elf trader was happy to come to town tomorrow, claiming that he had a new form of transportation. The alchemist could only imagine what that was, but pushed the thought aside. He finished his soup as the pair continued to argue, content with the day. Slowing down had its merits, but he knew that. Only after he had finished his soup did Tresk tug at his arm, urging him toward the door.

"Let's take a walk," Tresk said. "There's still daylight."

"It's raining," Theo said, poking his head out of the door.

"Hush, it's fine," Tresk said.

Theo reluctantly joined her under that deluge, feeling his clothes soak through immediately. She dragged him east toward the river, refusing to let him stop to harvest herbs. They just stood there at the bank of the river, casting their gaze over the raging water. The alchemist felt his thoughts join together in that moment. The rain let up, the constant sheet of water reduced to a light drizzle.

"This is good," Theo said, nodding. "I've been busy for so long, but there's a lot I need to think about."

"Like what?" Tresk asked.

"I have theories about core progression. Things that should be written down," Theo said. "Or perhaps it's just my cores."

"Well, I'm all ears," she said, wiggling her fluffy pink ear-things.

Theo explained his idea of core progression. The closer a core got to a level threshold, the more knowledge unfurled in the user's mind. He gave examples based on what Perg, Luras, and Ziz had told him. Their examples weren't as extreme as his, but there was still something there. It was enough for him to lock that theory in his mind, but he had doubts.

"There are mountains of books on the subject," Tresk said. "But I personally don't know much about it. I'll say this. I didn't experience that with my original common—grade rogue core, but my Assassin's Core is much more sensitive. When I upgraded my original core, it was like a rush."

Theo nodded. There was another layer he didn't understand about cores. The rarity had some effect on his theory, but he didn't have enough information to figure it out. There was that confluence again, staring him right in the face.

"Do you know where we're standing?" Tresk asked.

Theo looked around. He'd been here a hundred times before, collecting the Water Lilies from the bank of the river. "The river," he said, grinning.

"This is the exact spot where Sulvan Flametouched came to slay the Drogramath Dronon known as Theo Spencer," Tresk said.

Theo took his Mark of the Burning Eye between his fingers, rolling the emblem over so it caught the fading light of the day. He remembered Sulvan better than most, though he wished he could forget. The alchemist remained silent as he played that memory over in his head. It ended well, but he didn't want that to happen again. He felt vulnerable outside the town's walls.

"I remember you screaming in my mind," Theo said.

"He was scary," Tresk said. "He came into town looking for you, but you know what? It was fine."

"You tried to attack him," Theo said, smiling.

"I would drive my daggers into the heart of a god for you, Theo," Tresk said.

"I would helplessly toss a potion in its face for you, Tresk," Theo said, chuckling.

A rush flooded through Theo's chest.

Tara'hek Core gained experience (10%).
Tara'hek Core reached Level 7!

"Hey, we got a level," Tresk said. "But, I had a point. You told me about that confluence. Stuff coming together to make something else."

"It's the only thing I've been thinking about for a while," Theo said.

"But the thing it made was better," Tresk said. "From your dying world to a renewed town."

Tresk was getting at something, but Theo couldn't figure it out. She did this sometimes. He played along, for now. "I've suspected there's something more to my arrival in Broken Tusk. Likely the magic from the Harbinger."

Tresk sighed. "I want to make sure you're happy. I want to know that you don't have any plans."

There it was. She was worried about something, but she wouldn't voluntarily say it aloud without some prodding. His Wisdom allowed him to see through most things, giving him supernatural insight into most topics, but most of the time, the marshling was a mystery. "What plans would I have?"

"Sulvan, the Harbinger, or Drogramath. I just want to make sure you know that this is your home. You don't have to go on a crusade for either of them," she replied.

Theo let out a bark-like laugh. *That's* what you're worried about? No, I owe them something. Drogramath doesn't seem to care what I'm doing, and the Harbinger enabled this life. I don't have an interest in either of them," he said, grabbing Tresk's clammy hand. "I've got everything I need, and I intend to defend it no matter what."

"Good," Tresk said, resting her head on his arm.

Theo knew that wasn't the reason she really brought him out here. She wanted him to see that life wasn't just about grinding potions and clearing dungeons. The little things made up the fabric of life, while the exciting bits only served as bumps on the surface. He had to slow down to appreciate what he had, but there was still more to it. Those slow moments gave him a chance to reflect and let his thoughts settle.

They picked an ambling path back to their home, talking about all the things they had done since Theo arrived. Tresk explained why she came on so strong, theorizing that the Tara'hek was a powerful force that brought people together, even if they didn't know they wanted it. This furthered his idea about the power of cores and how far they would go to alter a person's perceived free will. How much of Theo Spencer, the killer, was still left? Those impulses and memories were left tattered underneath the new tapestry he had woven. These little moments blanketed his old life like a cloak, shielding him from that past.

Theo and Tresk found their way to the bedroom, using the Cleansing Scrub and crawling into bed as the setting sun gave way to twilight outside. The alchemist's thoughts stirred, even as the marshling's snores filled the room. Fenian would arrive in town tomorrow, giving way to his new gambit. If he knew the elf well, which he did, he would come with prices on the automated defenses. It would be the first step in his grand plan, something that robbed him of sleep for some time.

Chapter 47
Payday

Theo could have bolted out of bed, downed his breakfast quickly, and got to work on more potions for Fenian. Instead, his soft covers enveloped him for minutes that stretched on without end. Even after Tresk rose to prepare breakfast, he remained in bed. The money he would earn from this job wasn't enough to satisfy the hunger of the town, but he didn't care. He vowed to take it slow, if only for a day.

"What's your plan?" Tresk asked once he finally rose.

"My plan is to make a plan," Theo said, smiling. He sat at the table by the window, propping it open to let some of the relatively cool night air in. The sun hadn't risen yet.

Tresk responded with a grunt, working her pan to cook two wolf steaks. The tea bubbled away, filling the room with that comforting, earthy scent.

"Once we turn this page, it'll be a different game," Theo said, nodding to himself. "I should focus on the farmers now that I have the Spriggan Hearts."

"You need to focus on leveling. That's what you really need," Tresk said.

"Of course. It feels like I'm getting less experience with these potions. Even when I craft a thousand of them, I'm not getting levels," Theo said.

"It's like if I tried to get experience fighting Level 1 monsters," Tresk said, flipping the steaks. "Since you don't have access to anything higher, you're hitting a wall."

Theo nodded, taking the kettle off the fire and setting it aside. He laid out two cups, pouring the steaming liquid inside. He had no plans to work in the lab today, but there was a lot to be done. Rounding up the mercantile seats was hard enough, but with Fenian in town, it would be a madhouse. The elf trader liked to make his way around the town, trading with everyone for anything imaginable. Even the lure of his new ring couldn't get the alchemist to break the promise he had made to himself.

It was a fact of the mayor's position that they would have to spend days doing things they didn't want to do. Broken Tusk was evolving in front of everyone's eyes at an impossible rate, and the administrative duties were aplenty. They mostly involved making sure everyone was happy, or selling land to prospective citizens, but the new housing project was an example of large-scale work that needed to be done.

"You're joining me today, right?" Theo asked.

"Of course. That'd be hypocritical of me if I just ran off to the dungeon after badgering you about taking a day off," Tresk said. She finished with the steaks, putting them onto the plates. "There's so many projects that you want to do, but we need to take it one step at a time."

"I wonder when we'll have time to upgrade this place," Theo said, casting his eyes around the lab. The Newt and Demon was still only at Level 10. Whatever monster cores they had would go to the town in their mad scramble toward Level 15.

"I've never seen a town with walls, let alone the defensive upgrades," Tresk said, shoving a large piece of steak in her mouth. She said something after that, but Theo couldn't understand it.

"We need more information," Theo said. "Seems like we're experiencing something mostly unique."

"Well, you can hire scholars from the bigger cities, but they're expensive," Tresk said, finally swallowing the food in her mouth. "Some people like to hold information close to their chest."

"Drogramath would fit in with them," Theo said, remembering the riddles in his book. "Whoever wrote that Drogramath alchemy book obfuscated the information behind poems."

"I hate poems," Tresk said, scowling.

"But, as with most things, I have a theory for that," Theo said. "A built-in defense measure to make sure the wrong hands don't get the information. I think the poems will decode themselves on their own as I level my Drogramath Alchemy Core."

"Goes along with your *other* theory," Tresk said, grinning.

"I have a few theories, don't I?" Theo asked, nodding. "Maybe too many."

"Yeah, focus," Tresk said, taking another bite. "One thing at a time."

Theo took that to heart, turning his attention to the food and tea before him. The pair sat in relative silence, saying a few words here and there through the Tara'hek Core. When they were finished, they split up to collect the mercantile seats. They would meet in the Newt and Demon, as the floor of the shop was large enough for a handful of people to stand. That would also solve the problem of finding Azrug, who would come to work at the shop when he was ready.

"Good morning, Perg," Theo said, surprised to find her outside. He raised an eyebrow when Luras emerged from inside the tannery.

Luras winked. "Tanner business."

"I bet," Theo said. "Meeting today. I'm going to fleece you guys for money."

"At least you're honest about it." Perg laughed.

"Money for defenses." Luras grunted. "Aarok has been going on about it for a while. He's been hoarding the adventurer's guild earnings, refusing to join the larger guild network."

"He's consumed by the monster wave problem," Theo said with a nod. "I can't bankroll the entire operation like I'd want to."

"If we divide the costs, it shouldn't be a problem," Perg said with a shrug. "How much do we need to spend?"

Theo didn't have an answer to that question. Four defensive platforms, minimum, one for each gate, but the price was a mystery. The function of those defensive structures was also a bit of an enigma. Fenian would need to explain it to him.

"At least 40 gold between us," Theo said. "It might be more, but we might get a bulk discount—I don't know. I think these people are accustomed to dealing with larger governments, not some backwater town."

"Shouldn't be too hard," Luras said. "We could settle for just two gates covered, if need be. Wouldn't that cost 20 gold?"

"Yeah, something like that," Theo said. "That's a good idea."

"You need to talk to Aarok," Luras said. "He has a better idea of our combat capabilities. We have many people over Level 10 now. Some are approaching Level 20 even."

Luras and Perg shared a look, then smiled.

"We also have a secret weapon," Perg said, grinning. "The adventurers who have gone into the dungeon with Tresk say she's a horror. She jumps from the shadows, spinning like a wild dervish before eviscerating the monsters."

Theo knitted his brow. Tresk was at Level 11, and he had wondered how she was getting so deep in the dungeon. He remembered her saying something about clearing the fifteenth floor, and from what he understood, the floors of the dungeon scaled to the levels of the people attempting them. He didn't consider how much of a powerhouse she was, but it made sense. The more he understood about the power of cores and their levels, the more he understood the power of her Assassin's Core.

The alchemist felt a buzz from his inventory—a disconcerting haptic vibration that sent him fumbling for Fenian's crystal. He withdrew it, clasping it tightly in his hand.

"Theo, are you outside?" Fenian asked.

"I'm down by the tanner," Theo said, raising a single brow. *"What's going on?*

"Watch this," Fenian said, suddenly hanging up.

A sound like thunder rolled in from the north, shaking the ground under Theo's feet. Luras turned on the spot, narrowing his eyes on the horizon and drawing a bow out of nowhere. He nocked an arrow, his eyes going wide. Barreling down the cobbled street was a team of steeds unlike anything the alchemist had ever seen. Four horse-like creatures wreathed in purple fire galloped down the road. Their six multi-jointed limbs clattered over the hard cobbles as they reared their horned heads.

"That would be Fenian," Theo said, his heartbeat hammering hard in his ears.

The black carriage, similarly surrounded by an ethereal fire, came to an impossible stop. The creatures simply stopped moving without warning, coming twenty paces away from the ground. Luras let his bow fall to his side, both his and Perg's mouths agape. A door opened on the side of the carriage, and Fenian stepped out, his arms open wide. He wore his traditional attire, complete with too many frills and ruffles. The bangles hanging from his arms clattered together melodiously.

"Well, what do you think?" Fenian asked with far too much excitement in his voice.

"I think I need to sit down," Luras said.

A crowd gathered from the north. Theo spotted Azrug among them, his eyes wide.

"What good is a traveling merchant without a magical means of conveyance?" Fenian asked, slapping the rump of one beast. The carriage jerked to the east and took off. "They're thirsty."

"You know how to make an entrance," Perg said, laughing. "I've never seen such beasts."

"I wouldn't expect you to," Fenian said. "They're a rare breed. A distant cousin of the Karatan, thought long lost. Not anymore. Powerful magics—unknown to mortal minds for eons—come together for my personal transportation."

Newt and Demon

Theo didn't want to deflate Fenian's ego. The elf had a lot of pride in those horse-things, but to the alchemist, they were just horrifying. He turned to Perg and Luras before moving to greet the trader properly.

"Could you round everyone else up?" Theo asked. "Have them meet us at the Newt and Demon."

They both simply nodded in unison, moving past the elf with suspicious eyes.

"Nice to see you, Fenian," Theo said, reaching out a hand. The elf clasped it tightly, shaking with force.

"Very nice to see you, my friend," Fenian said. "You're making me richer by the day. By any merchant's standards, that makes you family."

"Someone said there are demons in town!" Tresk shouted into Theo's mind.

"It's just Fenian. He has some magic horses," Theo said.

"What's a horse?"

"Later."

"Well, let's get our business out of the way," Theo said, gesturing to the Newt and Demon.

Theo locked the door behind them, ascending to the second floor to avoid prying eyes. He didn't mind if everyone knew how much money he made, but he still enjoyed his privacy.

"What a long way you've come," Fenian said, letting out a wistful sigh as he sat down near the window. "You'll be happy to know I've sourced some defensive artifices for your walls."

"That's very good news," Theo said. "We'll meet with the others about that later. For now, business."

"Right," Fenian said. "I have an annoying noble breathing down my neck, asking for updates by the hour."

Fenian opened a trade window, and Theo put his potions inside. Two thousand of each restoration potion, 200 Wisdom-boosting potions, and 700 Vigor-boosting potions. The alchemist knew the merchant's ability to do math mentally was superior, and the sum appeared on his side almost immediately—20 gold. It seemed too high. The elf accepted the trade before Theo could object.

"Yes, that was too much gold," Fenian said, "but it's a bonus. Scarcity is the name of the game up north. A reputable vendor would ask 50 copper per restoration potion before, but they're pushing toward a silver each. They won't get it, though. People are tight-fisted with their coin—except these nobles, that is—and only those with connections are making sales."

"I'm glad I have you to trade with, then," Theo said.

"You're very lucky, indeed," Fenian said. "The world of trade is harsh. Add a war, and things get strange. Vendors ask for more money, and people don't pay it. The vendors who aren't greedy make decent coin, while the greedy ones starve. I won't bore you with it."

"So, the supplier you found for the defensive things," Theo said, realizing he knew little about them. "What kind of cost are we talking about?"

"Over your budget, I'm certain," Fenian said. "Let me lay something out for you, my friend. From the moment we met, I only wanted to see you rise above the others. For every gold I spend on your order, I make one. Even at wholesale prices, I double my profits. Why wouldn't you deal with the buyers directly? Because you're not in Qavell. These nobles aren't good people. If you're not used to the way they do business, they'll take advantage of you. You need a middle-man to get the job done."

"You make me sound dependent," Theo said, laughing.

"Perhaps, but you've found an honest trader to tie yourself to. *That* is a stroke of luck if ever I've seen one," Fenian said. "Another trader might have offered you what you charged at the beginning. Five copper for a potion; what were you thinking? The price of your next-tier healing potions is going to be obscene."

"But the process might be more difficult," Theo said.

"Worry about that later," Fenian said. "I had a point there, somewhere. Right. I make a fortune from you. For the sake of the future success of Broken Tusk, I'll source the defensive structures at cost. That means whatever I pay for them, you pay for them. I won't make a profit, but I'll have assurance."

"Assurance that Broken Tusk won't fall to whatever is coming," Theo said, his mind drifting. He could normally read other people, but the elf was impassive. Still, he had his suspicions. "You know something about the monster wave, don't you?"

Fenian smiled. "Monster *waves*. That's why I got those magical Karatans outside. We're staring down an event never seen before. If I was a betting man, I'd put money on a worldwide monster wave."

"Okay," Theo said, feeling ice form in his blood, "this is bad."

"It truly is. Great for business, though," Fenian said. "I've made a tradition out of this, but here you go—a gift."

Fenian withdrew something from his inventory and set it on the table. Theo recognized it as a seed core in appearance but inspected it anyway.

[Chain Lightning Tower]
[Defensive Artifice]
Epic
An artifice that can be attached to a defensive slot on a settlement's wall. Consumes motes to generate a bolt of lightning that skips between enemy targets. Comes with a recognition system that allows for distinguishing between allies and enemies.

"Fenian," Theo said, shaking his head. "I want to buy it from you."

"And you will," Fenian said. "This is the goodwill I bring to you, my brother. Not by blood, but by bond. Whatever else you need, I'll sell at cost—10 gold each at the moment. Now, shall we trade?"

The pair spent some time going through the items he had. Theo needed a few things more than others, namely house seed cores. Fenian honored their old price of six houses for 1 gold, trading twenty-four for 4 gold. The alchemist got another defensive artifice for 10 gold and ten Level 30 monster cores for 2 gold. This left him with 4 gold and a smattering of change.

"Always a pleasure to watch my gold flow back into my pocket," Fenian said, winking.

"This is massive, Fenian," Theo said. "Well, I've asked the mercantile seats of the town to join me for a meeting downstairs. I was intending to negotiate for a better price on the defensive platforms, but you've seen to that."

"Ah, well. It will be good to see everyone," Fenian said, smiling. "I'm growing quite fond of this place."

Chapter 48
Power Draws Power

The Newt and Demon's shop became a place cluttered with bodies. The lack of chairs didn't help things, but Theo cast his eyes over those assembled. There was a loose definition of what determined a mercantile seat, but it came down to who had influence and who had a seed core building within the town. Zan'kir stood, chatting with Azrug near the entrance. Throk stood with Banurub, Tresk, and Fenian near the wall of potions. Miana, Luras, Perg, Ziz, and Aarok stood near the counter. The mood was light, despite the alchemist's expectations. He thought it would be a grim day.

Theo was happy to be wrong. While they were facing down a difficult situation, things had already been set in motion. Any sense of disquiet vanished the moment he saw everyone's smiling faces, greeting him as he descended the stairs. He held up a hand for silence, which he got without question.

"What an odd bunch," Theo said, trying not to laugh. "We carved something special here, haven't we?"

"Yeah, we did!" Tresk said, pumping her fist in the air.

"There's a long road stretching ahead of us, but I'm trying to take it slow," Theo said. "I have a lot of experimentation coming up, so my schedule is going to be tight."

"Get to it," Miana said, flashing a roguish grin.

"Fenian thinks we're in for a battering," Theo said. "Aarok can confirm that with the research he's done. A worldwide monster wave is looking more likely by the day, but I imagine Qavell already knows that."

"Knows it and won't tell a soul," Throk added, nodding to himself.

"Those jerks!" Tresk shouted.

"Right. Fenian agreed to supply us with defensive platforms at cost," Theo said. "Ten gold each, and I already have two—thanks to his generous gift."

"I have an interest in this town," Fenian said. His voice always had an air of authority. "Qavell is small, relative to the other holdings. Their resources will run dry before long. You'll be on your own out here."

"That doesn't change much," Aarok said. "They send us pocket change to defend the town."

"They're doing their best," Perg said, shrugging. "I can't imagine the cost of a war."

"It's extremely expensive," Fenian said, grinning. "But there's money to be made. Potions are in demand, of course, but so are leather, food, and other goods."

"What he's trying to say is that we need to become a crafting town," Theo said. "The resources around Broken Tusk are absurdly rich. It's amazing they haven't been tapped into before."

"Well, there might be more to that than you think," Aarok said, withdrawing a notebook from his inventory. "Ogres don't keep good records, and half-ogres aren't much better. From what I gathered, it was never this rich. The fishermen have pulled in record hauls. There's a record from a Qavelli surveyor about the mineral deposits. *Poor* quality of marble. That's what they said."

"Our stone is of *perfect* quality," Ziz said, puffing his chest out.

Zan'kir cast his gaze on Theo, which made the alchemist's heart beat faster. Theo long suspected the adventurer knew more than he was letting on.

"There is a story among the Khahari—specifically the Khahari'-dul'te, holders of the oasis—about a confluence," Zan'kir said. "Portents of the Apocalypse, or the harbinger of a new world. It is quite poetic, so no one knows how much of it is true."

"A confluence," Theo said, feeling his heart skip a beat. His mind tickled when the cat person said "harbinger."

"Of course," Zan'kir said. "In this tale, power seeps through invisible cracks. It bleeds into this world, 'changing' things. For better or for worse."

"That seems a little too close for comfort." Luras grunted.

Theo thought about all the things that had gone well for them in Broken Tusk. The stone was one thing, but the way his reagents regenerated so quickly was another.

"An interesting tale," Fenian said, waving a dismissive hand. "Cautionary, but likely factual. Broken Tusk is prepared, though. Theo has done more to work out defensive measures than you could hope."

A silence settled over the crowd like a sheet. The air in the room turned heavy for a moment.

"We are ready," Azrug said, breaking the silence. He stood as tall as his adolescent form would allow, puffing out his chest and grinning.

"We will be ready," Aarok said. "We can worry about what's coming, but we're preparing."

"So, the reason we're gathered here," Theo said, clearing his throat. "I need help funding the remaining defenses. At least two more Chain Lightning Towers. Twenty gold."

"I'll pitch in," Azrug said, not missing a beat.

A murmur of agreement spread through the group. Whatever reservations they had about sharing their personal finances fell away in an instant, giving way to a sense of charity that made Theo's heart swell. After a whirlwind of shuffling funds and a few arguments, the group produced the coins, handing them to the alchemist willingly. The guilt he felt was washed away by the thought of that confluence. Before they continued the discussion, he had four Chain Lightning Towers in his inventory.

"I'll say this before I depart," Fenian said, his tone suddenly somber. "You've built something worth defending here. Whether you realize it or not, you've taken steps to defend yourself from more than monsters. There's a saying I'm quite fond of, although I cannot remember its origin. Perhaps in the Zalabar Empire—but that's besides the point. 'Power draws power.'"

That statement was enough to turn Theo's spine into a column of ice, the icy chill seizing in his veins. He knew it was true. Simply considering the threat of war and the invasion of bandits, it was easy to imagine how a group would want to take Broken Tusk for their own. Qavell wouldn't help; they simply couldn't spare the resources. Everything fell on the people in this room, who looked at the alchemist as though he were their rightful leader. He didn't feel like he deserved the position.

"Let them come," Tresk said, drawing one of her knives. "I'll stick 'em myself."

"Me too," Azrug said. He had nothing to brandish but scowled.

A chorus of voices joined in with empty threats to an invisible enemy. Theo smiled. Their business was done for the day. It was an informal meeting that turned into a rallying cry for the town. When the voices died down, he held up a hand to silence them completely.

"That's all I have for today," Theo said. "You're welcome to stay, but I have nothing more to say on the matter."

The group managed a collective shrug. They lingered for some time, discussing topics not related to the end of the world. Eventually, they filed out of the Newt and Demon, leaving Azrug, Theo, Tresk, and Fenian. It was awkward, at first.

"You're coming into your own," Fenian said, patting Azrug's shoulder. The boy blushed under his admiration.

"I'm getting better," Azrug said.

"He's a natural," Theo said. "Tell him about your cores, Azrug."

Newt and Demon

The boy did just that, going into length about what cores he had gotten and how useful they were. Theo bid farewell to Fenian, promising to keep in contact with him. Tresk joined the alchemist outside, tracing a winding path through the town. They found their way up the battlements on the walls, tracking an aimless path along the perimeter.

"What's your take on all this confluence talk?" Tresk asked.

"I think they're right," Theo said.

Theo peered over the crenelations of the western gate, watching as a group of adventurers went out into the swamp. That marsh seemed like such a dangerous place to him, like everywhere outside the walls. The privilege of safety didn't come cheap, but it was a constantly evolving thing. There was a lot of work to be done, but today was a day of rest.

"Do you think we'll survive?" Tresk asked. She sounded vulnerable for once.

"We'll be fine," Theo said. "There's no other option."

"Well, we're ahead of where we would be without you," Tresk said.

Theo continued his journey along the wall, starting his ascent to the north of town. He spotted Zan'kir's house in the distance, a steady stream of smoke rising from its chimney. Even at this distance, he could hear the voices of the man's children playing. It was a sound he never thought he would appreciate. It was the sign of a thriving town. He paused before the wall turned east.

"I've done a lot, but not alone," Theo said.

As the wall turned east, the path got dangerous. Theo slipped several times, caught only by Tresk's deft hands. The rising hills to the north forced the wall to pitch at a tricky incline. From the northern gate, all of Broken Tusk was laid out for them to see. The people looked like ants from that vantage point.

"Have you been to the Hills Dungeon?" Theo asked.

"Nope," Tresk said. "Other adventurers have, but it's still pretty low-level."

"We should keep information about each dungeon," Theo said. "Make sure we're clearing the overflow."

Tresk didn't respond as they hooked along the bend, heading south. The sound of chisels against stone chased after them, fading into the distance as they went. Rushing water came next, followed by the sound of the powerful eastern river. The water was a hundred paces from the wall, giving them a splendid view of the lowlands to the east. The alchemist perched atop the eastern gate, letting out a sigh.

"The River Dungeon is also concerning," Theo said.

"Maybe you can make a potion that allows for underwater breathing?"

She was thinking more like him. Potions had been his solution to everything, but that was fading. He sat for a moment, reflecting on the encounter with Sulvan down by the river. There were beings that were impossible to overcome in this world. Things that could kill him on a whim. That kind of world didn't seem very inviting.

Theo and Tresk continued south, coming to the next bend. Rising hills blocked any sight of the ocean in the distance. He knew it was there, even if he had never seen it before. The alchemist imagined the calls of seabirds and the rush of waves as he looked over the southern gate. He sat, dangling his legs over the inward ledge, and smiled. The view from the southern gate was the worst, but it had its charms. The southern section of the town was mostly undeveloped thanks to Perg's tannery. Now that the smell was gone, that was certain to change.

Each stop on the wall was a milestone, a brick laid in the road of Broken Tusk. Every memory sat in a special place in his mind, bringing that webwork of stone tighter. It laid over the man he used to be. Theo Spencer died a long time ago, leaving Belgar in his place. Why he held onto that name was beyond him—perhaps some vestigial piece of himself that his mind refused to let go of.

"Gonna sit here for a while?" Tresk asked, plopping down next to him.

Newt and Demon

Theo withdrew a journal he had only used for notes, a quill, and a pen. He smiled, looking over his town. "For a while."

The sun rose over the proud half-ogre town of Broken Tusk. Theo pressed the quill to the paper and wrote his thoughts.

Epilogue

Theo Spencer,
23rd Day of the Season of Blooms,
873rd Year of Balkor's Betrayal

I'm writing this message in the old Drogramathi script. If you're reading this, you're a Dronon. Hello, fellow demon. How are you?

It's a curious thing. To be ripped from your previous life just to be deposited in a new one. I don't know who is going to read something like this. Perhaps it's just for me, but I feel the need to express my thoughts. As I sit on the walls of my town, looking down at the meager lives these people lead, I can't help but feel a sense of pride. My Tara'hek, Tresk, sits beside me. Every moment with the woman is a surprise, but she is a rock that I can tether myself to.

Half-ogres don't live up to their name. I've never met an ogre, but I have to imagine they're not very bright. I'd also wager that they're mean. The people of Broken Tusk, who are a mix of marshlings and half-ogres, are kind, however. They're intelligent

Newt and Demon

in a way that I could never be, and they have a sense for community and the world as a whole. My mind goes back to my first encounter with one. Her name was Miana Kell, and, admittedly, my first impression wasn't the best.

Miana is a hard-headed woman, I know that, but she has her reasons. I never pry into her business, but it's clear that the mantle of mayor was thrust upon her at an early age. Before the confluence, the people of this town were scraping by. They could barely survive.

Luras was my next introduction to the race. He is a man without equal. His kindness in my early days shows the mettle of the half-ogres. He is selfless to a fault, and nothing I can do will properly repay him.

On the topic of marshlings, they are the most curious of the races I've seen so far. Elves might be the most similar to their fantasy counterparts, but marshlings are chaotic. They speak their mind, even to their detriment, but are fiercely loyal. My Tara'hek attacked a Level 130 inquisitor. He could have crushed her with little effort, but she did it. Her father, Throk, is equally fierce in his convictions.

Elves, as far as I can tell, are kind people. My sample size is small, but Fenian has been a blessing I could have never imagined. I'll write more about the man once I figure him out.

I'd like to write about the Harbinger, but I'm afraid I know little about him. Or her, I now realize that it's impossible to tell. Between that entity and Drogramath, I keep looking over my shoulder.

A thought lingers in my mind as I write this. My Tara'hek left me to my scribbles while she runs around town. I sit here alone now.

Edwin M. Griffiths

There's something I wouldn't even admit to her. I have a strange hope that Yuri Valkov, a man I knew far too little about, might yet still live. I'll write more about him later. He was a hilarious guy. That squad we found ourselves in was meant for a single purpose. A suicide mission against some unknowable enemy. If the nukes couldn't kill it, why would a few soldiers with guns?

I was born into war, if you could call perpetual conflict that. I didn't know what peace even looked like until 2345. They found me at an early age, in the summer of 2305, if I remember correctly. My father had already fallen into that never-ending machine, and my mother was looking for work. Military indoctrination from an early age—that's something to think about. It reminds me of Luras and Aarok applying to the Qavelli Irregulars. I wonder if they would sleep as soundly as I do with so much blood on their hands. But I'm rambling. The famine took my mother from me, and then I saw the beauty of peace. Through old media, of course, the kind of thing they held as contraband. The scales might have fallen from my eyes, but the end was already near. My mother was dead, and the sun was expanding.

The only thing I could do to honor those times of peace was to not pull the trigger. I didn't fire on the Harbinger. If this is my reward for pacifism, I'll do everything I can to do right by that strange entity.

Who will read my story?

Who, among the countless beings in this world, will care about what an alchemist did in the southlands of a fading kingdom?

I hope that, if you're reading this, you understand that I did my best. I worked as hard as I could, turning this ball of mud into something worth talking about. I worked so hard to change who I was, pushing those thoughts out of my mind as hard as I could.

Newt and Demon

Maybe I washed some blood off my hands that way, maybe not. Either way, I think the Harbinger would be pleased.

I'm not much of a writer. Never have been. These simple thoughts have taken me hours, and I'm afraid I have too much work to do. I have a barrier to break through. Perhaps, one day, there will be enough time for my story to be told. By whom, I cannot say. Until that time, there are potions to make.

～

**Newt and Demon
continues in Newt and Demon 2!**

～

Make sure to join our Discord
(https://discord.gg/5RccXhNgGb)
so you never miss a release!

Thank you for reading Newt and Demon

We hope you enjoyed it as much as we enjoyed bringing it to you. We just wanted to take a moment to encourage you to review the book. Follow this link: Newt and Demon to be directed to the book's Amazon product page to leave your review.

Every review helps further the author's reach and, ultimately, helps them continue writing fantastic books for us all to enjoy.

ALSO IN SERIES:
Newt and Demon
Newt and Demon 2

Want to discuss our books with other readers and even the authors?

JOIN THE AETHON DISCORD!

You can also join our non-spam mailing list by visiting www.subscribepage.com/AethonReadersGroup and never miss out on future releases. You'll also receive three full books completely Free as our thanks to you.

Don't forget to follow us on socials to never miss a new release!
Facebook | Instagram | Twitter | Website

Looking for more great books?

Join the quest to become the greatest farmer of all time! *Violet, an orphan from Earth, was just about to apply to a college when she was transported into the world of her favorite game, Adventure Incarnate. Thankfully, Adventure Incarnate is a cozy farming adventure RPG, and she has an awesome cheat—her inventory is full of raw materials that she can use to level up and craft legendary items.* **Join Violet in her lighthearted quest to become the greatest farmer of all time in this quiet living, slice-of-life LitRPG about farming, low stakes adventure, a bit of romance, and so much more. It's perfect for fans of Casual Farming, Small Town Crafter, and Oh, Great! I was Reincarnated as a Farmer!**

Get Emberstone Farm Now!

Ever wonder what it's like be a disposable Minion forced onto Quests by Summoners? *It was supposed to be another boring day at the insurance office for Rico Kline, but powerful forces had other plans for him. Finding himself repeatedly summoned to other worlds as a disposable minion, Rico must face deadly foes, disarm insidious traps, become a test subject, and run the occasional errand for his various summoners. At least when each summoning is over, he's rewarded and sent back home. But being back home has its own set of problems, and he'll need to grow stronger to face it all.*
Bestseller Dean Henegar returns with this unique spin on isekai LitRPG, about a MC turned into a summon minion who has to complete tasks for random summoners, allowing for a variety of adventures, foes, and missions as he progresses in power each time... But is any of it random?

Get You Are Summoned Now!

The secrets buried below can make him a Hero above... if he can find them. *Milo lives in a steel cave within a man-made mountain of steel and concrete. He spends his days repairing the machinery that keeps the habitat livable and tinkering with the prosthetics that help his twisted body move about through the small tunnels and air shafts that are his world. He's as much a piece of discarded machinery as the equipment he keeps running. An escaped lab experiment living in a hole. Given a chance at being someone different, will he become a hero and live in the sunlight? The light beckons, but there are secrets buried in the ground. Ancient mysteries left by races that delved deep and stayed below. Maybe only a tunnel rat can discover them...* **Don't miss the start of this unique spin on LitRPG featuring an unusual MC you can't help but root for. Featuring plenty of humor, action, thievery, ninja abilities, a detailed world and System, science skills, magic tinkering, item invention, and more originality than you can shake a rat tail at!**

Get Tunnel Rat Now!

For all our LitRPG books, visit our website.

Made in the USA
Coppell, TX
31 January 2026

70221019R00298